PENGUIN BOOKS

full-time and can be found across social media @grjbooks.

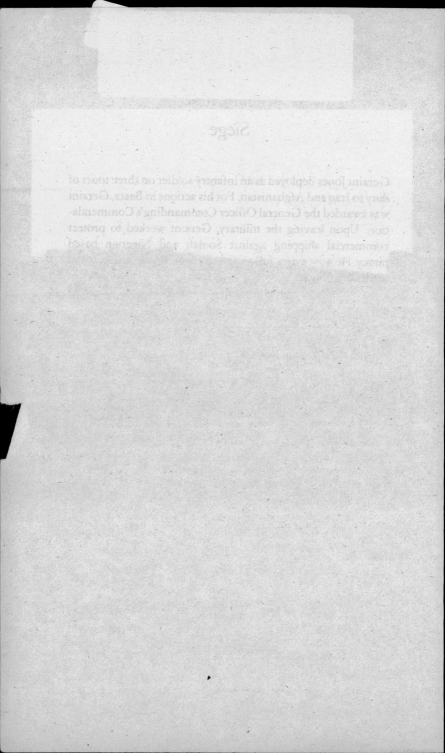

# Siege

### GERAINT JONES

PENGUIN BOOKS

PENGUIN BOOKS

UK | USA | Canada | Ireland | Australia
India | New Zealand | South Africa

Penguin Books is part of the Penguin Random House group of companies
whose addresses can be found at global.penguinrandomhouse.com.

First published 2018

001

Set in 12.5/14.75 pt Garamond MT Std
Typeset by Jouve (UK), Milton Keynes
Printed and bound in Great Britain by Clays Ltd, Elcograf S.p.A.

A CIP catalogue record for this book is available from the British Library

ISBN: 978-1-405-93161-8

www.greenpenguin.co.uk

To Dad

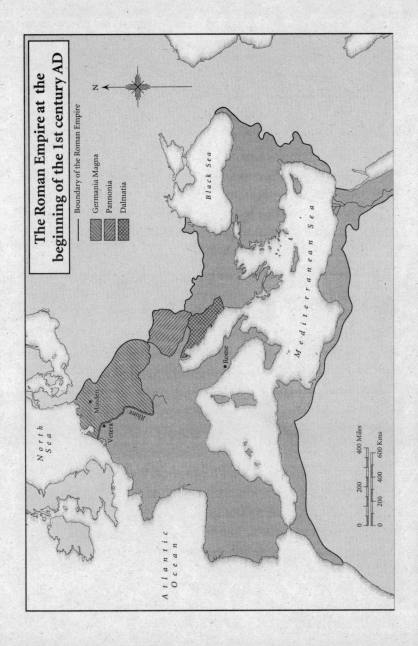

The Roman Empire at the beginning of the 1st century AD

— Boundary of the Roman Empire

Germania Magna
Pannonia
Dalmatia

N

North Sea

Atlantic Ocean

Minden
Vetera
Rhine

Rome

Black Sea

Mediterranean Sea

0    200    400 Miles
0    200    400    600 Kms

# Prologue

The soldier was dying. Wounds and starvation were bringing him to his knees. Death had shadowed him from the moment he had entered the forest, and through a thousand cuts and days of agony it now reached out to claim its victim.

The soldier spat in its face.

He could feel it on his heels – it snapped at them. Grasped at him. Its cold touch was on his shoulders. He ran from this cloying force, every painful mile of the race worn on his uniform like a decoration. Every rip, every stain told a story.

It wasn't a happy one.

What was left of his clothing was torn and filthy; a broken sandal flapped against a foot rife with blisters.

As the soldier broke through the forest's branches, the final stitches of his footwear pulled away. He cursed as his bare foot hit wet grass and slid outwards. Feeling the screaming of his tendons that warned of rupture, he gave into gravity. His body slammed down on to the slope, where it gathered momentum. The man grimaced as he felt a sharp stone rake across his back, and then he hit the ditch, feet plunging into the stagnant water. He used his battered knees to absorb the impact, his backside sinking down towards his ankles, the breath forced out of him as the cold water reached his waist.

Instantly, the soldier looked up the slope.

His eyes were wide. He was scared – very scared – but it was not a fear born of cowardice. For the past few days, his life had been measured by hours and miles. The fact that he drew breath meant that he had won the race so far, but the broken sandal, and now the slip, had cost him time.

He spat, and prayed that it would not cost him his life.

The soldier searched his surroundings. There was no sign of them, but that meant nothing. The men that chased him were mounted, and this was their land. They could predict where he would run, and be there to greet him with spear-points and smiles. Maybe, if he was lucky, they'd be forced to kill him in the chase. If they caught him . . . He spat again to clear that image from his head. The soldier still carried a blade, albeit a short dagger. It was no match for a sword, let alone a cavalryman's spear, but it would be good enough to nick his own throat and deny the enemy their entertainment.

The soldier scooped up a mouthful of ditch water to slake his thirst. 'Fucking goat-fuckers,' he growled.

The words and the rage warmed him. He was intelligent enough to be scared, but he was also angry enough to be dangerous. 'Fucking goat-fuckers,' he mumbled again, looking out in frustration across the open ground ahead of him.

It was cultivated farmland, seemingly abandoned now that blood was flowing in the province. To attempt to cross such a killing ground was an invitation to the afterlife, and so the soldier knew what he must do to reach the smudge of smoke creeping up on the horizon.

He would have to crawl.

Day became night. Night grew to dawn. Hour after hour, the soldier moved through the ditches like a rat. Farmland became a patchwork of fields and wooded groves. Concealment became easier, but the soldier's vision began to swim from fatigue. The thought of a forest of corpses kept his limbs moving.

At some point during the second night he collapsed on to his face. When he woke in daylight he tasted blood. A tooth came away from the gum. The soldier threw it into the grass, angry at his body for giving way. Angry because it was a sign of the end.

And then he saw the smoke.

It was no smudge now, but a stark tower of soot that rose from behind thick wooden walls. Thick wooden walls that were studded with guard towers set beside an open gate.

*An open gate.*

The soldier's stomach lurched into his throat. *No!*

'Close it!' he tried to shout, but the words fell pathetically from his lips. He stumbled, cursed, crawled. The fires within him began to burn stronger. He had come so far. Too far to fail.

The soldier dug his fingernails into the dirt. Finally, words formed: 'Close it, you idiots!' he roared. 'Close the gate!'

But it was too late.

He could hear the hoof beats. He could *feel* them through the soil.

*Bastards!* he screamed in his mind. *Fucking goat-fucking bastards!*

In that moment the soldier knew that it would be death

for him. He could no longer run from it, not even crawl from it, and so he drew his blade, pushed himself on to his knees, and saw the horsemen for the first time.

He tried to swear, but his tongue had become dry at the sight of them: a charging wall of armour and beast. A tide of murder.

The soldier drove his dagger into the dirt, and gave himself to death.

# PART ONE

# I

I thought I knew fear.

I had seen it: men screaming and wailing, bodies whole but minds shattered through combat. I had smelt it: the piss, shit and puke that came with every battle. I had felt it: my muscles dancing and quivering like netted fish. I had even tasted it: the rank acid that burned my throat as my insides churned and retched.

Yes, after years of bloodshed – years of the butchery I was told was soldiering – I had thought I knew fear.

I was wrong.

It was not battle itself that now had me shaking like a child, a dribble of tears cutting paths through the grime and blood coating my hollow cheeks.

It was what was to follow.

I stood in a field of corpses, the carpet of dead so thick that a man could step from one body to another as children would dance on stones in a river. I watched as these cold Roman bodies were hacked apart by the German blades and feasted upon by crows that owed allegiance to none but the gods.

We numbered a few hundred. A few hundred miserable, half-starved, blood-drenched creatures. The sole survivors of a Roman expeditionary force that had marched into Germany with the might of three legions, only to be torn apart inside an endless, vengeful forest. Brutal hurricanes of wind and rain had been followed by murderous storms of German steel, and on those blades I had seen my comrades die. Only Stumps, right ear half hanging from his head, stood beside me now.

Yes, I had thought I knew fear, but no skirmish or battle could compare with the terror that now filled my mind, because it was no longer death that I dreaded.

It was life.

The life of a prisoner.

The life of a slave.

'We have to escape,' I whispered to Stumps.

My comrade stared back blankly.

I had not fought my way through the war in Pannonia, and through Arminius's treachery in the forest, to live and die a slave. 'We have to escape,' I repeated.

'You're right,' I heard behind me. The Latin words were accented, and I turned to see the face of a Batavian auxiliary, one of the light-infantry soldiers recruited into the army from provinces under Rome's control.

The man was tall, thickset, with a scruff of blond beard covering his face and throat. Batavians were as German as the men who guarded us, but keen allies of Rome; they had chosen the losing side of this battle.

The man spoke to me, his blue eyes wild and lively. 'We have to act soon, whilst we have the strength.' A fighter, who could not conceive of defeat even when the savage evidence of it surrounded him.

I said nothing, simply looking towards the ring of warriors that watched us as wolves eye a tethered goat. Cries of agony rang out from the few Roman officers who had not yet succumbed to their torturers. German jeers rose with each scream.

'No,' I told the stranger. 'Look at them. Their blood's up. Their energy. And look at us.' We were the opposite, beaten down and dying on our feet. 'We have to wait for the moment. Gather our strength. They're taking us as slaves, and slaves are only useful if they can work. They'll have to feed us eventually.'

The Batavian snorted in frustration, but any man could see that action in our present position would result in certain, drawn-out death. 'And until then?'

I gave no reply, because he didn't need one. The man just needed to be heard. To be on the offensive, at least mentally, whilst others gave in to fate. He knew as well as I that our crowd of prisoners would become thinner by the hour as men died of wounds, exhaustion, hunger and thirst. This was a battlefield, not a slave market; we would be marched away from here, and many of us would fall.

The Batavian spoke, breaking me out of my dark thoughts. 'Something's happening.'

Orders were being barked. The German army was stirring.

'They're getting ready to move,' my new companion translated.

'What's your name?' I asked him, knowing that to survive I would have to look beyond myself.

'Brando.' He then gestured to a pair of Batavians who sat silent on the soil. 'This is Folcher and Ekkebert. We're from the same cohort.'

'Felix. This is Stumps. Same section.' I didn't need to

explain to him what had happened to the rest of our comrades. Rufus had disappeared from our camp and was found hanged from a tree, his innards piled beneath his swaying feet. Chickenhead, the salted veteran, had died attacking the enemy's final barricade. Young Cnaeus had bled to death as I stood helpless above him, blood bubbling from his opened throat. My centurion, Pavo, had vanished beneath the clattering hooves of an enemy horse. Of Moonface, and the boy soldier Micon, there was no sign. Titus, commander of our eight-man section, had melted into the forest when the army was shattered and all hope was lost.

'Boys.' Brando gripped his friends by the shoulder. 'On your feet.'

I soon saw what the taller man had spotted: German warriors prowled hungrily at the edge of the mass of prisoners, the shoal of slaves shifting like mackerel disturbed by a shark. Grasping the enemy's intention, I pulled Stumps close to me. Seconds later, I heard the familiar sound of an axe chopping into flesh.

Brando grimaced. 'The badly wounded.'

There were no cries of protest from the prisoners. Each man knew that to open his mouth was to die, and hope kept their lips tightly shut. Hope that they could live to escape slavery, and reach home.

'At least it's over quickly,' Brando offered, and I nodded in agreement. The death of our officers had been drawn out over hours, only ending, I imagined, because Arminius was keen to march his army from the field and capitalize on his great victory.

Arminius. A man I had thought was a Roman leader to be admired, only to discover that he was a traitor who had carefully engineered the destruction of Governor Varus's legions, and so, too, the death of my friends.

'You're smiling?' I heard the German speak. His face was neutral.

'I am,' I realized, catching myself.

'Why?'

I tried to shrug, but I suddenly began to weep instead. I was still weeping when our German captors stripped us of our armour and we were herded into a mass and shuffled northwards from the carpet of corpses.

'They're all dead,' Stumps finally moaned beside me.

It was an inadequate eulogy for our friends, but in that moment, it was all we could offer.

Our life as slaves had begun.

# 2

The human body and mind were created to endure. I often wonder why that is so. If, as we are told, we were created by the gods, then they must be black-hearted bastards to allow us to struggle through so much misery. Endurance is a curse, and hope is intoxicating. Combined, the two were an elixir, keeping us upright and marching from the battle-field. It was the same poison that had carried me away from a past that I had hoped forgotten, only for it to be uncovered by Arminius when he had revealed me to be Corvus.

*Corvus.* The heroic soldier who had abandoned the Eighth Legion to stand in defiance of the Empire. That insurgency had all but collapsed, and now I was no longer a rebel, simply a traitor. The word burned inside me as painfully as any spear-point in the stomach, but why? What was I a traitor to?

Fuck Rome. I didn't care for the place I had never set foot in. It was no more my home than Arminius's forest. And fuck the Emperor. His supposed divinity was nothing but a political ploy of the senators who suckled from his gift-giving teat. Fuck the Legions, too. Fuck their campaigns, and the 'enlightenment' they brought to new frontiers. Fuck them all.

But my comrades? My friends?

I was a traitor to them too. I had tried to forget, but the unforgivable acts had stalked me across a continent. I knew now that this slavery was my punishment. It was the penalty for my abandonment of Varo, Priscus and Octavius. It was vengeance for Marcus.

Marcus . . .

I fought down the rising tide of puke. Desperate as I was, I needed every drip of my body's fluids to survive.

'Stumps,' I hissed. '*Stumps.*'

I had to grab his shoulder and pinch the flesh before he half turned to acknowledge me. 'I won't leave you,' I told him suddenly.

He made no reply.

'I won't leave you. What I did before, I won't do it. Not to you,' I promised.

For a split second something of the old Stumps moved beneath the surface. A twitch around his eyes. A battle for the return of his merciless banter.

But then it was gone. 'What does it matter?' he told me. 'We're dead men.'

'We're not,' I protested in a bid to convince myself. 'We survived the forest. I'm going to get us out, Stumps, I promise.'

He looked at me as if I were a child. 'Save your energy, Felix.'

'My name is Corvus.'

'It's Felix. Anyone who knows differently is dead. You can hold on to your secret a little longer, until we join them. Or don't.' He shrugged my treason away. 'Won't change things for you.'

I looked at our surroundings. The forest had thinned to copses of woods and fields – the open ground Varus and the legions had been seeking to set our battle lines. The army

13

had died within miles of salvation, and now what was left of us, a few hundred men, were being herded to what could only be slave markets, and a short life of misery.

The march that day lasted only a few more hours. The dusk came down with a violent pink that matched the drenched soil we had left behind, the September sun setting on our right flank as we marched south into the German hinterland. The ranks of prisoners were silent, but our guards were in full voice, braying what I could only assume were songs of victory. The three Batavian men alongside me could understand the words; Brando's face twisted in growing fury with each chant. With such obvious contempt for his new masters, the man was unlikely to survive long in captivity.

There was no order to halt. The Germans simply ceased to herd us. Seeing them set to work on their campfires, Roman legionary and auxiliary soldiers dropped to the ground. Many were asleep within moments. I wanted to follow their lead, but sleep, like death, was not interested in taking me.

Stumps was also trapped by his thoughts. He was lying beside me, voice calm but raspy from thirst. 'Felix. We didn't bury them.'

'No,' I agreed eventually.

'We didn't bury them.'

I knew what was in his mind. Stumps was picturing our comrades being pecked at by crows. Gnawed at by wolves and foxes. They deserved better, but they would not receive it at the hands of our enemies. That was war. Unless it was to prevent the spread of disease, the Roman army did not extend the courtesy of burial to its victims either.

'When we get back to the Rhine, we'll honour them,' I encouraged my friend, hoping that my words would not betray my true feelings. 'We can dedicate a shrine to them.'

'The Rhine?' Stumps snorted miserably. 'We'll never see those forts again, Felix. We'll never set foot in the Empire. They're taking us south. We're going to their towns, and the slave markets.'

But Stumps was wrong, for the next morning, after we were roused viciously to our blistered feet, we were marched westwards.

Westwards, and towards Roman lands.

# 3

Hope burned bright in me during the second day of my enslavement. A voice in my head began to whisper that my captivity would be short-lived. That Arminius was looking to come to an accommodation with Rome, and that we prisoners would be returned to the Empire as an act of good faith.

I battled against that voice, but with each mile west it grew louder, and I dared to dream of food, open fires and a bed.

I was a fool.

The evidence of my stupidity was a small Roman fort that burned savagely beside the River Lippe, where it had likely been erected as part of the army's supply chain. There were screams coming from within, behind its low wooden palisade. They came from those who had sought to hide, and were now being consumed by flames. Piled in front of the blaze were the bodies of those who had tried to fight.

Varus, convinced by Arminius that the province was peaceful so long as it was garrisoned, had sent detachments from his legions and auxiliary cohorts to man a series of forts along the river. These forts had been designed to resupply Varus during any punitive campaigns against the tribes, but Arminius had again used his relationship with the governor to convince him to abandon the supply route, and to instead push the army north and into the forests.

Now, it seemed, Arminius was eradicating what was left of the Roman presence east of the River Rhine.

'Arminius isn't going to stop.' Brando shook his head, his granite jaw twitching. The trio of Batavians had stayed beside me during the march, though they had stayed silent until now. Like us, their unit had been decimated in the battle of the forest, and so he had seen enough of Arminius's treachery to guess at the German's intent. 'He's not looking to bring Rome to the table,' Brando went on. 'He wants her on her knees.'

I said nothing.

'The garrison hardly put up a fight.' Brando spat, looking at the one-sided battlefield. 'They didn't know what was coming.'

The evidence of his words was in the bodies. They all wore Roman uniform – no Germans amongst the dead. Behind them, the gate of the small fort yawned open and belched flame.

'They surprised them,' I guessed. 'Unless a survivor made it here, there's no way they'd know about the forest.'

Brando grunted in agreement. 'As far as Rome knows, Arminius and his men are still allies. They probably rode straight in through the open gate.'

'How many forts on the Lippe?'

'What's it matter? None of them will know what's coming. He'll do this one by one, until he hits the legion's main forts on the Rhine.'

It seemed that Brando was right, for the next day, having been marched beside the river, we reached a second small fort. The garrison had been defeated, but the fort stood intact, its gates spread invitingly wide like a camp whore's legs. A pair of auxiliary soldiers lay dead in the churned dirt beside them, whilst a few dozen others were being herded out to join our growing number of slaves. These latest captives were sped onwards by the screams of their former commander – a half-dozen German warriors were finding great hilarity in skinning him alive. We looked on at this new torture with numb eyes.

German voices began to bark orders. Threatening spear-points enforced them.

'They want us to strip the fort,' Brando translated. 'They want the good timber.'

We were jostled towards the barricade. The Germans were crafty enough not to trust their prisoners with tools in their hands, and their own warriors set about the task of cutting ropes and pulling away nails. Then, with muscles already aching and spent, we slaves lifted the timbers on to our sagging shoulders and made for the bridge that crossed the river.

It was a place I remembered well.

I turned quickly to look at Stumps behind me. We had been here before. We had *built* this bridge, and I had spilled blood on its boards when Germans had ambushed our work party.

Thinking of that fateful summer day, my mind began to play tricks on me. I could hear the sound of blades clashing. I could feel the resistance of the German's skull as I had driven a blade into his brains, and then the choking water in my lungs as Titus threw me into the river. So strong was my nostalgia that, for a moment, I pictured the boy soldier Micon struggling to carry his own timber across the bridge.

'Felix?' he asked me, feeling my eyes on him. 'Stumps?'

It was no illusion.

'Micon,' I managed, taking in the boy with my gaze and fighting back the urge to drop my burden and embrace him. 'Don't drop your log!' I warned, worried that he would be thinking the same, and would incur the guard's wrath.

I drank in the sight of him. Like us all he was battered and bloodied, his limbs drained and empty, but his face still retained the same idiot, confused smile he had worn since the day I had first come across him, polishing armour outside of the section's tent.

'We'll talk when we stop,' I promised him. 'I'll find you.'

Holding to my word was not easy. Darkness had fallen by the time we were allowed to stack the cut timber beside the river and halt for the night. The burdens had grown heavier by the hour, and a constant stream of fire had poured down from my shoulder and into my hip. Men had groaned or prayed to get through their own pain; I saw a legionary on his knees plead for mercy before a blade was driven between his chattering teeth. I saw other men drop to the floor unconscious, or simply because they ceased to value their own lives. I didn't blame them for giving up. A part of me envied them, but I was more afraid of the mystery of death than the certainty of pain. I had found life to be brutal and uncaring. Why should I expect the afterlife to be any different?

'Micon,' I called quietly, picking my way across the prone soldiers who hadn't moved from where they had fallen. 'Micon?'

'Felix?'

I could make out his young face in the moonlight,

innocent as a lamb despite all that he had seen and endured. It was as if the reality of the situation had yet to dawn on the boy soldier. I wished in that moment that it never would. Let him be ignorant. It was a blessing.

'Follow me. I'll take you over to Stumps. We'll look after you.'

He followed. I stepped carefully over sore limbs, using the position of the German campfires to guide me back to where I had left my comrade. Micon was not so nimble, treading on hands and feet, leaving a chorus of tired insults in his wake. Perhaps it was this that drew the Germans' attention.

I heard a harsh word barked in our direction. From its force, I took it to mean 'halt'. We did. Looking over my shoulder, I saw a huddle of Germans approach. Several of them began rousing sleeping Roman figures to their feet. The light of torches played from their blades as the enemy shoved a handful of prisoners towards their campfires, the tribesmen talking excitedly amongst themselves.

'What are they doing?' Micon asked me as rough hands took us by the shoulders and pushed us on after the others. 'Felix? What are they doing?'

I didn't answer him, because I had picked out one Latin word amongst the excited laughter. One word known across the Empire, and beyond.

It froze my blood to hear it.

*Gladiator.*

# 4

The Germans pushed us on to our knees. There were half a dozen of us in the dirt, surrounded by a wide circle of German warriors, their smiling faces golden in the torch-light. Perhaps thirty of them. Young, their beards thin and eyes defiant.

I knew what was to come.

'Felix?' Micon chattered beside me. I ignored him, scanning quickly for any chance of escape, no matter how slim.

Nothing.

In the same moment, a warrior stepped from the crowd and towards the prisoners. He was young, but huge, his muscular arms as thick as marble pillars. He carried fresh scars, showing his experience of the battle in the forest. The skin of his face was stretched tight by an ugly smile.

'Gladiator,' he said in thick Latin. Then he raised his blade to point out a tall legionary who knelt beside me. 'You.'

A sword came from the crowd to land beside the Roman. He looked from it to the warrior in the circle's centre, and he knew in that moment that his life had run its course.

He turned to me and spoke. Rarely have I seen a man accept death with such strength. 'My name is Seneca, from the Nineteenth Legion, born in Ostia.' This soldier understood that no man should die amongst strangers.

'Felix,' I said, meeting his dry brown eyes, desperate to help him find some honour in the spectacle of his death.

The legionary then pushed himself to his feet, sword in his hand, fingers dancing on the pommel as he shook to loosen his grip. There was no quake in his muscles as he raised the weapon and assumed his defensive stance. German smiles slipped slightly at this show of courage, but cheers returned moments later when the muscled champion moved as gracefully as a dancer, his flurry of lightning blows driving the Roman backwards, and then the blade from his grasp. Two breaths and a strike later, Seneca was on his back, blood bubbling from his throat as he gasped away the final seconds of his life.

The German warrior used his feet to flick the fallen blade up and into his hand. He was clearly a master of the sword, trained since childhood for the glory of single combat. We Roman soldiers were cogs in a killing machine, skilled at taking life in formation through repetition, not grace. This warrior would kill us one by one, delighting in the irony that the world had been turned on its head – that the Roman army was beaten, and that Romans citizens would now provide the entertainment in death that they themselves had enjoyed as spectators in the arena.

The warrior grinned and held out the blade, inviting one of us to take it. Inviting one of us to our deaths. I looked at Micon. If I could buy time . . .

A Batavian auxiliary was not so indecisive. He stood behind me and stepped forwards, letting loose a torrent of curses in German. He spat at the warrior's face as he took the offered blade, but the action provoked nothing more than a deep laugh.

The brave Batavian didn't wait to be attacked, but lunged at his opponent. The move was slow, the man's muscles spent from his captivity. Not so the tribesman, who sidestepped quickly, flicking his blade to nick the flesh of the Batavian's arm.

I swallowed the lump in my throat. This would not be a quick death. He was toying with him.

The auxiliary tried to attack again, screaming defiance as he brought the blade across in a swinging arc. It was blocked easily, the German warrior bringing his thick skull down in a vicious and unexpected head-butt. It dropped the Batavian to his knees and the German swordsman took the man's head from his shoulders with a skilful backwards swing. Jets of blood spurted into the air, the cut so swift and clean that the body remained on its knees. The onlookers cheered, and a teen broke from their ranks, rushing to the body and undoing the rope that held up his trousers. The watching tribesmen doubled over in laughter as the boy then aimed a stream of piss into what had been the Batavian's neck.

As the braying laughter finally faded, the warrior picked up the severed head and spat into the Batavian's dead eyes. This time, when he held out the challenger's sword, I did not hesitate. My victory would come from buying more life for Micon, however short.

The huge man grinned as he saw my haste to take the blade, mistaking it for a desire to meet my inevitable end quickly – he had no idea that I wanted to draw out every bloody second.

I stepped back and felt the weight of the weapon. It was a long sword, and heavy. Exhausted as I was, I would struggle to swing it with enough speed or force to break the big German's defence, but I had no intention of doing anything so clumsy. I would use the point to jab and parry. He would fight to cut, and I would fight for time. Even if I were fully fit and could defeat the man, I would never leave this circle alive – any Roman that killed this warrior would be cut down by his friends, and so my victory would be counted in breaths and heartbeats only. Maybe I could buy sufficient time so that enough of them grew tired of the sport. Even then my survival was not assured, but what guarantee is there in life, other than death?

And so I let out a cry.

I had been holding it within me since my enslavement began. The shout had festered within my chest; I had been unable to unleash it for fear of the fate it would bring. I had no such reason to hold back now, and all of the anger, the frustration, the hate burst out of my lungs with such ferocity that the watching Germans stepped backwards, some uttering protective oaths to their gods.

I screamed again; then I laughed. I laughed at the world, and my place in it. I laughed because, with a blade in my hand, I had regained some measure of control over my life.

'You stupid ugly cunt! You fat piece of shit! Come on – come and die. Come and die!' I challenged, grinning at the German warrior.

He didn't die. Instead he danced about me, and I struggled to keep my eyes on his blade as it blurred through the torch-lit air, the singing steel missing me by inches and moments. Our blades clashed, and I knew that my life was coming to an end as my strength ebbed with every ringing parry. Every panted breath.

'Die, you cunt!' I shouted, and then let loose a high-pitched wail that made the warrior wince – I was alien to him, and superstition was creeping into his tribal mind: the stories that crones had whispered at the fire's side; the tales of wicked spirits that had been burned into his soul.

The German roared his own challenge at such evil and attacked. Our blades met. So did our eyes. I could see in his that he knew he had beaten me before the fight had begun. What did he see in mine, in that moment where I knew that death was moments from taking me? I could even feel its hard grip on my shoulders, pulling at me, tearing me back off my feet.

I landed in the dirt, the last of my breath choking from my chest. A chorus of shouted German erupted, and I looked up; the warrior stood with the blade by his side and his eyes on the floor. An older warrior was inches before him, screaming oaths, spittle flying into the younger tribesman's face. I couldn't understand the angry words, but from the pointed fingers to myself and to the bodies of the warrior's victims, I could guess their meaning – slaves have a price, and this man had not paid it. We belonged to Arminius, and so long as we were useful, we lived.

I wasted no time, and began crawling towards Micon. Strong kicks from German legs propelled me on my way. Hissing at my comrade to move, we skulked back to the mass of prisoners, leaving the bitter tribesmen arguing in our wake.

We would survive the night.

# 5

We survived longer than the night. In the morning, after being roused by insults and kicks, we were fed and watered by our German masters. The water tasted foul. The meat was tough and stringy.

Never have I enjoyed a meal more in my life.

Stumps smiled, the ghost of his true character rising. 'Must be my birthday.' The most basic of medical supplies had come with the food, and Stumps had subdued his pain as I stitched what was left of his ear together.

Funny how the ways in which we find happiness can change so quickly. I'm sure there are filthy-rich senators in Rome whose day is ruined by a stained toga, or too much seasoning on the third course of a meal. I have been guilty of such pettiness in my past, but that morning, for a brief moment at least, my situation was somehow forgotten. I had enough food in my shrunken belly so that I felt like a new man. The sun came from beneath the clouds to warm me with its rays, and beside me were two dear comrades. Yes, for a short time at least, I was a slave and I was happy. Life is strange.

We marched from the campsite with our shoulders a little straighter, our eyes a little more lively. The timbers were left in our wake, to what end I did not know, nor did I care. My near cheerful mind-set remained until we crested a wide ridge, and for the first time, I was given a glimpse at the scale of Arminius's victorious army.

It was massive. The tribes had gathered and spread like a cloak across their land.

I turned to Brando. The Batavian had become a fixture beside me, and there was a reassurance in his solid presence.

'The chieftains are lining up behind him,' I said. 'He's shown them that Rome can be beaten.'

Brando nodded. 'Germans like a strong man.'

And who was stronger than the prince who had destroyed three of Rome's legions?

'As long as he's winning, they'll stay with him,' the Batavian added.

I looked at the winding snake of men that stretched ahead of us. It didn't march with the same rigid formality as a Roman army, but it engendered the same kind of fear. What chance did the forts on the Lippe stand against such numbers? It looked as though nothing could stop Arminius until the Rhine, where numbers would count for far less as he would be forced to face Romans behind stone walls. Should he triumph there . . . what force would stand between him and Rome itself?

There was none.

Something had to stop Arminius and his army. Someone had to stand and fight.

It was another three days until we found them.

For three more days we marched beside the river. We passed forts reduced by the German vanguard, the pattern familiar: bodies lay in the dirt; screams rang out as men were tortured and women were raped; prisoners were taken; valuables were looted; at times our labour as slaves was called upon, and we dug graves or carried burdens. It was not a happy time, and for the most part men withdrew into themselves. Conversation was stifled as we sought to conserve our energy and minds.

The German army was not so inhibited. They sang as they marched. They sang as they killed. They sang as they looted. This was their hour, and they knew that, should they cross the Rhine, the innards of the Roman Empire were ripe for gutting.

And then, a week after the collapse of Varus's army, something changed in the ranks of the German tribes. It was a feeling – untouchable, but it was there. The singing died away. There was less laughter. Rigid shoulders showed signs of nerves, not bluster.

'Something's happened.' Brando sensed it also. 'Bad for them and good for us.'

He made a gesture, and I shuffled with him so that we stood on the outside of the cohort of prisoners. We had been brought to a halt, and I watched as German dispatch riders sped by our flanks on flogged steeds. Brando strained his ears for snippets of conversation. Eventually, he heard enough to smile.

'A fort's closed its gates. A big one.'

'Arminius can't leave that on his flank,' I thought out loud. The German prince had proven himself to be a masterful tactician so far. He would not make the blunder of leaving a Roman garrison in his wake, where it could raid his baggage train and supplies.

'No,' Brando agreed. 'He's going to attack it.'

I bore no witness to that assault, only to its aftermath. The Germans were not singing, now.

They were screaming.

We saw their wounded carried back from a battle that raged a mile away from us, the action obscured by a thin treeline. The fight had begun with a roar from German voices, but that defiance had quickly turned to pain. I saw that many of their wounded had shafts of arrows protruding from their red flesh.

Eventually, the clash of arms died to nothing. The screams of the wounded and the dying continued. I heard one word repeated over and over by the maimed as they passed our position. I asked Brando what it meant.

'Mother.'

They started to carry the German dead from the field; I stopped counting at a hundred. Brando was smiling. I warned him to hide his emotions if he did not want to join his enemy in whatever afterlife the Germans believed in. He thanked me, suppressing his glee.

'Germans don't know how to lay a siege,' the Batavian said. 'The fort must have been ready for them, and now they're fucked.'

But Brando was wrong. The German tribesmen may have been ignorant of siege warfare, but Arminius had served in the Roman ranks as a brilliant staff officer. In Pannonia he had seen war in all of its forms: open battle, skirmish and siege. He knew how to crack a nut, and he had hundreds of other trained men at his disposal – his Roman slaves.

Dusk was falling as we were herded forwards and tools were thrust into our hands. Germans with a grasp of

Latin barked orders, and we began to dig. From the positioning of the earthworks, I could see that Arminius was attempting to set a ring of defensive positions around the fort, and of that bastion I now had my first sight.

The river, silver in the dusk, ran close to the southern wall, rendering that flank near impossible to attack. The fort's palisade was thick and wooden, with guard towers flanking a wide gate that was barred in the face of the enemy. An enemy that lay dead beneath the defences, a thick carpet of the chequered cloaks and painted shields of the tribes.

'What fort is this?' I asked aloud.

'Aliso,' a veteran of the Nineteenth answered. 'I've been here. This is my legion.' He spoke with pride.

I looked from him to the German dead, and then to their living. They had been repulsed, but they were not beaten. Battle lines were being drawn, and blood would flow.

I intended to be within the fort's walls when it did.

It was time to escape.

# 6

Arminius's men worked us into the night. By torchlight we scooped out the soil of his growing defensive works, and by that same light I saw the animated faces of my comrades. The labour was hard and jarring, but the presence of a Roman force so near had given our muscles and minds the fuel we needed to go on. Questions burned inside our heads, but we kept them buried whilst our masters were close. They were angry after their first taste of defeat, and we didn't want to give them an excuse to avenge themselves on Roman flesh. Brando looked cautiously over his shoulder, seeing our guards deep in animated conversation – it was time to talk.

'What's the garrison's size?' Brando asked the soldier who'd named the garrison as Nineteenth Legion, his parent unit.

'Don't ask me stuff like that,' the man shot back quickly, glancing towards the guards. 'They could speak Latin for all you know. I'm not looking to be tortured.'

The soldier had a point, but I shook my head. 'Arminius knows who and what's where. If he didn't, he'd have been pulling men out of the ranks to find out before we ever got here.'

The man kept his lips shut, unconvinced.

'Look what he did to our officers,' I pressed. 'You don't kill them all out of hand like that unless you already have the information that's in their heads.'

This time, the legionary shrugged his shoulders. After wiping the back of a muddied hand across his face, he confided in us with his voice low, his eyes never leaving the guards: 'Last time I was here there was a cohort.'

A cohort was a subdivision of a legion, further divided into six units, know as centuries, of eighty men. Close to five hundred heavy infantry on the fort's walls would be a formidable force.

'Was the cohort full strength?' I asked.

'I don't know,' the man admitted. 'I doubt it. Varus was sending us every which way, wasn't he? Garrisoning every fucking mud hut with a goat.'

All with Arminius's insidious encouragement, no doubt, spreading the occupying forces thinly enough so that they could be destroyed piecemeal by the tribes.

Until now.

'There were arrows in the German wounded, weren't there?' I asked, as this was unusual. Legionary units them-selves were not manned with archers, and these specialists would come from auxiliary cohorts. Units drawn up on the outside of the Empire, the soldiers recruited with the promise of Roman citizenship at the end of their twenty-five years' service.

'Weren't here when I passed through, but that was beginning of summer. Could be all changed now.'

'What's your name?'

'Vinicius.'

'Do you know a way into the fort?'

The soldier laughed, guessing at my meaning. 'Sure. Through the gate or over the wall.' He half snorted. 'Don't try anything stupid, my friend. I don't want to die in this ditch.'

I caught Brando sneering at the comment, then saw his eyes come to rest on the form of his comrade, Ekkebert. The Batavian's cheeks were hollow and grey, his eyes shrunken. Ekkebert's strength had ebbed quickly during the march, and the sight of a fighting Roman force had done nothing to revive it.

Brando asked the man something in their native language. There was no reply. When Brando turned away, I saw the concern for his comrade etched deep into his own drawn face.

We dug on in silence. Silence except for the sound of metal breaking into dirt and the hard breathing that went with it. Deep into the night, a German adorned with a thick golden torque about his neck passed by where we laboured. The wealth marked him out as a man of station, and his visit appeared to be an inspection of the work. It seemed as though we had passed, for our guards then came forwards with drawn blades and their customary insults. For a moment I feared we had dug our own graves, and was loath to drop my shovel, my last feeble line of defence. Brando sensed my hesitation, and spoke quietly as he threw his own tool into the dirt.

'They won't waste graves on us, Felix.'

Of course he was right. I dropped the shovel. The tools were collected, and then we prisoners were herded together and marched away from the fort. Thus far into our enslavement we had been held unbound, the promise of hideous torture enough to keep us in our place, but Arminius and his leaders must have known that the sight of Roman defiance would lift our spirits, and so that night we were tied tightly by our hands, six men to a rope. I found myself between Micon and Brando, our shoulders pressed together so snugly that I could feel the twitch of their muscles.

Micon soon spoke up. 'I can't feel my hands.'

A week ago Stumps would have jumped on such a statement. *Can't feel your brains, more like,* or some other insult would have passed his lips. Not now. Stumps was enduring his captivity with the quiet detachment of a condemned man. We missed his humour. A warrior had to find absurdity in suffering. How else could he repeatedly face it?

With Stumps silent, it fell to me to try and distract Micon from the pain in his hands and the cold that made his teeth chatter in the darkness. 'You're from Pompeii, aren't you?'

'Y-y-yes,' he stammered eventually.

'I've never been there. How is it?'

'It's a-a-all right.'

'Pretty girls?'

'Some. Yes.'

So it went on. Then, sometime during the early hours, my body graciously gave in to sleep. When I woke, my limbs were concrete in their joints. My throat was dry, my empty stomach churning. I felt every mile I had carried since the day of my enlistment into the legions. Every wound, every bruise, every fall. I just wanted to sleep, but German threats and spear-points persuaded me otherwise.

They marched us towards the fort. All about us I saw the tribal war bands with their painted shields and thick beards. These warriors were stirring in the grey dawn, but there was no sense of urgency or purpose to their movement. Fires were being lit, and animals butchered, the reek of smoke and beast thick in the air. If another attack on the fort was coming, then it was not imminent.

Our guards halted us at the ditches we had dug the previous day. These defensive works were now manned by tired-looking German sentries, posted there to guard against breakout or raid by the fort's garrison.

'Slaves, look at me!' a German voice commanded in Latin. I turned in the direction of the sound, seeing a barrel-chested warrior, his beard a rich chestnut. 'You will dig, like this!'

The German pointed his sword towards the fort, and then used the blade to cut a zigzagging line in the dirt. I grasped his intention. Having been savaged by the archers on the fort's wall, Arminius would use the trenches to creep closer, and minimize the time his men were exposed to the missiles. Spoil from the digging would be placed on the fort-facing side of the trench to add further cover from both view and arrows. The basic siege work would be highly effective in giving protection to the assaulting troops.

Of course, someone would have to dig the trenches first.

Shovels were thrust into our hands. Spear-points were levelled at our waists. Our choice was simple – risk Roman arrow, or suffer certain German spear.

We began to dig.

The progress was good. Even knowing that each yard brought us closer to the risk of arrows, there was an irresistible pull in knowing that we were inching closer to a Roman bastion. I knew that the digging of this trench would provide my best chance of escape, but, out of range of the archers, our German guards prowled over us on the ditch's lip, and that first day provided no opening, only burning muscles and parched throat. Then, as dusk was approaching, I heard the sound of a body hitting the floor.

It was Ekkebert.

'Felix, help me!' Brando whispered, desperate to get his exhausted comrade on to his feet before the guards spotted the useless slave. I shuffled towards the Batavians and grabbed a piece of Ekkebert's tunic beneath his armpit.

We began to lift. But we were too late.

A half-dozen German warriors appeared instantly on the lip of the trench. They looked down at us with uncompromising disdain.

Brando spoke to them. I could not understand the words, but they were respectful. Almost pleading.

The enemy laughed at his hope. Three of them dropped into the trench beside us. My hands were on Ekkebert's tunic, but my eyes were on the spear-points above us.

Brando whispered something to his ruined friend, doubtless urging him to his feet. The words fell on deaf ears. Then a German hand gripped me by the shoulder. I saw another grab Brando by the hair. They pulled at us, and in that second, we were forced to make the choice between dying with a comrade or abandoning him.

We let ourselves be pulled back.

I looked at Brando. He closed his eyes. A moment later, a dagger was driven into the base of Ekkebert's skull.

That night, as we lay huddled and tied together, I whispered to Brando beside me: 'I'm trying tomorrow.'

The big Batavian grunted, 'I'm with you. I can't do that

36

again. I . . .' His words slipped away with the same tired struggle that Ekkebert's life had ended.

Then: 'Why us, Felix?' he asked me.

I gave no reply, for I had none. Instead I willed myself to sleep, and to hope.

# 7

The next morning we were returned to the trench. Again the German army stirred but did not appear as if it would strike.

'Do you think they know yet? On the Rhine, and in Rome?' Brando asked, swinging his pick into the dirt with simmering anger.

'I think so,' I answered. I'd considered the question, and come to the conclusion that the mobilization of the tribes was too great an undertaking for word of it to not have filtered back to Rome through spies, traders and sympathetic allies; not all of the German people would stand behind Arminius. The Batavians alongside me were proof of that.

'So now what?' he asked.

I had no idea. To my knowledge, a large portion of Rome's military might was still in Pannonia and Dalmatia, putting out the final embers of rebellion that had raged for three years, drenching the provinces in blood. Even with immediate notice, it would take weeks to reach a position where it could block Arminius should he cross the Rhine and advance into Gaul.

'There're two more legions on the Rhine.' Brando spoke up, mirroring my thoughts. 'But they're spread out in the forts, and to the south.'

'They don't need to be together to hold him at the

river,' I suggested. 'They just need to cut loose the pontoon bridges.'

'And then what happens to us?'

I said nothing.

After a morning of labour, we were granted a short rest in the dirt of the trench. Eyeing the fort's walls ahead, I could see that we were almost within range of the archers – the reeking bodies of German warriors, shafts protruding from their decaying flesh, were proof of that.

The sight of the dead put our guards on edge, and they abandoned the high ground to join us in the relative safety of the zigzagging trench. As a waterskin was passed from one pair of cracked lips to another, I knew that the time to attempt an escape would be soon, or never.

Our guards grunted orders. Our toil resumed. With every swing and bite of the spade, our shallow trench crept closer to the fort. The first shaft of an arrow hissed over shortly after. Men took to working on their knees. Our guards took to crouching, and I saw the opportunity that I had been looking for.

It was dusk before I took it – I needed the long shadows. Until then, I dug like a dutiful slave. When I judged that the moment had come, I looked back over my shoulder.

'Brando,' I warned, my look giving him all the instruction he needed. Then I dropped to my knees and hissed in pain.

The closest guard came towards me a second later. Another tall tribesman, he was stooped awkwardly to avoid arrows. There was a blade in his hand, and his blue eyes were dangerous.

He didn't see the stone I had left half-buried in the

mud. Crouched as he was, the trip was enough for him to lose balance, and as his body tipped forwards, the German's eyes looked to break his fall, and not for an attack – it gave me inches.

It gave me enough.

I looped the spade over in a wide arc. I held it side on, and the angled steel of the head dug into the back of the man's skull with a grotesque crack. The shape of the zigzagging trench hid my actions, and now bought me seconds before the body was discovered – I hoped it would be enough.

'Run!' I hissed into Micon's face, half throwing him with Brando on to the lip of the trench. Stumps needed no such help, and took off like a hare. Brando and Folcher were soon close on his heels. Beside me, Vinicius of the Nineteenth climbed out from the dirt.

'You stupid bastard!' he hissed at me as we took off, and I begged my legs to sprint.

I never felt so slow in my life. Nor, having left the confines of the trench for the open field strewn with corpses, did I ever feel so exposed. My muscles screamed at me that they were empty, and needed to stop. My mind cried that I was a fool. Behind me, German voices snarled. I did not turn to look. I simply ran.

'We're Roman! We're Roman!' I tried to shout as arrows began to hiss through the air.

The others quickly took up my call. Beside me, Vinicius's cries were cut short as an arrow buried itself in his face. He was dead before he hit the floor, and I assumed that I would follow a moment later.

I was wrong – the fire ceased, and we covered the remaining ground panting and ragged.

'Run then, you fuckers!' came the encouragement from the walls.

We ran. We ran, we stumbled, and we closed on the gate that we thought would be our salvation.

'Open the gates!' Stumps cried, the first to reach them, his arms banging feebly against the thick wood.

The others took up the calls. 'Open the gates! Open the gates!'

I raised my eyes to the gatehouse above me, where I saw a dozen arrows pointed at my face.

Their message was clear.

The gates would stay shut.

# 8

I pressed my calloused hands against the wood of the gate. It was solid. Immobile. Blood pounded in my ears. Breaths rasped against my throat.

'Open up, you arseholes!' Stumps roared, defiant in the face of the archers.

I turned to look behind us, expecting that a wave of Germans would have followed in our pursuit, but there was nothing. Aside from the thick smudge of movement in the German camp, all was quiet and serene. Having gone from death to such tranquillity in an instant, I wondered for a moment if this was the afterlife.

'Who are you?' a voice called out from above, reminding me of where I was.

I stepped back from the gate so that I could see the man who addressed us. He was a centurion, marked out by the transverse crest of his helmet. His face was open and smiling. 'Speak up, boys. These archers have got a competition going on for most kills, and you lot are looking tempting.'

'We escaped, sir,' I managed.

'Yeah, I saw that.' The centurion grinned, before he remembered that one of us had died in the attempt. 'Sorry about your friend, but the fort comes first. No settling debts if you come in, all right?'

'If?' Brando blurted out, unable to contain himself.

'Fort comes first,' the centurion repeated. 'Now who are you?'

One by one, we gave our names and unit, and then the centurion quizzed us until he was happy that we had indeed served beneath the eagles as we claimed. Stumps was irritated, but the mild interrogation did not surprise me. What did was that the centurion made no attempt to quiz us on how we had come to be slaves of a German horde. News of the lost legions had arrived before us.

'Look, boys.' The man spoke up. 'Just sit down there and rest. Here.' He smiled, dropping down a wineskin. 'Relax. These gates aren't opening even for a parade of half-priced whores, so I've sent for ropes. We'll lift you in.'

With nothing to do but wait, I took the officer's advice and sat back against the timbers. The wineskin passed from hand to hand, eventually arriving in mine. The liquid was beautiful.

'Cheers,' Brando offered, passing it to me for a second time. 'You know, I thought I'd be relieved when we made it here,' he confided, 'but looking at that . . .' His arm swept out to encompass Arminius's sprawling army. The vast body of men was thick on the ground surrounding us, cloaking any rise in the terrain – it was a formidable sight.

I thought to answer, but at that moment, ropes came tumbling from the top of the defences.

The Batavian shrugged as he took hold of one and tested its strength. 'At least now we'll be on the right side of the wall.'

It took some time before we made it on to the fighting step of the fort. We were too weak to climb, and so the centurion had his men fashion loops in the rope into which we could place our feet, then be hoisted upwards. When my own turn came, I spilled on to the wooden boards of the step with as much grace as a netted carp.

It was the centurion who helped me to my feet. 'My name's Hadrianus,' he said. 'But my men call me H. Sorry for the delay, but I've ordered the cook to get you some scoff on. Hot scoff. Doesn't look like you lads have eaten in a while.'

There wasn't much to say. In truth, we were still in shock that we had escaped. The reality that we were no longer slaves had yet to sink into already battered minds. In this stony silence I followed H from the battlements, casting my red eyes over the fort; it was large enough to hold several cohorts, though the sentries on the wall seemed to be spread thinly. Civilians sat huddled between the buildings, evidently cowed by what waited for them beyond the ramparts. Many looked to be in the same state as myself, and I guessed that these were refugees who had fled in the face of Arminius's army. It was a question for H, but it could wait. I just wanted to eat, to drink and to sleep.

H offered me something else. 'You lead this lot?' he asked. I hesitated, but Brando spoke up for me.

'He does.'

'Well, that's good. You can keep command of your mates. Our cohort's understrength, and I don't want to break you lads up after what you've been through. You'll be Seven Section in the Fifth Century, which is mine. We don't have an Eight Section,' he added.

I had nothing to say. We were back in the folds of the army, such as it was, and I had clearly been given an order, no matter how friendly. H turned to address Brando and Folcher.

'Don't worry about you lads being Batavian and all that. We just need you to stand watch, and fight from the walls. Plenty of time to learn the heavy infantry ways when we get out of here.' H sounded happy, as if we were not surrounded by a swarm of the enemy. 'Besides, plenty of dead men's shoes. We just need to be a little creative on the record-keeping. Find you a Roman name you like. Anyway, welcome to the Fort of Aliso, boys. Welcome to the Nineteenth.'

# PART TWO

# 9

All I had wanted to do was eat, drink and sleep, but a soldier has about as much choice over the direction of his life as a slave, and so, after a legionary was directed to take my comrades to barracks and see that they were fed and watered, I did as I was ordered and followed Centurion H towards the headquarters building.

Like all Roman bases, the HQ stood proudly in the camp's centre, and we followed the wide road that led directly from the camp gate. Huddled groups of civilians lined the way. They were miserable-looking creatures, shoulders stooped and their eyes on the floor. Even the children – usually the most optimistic and active no matter the circumstances – were subdued; what had they endured to get here, and reach the safety of the walls? What acts of war had they already witnessed at such a young age?

H spoke up. 'Look terrified, don't they?'

I gave no reply, for it seemed so obvious.

'It's not just the goat-fuckers,' the centurion went on to explain. 'There was a murder last night. Young girl, twelve years old. Fucking brutal. Now we've got to start night patrols inside the walls as well as on them. As if we didn't have enough to do.'

My attention was then drawn from the sunken-eyed children to a group of dark-skinned men who marched towards us. They were bundled tightly up as if for deep winter, though there was some warmth in the September day. The bulky clothing made it hard to judge their size, but they were not tall men. All had short, jet-black beards. In their hands were the bows that had caused such murder from the battlements.

'They're from the East?' I asked H.

'Yeah. Syrian. We've got a cohort of them here. Probably them that killed the little girl, to be honest. They're not much better than the goat-fuckers, really.'

Despite H's words, I felt my spirits threatening to rise; a cohort of archers on the walls would punish Arminius heavily in every attack. How many men was he willing to lose? More to the point, how many were the tribes willing to lose? Arminius was only their leader so long as they decided to stand with him. The Germans had been roused for war, and had won a great victory in the forest, but with my own eyes I had seen that they had paid heavily for it. Were they willing to lose more of their youth to press on further into Roman lands, or would Arminius and his collective of chieftains be content to push Rome back beyond the Rhine before making peace?

The headquarters building loomed ahead.

'Fort commander wants to be debriefed by you,' H explained. 'I'll try and speed him up as much as I can. Don't want you dropping dead in his office now that you made it this far.'

I muttered thanks as we passed the two sentries that stood at the headquarters building's door. Like the other structures in the fort, it was crafted by legion hands from wood – Varus's Lippe garrisons had been intended to be semi-permanent, before strong stone forts such as the ones on the Rhine could be built in their place, or the need for them moved deeper into Germany. Surely those dreams of expansion had died in the forest with the three legions.

I suddenly felt anxious, and realized that it was my unfamiliarity with being indoors. It had been weeks since I had stood within a structure that shielded me from the elements, and reminded me that people lived in towns and cities, where a wet blanket beneath a tree was not considered a good bed for the night.

'Been a while, has it?' H smiled, catching my darting looks at the tables and chairs.

'Minden,' I mumbled back.

'I liked it there,' he told me. 'Spent a lot of my children's savings on a beautiful blonde whore. Money well spent, it was. I didn't even catch a thing.'

I'm not sure quite how I looked at him, but H felt moved to give me a friendly tap on the shoulder. 'Don't worry. I'm not that much of a bastard! I only spent it when my daughters died.'

'I'm sorry to hear that,' I mumbled.

'Ha! You're too easy, you are.' The man laughed, shaking his head at my naivety. 'Sharpen up, eh? Children, my arse. What a waste of good money. Go on. In you go.'

I was ushered through the doorway into a small office space. One officer waited inside, his hair silver and eyes blue. Despite his advanced years he was athletic and vital.

'Come in, soldier,' he encouraged me. 'Sit down. Relax. I'm Prefect Caedicius. I'm the fort's commander,' the officer introduced himself before looking to my escort. 'H, can you go and get this man some food and water, please? Not too much, though.' Caedicius turned to me with an apologetic smile. 'Body has to get used to it again.'

I nodded, and took the chair that he gestured me into. I looked again at the man in front of me. As a prefect, Caedicius held the third highest rank in a legion, and the highest that could be reached by a soldier who had started at the bottom as a simple foot-slogger. Caedicius would be an experienced soldier, but he was also a lucky one; he had been here behind Aliso's walls whilst his legion had been butchered in the forest.

'What's your name, soldier?'

'Legionary Felix, sir. Second Century, Second Cohort, Seventeenth Legion, sir.'

'And the Second Century, where are they now?'

'Mostly dead, sir.'

'Mostly?'

'There are some other survivors, sir. Two came in with me.'

'So as far as you know, there are three survivors from your century, and the rest are dead.'

'Yes, sir.'

'But you didn't die with them.'

Fuck. I should have expected this. Caedicius wasn't seeing a survivor in front of him. He was seeing a deserter. This was the Roman army, after all. If the eagles fell, we were expected to follow suit, and to have the decency to die in their defence.

'We were taken as captives, sir.'

'Tell me how.'

I did. I began with telling him how, once Varus and his staff officers had taken their own lives, a prefect named

Caeonius had rallied the army, and made one last attempt to break out of the forest. That attempt had died trying to overcome the Germans' wall, and then there had been the last stand beneath the eagles. Finally, a band of a few hundred Romans was all that was left of the great army, and to this group Arminius offered the terms of surrender and enslavement. Caeonius took it. Then he and all the other surviving officers were murdered in the most hideous ways. The rank and file, myself amongst them, were marched into slavery.

As I told the story, Caedicius's eyes never left me. My own eyes were fixed on to the wall. It was the first time I had played over the events of that final day, and the memory of the stink of blood and shit tried to force its way into my nostrils. When I had finished with my tale, my hands were as white as marble. For the first time, I noticed that one of my feet was tapping uncontrollably. I fought to stop it, but the twitching muscles would not obey.

Caedicius walked away from me then. When he returned, it was with a thick cloak that he placed kindly over my shoulders. The door opened, and through eyes moist with shocked tears, I saw food and water placed before me.

'Eat,' Caedicius ordered gently.

I struggled to hold down the bread and the broth that H had brought for me. My stomach had become conditioned to its empty state, but my difficulty was more as a result of retelling the last moments of the forest battle – it had shaken me to a point where my mind swam and blood pounded in my temples. I was nauseous, and it was a long time before the food was gone, and the patient prefect spoke.

'I knew Prefect Caeonius well. He was a great friend,

and always did care more about his men than his reputation. He died well?'

'He did, sir. It was quick.' I tried not to think about how the blade had cut the man's head from his shoulders. How the blood had pumped from the stump.

Caedicius then questioned me in more detail: had Varus truly taken his own life? Were the eagles lost to enemy hands? What number of enemy casualties? What of their tactics? I answered to the best of my drained ability, careful to avoid any trap that would reveal something of my own past, and relationship with the enemy's leader.

'I always liked Arminius,' the prefect then grunted. 'He was the most promising officer on Varus's staff, and always seemed more Roman than a native. He could have been brilliant.'

It was not my place to point out that the German *was* brilliant. That he had orchestrated one of the greatest victories against the Roman Empire for decades, and had proven himself a master tactician and strategist.

'You're not the first survivor we've had come in,' Caedicius then explained. 'But . . . three legions? It's beyond comprehension. Until the bastard arrived with his army, I still believed it was the made-up fairy tale of some cast-out civvies and a bloody deserter.'

Caedicius then stood straight, turning his full attention to me. 'Centurion Hadrianus tells me he's taken you into his century?'

I gave a shallow nod.

'Good. Go get some rest, Felix. Dawn will be here soon, and I expect Arminius and his scum will be coming with it. Be on the walls to meet them, soldier, and show them Rome's vengeance.'

# IO

Centurion H escorted me from the headquarters building. Prefect Caedicius had insisted that I keep the thick
cloak, and I pulled it tight around my bony shoulders as
we marched through the camp to the barrack block that
would be my accommodation. The block was of the same
design as any in the Empire, broken down into ten sections: one for each of a century's eight sections; one for
the optio, the century's second in command; and a large
section for the centurion, including an office and living
space.

I entered the doorway of Seven Section's accommodation, walking first into the partition that housed the
soldiers' equipment. My eyes grew accustomed to the
dark, and I could make out the rounded shape of shields
and the points of javelins that shone dully in the ambient
light.

'All your kit's here,' H whispered. 'I'm just going to hold
you in reserve tomorrow. I'll only use you if they get over
the walls, in which case you don't really need to be in any fit
state to fight anyway, because it'll all be over. Goodnight.'

I saw his white smile flash in the darkness, and then I
was alone. I pulled back the flap that separated the storage area from the men's sleeping space, and quietly
stepped within, careful not to disturb my comrades, who
snored on the bunk beds. I found a lower one that had

been left unclaimed, and exhaled gently as I lay down on the straw mattress.

Within a breath, sleep had claimed me. Perhaps I slept for hours, but I did not even feel as if I'd closed my eyes when an unknown legionary shook me by the shoulder and uttered the words that every tired soldier dreads to hear: 'Stand to.'

There was no point in fighting it. I swung legs of lead from the bunk and began to wake my section.

'Micon. Get up.'

'Where are we?' he asked. Half dead with fatigue as we were, I did not hold it against him.

'Just get up and put your kit on. Wait outside.' I turned to where Stumps still snored deeply. 'Stumps. Wake up.'

'It's not my duty,' he mumbled, reciting automatically the defence of every woken soldier. 'You got the wrong bed.'

'Arminius is coming at dawn, Stumps. Do you want to be in your bunk when he gets here?'

The veteran finally opened his eyes. His answer was deadpan: 'Yes,' he told me, unblinking.

I thought about reasoning with him. I thought about telling him how we hadn't come this far for him to be imprisoned for refusing to fight. I thought about saying all of that, but instead, for the first time in as long as I could remember, I laughed. I laughed so hard that it did the job of waking the others, and even persuaded Stumps that sleep would now escape him.

'Fuck it then. I'll come. May as well die on the wall with you and get it over with, you cunt,' he grumbled, and my tired spirits rose to see his own character returning. I caught the feeling and wondered at it; by what right was I laughing – and hopeful? Surrounded and cut off, we were surely soon to be assaulted by Arminius's savage army.

And yet I *was*. I was hopeful. Why?

We had walls, and we had archers, but neither guaranteed victory, nor even short-term survival. It was as I helped Micon pull his heavy chain mail over his head that I discovered the reason; it was as I watched Brando and Folcher check each other's equipment, pulling straps tight and testing the fit of their armour: I was amongst comrades, but more than that, I was responsible for them. I was a commander again, if only of a small group, and for a short duration. It wasn't from vanity or glory that this position lifted me, but because I felt as if I now had a good chance to protect their lives.

I hadn't risen to be standard-bearer of the Eighth Legion because of my looks. I hadn't dragged out a rebellion against Rome because I was skilled as a shepherd, or fishmonger. I hadn't survived the forest because I was a man of words, or art. No, I was a survivor, but more than that, I was a killer, and as I accepted that truth, the weight of the armour lifted from my shoulders. The concrete holding my tired limbs began to break away.

I was a killer.

In the grey light of the dawn, I looked at the four men surrounding me, helmeted and armoured, the last taint of our slavery cast off as we took command of sword and javelin. We were soldiers again.

In that moment, I felt the need to explain myself to

these men, but then I remembered the words that Marcus had once taught me on a bloody mountainside, a continent away: 'Leaders don't talk. They lead.'

And so I led.

The century was beginning to form up outside of the barrack block. It was a small force, as two sections were already deployed as part of their guard duties.

'Morning, Felix,' Centurion H greeted me. 'Ready to make widows and orphans?'

I grunted something to the affirmative.

'Won't be much need for that, I don't think,' H went on. 'I just need you and your boys in that south-eastern corner there. There's a nice big pile of stones at the bottom of the stairs, so you'll run them up to the top if the piles on the wall get small. Didn't have to use any the first time they attacked, thanks to the archers, but we'll see. Have fun.'

With that we were dismissed, and I led my small band to the fort's corner. Other knots of soldiers moved in the fading darkness. Most conversations were hushed, but some voices carried to my ears, full of bravado. These were the men who were more afraid of being *discovered* afraid than of the source of the fear itself.

We reached our assigned position; the rocks were the size of a child's head, or bigger. No doubt they had been diligently scrounged from every corner of the camp and the river. I looked up at the sky, which was slowly lightening to grey. Beside me, I felt the impatient energy of Brando as he shuffled from foot to foot. Doubtless he was eager for the chance to spill the blood of the enemy who had murdered his comrades.

'I'm going on to the wall to look,' I told the section, wanting to know where our resupply would be needed.

At least, that was how I justified leaving our position. In truth, I wanted to see the enemy coming if they attacked. I did not want to be a bystander, like the civilians who were peeking nervously from doorways and alleys.

'I'll come with you,' Brando offered, as I was certain he would.

The other men remained where they were, Stumps lying on the ground and using his shield as a pillow.

'I don't want to be down there,' Brando told me, echoing my own thoughts as we climbed the steps that led to the wall's top. 'I want to kill, Felix. I want to capture them, and treat them like they treated us. I want them to suffer, and then I want them to die.'

I wasn't sure how to respond to the man's bloodlust. 'You'll get your chance,' I said eventually.

We reached the top of the wall and I looked about me. The men of the watch were cloaked spectres against the battlements, the slightest trace of their breath visible in the dawn. Veterans amongst them stretched their limbs, preparing their bodies for combat. Syrian archers tested the pull of their bows, and placed arrows close at hand.

The sight of those archers did a lot to explain the smell that now came to me. It was the pungent, sweet aroma of death; the bodies of the decaying German dead were visible as dark marks on the field. None had made it to the double ditch that ran below the wall, or on to the rampart that had been created from its spoil.

'They didn't even get close,' Brando snorted. 'We won't be bringing any stones up here.'

I didn't share his optimism. Arminius was no fool, and I did not believe that he would be content to follow one failed attack with the same tactics as the first.

He decided to prove me wrong.

It was Brando who first spotted them. The sun was slowly cresting the eastern horizon, and below it was the unmistakable movement of a large body of troops.

'He's hoping the sun will blind the archers.' Brando smiled. 'Maybe we will get to kill some of the fuckers.'

It was no sneak attack. No surprise. Men do not willingly run at a wall of death without coaxing, and we could make out the braying of orders, the deep boom of chants as men built up their courage through drink and song. The sun was steadily climbing. It came to a height where it was now or never for Arminius. Light in the archers' eyes was his slim hope of avoiding another massacre. Knowing him as I did, I expected him to lead by example, and initiate the first charge.

It was something to see.

War is a brutal thing, a plague, but it is a sight to behold, as beautiful as it is terrifying. As the charging carpet of German warriors rolled towards us, the breath caught jaggedly in my dry throat.

'I'll get the stones,' Brando whispered, leaving me to watch the smiling Syrians as they began their own chants and mantras, nocking the first of their arrows and calling to one another what I imagined were challenges of competition and marksmanship.

I squinted into the sun, the shape of the attacking men a blur. Could the archers identify single targets? What did it matter, when the enemy host was so thick?

The slaughter began seconds later. The Syrians could not miss. Screams pierced the calls of challenge and defiance. Stricken bodies sent others tumbling to the ground as they fell. I watched an archer pull and loose. Pull and loose. He was smiling. He had been born for this day. Trained for it since childhood. There were no enemy archers to threaten him. This was a target range for him, and nothing more.

For the Germans, it was a slaughter.

Through sheer strength of numbers the first of them reached the earthen rampart across the ditches, but as these men climbed they were plucked from their feet with arrows. Other brave men charged by. Within moments, the ground below us was filled with snarling faces that fought for handholds on the wall.

'They don't have ladders!' A legionary laughed, then whooped in joy as his dropped stone found its mark.

'Legionaries! Stones on the ditch!' a strong voice commanded from the gatehouse. 'Archers! Fire beyond them!'

The soldiers of the Nineteenth set to work on hurling their burdens over the wall; German heads were shattered like eggs; shoulders crumbled. I risked a look over the wall, seeing a ditch that was filling with the dead and dying.

'More stones!' a voice called.

I ran to the stairs. Brando and the others were already making their way up it, their arms full.

It wasn't the last time they ran up and down them. By the time the killing was done, we were slathered in sweat. Outside of the walls, the cheering of the enemy had gone. Only the dead and dying remained, and their wails and groans forced me to raise my own voice as I instructed my men to wait for me on the dirt at the foot of the stairs; I had seen Centurion H on the wall, and wanted to report in. Now that the attack had been broken my adrenaline had drained quickly, and I hoped that the centurion would dismiss me and my comrades to our beds.

I wanted to escape the screams. So too, evidently, did some of the archers – arrows struck down into the wounded who lay gasping and howling in the ditch.

'Hold your fucking fire, you lizards!' a voice boomed, and I turned to see a tall centurion striding the battlements. Centurion H was behind him, smile gone now as he scanned the carnage beneath the wall.

I turned my eyes back to the taller officer, working out by his decorations and manner that he was the cohort's commander, the Pilus Prior. Confidence came from him in waves. The Syrian archers almost bowed as he addressed them.

'Don't waste arrows on these cunts, understand? Where's the interpreter? Come here. Tell them that these screams send a message. They scare the other goat-fuckers, and scared goat-fuckers mean you lizards will live through this. You start feeling sorry for them, go and speak to the survivors of the army that came in last night. Ask them how the hairies treat our wounded. Our prisoners.'

Centurion H had noticed my presence, and came over. 'That's the cohort commander, Malchus,' he explained. 'All your lads all right?'

I nodded, my eyes scanning the distance – there appeared to be no stirring for a second attack. The morning's massacre had taken the fight from the enemy, at least for now.

'We didn't lose a man,' H told me, recognizing the same. 'Not that I'm complaining of course, but . . . fuck. You almost feel sorry for them.'

I said nothing, and the officer took that to mean he had offended me.

'I'm sorry, Felix. I wasn't with you in the forest. I didn't mean it like that.'

I shook my head. 'No warriors deserve to die like cattle.'

We fell into silence then, distracted by the agonized cries of the dying.

Centurion Malchus paced over to us. He towered over me, a formidable presence. Slate-grey eyes peered intently from his rugged face. 'You're the one that came in last night? What's your name?'

'Legionary Felix, sir.'

He surprised me by offering his hand. 'You've got some bollocks on you. I hope you got the chance to get stuck into the bastards this morning?'

I realized then that I had taken no direct part in the dawn's killing, but I was under no illusion that my hands were clean, knowing that the rocks I had carried to the battlements had been used to split skulls and crush bones. I was not ashamed of that – survival of my comrades was my first and only concern – but that gave me little solace as the pleading screams for mercy droned on.

'We can only hope to do our duty, sir,' I finally said.

'Come with me, Felix.' The man gestured, surprising me again. He then turned to my own centurion. 'H, make sure the lizards don't waste any more arrows. This isn't a place for weakness.'

'Will do, sir. Do you need any more men?' he asked. There was an edge of confusion to my own centurion's tone, wondering what the cohort commander could want with me.

'Just him,' Malchus replied with a grim smile. 'He's going to help me kill Arminius.'

## 11

Malchus was silent as he strode towards the fort's centre. I followed in his wake, watching as lone soldiers ran back and forth to the ramparts. These runners were the fort commander's eyes and ears during the battle. They were all young, as they needed to be fit, but it wasn't a responsibility that could be handed to any boy soldier. Delivering the wrong message could bring disaster, and I made a mental note to never allow Micon to be drawn for the duty within our own century. It was as much for his own good as the safety of the fort.

The imposing officer found Prefect Caedicius in the headquarters building, which was still lively with chatter following the morning's attack. In the centre of the room stood a table on to which had been drawn a diagram of the fort. Numbered stones showed the disposition of the Roman forces, and I expected I had been brought here to help the officers learn more about the enemy's. Seeing me beside Malchus, Caedicius came to the same conclusion.

'I've already debriefed him, Malchus.'

'Not about their army, sir,' the centurion explained, removing his helmet. 'Arminius himself.'

*Arminius himself?*

I don't know what they saw on my face in that moment, but my mind screamed in alarm; how could Malchus know that I had knowledge of the German personally?

Had I let something slip as I'd talked to H? What about to Caedicius? He appeared unwitting, but had he set the trap, and was he now readying the noose for my neck?

Malchus turned to me, pressing a cup of wine into my hand. When he spoke, I almost fell to the wooden floorboards in relief.

'This soldier's seen Arminius as a general at work, sir. Not just the numbers in his army, but how he drew Varus in. How he broke the legions. The tactics. The tricks.'

Caedicius now gave me his full attention. 'True,' he agreed after a moment. 'But he's not the only survivor we've brought in.'

'He's the only one that escaped his army. And I know a veteran when I see one.' Malchus turned to me. 'Got more scars on your arms than hairs, eh? How long have you served?'

I plucked a number from the air. 'About ten years, sir.'

'Done a lot in that time.'

I held my silence, and hoped that hiding my past would be interpreted as modesty.

It was.

'Good lad.' Malchus smiled before turning back to the prefect and coming to the point of his visit: 'I don't like how this morning went, sir.'

Caedicius looked about the headquarters; then he raised his voice so that it could be heard by the half-dozen clerks and runners. 'Clear the room,' he ordered. 'You stay here.' He gestured towards me as the room quickly emptied.

'My runners told me you butchered them?' Caedicius then asked of his subordinate.

Malchus nodded. 'We didn't lose a single man, sir.

There're at least a hundred dead goat-fuckers in the ditch. Probably another hundred more on the rampart and in the field.'

'But?'

'But Arminius didn't destroy three legions by throwing eggs at a brick wall, sir. The bastard's got brains, and we can't expect that he'll keep doing us a favour and let us kill all of his men.'

'His trenches are getting closer,' Caedicius thought aloud.

'That buys him some distance, but we'll still slaughter them in the ditch,' Malchus explained. Then he turned to me. 'You saw what he did to the other forts. Tell us what you think. Speak freely.'

And so I did. Not because of any misplaced sense of duty, but because my mind was aligned with Malchus's; Arminius was not just good, he was brilliant, and to survive in the fort we would need to find our own weaknesses before the enemy did.

'He didn't expect two things here, sirs,' I began. 'The first is that you would be ready. The second is that you'd have archers.'

'A little fortune on both counts,' Caedicius agreed. 'Go on.'

'Arminius's success in the forest came because his forces were lighter than ours, and that suited the terrain where we could never set our formations. When we set our lines in the open, he was content to hold us there and wait for us to starve.'

'He won't do that here.' Malchus spoke up, rubbing a hand over his jutting jaw. 'In the forest he knew that

67

Varus had a week or two of supplies at best, and the army was deep into Germany. He has no idea how well supplied we are here, and the Rhine legions can march to us if he digs in to starve us out.'

Caedicius chewed over Malchus's words. I could see by the worried crease of his temple that he had come to the same conclusion as I: that holding the crossings on the Rhine was the best guarantee of Rome's protection against Arminius. Crossing them to break a siege and fight on Arminius's terms risked too much, at least until the frontier could be reinforced.

'Sooner or later, there will have to be a reckoning with the German.' Caedicius spoke as he paced, the room silent but for his words and the tap of his hobnails on the wood. 'We have no idea when that will be, but what we do know is that the German tribes do not easily come together. Nor are they easily held together. After his victory over Varus, Arminius has momentum, but he must keep it if he wants to fight on.'

Malchus nodded. 'Agreed, sir.'

I agreed silently in my own mind. Knowing Arminius as I did, I believed he would have simply bypassed the fort had he known how much blood it would cost him. He could have kept the garrison contained with a small force of his own, but now that battle had been initiated, pride and the need to keep up appearances would ensure that some kind of victory must be reached. But how?

And then I remembered the blaze of that first fort. How the flames had danced into the sky as the sizzling thatch of buildings hissed and popped.

'He could burn us out, sirs.'

Malchus nodded gravely. This was his own conclusion. 'Those trenches can't get him over the walls, but they can get him close enough to them to build fires. He just needs enough fuel to get it going, and half of Germany's a fucking forest.'

Caedicius surprised me then by smiling. I realized he had recognized a look in his senior centurion, and I took it in myself – it was a fearsome snarl. A look of a man who lived for the chaos and terror of battle.

'You have a suggestion, Malchus?' Caedicius indulged him. 'I expect it's a violent one.'

Malchus grinned savagely, one hungry shark to another. His words were simple, but in that simplicity was written the deaths of dozens. 'A raid.'

For a moment, Caedicius said nothing. Finally, he shook his head. 'This inaction doesn't sit well with me either, Malchus, but we can't afford to lose the men in a raid. We're slaughtering them at the wall and not losing any of our strength.'

'The raid's not for killing, sir,' Malchus countered, to the prefect's surprise. 'It's for stealing.'

Caedicius grasped the raid's intention a moment later. He laughed, full of pride in his subordinate. 'You want to steal his wood, you bastard!'

Malchus nodded. 'If we can convince him we're desperate for fuel, maybe he won't pile it against our wall. Not only that, but if it looks like we're settling in for winter, perhaps he'll think we know something he doesn't, and that there's a relief force coming. There's no guarantee, but . . .'

I found myself looking at the centurion in admiration.

He was right; there was no guarantee of success, but the only guarantee in war was death and misery. Given the way the dice had rolled, it was an ingenious idea by Malchus. It was also one that was certain to be deadly.

So why did I volunteer to lead it?

# 12

'I'll go,' I heard myself say. 'I can show them into the camp.'

Malchus laughed. 'Well, that saves me the trouble of ordering you to do it.'

I took no offence from his words. As I had expected, the centurion would want guides for his raid, and who better to guide him than a man who had lived within the enemy's host? The fact that I was a half-starved survivor of the forest massacre was of no concern to a killer like Malchus. I had known many men like this warrior, and to them, pity and weakness had no place in the legions. Sacrifice and honour was all.

'We'll take the rest of the group that came in with you too,' he added, to my alarm. 'They good lads?'

I thought quickly of a way to dissuade him. 'I don't want to speak badly of my comrades, sir,' I finally confessed.

Malchus frowned, and urged me to speak.

'I'm worried they'd be more of a liability than an asset, sir,' I lied, except in the case of Micon, who would doubtless be a disaster. 'If I can be honest, sir, I don't know how they made it this far.'

'I expect I know.' The tall centurion smiled down at me, respectful of my tact and of my service. 'I'll go with your instinct on this one, sir?' he asked of his prefect.

'Sounds right,' Caedicius agreed. 'Take him, Malchus. How many others will you need?'

'A century.'

Caedicius shook his head. 'That leaves us with no reserve. Take a half instead, handpicked or volunteers.'

'Yes, sir.'

'You'll go tonight?'

Malchus nodded. 'With your permission, sir.'

Caedicius gave it. 'Make the preparations. Fully brief me at the end of the next watch.'

Malchus saluted his superior officer; then he placed a hand on my shoulder. 'Let's find some food,' he said, and I followed his wide shoulders through the doorway.

Malchus acquired bread and cheese and ordered me to sit and eat beside a table in the headquarters building. Then I was interrogated about the enemy's camp, Malchus writing notes and drawing sketches from my memory.

'Don't want to lose all this if your head comes loose,' he joked darkly.

I could tell that the centurion was fond of me. He had only slightly exaggerated when he said that there were more scars on my arms than hairs. One of a warrior's greatest tools for survival is identifying fellow killers, and Malchus was certain he had found one in me. Doubtless he thought I had volunteered to join the raid so that I could accompany him in spilling blood.

He was wrong. It was the conservation of life that had led me to open my mouth. To see that Stumps and Micon remained within the wall. Brando and Folcher too, for these Batavians were now my responsibility by rank. More than that, they were my comrades.

I finished my last mouthful in silence as Malchus

absorbed the work of his hand. His gaze was so full of intent and heat that I worried the paper would burst into flame. Finally he rolled up the diagrams and handed them to a clerk. I expected then that I would be excused, and returned to my century.

I was wrong.

'Three legions.' Malchus finally spoke. There was some anger in the words, but mostly it was disbelief, and grief.

I remained silent. Malchus did not. 'I need you to understand something, in case you haven't already. What you were involved in, Felix, is going to change the Empire. We can't lose three legions. We simply can't. All the plans for Germany, it's all going to change. This frontier isn't about expansion any more, you understand? It's about survival.'

I held my tongue. I understood every word, but not why they were being directed towards a legionary by a cohort commander.

Malchus enlightened me. 'Have you ever been involved in a siege, Felix?'

I had, and I had no wish to recall those memories: the stench of rotting flesh; the empty pain of hunger; the misery of knowing that death waited patiently beyond a wall; the terror as voices screamed that the final defence had been breached, and now enemies swarmed in for the kill.

'No, sir.'

'In a siege, people need hope. Now, everybody in here knows what happened to Varus's army, but they don't *know* what happened to Varus's army. Do you understand me, Felix? Do you see the difference?'

I nodded. Malchus went on.

'Three legions. Fifteen thousand men. It's just too big a number for them to grasp. They know it's bad, but they can't get their heads around how much of a fucking disaster this is. Understood?'

'I understand, sir.'

'I think you do,' Malchus said. 'And so you know why it is that I can't have stories getting out about what happened. Stories these people *can* understand. Because when they *do* understand, Felix, there will be no hope in this fort. There's just going to be panic, and when that happens, we die.'

'I won't speak of it, sir,' I answered. 'Nor the others.'

'Good. We have to stand strong, and united.'

I could see that the centurion wanted to say more. He almost bit it back, but something in my wretched manner caused him to confess, and issue a warning. 'If we survive here, Felix, then be careful, all right?'

He got to his feet then. Our conversation was over. 'We'll form up at the west gate at dusk. Go and sleep.'

I saluted and left the room. Early autumn sunlight hit my face as I stepped through the doorway. It was beautiful, but as I closed my eyes to embrace it, I caught the sound of screams – the wounded outside the walls still toiled in their agony. I tried to let the thought of them slip from my mind, thinking instead of what Malchus had told me.

*Be careful.*

He had no idea how close to the truth he was. If I survived Arminius's siege, my past was only a chance encounter away. Whilst I remained in the Empire, I lived on the precipice. For the first time in days I thought of Britain beyond the sea. Instantly I felt the familiar pull to break free of Rome's chains, and to chase the ghost of a new life beneath the white cliffs of that island. To chase the ghost of the one blissful memory in my past.

I snapped from my daydream. The screams would not cease. Before I could ever be rid of them, I would have to survive.

# 13

The hillside was a carpet of plant life, deep green and vibrant. I sat high up in its reaches, the rocky clearing a refuge since my childhood. Below my sanctuary stretched the sea, its purest shades of blue teased by the wind.

'I don't want to leave here,' I told my friend.

He sat beside me on the stone on which we'd once carved our names. His face was handsome and vital in profile. 'You don't have to.'

I snorted a laugh. We both knew it was a lie, and so instead of speaking I strained my eyes to stare hard at the horizon, willing them to see what was beyond the waters. Willing myself to see the majesty of Rome.

'You'll go there one day,' my companion told me. My most loyal friend, he had always known what was in my mind.

'I don't know if I want to,' I answered, surprising us both. 'Why?'

I thought then about love, and expectation. I thought about dreams, and hope, and how they never survived the reality of our lives. Did I want to shatter an illusion?

'What are we doing up here, Marcus?' I said instead. 'This is home. We shouldn't be here.'

A soft laugh, and then my friend turned to face me, revealing the side of his face that had been hidden.

I jumped back as terror shot through me – his jaw had been unhinged from a sword's bite. It flapped useless and red beneath his face.

'Don't you miss it?' he asked me, his voice now rasping. With each breath, his thick tongue lifted below his opened mouth.

I recoiled, reaching desperately for my weapon.

I found nothing.

'Don't you miss it?' he asked again.

'What are you doing here?' I gasped.

He stood in answer. A hand held against his split stomach was all that kept him together.

'I miss it.' His voice grated, eyes wandering from me to the horizon. 'I miss the sea. I miss the hills. I miss the wind.'

'Marcus . . .'

His stare shot back to me, eyes full of furious vengeance. 'I miss my sisters. I miss my parents. I miss my friends . . .'

'Marcus . . .'

'Do you miss your friends, Corvus? Do you miss your friends?'

He stood over me now. Blood from his wounds dripped on to my face.

It was cold.

'Do you miss me, Corvus?'

'Marcus . . .' I stammered, beginning to cry. 'I'm sorry.'

'DO YOU MISS ME?' he roared.

And then the droplets became a downpour, the blood cascading over my face, washing into my eyes, choking me as it clogged my throat.

I was dying. Drowning.

I tried to scream.

I tried to cry out.

*Marcus . . .*

But there was only blood.

# 14

It was Brando who had thrown the water over me. I woke gasping, seeing the Batavian look back at me with a wide-eyed Folcher on his shoulder.

'I told you to just let him get on with it,' a voice grunted. It was Stumps, lying flat on his own bunk. 'Mattress is fucked now.'

Brando ignored him, and looked apologetically from me to the empty bucket. 'It used to work with my father.'

I swung my feet from my bed and on to the concrete floor of our barrack block. Micon's snores droned from the bed above me. 'How long was I asleep?'

'Six hours,' Brando told me. 'It's almost dusk. The raiding party's beginning to form up,' he added, and I noticed then that both Batavians were wearing their armour.

'You're not coming,' I told them flatly.

Brando ignored me. Instead he passed me a bowl of hot soup and a wedge of bread.

'You're not coming,' I insisted.

'With respect, Felix, we lost hundreds of our brothers in the forest. We'll do what we like.'

I didn't try to argue. Not yet. Instead I quickly finished the food, grateful that I had something to concentrate on instead of the blood that pounded inside my skull, and the lingering touch of the nightmare.

'I heard you volunteered to go on this raid.' Stumps

spoke up from his bed. I said nothing. 'You're a fucking idiot, Felix. Stop looking for ways to get yourself killed.'

I had no desire to argue with my comrade, but I felt the need to calm him. It could be the last time that I saw him, and if this was to be the parting of our ways, I wanted it to be on good terms.

'I'm just going as a guide.'

'You're guiding yourself into a hole in the dirt.'

'I'll see you in a few hours.'

Stumps snorted at that, and rolled on to his side, his face hidden from me.

'I'll see you in a few hours,' I repeated; then I walked into the dusk, collecting my short sword as I went.

Folcher spoke up. 'Felix. Your armour.' Having been fed and given some measure of rest, the Batavian had finally found his tongue; it was thicker in its handling of Latin than Brando's.

I shook my head. 'Not for this. Light and silent.' I hoped my words would encourage the men to remain behind me, to discard their own armour, but they stayed on my heels as I made my way towards the western gate.

The civilians I passed on our way were cowed and fearful. Their manner surprised me, given our victorious slaughter of the dawn.

'Did something happen?' I asked Brando.

'Nothing unexpected,' he answered cryptically. Folcher was only slightly more helpful.

'Arminius was killing.'

I asked them to be more specific. The actions of the day could affect the course of the raid.

'Two dozen horsemen came out of his camp,' Brando

explained. 'They stopped just out of the archers' range. They had heads on their spear-points.'

News of the grotesque display was not surprising. Arminius would want to dampen the Roman spirits that had been raised by the morning's repulse of his attack. I hoped that the owners of the severed heads had not suffered too greatly before the parade, but knowing the enemy, the deaths of the victims would have been long and agonizing.

Sword in my own hand, with bloodshed imminent, I thought then about how quickly it could all end. How years of a soldier's life, and all the memories and moments he had treasured, could cease far from his home surrounded by strangers, and in a strange land. How mothers would never know that their boys cried for their comfort as life slipped away into dirt or sand. The families of the fallen would never know the detail of their loved ones' end, and that, at least, was a mercy.

In the fading light I saw the body of the raiding party forming up. Drawing closer I took in their faces. All were volunteers, and it showed: narrow eyes and set jaws. The mark of men set on killing.

I sought out the crest of Centurion Malchus. He found me first. He was inconspicuous in his dress – a simple tunic. His weapons were sheathed in the scabbards on his crossed belts, his skin darkened with dirt. All about us, the men of the raiding party followed his example.

Brando spoke up quickly. 'Sir, I beg that we may volunteer for the raid? We speak German, sir. We can help.'

Remembering our earlier conversation about my comrades' capabilities, Malchus turned his grey eyes to me. Set back in his darkened face, they made for a formidable sight. I met his look, and gave the slightest shake of my head.

'Just you,' Malchus ordered Brando, sending Folcher's shoulders slouching with disappointment. 'You'll stay next to me at all times, you understand? Send your armour back with your friend.'

Brando obeyed quickly, stripping out of his mail with the help of his comrade. Then the two Batavians embraced, exchanging words in their native language. Stooped with frustration and worry for his friend, Folcher slumped away in the direction of the barracks.

'Did you hear about the parade this afternoon?' Malchus asked me.

'I did, sir.'

'He's trying to rattle us. Keep a cool head,' he warned, apparently still convinced that I yearned for battle. Given the evidence of my life, perhaps he was right. Perhaps he saw something that I did not, or at least that I refused to acknowledge.

'You.' Malchus addressed Brando. 'What's German for *goat-fucker*?'

Brando told him, and the centurion laughed. On the eve of danger, he seemed serene in his happiness. 'Stay here. I'll find you when it's time.'

Silence held between myself and Brando. Elsewhere there was the hushed sound of talk between comrades. The nervous laugh; the whispered promise; the most mundane conversation, offered as distraction from the inevitable.

'Soup, sir?' a voice asked from the darkness. He was an older man with crumpled skin. His Latin was clear, but accented. A slave.

'Thank you,' I answered, taking the broth and observing the man.

As a Roman citizen I had spent my life surrounded by slaves. They had cooked my meals, cleaned my home and died for my family's entertainment in the arena. But never had I seen them as I did now, following my own captivity, however brief it might have been.

'Felix. I'd like some.' Brando took the cup that I'd held on to as I daydreamed.

Brando took a deep mouthful and then passed the cup back to the slave, who slipped away into the darkness. I thought about him as we awaited the order to creep away ourselves: where had he come from? Who had he been? What were his dreams, before slavery had taken him? How did he feel serving men who enjoyed rights and freedoms that were denied him? How did he do it with a smile on his face? And why had he not escaped, or died trying?

'Felix. It's time,' Brando told me, seeing Malchus's towering silhouette approaching. I watched it, noting how the centurion paused to talk to each of his volunteers: cementing their confidence; pouring fuel on to men's anger, or dousing it, whichever was required by their temperament. I had seen many leaders in war, and Malchus was proving himself to be amongst the more natural. Of course, the real test would come beyond the wall.

'Let's go,' he ordered, and I followed to where ropes were being dropped into the darkness and men crowded and hushed on the fighting step, their eyes bright in blackened faces.

As guide, I took hold of the closest rope, and made to

be the first down the wall. Malchus stepped forward and put his hand on mine; he would lead the way. Seconds later, he had been lost to the night.

I felt Brando's presence on my shoulder.

'Are you ready?' he asked me.

'Yes,' I lied.

And then I took the rope in my hand, and crept down into the darkness.

# 15

The muscles of my shoulders ached as I slowly lowered myself down the face of the wall, feet padding gently against the facade to control my descent.

Malchus was already on the ground, his tall frame coiled like a serpent preparing to strike. I joined him as the black shapes of the raiding party began to descend the wall either side of us. We were using ropes for the security of the fort, so the gates could remain shut, but it would make the extraction of the wounded difficult, if not impossible, and so Malchus now gave me the same pragmatic advice as he had given his men.

'If you're hurt badly, just accept it and finish yourself off. We need every able-bodied man we can to defend the fort, and it's not fair to get someone killed in a rescue attempt, just because a soldier can't find the guts to do the right thing. Agreed?'

I could think of little to say, and so I simply nodded in the darkness.

'We've seen what they do to our wounded, sir,' Brando replied for the both of us.

'Good man. Is that everybody down?' Malchus whispered. 'Form up in single file behind me. Not a sound from here. Felix, take us to the bastards.'

There was little point in hesitating, and so I moved off at a crouch across the flat field, pausing regularly to listen for the tell-tale clink of weapons and armour, or the suppressed word or cough from a loose mouth. Arminius's forward picket line was set far back from the fort, and was not manned in strength; who expected the men within the fort's walls to leave its promise of safety and sally out against an army that numbered in the thousands? Still, there was always the chance of encountering scouts, or men desperate to retrieve fallen or wounded friends. With my own eyes, I had even seen men risk death in the darkness to loot the bodies of their dead comrades. I did not doubt that there were such opportunists within Arminius's ranks. Nor did I doubt that there would be Roman soldier, civilian and Syrian archer leaving the fort's walls to plunder the bodies that filled the eastern wall's ditch.

Pausing again, I slowly scanned from left to right, certain that I could now make out the black line of earth that marked the lip of one of the zigzag trenches. During my talk with Malchus he had asked whether I thought it viable to use the earthworks as a means to approach the enemy camp, but darkness gave us the cover and freedom that we needed. Confined in a trench, sound would be dampened. Sight would be limited. I had fought in siege works before, and there was no battle more horrid than that conducted beneath the soil.

I looked up to the sky. A high blanket of cloud continued to contain the moon. So much the better for us. The sixty men were silent except for the escape of breath, and the gentle splash of a piss that could no longer be held. Perhaps two hours passed as we inched our way across the field, considering every yard.

The enemy were not so concerned with concealment.

As we drew closer, the red smudges of their campfires could be made out by the detail of the blazing branches. The silhouettes of tall men stood about the flames, some engaged in conversation, none in song. The morning's slaughter had shaken them, and tonight would be a time for remembering those who had died spitted by arrows or crushed by rocks.

I froze as I felt Malchus's hand on my shoulder. He then cupped it to my ear and whispered, 'Two sentries. Fifty yards. Look ahead, and then come slightly to your left.'

I strained to hear the words, and followed the instructions. Sure enough, Malchus's predatory eyes had picked out the outermost screen of Arminius's sentries.

I felt a prodding in my ribs. I looked down, and saw that it was the centurion's dagger. I met his look, and understood his meaning; we would go forward alone, and take out the enemy's eyes.

With a gesture Malchus ordered the others to remain in place. Then, as seamlessly as an otter slips into the river, Malchus was on his belly and silently crawling towards the Germans.

These were tribesmen, not trained soldiers. They had been rounded up by their chieftains and told that it was war. They were amateurs in a deadly game, and Malchus was a professional who lived for nothing else but to play it. I was not so enthusiastic in giving death, but I could not deny that I was the centurion's equal in practice.

We crawled out and around so that we came from behind the German guards. This close, I could smell the stink of their furs, and the stale ale on their breath. Their voices were hushed, and high. Nervous young men who would never live to learn from their mistake.

I felt the silhouette of Malchus rise beside me. I matched the movement, slowly bringing my hand outwards so that it could be clapped over the sentry's mouth. In my left hand I held the dagger. It was angled high, ready to plunge into the base of the sentry's neck. My breath was held in my throat. The Germans talked on. One of them laughed. And then they died.

Malchus made the first move, but I did not watch his action, needing only to feel the movement. Once I did, I swept my hand out to quickly trap shut the German's mouth, and within the same breath I drove my blade into his skull, fighting against the bones of the spine as I struggled to dig it in deeper, and to kill the man before he could recover enough to bite at my hand and scream.

There was a brief flash of rigidity, and then his body was limp. Blood gushed out from his mouth as I took my hand away and slowly returned the body to the floor.

Malchus wasted no time, creeping at speed to summon the raiding party forward. They rejoined me at the bodies.

'Faster now, Felix,' Malchus whispered, his teeth flashing brightly. With blood on his hands, the centurion seemed eager to unleash more death on to the enemy.

I did as he ordered, moving quickly at the crouch, anxious to pick the trail that gave us the most cover from the dancing light of the enemy fires.

'We need to get some of those flames,' Malchus ordered one of his men, and dispatched six of them to take care of it. 'When it all gets noisy, torch whatever you can.'

I had expected to find more sentries in our path, but soon we were on the edge of the German camp, its tents, shelters and fires clear in the torchlight. Tribesmen were present beside the flames, but it appeared as though most of Arminius's army was sleeping.

Malchus almost seemed disappointed at the ease with which we pushed inwards into the camp, the smell of burning wood, slaughtered goats and open latrines wafting into our nostrils.

'There's some,' I whispered, pointing to a large stack of timber beside a goat pen. Moving closer, I could smell the sawdust and see the fresh saw marks. Arminius was either settling in for a siege, or preparing to fire the fort.

'Grab it,' Malchus ordered his men.

The raiding party's soldiers came forward in pairs. Their instructions were to carry what they could, then make their own way back down the route that we had followed into the camp. If that path was blocked, then they were to fight their own way back to the best of their ability. Failing that, they were to single out the enemy leaders marked by the wealth of gold that the Germans wore so fondly, and attack them. The soldiers were not expected to survive such attempts, but dead German leadership would cause internal disputes within their tribe, and any conflict that drew strength away from Arminius's campaign was welcome.

'Sir.' A voice spoke up beside me. It was Brando; the Batavian crouched beside us, his eyes on Malchus.

The centurion's look gave him consent to speak.

'Sir, I beg permission to try and rescue prisoners. They won't be far from here, sir. I know I can get some of them.'

Brando's eyes were pleading. The big man was set on this task, I could see. He was willing to die for it.

Malchus recognized the same bravery, but shook his head. 'This is about Rome, not us. Arminius had to think we came for this,' he said, gesturing to the timber.

Brando's strong jaw flinched as he bit back his ambition to free the prisoners. 'For Rome, sir,' he muttered, and I was about to tell him to keep quiet, and concentrate on keeping watch, when all thoughts of stealth ceased to matter.

A guttural challenge rang out in the night. It was followed by a clash of steel, and then a scream.

Malchus flexed his shoulder and tested the weight of the blade in his hands. 'They're awake,' he snarled.

And then the killing began.

## 16

The German camp woke slowly to the bloodshed. Many of their men had drunk themselves stupid after their failed assault that morning, and they snored away in ignorant bliss of the presence of Romans amongst them. Those who had found resting places close to the fires would never wake again: Malchus ghosted from one to another, slitting throats and cutting spines. I followed in his wake, my sandals slipping in blood.

'You two, stay close,' Malchus ordered me and Brando. 'The rest of you split up!' he told the men that had yet to collect timber. 'Grab what you can and make your way back to the fort. Try and kill some of the fuckers on the way!'

The sound of blade on blade was growing now. So too were the screams. One must have come from a horrific wound – the agonized wail was never-ending.

'You! Batavian!' Malchus called to Brando. 'Start shouting commands in German. Confuse the fuckers! Call them to rally here.'

Brando obeyed, and within moments a pair of young spearmen rushed to his call. There was a split second to register the confusion in their eyes before Malchus drove the point of his sword into a stomach and I took the other with a driving stroke into a thin chest.

'They've lit fires,' I pointed out to Malchus, seeing tents

erupt into flame a hundred yards away. The centurion had ordered a group of soldiers to fire what they could, and the blaze was quick to spread in the tightly packed German camp. Many tribesmen stumbled out of the tents in panic, unarmed and unprepared. This was not a time for mercy, but survival, and so I cut through them with quick sword strokes. My blade bit into the bones of their forearms as they tried in vain to protect themselves.

'Leave the wounded,' Malchus ordered, seeing Brando sawing through beard and throat, his revenge at hand. 'The more wounded they have the better! Come on. Keep moving.'

We moved. We moved between tents, through pens and over bodies. The tribesmen in our path were drunk or disorientated, and they died easily. So too did their women, but none by my own hand. I saw their bodies stretched out in the mud, golden hair stained red.

'Plenty of women back in camp,' Malchus had teased me, catching my look.

'Enemy left!' Brando called.

I turned, seeing the first pocket of real resistance: a half-dozen tribesmen with swords and spears, their beards and eyes wild in the light of the fires.

Malchus snatched a German spear from a corpse and hurled it like an Olympian, the point burying itself in a chest.

And then he charged.

Instinct rather than duty told me to follow on his shoulder. When faced with greater odds, do what the enemy don't expect. Outnumbering us as they did, a charge from the bloodied centurion was not what they'd foreseen. It was that split second of doubt which gave Malchus his opening, and then he was in amongst them.

He was fast. Perhaps one of the fastest I had seen. His sword was just a blur to me as I concentrated on my own fight, parrying the thrust of a spearman to my side and using my momentum to swing an elbow into his face. I felt his cheekbone buckle beneath the blow. I tried to punch him as he fell, but caught only his shoulder, the sting from my knuckles shooting back through my arm. As the man hit the floor I stamped with all of my force on to his head, my eyes already on my next opponent, who swung wildly with his sword, and it was a simple move for me to feint back before lunging forwards and up beneath the swing, my blade cutting through the soft belly, the heat of his guts steaming as they burst out on to my hand.

I let him fall then, as good as dead. Malchus and Brando had taken care of the others. I assumed we would move immediately, and prepared myself to run.

'Wait a minute,' Malchus ordered, dropping to his knee alongside the largest of the Germans. The centurion must have dropped the man with a combination of blows: the thick German chest had been cleaved open and hissing air escaped from torn lungs. The warrior was not long for this world, but before he could move on to the next, he would have to suffer the pain of Malchus cutting the ears from his head.

'Why, sir?' Brando asked, more in confusion than revulsion.

'Why not?' Malchus laughed. 'Come on. Let's go.'

I had no time to think about our commander's trophy-collecting. Fires raged around us, and where there was no fire, the enemy were forming up in groups bent on killing.

As we ran, we passed the first of our own dead.

'Check that he's done,' Malchus ordered, wanting to save our men the agony of torture.

I turned the soldier over. A German axe was buried deep in his chest.

'He's dead.' I had to shout to be heard. The sound of fighting was scarce, but barked commands were everywhere. So too was the crackle of flames. Goats bleated in fear of the blaze. I saw men and children running with buckets, whilst the intent of most tribesmen seemed to be the protection of their meagre assets rather than the capture of the raiding party.

'They're not interested in us now,' Malchus said as he took in the rippling flames that licked about us, the soot of his face streaked by sweat.

It wasn't until we had sneaked and sprinted our way to the outer edges of the enemy encampment that we realized the Germans had proved him wrong Between the enemy camp and our safety stood a strong skirmish line of German warriors.

## 17

The light of the fire shone back from a hundred iron shield bosses of German warriors positioned between ourselves and safety.

'Remember your way to that trench?' Malchus whispered.

I did. It was our only chance to sneak by the line of enemy, though I had little hope that there would be anything stealth-like about our movements. The enemy were certain to have guarded it and, trapped in the narrow confines of the zigzaging trench, we would have to take them head on, and hope that spearmen did not appear above to spit us like fish.

I led the way back into the warren of tents. The blaze was coming under control. We had to use the last of its distraction whilst we still could.

'Just run,' Malchus ordered.

'Wait!' Brando insisted instead. Without waiting for acknowledgment, he ducked inside a tent. A high-pitched plea from within was followed by a gurgle. Brando emerged seconds later, his blade bloodied and cloaks in his hand.

'Good lad.' Malchus smiled, taking one. I wrapped the other about my shoulders.

'You can lead the way?' I asked the Batavian. He was our best chance of navigating the camp now.

He nodded sternly and we hurried on, the raised bank

of the outer earthworks visible in the light of the flames. A few solitary figures paced this higher ground as we drew closer, but none paid attention to the three cloaked figures who strode brazenly towards the opening of a zigzag trench.

We dropped down into mud. The smell of wet soil filled my nostrils. The walls of the trench dampened sound, the noise of the camp's chaos instantly muted.

'You done this before?' Malchus asked me.

'I have.'

'Take the left wall. I'll take the right.'

I did, sticking close to the soil, Malchus a half-pace beside me on my flank. Brando walked backwards behind us to watch our rear, occasionally peering above the lip to check that we were not placing ourselves like eels in a wicker trap.

We came to the first zigzag of the trench. It angled to the right as we faced it, which placed me on the exposed side. If there was an enemy warrior waiting in the shadows he would see me first, and lunge. Malchus, tight on the right, would have a moment to strike as the man came at me and exposed his own flank. When the trench turned left, our roles would be reversed. A heartbeat of hesitation from either one of us could see the other dead.

The first of the enemy we encountered was still raising his blade when Malchus's sword chopped through his throat. I moved past the fallen man quickly, his companion's wide eyes flashing with terror before I plunged the blade into his heart. It stuck deep, and it took my foot on the man's chest to pull the blade free from the body's suction, air gasping as I finally succeeded.

We moved onwards. Inch by inch, mouths dry, hearts beating. Eyes adjusted to the gloom, but visibility was still measured in yards.

I took the wide sweep on another right angle. There was a brief flash as the axe flew by my head, and buried itself in soil. Then there was a scream as my blade found guts, and blood jetted out over the tribesman's beard.

It had been a loud scream.

The cries of alarm followed a heartbeat later.

'Fuck it!' Malchus ordered. 'Over the side! Go!'

We obeyed, Brando pushing my legs up and over before I turned to help pull him out. Malchus came out alone, vaulting clear like a thoroughbred horse.

We had cleared the enemy's skirmish line, but only just, and warriors now came at us from the darkness, screaming revenge and murder.

'Go!' Malchus shouted. 'Run! Get to the fort!'

And so, for the second time, Brando and I ran from the German trench. On this night, the enemy were not about to allow our escape without pursuit.

Fuck, some of them were fast. I imagined these were the youngest and the most headstrong, eager to make a name for themselves and desperate to wipe clean some of the humiliation that the tribes had endured that day. Two of them cleared ahead of their pack like cheetahs, axe heads flashing as their arms pumped in stride.

'Keep going!' Malchus ordered us, before turning to face the enemy.

The German pair had been fast sprinters, but that counted for nothing once they closed on Malchus, who had speed where it counted: in his sword arm. I heard their screams, but I did not stop to look. I would not stop, I promised myself. I would not stop.

But my body thought differently.

My legs buckled.

I went down hard, my head bouncing from the dirt. Brando stopped instantly and turned to my aid as Malchus rushed to rejoin us, the enemy close on his heels.

'Get up!' he screamed. 'Keep going!'

I tried, Brando grunting as he hauled at my tunic, but I managed only a single pace before my legs failed me again. All the miles, all the wounds, caught up with me now to condemn me before the fort's walls.

'Go,' I begged Brando.

He would not.

Malchus arrived beside us. His eyes flashed from me to the enemy. Less than ten breaths and they would be on us.

'I know, sir.' I gasped for air. As Malchus had ordered, I would die by my own hand. I would not be a plaything for the Germans. 'I'll finish it myself,' I told him.

'Shut up and run!' the centurion roared at me instead.

I tried – fuck, I tried – but I had reached the end of my road, and so as I collapsed on to my back, I took the point of my blade and pressed it into my throat, praying that I would have the strength to push it home before the enemy took hold of me.

'Go,' I pleaded, readying myself to end it all. '*Go!*' I barked.

They would not.

And then the sky rained fire.

# 18

My eyes were closed. I was picturing the fire arrows that had streaked through the sky above me as Malchus and Brando had grabbed my tunic and dragged me like a corpse to the fort's wall. There I had tried to stand, but my limbs had mutinied, failing to obey the simplest command. That did not condemn me, for the awesome display of force from the fire arrows had deterred the German pursuit, and so we were unmolested as ropes were lowered, and I was trussed up like a calf to be lifted on to the battlements and carried to my barrack room.

I opened my eyes to daylight, finding three pairs peering back at me: Folcher, Brando, Stumps.

'You daft cunt,' the Roman grunted.

I sought out Brando. 'Thank you.'

The Batavian shrugged his shoulders.

'You should eat,' his companion urged.

I shook my head. From the tight feeling of my skin, I knew that I was decorated in dried blood. I wanted it off me. The gnawing hunger in my stomach could wait.

'You look happy?' I asked the Batavians cautiously as I got to my feet. The two men were poised to come to my aid should I falter, but they beamed at the news they delivered.

'The raid worked,' Brando exclaimed. 'Arminius's men are cutting down every tree they can find.'

'And moving them that way,' Folcher added, pointing to the distance. 'Not this way.'

'How many made it back?' I asked.

'All but twelve,' Brando answered with a shrug. He wasn't being callous. Men died in battle, and a dozen had died that night in an effort to buy life for hundreds within the fort. In the economics of war, it was a profitable trade.

'I hope it was quick,' Folcher added, grave.

Brando explained to me that Centurion H had excused our section duties that day, and that we should expect a few more men to join us soon, when they were released from the fort hospital's care. I told my comrades to wait for me in the barracks, and went in search of the nearest well.

It was easy to find, as dozens of civilians moved back and forth to the ramparts carrying buckets. These they were using to fill a wide range of containers, from wine barrels to vases, all stored beneath the fort's walls. If Arminius was carrying out his own ruse – and the removal of the timber was a feint before using it to attack the fort – then Prefect Caedicius would do what he could to douse the flames. At the gatehouse, soldiers poured water over the ramparts to keep the gate's timbers sodden.

Seeing such industry within the camp, I expected I would have to wait some time for my turn at the pump. Of course, I had not taken my appearance into account, and when the civilians took in the bloodied and muddied figure that arrived among them they soon moved away, their eyes either fixed on the dirt or drawn irresistibly to the story painted on to my skin.

I had intended to wash directly beneath the pump, but

realized now that to do so would hold up the fort's preparations. Blood was thick on my forearms and had matted my hair, and I knew that I would not be clean quickly. I needed a bucket so that I could move myself to a quiet spot, and I turned this way and that to find one.

'Here,' a voice offered.

'Thank you,' I replied, taking the offered bucket from a young woman. She was perhaps twenty, her blond hair and accent betraying her German heritage. Her face was unremarkable, but her eyes flashed with the brightest blue; they reminded me of the waters of home. And so they compelled me to speak. 'You don't need this for the walls?'

'I can wait,' she answered, eyeing me with more than curiosity. I looked for what that was, feeling in her manner something more desperate than morbid fascination with a killer.

'You came from Varus's army,' she said. 'I saw you, when they brought your men over the wall.'

'I did.'

'I would like to ask you things, if that is fine?'

I wondered at her interest, but shrugged. 'It is. Let's move over here. I'm getting in people's way.'

That was a lie. I was simply sick of their stares. From the flash in her blue eyes, I saw that the girl understood that.

'What's your name?' I asked her.

'Linza.'

'Felix,' I offered; then I began to scrub the blood from my body. I thought I knew why this girl wanted to talk to me, and so I pre-empted the subject, suddenly uncomfortable with her attention. 'You know someone who was in the army?' I guessed.

'My husband. He is a Batavian.'

'Name?'

'Gildo. Fourth Cohort.'

I shook my head. 'I'm sorry, I've never come across anyone by that name, but two of the men that came in with me are Batavian. I could take you to them, if you'd like to talk to them?'

The slightest drop appeared in her shoulders. 'I have.'

'I'm sorry.'

The girl surprised me with her next words.

'I am hoping he is dead,' she said. Feeling my look, she pushed on to explain. 'Better to be dead than a slave. The things they do . . . I pray he is dead.'

There wasn't much I could say to comfort the woman. She was right. And what use are soothing words when they come from a man wiping blood from his hands?

'Thank you. I'll go now,' she said, though she made no move to leave, and her words were floated as a question. I had come to the well in search of some solitude, but a kind female presence was unlike anything I had experienced since Pannonia, and a voice whispered inside my mind that I should enjoy the moment while it lasted. The alternatives were the company of my own cracked mind, or my comrades in the barrack blocks: beloved to me, but certainly harder on the eyes and nostrils than this woman.

'Could you help me get more water?' I asked.

'I can.'

I could hear the relief in her reply; she was as desperate as I for an escape from her truth. Together, we could perhaps provide each other with the briefest respite from our realities.

And then Arminius appeared.

My first warning of it was calls of alarm from the ramparts. The mood of the civilians switched from confidence to the early stages of terror in moments. I put the bucket in the girl's hands without a word and made for the ramparts. I wanted to run, but the painful memory of my collapse was still fresh. I was a proud bastard, I realized then. It hadn't been the thought of my own imminent death that had stung me so deeply in the field, but the thought that I had, through my own weakness, endangered the life of my comrades who had been forced to carry me.

It took me some time to reach the western rampart. By the time that I did, the fighting step was thronged with off-duty soldiers come to join those of the watch.

'Get back to your fucking posts!' I heard Malchus roar. 'This isn't a fucking theatre! Get back to your posts, and stand by for your orders! Move!'

The tall man's face was livid, and soldiers ran quickly at his words. Malchus was astute, and did not want Arminius to lure our eyes to one spot, opening up our blind sides.

I was turning to leave myself, when the centurion's voice boomed again.

'Felix!'

A sweeping gesture of his arm was my invitation to join him.

'You don't need to be here for this,' he grunted as I

saluted him on the rampart. 'But, because you were there, I'll give you that choice.'

I wondered at his words, and then, as I looked out over the wall and into the field, I understood too well: Arminius had come, and he had not come alone. Three Roman soldiers knelt in the dirt.

'My men,' Malchus hissed.

Not all twelve of the missing had died in the raiding party. Now, mere yards out of archery range, they would die by inches before our eyes.

I heard a tramp of hobnails and turned, finding Prefect Caedicius and the small body of his staff.

'Swine,' the veteran cursed through clenched teeth. 'That bastard swine.'

He caught my eyes on him then and became a commander, rather than a man. 'Malchus told me what you did last night. I don't have an opening for an officer, but when I do, we'll talk.'

The suggestion of promotion bounced from me like rain on marble. Survival was my concern, not the career ladder.

After taking a moment to compose himself and appear rational, Malchus turned to his superior officer. 'Sir, let me go out there. Let me challenge the cunt, one on one.'

Caedicius shook his head.

Malchus pressed: 'Sir, I can finish him.'

'And if his men just ride in and kill you?'

Malchus would not be dissuaded. 'Then Arminius shows that he's a fucking coward, sir, and he loses support. I'll die for that.'

'I can't let you die for that, Malchus.'

The first scream echoed out across the field.

'Please, sir,' Malchus begged.

'The barbarians are out there, Malchus, not in here,' Caedicius explained, shaking his head sadly. 'We can't lower ourselves to their level.'

I expected that Caedicius simply did not want to lose his best soldier so easily, and for such little gain. Malchus would be deadly in single combat, but he would be more deadly still behind the fort's walls, orchestrating death for the enemy on the rampart and in the ditch.

A long wail cut short Malchus's retort. I chanced a look out towards the condemned men, and wished that I had not. One was tied by his arms, the length of rope fixed to a horse's saddle. His legs were tied similarly to another beast. The animals were being whipped in opposite directions, and so, slowly, the man was being pulled apart.

Malchus turned, his eyes full of fire and fury. 'Felix,' he ordered. 'Get down from here. Go to your section.'

I was happy to obey, my head swimming as I took the steps back to the dirt. The vision of the man and the horses seemed burned into my eyeballs, and would not leave me. Feeling light-headed, I sat back against the wall of a building. I saw Caedicius take his leave from the fighting step, but Malchus remained, an immovable statue as the prisoner's body and screams finally gave out, and the German host gave a cheer.

I tasted bile in my throat. I had been yards away from such a fate myself. If Brando and Malchus had left me, would I truly have had the courage to take my own life, or would hope, just the slightest touch of it, have been enough to let me fall to the enemy for a second time?

'I thought you'd be here,' I heard, and opened my eyes.

Stumps.

'Why do you do this to yourself, you soft bastard? You think any good is going to come from it? We're all gonna die, Felix. Stop trying to live with a blade to your throat.'

'Can you help me up?'

My comrade reached down, and pulled me to my feet. 'At least you're clean,' he mumbled.

'I met a girl at the well.' I, for some reason, felt compelled to tell him.

Stumps looked at me with new eyes. 'You know that's the first time I've ever heard you mention a woman?'

I shrugged.

'So what happened?'

'Arminius.'

'Ha! Thwarted by the German. He really is a master of grand strategy, the cunt.'

'She was looking for her husband. A Batavian.'

'Oh! That one! Yeah, she came by the block. Good shag, she was.'

I fell into the man's trap – my eyes betrayed my jealousy.

'You soft bastard!' Stumps cackled. 'She just came by, asked questions, cried, and then left. Probably the same outcome as a sexual experience with you, actually.'

'I'm glad you're feeling back to your old self.'

'I'm better than that,' my friend told me as the screams echoed beyond the battlements, 'because I've accepted that we're going to die here, Felix. And honestly, once you accept that, everything else seems all right. Even the fucking soup tastes incredible.'

'You need more rest.'

We walked on in silence. I knew that my comrade's elevated mood would not last. I had seen it in other soldiers broken by war. This optimistic fatalism would be followed by soul-crushing guilt, and then terror. I knew this first hand, and that was why I was only too happy to try and leave the screams behind us.

With one final look over my shoulder, I saw that the imposing silhouette of Malchus had not moved from his vigil – he would not abandon the men who had been trapped in the raid. Exhausted, but safe in the knowledge that I had such leaders to follow, I knew I could sleep well that night.

'Arminius is gonna know how understrength we are now.' Stumps's words were prompted by another scream of a man under torture. 'Probably that the raid for wood was a load of arse, too.'

I shrugged, though I expected he was right. 'We'll see.'

We had almost reached our own barrack block now. I felt my comrade's pace slow.

'Please, Felix.' Stumps was looking anywhere but at my face as he forced the uncomfortable words from his chest. 'No more stupid shit. I've lost enough mates.'

'All right,' I promised.

Stumps still refused to look me in the eye. 'All right then. I'm gonna go find a drink. Coming?'

A drink with a comrade. I think I might actually have smiled at the suggestion. At that moment, only one thing sounded sweeter.

'I'm going to sleep,' I told him, entering the barrack room and falling heavily on to my straw mattress.

Stumps said something as I pressed my body down into the bed. I caught the sarcastic tone, but the words were lost to me as my eyelids slammed down. Within a breath, I was asleep.

It was almost a day before I woke. The weak light of dawn was the clue as I stirred, half hoping that I would slip away again into slumber.

I had dreamed I was in Britain, an island that I had never seen, but which had been painted to me in stories when I was a young man. I wanted to return to those visions. The details of the characters in the dream were lost to me, but the image of white cliffs was seared into my sight. A serene feeling of calm had come over me, the sensation of which I had not experienced in months, nor did I have a right to when surrounded by enemies.

Enemies. I could not stay in my bed. My dreams were exactly that, and so I shook them off and opened my eyes.

The white cliffs vanished.

I was alone in the room, but that didn't alarm me. There was no sound from the walls. No shouts. No cries. The camp seemed tranquil.

I swung my feet on to the floor. My joints and muscles ached, but my mind felt vital for the first time in days. I smiled as I saw that bread and cheese had been placed beside my pillow. My stomach growled instantly once I'd laid my eyes on the food and I ate it quickly.

I stood and stretched, knots of muscle and bone popping and clicking. Pulling back the partition curtain, I saw that the arms and armour of my comrades had gone with them. I guessed that they had been assigned to some guard duty or other, of which there would be many. Arminius's assaults had been bloody, but those moments of a siege were the anomaly. The usual was the tedious nature of standing watch, the gnaw of hunger and the stress of confinement.

For the moment, however, I was happy to remain confined myself, and lay back on my bed. There would be more bloodshed, and to survive it I would need my strength. Guilt suddenly washed over me then, taking any lingering happiness from my dreams with it; I would not be a burden again, as I had been to Malchus and Brando. No one would die for me, I vowed. And with those thoughts, I felt the familiar darkness creeping back. Seeping into my mind. Telling me that I was scum. Telling me that I was a traitor. Telling me that Marcus—

I shot to my feet as I heard men enter the block.

'Brando.' I was so happy to see his face and its promised distraction from the poison of my thoughts. 'Where have you been?'

'Duty up on the northern wall. Centurion H told us to let you sleep.'

'Anything happening?'

'Nothing since the three executions. Centurion H thinks Arminius was using it as a chance to get a look at our numbers, and sneak in a little closer.'

H was probably right. Armed with the knowledge extracted from his prisoners, Arminius would now have a detailed picture of what stood in front of him.

'We've got three more for the section,' Stumps told me as he came in and clambered up on to his bunk. 'They've gone to get their possessions.'

The trio arrived soon after. Centurion H appeared with them.

'Felix,' he greeted me cheerfully. 'How are the legs? Went a bit wobbly on you, did they? I do tend to have that effect on people.'

I couldn't help but smile at the man's easy manner.

'I've got some new lads from the hospital to join you. They're all Nineteenth Legion. I'll leave you to get on. Whole century will form up at dusk, full armour. We're a reserve in case they try anything at dusk, and then we've got night duties. Sound good?'

'All good, sir.'

'Great. I'll leave you to it then.'

I heard the sound of arms and armour being shed in the storage partition of the block, and then the first of the men appeared. He was tall, friendly looking, and stammered like a man pulled out of a frozen lake.

'Ba-ba-ba-balbus,' he greeted me.

'You sound like a fucking sheep,' Stumps snorted from his bed. 'The Batavians will be trying to crawl into your arse.'

The newcomer and the German-born pair laughed. Clearly Stumps had already used the insult that day. It was a tired joke, but I smiled to see my friend's mind active, if only to create barbs.

'Take a bunk,' I told the soldier; then: 'What's your name?' I asked the second head through the doorway.

'Dog, sir,' the man replied.

I didn't need to ask why. His breath hit me like a battering ram. The source of the stench was his rotting gums. Two teeth perched in the meat like dirty fingernails. Dog Breath, a common name throughout all legions.

'Twisted my ankle, I did, sir,' Dog explained the reason for his time at the hospital, his words wet.

'Take a bunk,' I told him, glad that there was not one available alongside mine. Truly, the man's smell was more pungent than the rotting dead beyond the wall. 'And you don't call me sir,' I added.

'That's good then. Wasn't planning on doing it,' said the final man to appear. He was younger, and would have been handsome if his features hadn't been decorated with the scars of disease. The arrogance of his words jabbed at me, and from years of experience in the legions, I knew how I must deal with that display of self-importance – with violence.

Instead, I put out my hand. There was enough fighting beyond the walls. 'Felix.'

My hand was ignored.

'Whose is that bed?' the man asked instead. A flare of anger burst inside me, but I fought it down, and opened my mouth to talk.

But I was too late. Knuckles cracked into bone.

I looked down and saw the newcomer writhing on the floor, struggling to protect his head as kicks rained down.

They were not my own. Folcher and Brando beat the man as savagely as if he were the Germans who'd held them slave.

I let them be at first. The man had brought it upon himself. And yet . . . this was my section. I was the one that carried the burden of command and leadership. If you want to be a leader, you lead.

'Enough!' I thundered, and the two Batavians backed away instantly, their breathing heavy.

Finally convinced that the rain of kicks was over, the man slowly uncovered his head and looked up at me.

'What's your name?' I asked him gently.

'Statius.'

'This is my section,' I told him.

'I understand,' he whimpered.

'Good.'

And then I brought the hobnails of my sandals down on to his face. This time, when my men began kicking, I did not stop them.

It was only the sound of a voice in the doorway that brought the violence to an end. A hard voice, steel dragged over gravel.

'This looks familiar,' it said.

I turned to look at the man in the doorway.

I turned to look at a ghost.

*Titus.*

# 19

The slab of a man filled the doorway, his rugged face drawn into a smile as he surveyed the bloodied soldier that lay moaning at my feet.

*Titus.*

What did I expect had happened to the man who had commanded our section through the battle of the forest? Either that he was dead with the others, or rich beyond its reach. Rich with the legion's pay chests that he and I had found as battle disintegrated into massacre. Clear of the fighting and in the trees, I had made the choice to turn my back on the riches, and to instead seek out my surrounded comrades, and death. Titus had chosen life, and had melted into the forest with the pay chests. Both of our roads had led here.

'Fuck,' I swore softly. How else could I express the hundreds of thoughts and words that now bounced inside my skull?

Titus looked up to one of the bunks. Stumps was staring at his old friend with wide eyes and open mouth. He seemed paralysed.

'I'd shut that hole before the Syrians put something in it.' Titus smiled. 'Are you gonna come down here or not?'

Stumps did. As he embraced his friend, tears rolled over his cheeks. I thought I caught the sight of them in Titus's eyes, too.

'Everyone else out,' I ordered. This was a moment for

our old section. For the men who had stood beside each other in the forest.

Brando and Folcher understood. They grabbed Statius's limp form and dragged him from the room by his ankles. The others fell in behind them.

'Not you,' I said, grabbing Micon. 'You're a part of this.'

Stumps and Titus finally broke their embrace. Stumps made to speak, but only doubled over in tears. He buried his face in his friend's thick chest. Micon watched, his face blank.

'Still the brains of the unit, are you?' Titus grunted at the lad. 'But I'm glad you're alive,' he added with warmth.

'Thanks,' Micon muttered. He was out of his depth, and shuffled back into the room's corner.

'We thought you were dead,' Stumps finally managed.

Titus shrugged. 'We all thought we were all dead.'

He turned his eyes to me, then: 'I can't decide if you're the luckiest or unluckiest bloke I've ever met. You make a habit of falling from one death trap into another, but then you're harder to kill than a fucking cockroach.'

'Uglier, though,' Stumps chimed in, now conscious of his tears.

'How the fuck did you get here?' Titus asked us.

And so we told him.

Titus sat on the opposite bed to mine and listened patiently as I told him about our short time as prisoners. I left out my reckoning with Arminius, and how the German had revealed that I was more than just a simple deserter from the Eighth Legion, beginning instead with how I had found Stumps when the army had surrendered.

113

Once I had finished the story of our escape, Titus asked if we knew the fate of our comrade Moonface, or Centurion Pavo.

'I saw Pavo go under a horse,' I told him. What had happened to Moonface, none of us knew.

'They executed every one of the officers?' Titus asked me again.

I nodded.

'Lot of room for promotion now,' Stumps joked darkly.

'Maybe if there was a legion.' Titus shook his head. 'I still can't believe it. Three legions? How many people that I knew just disappeared in that forest?'

The answer was in the hundreds. The Seventeenth Legion had been home to Titus and Stumps for years. Their friends, acquaintances and enemies of decades had been wiped away in the space of days.

'I didn't think I'd ever see a legion fit into one barrack room.' Titus grimaced, looking around at the half-section that had survived the massacre.

Silence fell. It was time for him to tell his own story.

'Micon.' He pulled some coins from a purse. 'Go find us some wine. Good lad.'

'You know he'll be wandering around the camp lost as fuck?' Stumps asked.

That had been Titus's intention. He wanted total privacy for his own story. He had that confidence in Stumps, his old comrade. He had it in me, a witness to his secrets.

'When our battle lines broke, I was on my own. I was lost. I made it to the trees, but there was a group of them after me. I couldn't make it back to the body. I'm sorry.'

Stumps nodded. 'It was chaos.' he agreed, letting his friend know he understood, and held no grudge that Titus had made his own escape. 'Felix thought you were dead.'

I didn't know what to say. Titus filled the space.

'I took a spear and went down, but the mail held. You know what it was like. I probably looked dead.'

Stumps nodded again at the words. Evidently I was forgiven my own fictitious part in Titus's separation from his comrades.

'I got away from that first lot,' Titus went on, 'but when I came out of the forest my tracks were picked up by a group of horsemen. I could see them coming after me, but I kept my nose just ahead by going through rivers and trees when I could. I even crawled for a fucking day.' He spat, angry at the memory. 'I could see smoke on the horizon, just enough for it to mean life, not pillaging.'

'This place?' Stumps asked.

'This place. But the horsemen got me first. My legs gave up on me with less than a mile to go.'

'Then how . . .' Stumps began.

'They were Roman.' Titus laughed, enjoying the irony. 'I'd been running from Romans. They were out looking for Varus's army.'

'Why?' I asked.

'Remember when Varus abandoned the baggage train? A lot of civvies turned back then. The smart ones had even turned back before that. The hairies probably got most of them, but some made it here. The command here didn't know how bad things were with Varus, but they knew it was bad enough for him to abandon the baggage train, and so the camp commander sent out scouts.'

'You were the one that told them about Arminius?' I suspected.

'I was. They barred the gates then, and Prefect Caedicius loves me for it.' The big man grinned. 'Gave me any choice of post I wanted.'

'Let me guess.' Stumps laughed. 'You told him you wanted to be commander of anus inspection for the archers?'

'I told him I wanted to be quartermaster, you dickhead. Every fort has a black market, and a fort under siege is our chance to get rich.'

I think I smiled at that point. Titus had survived the massacre of the forest and had escaped Arminius's army by a whisker, only to become besieged by them, but money was foremost on his mind no matter his predicament.

'I've got plans if we survive this place,' the man grunted, feeling my look. 'And call it fortune if you want, but someone wanted me to be here. Stumps, *Metella* is here. She's been running the show since the army pulled out of Minden.'

Metella. I remembered the name, and the woman. She was as massive as Titus himself, with a mouth more foul. The industrious camp follower had run an inn in the town where the army had pitched its tents for the summer, and evidently her business did not stop with wine. As a friend of Titus's, I should have guessed as much.

'I'm the quartermaster,' Titus spelled out. 'And she runs the black stuff.'

Despite the death and the misery, fortune did seem to smile on this man who lived for coin.

'I'm glad you're in your element,' I offered. 'But why are you telling us this?'

Titus shrugged, as if it was obvious. 'I want you two in on it.'

'You actually think we're leaving here alive?' Stumps laughed.

Titus face's clouded over. His words were steel. 'We didn't come this far to die here. Do you want in on this or not?'

Stumps shrugged. 'I'll keep you company.'

'And you?' he asked, the question thrust towards me like a spear.

I held my tongue for a moment, looking into my comrade's dark face. 'Let's talk outside.'

We stepped on to the packed dirt outside the block, and walked in silence. I had no destination in mind, only that I wanted privacy with the man who knew that I had deserted from the Eighth Legion in Pannonia. For my part, I knew that Titus was a smuggler and a murderer. He was not the kind of person to hold secrets without considering them leverage, nor would he look on a loose end with favour.

'You still think I want you dead.' He half smiled, reading my thoughts or, more likely, my body language; I realized then that I was tense and coiled, as if waiting on him to strike. In truth, there was an uncomfortable tension within the fort that plucked at my senses. I wondered now if its cause had been Titus, watching me, and waiting.

'You're not a talker, *Felix.*' Titus said, stressing my new name to remind me that he was aware of my true identity, or at least part of it. 'You haven't even told Stumps about what happened.'

'I've told no one,' I confirmed.

'We're the two most honest men in the army.' Titus smiled. 'I'm a selfish bastard, and I'm all right with that. I'm not going to pretend that I give a shit about anything other than myself and a few mates. After what we went through in the forest, I think you fall into that second category.'

It was something I'd considered before. True, the forest had taken us from plotting each other's deaths to saving each other's lives, but that made us comrades more than friends. *Friend?* Could I call him that? Did I truly have his trust? Did he have mine?

The big bastard grinned. 'You were glad to see me, weren't you?'

I had been.

'Friends then,' I allowed, and the man snorted. 'What happened to the pay chests?' I asked, more out of curiosity than from any remote hope of touching them. For a moment, I had seen those coins as my passage to Britain and a new life. Now I expected they were scattered across the forest's floor. I was half right.

'I buried them,' Titus confided in me, with the same sense of sadness as if he'd buried his own family. 'Goat-fuckers were looking for survivors, so I found a spot by a river and buried them.'

'What about the donkey?' I asked suddenly, referring to the beast that had carried the chests.

Titus choked on a laugh. 'What about it?'

'I don't know. What happened to it?'

'I killed it, of course. Didn't want any witnesses . . . Fuck me, you're a strange one, Felix. I let it go. Didn't

118

want the hassle of its tracks. Bloody donkey.' He laughed again.

I had surprised myself with the question, but I was almost relieved to know the animal had been let loose.

'I remember how to get there.' Titus brought my wandering mind back to the hoard of coins. 'I have a life waiting for me outside of the army,' he reminded me.

He had told me briefly of that life. Shown me a ghost of it. A son, presumed dead at sea, now alive and in trouble. What kind of trouble, Titus had not said, but I could see that the man was resolved to end it. If Titus did live through this siege, then I doubted it would be the last time he saw bloodshed, or that he would die peacefully in his own bed. Some men were born for violent death.

'I don't think Arminius can get over these walls,' Titus asserted. 'He's going to try and starve us out, but we'll be all right. We'll find a way, and then you, me, Stumps – and a few others we trust – we go back for the chests. What are your new lads like? The two Batavians look handy.'

I kept silent. Titus took that to mean I was turning down his offer. He had no idea that I was picturing the white cliffs of Britain, and the ship that would take me to them.

'Felix, I know you still have your doubts about me, but if we're not blood brothers after the forest, then what are we?'

I turned to look at the man who had stood by me through the worst of it. There was no denying that I had missed his dangerous presence.

'You've seen what's outside of those walls?' I asked, a genuine smile creasing my cracked cheeks. 'What we are, Titus, are ghosts.'

# 20

I stood on the eastern wall with a solitary companion. The night around us was cold and moonless. I pulled my scarf tight around my face to fight off its touch.

It was deep into our watch, and a light wind had pushed the cold inside my bones. I rolled my shoulders in their joints, and flexed my fingers against the shaft of a javelin. My shield rested against the wall, and now I reached for it.

'I'm going to check the others,' I told Micon beside me. The rest of my section was spaced out to cover ground, but I kept the young soldier within arm's reach as we stood watch. 'Don't move.'

I made my way from man to man. The section covered a hundred yards of wall. More than eight men should have been assigned to such a stretch, but the fort was under-strength. Arminius would want the soldiers on the walls to burn out through fatigue, but Caedicius was refusing to indulge him, instead gambling that he could rest his forces and have enough warning to reinforce the wall in case of an attack in the night.

It was a tactic I hoped would not be put to the test.

'Black as a Syrian's arsehole,' Stumps greeted me, looking out into the darkness.

'You seem to have their arses on your mind a lot,' I responded. Stumps was silent. He never knew how to take it when I tried to make a joke.

'Fucking cold,' he said instead. 'If it is a siege, it won't be much fun. German winter's savage.'

'It'll be savage on his own men, too.'

'Yeah, but something about being uncomfortable in your own country makes it a bit easier to put up with, don't you think? Not like they're going to go short of supplies or firewood.'

I couldn't argue with the man. 'Firewood's one thing we've got. Even with the civilians housed there're still enough empty buildings we can tear down.'

'We'll see,' Stumps conceded. We lapsed into silence for a moment. 'I'm so glad he's alive,' he then told me, referring to his old friend, Titus.

'Me too.'

There was a moment before he spoke again. 'You said you saw him die,' he said. The words were simply stated, but accusation simmered beneath the calm tone.

'I thought I did.'

Stumps said nothing. I decided it was time to leave, and began to turn.

'Did he run?' he asked me. 'Just be honest with me, Felix. Did Titus run?'

I turned back to face the man. It was too dark to make out his features. I expected his eyes would be filled with anguish. Worry and doubt that his friend had saved his own skin, and left his comrades behind.

No good would come of the truth.

'I thought he was dead,' I lied. 'I'm glad that I was wrong.'

I walked away then and returned to Micon, relieved to find the young one where I had left him. Lying to Stumps was not something I enjoyed doing, but it was necessary. He had cheered in the days since we arrived in the fort, but his mind was fragile. He didn't need the truth of his friend's desertion placed atop the other traumas. I wondered how Titus would approach the truth, should he and Stumps survive to retrieve the pay chests, and the coins that Titus had chosen over what he had thought would be death with his comrades.

'What was that?' Micon spoke up in the darkness, breaking me from my thoughts.

'What was what?'

'I thought I heard something.'

I said nothing. The fort was a noisy place, even at night. Wood creaked. The waters of the river rolled by. Dogs barked, and cats screeched. It wasn't a place that made a man feel comfortable, and I was certain that young Micon—

'There it is again!' he hissed.

I held a finger to his lips, and controlled my breathing. I strained to hear. Nothing. Nothing, until—

A soft bump against wood.

It came from our left, on the stretch of wall held by the next section.

'Don't move,' I whispered, stepping off. 'Six Section?' I hissed. 'Six Section?'

'What?' a soldier answered from along the battlements.

I ignored him; the sound had come again. It was wood against wood, and I knew then that death was about to follow in its wake.

'Ladders!' I shouted at the top of my lungs. 'They're putting ladders up! Find them!'

I rushed to the edge of the wall, looking downwards. It was a carpet of black, but alive and rolling like a night sea. My silhouette above drew a spear that cut through the air to my side, and then I was running, looking for the ladders.

A soldier of Six Section found one first. He hurled his javelin into the darkness and I heard a scream. I joined the man, and we pushed the ladder back and into the night with ease; the first casualty must have cleared the other tribesmen from the rungs.

'Report! Report!' I heard Centurion H's voice below.

'They're on ladders! We need more men!'

I could already hear the cries to rally within the fort. Caedicius had ordered that half the men rest in full battle order, and these readily equipped troops were now being rushed to the battlements, sleep in their eyes and nervous energy in their muscles.

I ran back towards my own section. The sound of battle was growing from the opposite end of the camp, and all need for tact had gone.

'Seven Section!' I shouted for the ears of my own men. 'Watch for ladders! Watch for ladders!'

A reserve section was running up the steps and on to the battlements. A dozen Syrian archers were with them, some carrying torches that they now pitched over the walls. Following the fall of the flames, I saw for the first time the assaulting enemy: dozens of them, ladders in hands and faces tight with nerves. Now uncovered, they screamed curses and threats as arrows began to thump into their bodies.

'Seven Section, use the rocks! Save your javelins!'

I reached for one of the piles of stones, picking out a

rock that was the size of Titus's fist. I hurled it down, seeing a head snap back.

I felt a shove in my back and cleared the way as more archers appeared. I watched them work, shaft after shaft unleashed into the men below. By the firelight I scanned either way along the wall; I saw no ladders leaning against it, and thought that the enemy had been stopped from making it on to the fighting step.

The clash of steel on steel told me I was wrong.

It was coming from Six Section's stretch of wall. I had been assigned my own duty, but hearing cries of challenge and pain, I made the decision to abandon my post. The archers beside me were murdering the men below them, and with their presence it would be near impossible for the enemy to place ladders against the wall.

But if they were already on it . . .

'Seven Section! On me! On me!'

Through the darkness the shapes of my section appeared. The fighting step was deep enough for two men to overlap their shields and advance, and Brando fought to be the one alongside me as we pushed towards the sound of ringing blades.

We were too late to save the last legionary standing. He went down with a spear in his guts, and joined two of his comrades and a few of the enemy on their backs. A dozen of the tribesmen were on the rampart, some calling down to their comrades, frantically gesturing for ladders and reinforcement.

'Wait for the archers!' Statius shouted from behind me. 'We can pick them off!'

He was right – the Germans were exposed – but then I

saw the head of another ladder thump against the wood. There was no time to wait.

'Javelins!' I shouted. 'Javelins! Loose!' At the order, the men at the rear of the section dropped back to gain space, and hurled their shafts ahead. One sailed over the wall. The second dug into a thigh. The German howled, and we advanced.

There were only ten yards to cover. Ten yards where I pulled my shield tight to me as if it were my long-lost child, and dipped my head so that my world was reduced to the slit between shield and helmet brim.

'Second rank, shields up!' No sooner had I called the order than a throwing axe dug into the shield held above me.

I watched the Germans now, seeing them jockey for position and honour. None had become the first on to this wall because they were cowards, but the sight of an advancing tide of shields gave them pause; how to attack a formation where the only break in cover revealed the pointed blades of short swords?

Faced with the challenge, the tribesmen did what they knew best.

They charged.

'Brace!' I called, grinding my hobnails into the wooden planks.

The warriors hit our shields a second later. The force of it jerked me back and sent a shock of pain along my shield arm, but our formation held firm. I pulled my sword arm back, freeing it from a man who had punctured himself on the steel by his reckless momentum.

Through the narrow slit between my own shield and the one held above me, I saw bearded faces screaming and biting. Spit and blood flecked my face. Fist and axe hammered against shield and my head in the savage drum of battle. The enemy were vicious, brave and ferocious, but they could not break apart our shields.

Beside me Brando screamed oaths, his sword arm sawing in and out, back and forth. My own blade bit flesh, hot blood shooting from a German mouth and on to my neck.

'Push!' I shouted at the men behind me. 'Push!'

It was a wrestling match now, our shields against theirs, and as our short swords punctured the stomachs of their leading warriors, there could be only one result.

They broke. They ran from us, seeking their escape over the wall.

'Break formation,' I managed, panting.

I looked left and right along the wall, which was now well lit by torches. Below us, civilians raced to replace the flames and stockpiles of stones. Archers sought out targets beyond the rampart, but our stretch of the fighting step was clear. Clear, but not out of danger; the sound of battle still echoed from the far side of the fort.

Centurion H came running towards me. He ignored the leaking bodies at his feet. 'Re-form your section on this stretch. They're attacking in force on the west side, but they could come back up here. I'm sending half of these archers back inside the fort as a reserve. The rest will space themselves out.'

A nod was enough to acknowledge the orders, and then H was away to see to his other sections.

'Are they all dead?' I asked Brando. The Batavian was busily checking the German bodies and pocketing their coins.

'They're dead,' he replied, spitting at one.

'Put them over the side when you're done.'

Folcher and Balbus came forward to help the big Batavian lift the bodies over the battlements, dropping them into the ditch below. The final 'corpse' gave a cry of pain as he landed in the darkness.

Brando smiled at me. 'Dead enough.'

Folcher grinned, and then cocked his head. 'The fight is smaller,' he said. Sure enough, in the west, the clash of arms and cries of pain were growing quieter.

'Look to your front,' I ordered my comrades, expecting another attempt.

It came soon enough, but this time, with torches on the walls and archers on the fighting step, the assault died before it had even reached the ditch. The tribesmen knew that they had blown their chance, and so, as the first shafts punctured flesh, the warriors turned and ran. Syrian, Latin and German taunts followed them.

'What did you say to them?' Dog asked Folcher after one particularly long and breathless barrage.

'That I will rape and eat their mother, then feed my shit to their children.'

'Fuck me.' Stumps whistled. 'If soldiering doesn't work out for you, there's always poetry.'

We waited on the battlements until dawn had come and gone. Centurion H was an astute and caring officer, and sent civilians up and down the line with water and soup.

'Where's the wine, sir?' Stumps had asked.

'Wine's for winners. You can have some when all the hairies are dead.'

As well as bringing refreshments to the fighting men, the civilians also took away the dead.

I had seen a half-dozen of our own fallen carried away. Dozens of enemy bodies had been piled in the ditch and on the rampart. When Centurion H returned to speak with me, the grief for the loss of his men was beginning to sink in. His eyes were a little narrower. The angle of his chin had dropped.

'I hate this job sometimes,' he confided in me. 'West side got it worse though. Took Malchus and his reserves to keep them from the gatehouse. Lost a dozen dead and nearly double that with injuries.'

'We can't keep this up every night,' I said, and H nodded in agreement.

'But can Arminius?'

I had no answer for him. Only the German prince knew what he was willing to sacrifice to take the fort. Until he showed his hand there was nothing we could do but stand on its walls, and wait for death.

## 21

Dawn arrived, bringing with it the sight of dark red stains on the fighting steps. Balbus found a severed hand and tossed it casually into the ditch. On another day, perhaps the men would have found some humour or joke in the body part, but, drained by the night's cold and the enemy attacks, conversation was stilted, the men withdrawing into themselves as they looked out over the battlements with sunken eyes.

There was not much comfort to take from the view of our vantage point. We had beaten back the assault, but Arminius's host hung over the fields and gentle hills like a curse.

I stared at the gathering of tribes, wondering where Arminius himself was. What was the prince thinking? What was he planning? In a moment of self-importance, I even wondered if I featured in his thoughts.

I doubted that. His was a mind of singular vision and, having failed to live up to my part in it, I was certain I would have been cut out and cast aside like rotten flesh.

I turned and looked down into the fort itself. Preparing for a dawn assault, Caedicius had the whole of the garrison stood to and ready to fight. Many of these men were held back in reserve so that they could be directed to the point of attack, and so my section was once again spread thinly on the wall, a dozen Syrian archers split down into pairs as our support.

I walked from man to man. There was little to say, and so we simply stamped our feet against the nagging cold and exchanged tired looks.

I came to Statius, the soldier I had beaten for his disrespectful attitude. Beneath the rim of his helmet, his face was yellow and purple, lips swollen. I could imagine the pain he was feeling in his body, the agonizing stiffness of bruised limbs and ribs. I felt the beginning of pity for the man, but forced it down. His attitude had justified the punishment. Still, I felt it important to explain to him why he had needed to suffer violence.

'Individuals won't survive this.' My words caught him off guard. 'We're going to live or die as a section. If you don't understand that, I'll beat you again until you do.'

I saw the flash of anger in his eyes. A flash of arrogance, and pride. There was nothing he would love more than to spit me with his javelin, and yet . . .

'I'm sorry,' the young man apologized. 'New section and people I don't know. I thought I should stand up for myself, so I don't get shat on.'

'Look who's outside the walls,' I told him, jutting my chin towards the enemy. 'There's no time for the usual barracks bullshit here. No one's going to get fucked over and have to clean an entire section's kit. We're on the battlefield, Statius, not a parade ground.'

The man grunted an acknowledgment.

'Last night,' I asked him. 'Your first taste?'

Grudgingly, the man admitted that it was. He wasn't happy with that fact, but I was still unsure as to whether that was down to the feeling of inadequacy that plagues many young and ambitious soldiers, or because he desired to be anywhere else but in the killing grounds; I could hardly find fault if it was that second reason.

'Can I rely on you?' I asked him.

'Yes.'

It was not the most convincing reply I'd ever heard, but it would have to do. Centurion H called me from along the wall.

'I've got some of the women to go and find something hot for the troops,' he told me. 'I sent a runner to the new quartermaster but I've heard nothing back. Useless bastard, he is.'

I smiled. 'He's a friend of mine.'

H laughed. 'Why didn't you say so? Next time *you'll* go. It's always like getting blood from a stone with that lot. "Stores are for storing. Sign here. Account for that." There's a fucking army on our heads, for fuck's sake. What are you going to do? Beat them off with your ledger?'

I let the centurion's light-hearted rant run its course. He smiled at himself.

'I'm not sure how long the prefect will keep us stood to like this, but it seems pretty clear that the goat-fuckers aren't doing anything else for now. Once we get the order to stand down we'll go back to normal duties, and I'll rotate the sections so everyone can get a couple of hours' sleep at least.'

We both looked out at the German army. It was close enough for us to see the breakfast campfires and the movement of horses and men as the tribes licked their wounds.

'I've been on this frontier for sixteen years,' H then confided in me. 'And I've never seen the Germans stand together like this. I don't think it will last, Felix.'

I turned to face him. There was not a hint of a lie in his features. He really was that optimistic.

'The Germans love a few things,' he began to explain. 'Beards and goats, obviously, but then they're like us in loving victory and plunder. The difference between us and them, though, is that when we don't get victory we usually die trying, and when we don't get plunder we bitch and moan, but we still get on with soldiering. Not them, Felix. When they don't get it, they go home.'

I considered the man's words, and heard a resounding truth in them. Arminius had brought together the German tribes, but though they shared a common tongue and heritage they were not one people, as was supposedly the case in the Empire. Each tribe had its own agenda. Its own leaders. Its own politics. Those chieftains who had joined Arminius and brought men to his banner had done so for their own ends, and no one else's. Once they decided that their effort was being wasted, then they would return home. Some might even switch sides and pledge allegiance to Rome, if the tides of war shifted back into the Empire's favour.

'There wasn't much loot in the forest,' I found myself agreeing. 'The baggage train, but that was mostly camp supplies. Tents, rope, picks.'

'The same tents they're living in now, I imagine, but not exactly much to keep you at war, is it? They want gold and coins, not fucking tent pegs.'

H's prophecy began to materialize that afternoon. Relieved of our duty on the wall, we were stripping our armour in the barrack block when the news was brought to us by a civilian boy.

He beamed. 'They're goin'!'

Dropping the chain mail back on to sore shoulders, I ran to the rampart with Brando close behind me. My heart beat with anticipation as I reached the wall's top, and looked out over the battlements.

The child was right. The enemy were leaving. The host shifted and moved as large sections of the camp began to empty.

'Some of the tribes are leaving him,' the big Batavian guessed. 'They've had enough.'

The temptation to watch the enemy breaking camp was overwhelming, but I told myself that it could all be a ploy. We needed to be rested. We needed to be ready to fight.

'Come on. We need to sleep. Whatever happens is going to happen. Us watching won't change that.'

I was intrigued but I resisted the urge to stay at the wall. Deep snoring and Dog's rancid breath greeted me as I entered the barrack room. As I fell on to my mattress I noticed that Stumps's bunk was empty, but I dismissed the thought, assuming he'd gone to the latrines. When I woke to take a piss myself some hours later, there was still no sign of the man.

I knew that sleep would elude me. Perhaps for that selfish reason alone I took hold of my arms and armour from the block and set out to find my comrade.

It seemed likely that Stumps would seek out his friend Titus, and so the quartermaster's was where I headed to begin my search. As I walked the fort's wet streets I felt my soldier's instincts chafing – I was being watched. That didn't surprise me. From wide-eyed urchins to frowning crones, the fort was home to many who did not trust the very soldiers who were there to protect them. I did not begrudge them this fact, as I had seen many a legionary rape and rob those he might one day lay down his life for.

Such was life in the Empire. Still, the tension in the fort was palpable. Fear had a scent, and it was thick in my nostrils as I recognized Stumps's silhouette, his back to me as he looked at a construction of marble.

It was an altar, I realized.

I made my angle of approach wide so that my friend would see me in the periphery of his vision. I did not want to disturb a man deep in prayer.

'Felix.'

His eyes were open.

'I thought you might be praying.'

'Nah. Seems like a waste of time that, doesn't it?'

'This an altar?' I asked.

Stumps nodded. 'An altar dedicated to Drusus, the great general. He died when he got pissed and fell off a horse. A glorious end.' He chuckled darkly, and I realized then that the late Drusus was not the only drunk present.

'You should have told me you wanted a drink. I'd have come with you.'

Stumps pressed his lips together and made a noise. 'I like drinking alone. Only way I can be sure of good company and intelligent conversation.'

He then revealed a wineskin, pulling it from his cloak. 'Here,' he offered. 'I think the closest it got to grapes was a goat eating them, then pissing this, but it's strong.'

I took a mouthful. He was telling the truth, and the drink burned my parched throat. As I handed it back to him, Stumps poured a generous amount on to the altar.

'General Drusus is probably thirsty. You know Chickenhead fought under him?'

So that was what had brought him here – memories of his

134

friend who had died beneath the enemy's barricade in the forest. I held my silence. Stumps needed to be heard. I knew, because I had felt the same desire to unburden my soul.

'Every minute, it's in front of my eyes,' Stumps said. 'I see him when the spear went into his shoulder. I see him when the rock smashed his head open. I could see my friend's brains, Felix. One second he was there, the next he was dead, and now it's in my head, over and over. When does it stop?'

I said nothing. I didn't want to tell him that the pain was endless.

'You'd think it would get easier, wouldn't you?' he almost snarled. 'I saw two of my little sisters die. I watched my uncle shit himself to death. But Chicken . . . he was closer to me than any of them. He was my true brother, and . . . and I failed him . . .'

Stumps suddenly threw the wineskin violently at the altar. Crimson liquid dripped from the marble like blood as the man dropped to his knees and the misery of loss took him. 'I'm a piece of shit and I just want to die,' he groaned.

I went on to my own knee beside my friend. There were no tears – he was too exhausted for that; instead his chin hung limp on a heaving chest.

'I just want to die,' he told me again.

I put my arm over his shoulders, fighting for words that escaped me. I wanted to tell him that he could overcome it. That the visions would fade. That the pain would go away.

I wanted to lie.

'I feel like this every day,' I told him instead.

The chin lifted. He looked at me. 'For how long?'

135

'Years,' I admitted.

'The screaming? The nightmares?'

'Not spirits, Stumps. The same things you see.'

The man slumped back on to his heels. 'So I'm fucked, then? This is my head from now on? I'm as fucked up as you?'

He meant no offence with the words and I took none.

'Chickenhead told me how to get better,' I told him. 'He said you have to accept your memories. You can't run from them.'

'I don't want to feel like this forever,' Stumps pleaded.

I took hold of the back of my friend's head, and pulled him into my shoulder.

Stumps pushed back from me after a moment, suddenly conscious of his vulnerability. My own itched and bit at me like a swarm of insects as my comrade turned to look at the altar.

'It doesn't end, does it? War.'

How could I disagree? All of my life I had seen war's stain. Regardless of a campaign's outcome, there was no such thing as a definitive end. Victory was simply the sowing of seeds for the next generation's battles. Defeat was a grudge that would demand vengeance. No, it did not seem that there was an end to war itself, but one way or another it would end for the soldiers that fought it. Until then it would rage inside of minds if not on battle-fields. I did not know of a way to heal these wounds, but I knew of a bandage.

'Come on,' I told my friend. 'Let's go and find some more wine.'

## 22

Blood pounded inside my skull. My chest heaved. Bile was rising from my gut.

A voice laughed. 'He's going to be sick again.'

I puked. The purple-tinged liquid pattered the dirt floor. Wiping at my mouth, I saw my section laughing.

'Never again,' I swore to Stumps, the man my equal in degeneracy.

'Just kill me,' he croaked.

We had drunk late into the afternoon and then stood a very shaky guard during the night. Arminius's host had continued to shrink during the daylight hours, creating a jubilant mood in the camp, and so Stumps and I were far from the only soldiers wishing for death as an escape from our hangovers. Instead of that mercy, we were tearing down unneeded buildings for the fort's supply of wood for fuel and the construction of defences.

'Fu-fu-fuck!' Balbus called out, grabbing at a hand that trickled blood. 'Fu-fu-fucking splinter,' he explained as we tore away the wooden planks of what had been a storeroom.

'What do you think Arminius will do now?' Dog asked me, his hideous breath threatening to make me gag once more. I was in no mood to answer questions, but as I was the man's commander, some sense of duty compelled me to concentrate and string a sentence together.

'I don't know, Dog. He's left enough of a force to keep us contained, so I expect he's settling in for a siege.'

'There're only a few th-th-thousand of them out there,' Balbus put in, pulling at the splinter in his palm. 'Not enough to stop the Rh-Rhine legion when they come fo-for us.'

'Who says they're coming?' Statius asked, his face darkened by more than just bruises. 'Why risk leaving the bases to rescue a few hundred of us?'

'Because we're Ru-Romans?' Balbus answered, as if speaking to a child.

'Statius is right.' Folcher spoke up in his thick Latin. 'Rome must come first, not us. I hope that the Rhine legions stay where they are. Arminius must never cross there.'

Dog looked at the Batavian with a wry smile. 'You're joking, aren't you? You don't want that.'

'I do,' Folcher answered. 'Rome is bigger than all of us.'

'None of us are saying the Empire doesn't come first,' Dog allowed. 'But are you really saying you want it to forget about us?'

'Yes.'

'Bollocks.' Statius laughed. 'You're not even a Roman citizen. Why would you care?'

'Because I *will* be a citizen,' Folcher answered proudly. 'So will my children. So will their children.'

'I didn't realize it meant that much to you.' Dog shrugged, handing the Batavian a hammer.

'That is because it is not appreciated what you have. I will soldier for twenty-five years for this. Maybe I will die.'

'Have you ever even been to Rome?' Statius asked.

'No.'

'So you'd die for a city you've never seen?'

Folcher let his body language talk for him – he would.

Statius smiled. 'Rome's a cesspit. I was born there. If it's so great, then why does anyone from there leave and end up in the legions?'

'For duty,' Folcher answered without hesitation.

Statius laughed at his answer. 'Because they can't find work,' he told the Batavian. 'Because they hate being poor and hungry. Or, if the Empire feels like it, because they get told to join, and have no fucking choice.'

'Which were you?' Brando asked.

'What does it matter? I'm here. I'm just telling you, don't be so quick to die for a city that doesn't care.'

Folcher hit a plank of wood violently with the hammer, knocking it to the floor. 'I care,' I thought I heard him mutter.

The conversation died there, returning instead to the necessities of the task, and the ever-at-hand topics of the soldier: wine and tits.

I held my tongue, instead chastising myself for drinking, and thinking of what Folcher and Statius had said.

Rome. Folcher was not the only man in the section who had never set eyes on it. The centre of the Empire had controlled my life in one way or another since I was born, but I had never walked its streets, set foot in the forum or taken in its grand temples and palaces. And yet I had killed hundreds for that place. I had suffered for it, and inflicted suffering upon others. As a child and a young man I had looked on the idea of the city with love. Then, witnessing its true face, I had considered her the great betrayer. It was enough to say that I now hated the capital, the Empire and all that they stood for.

But here I was, sweating and labouring at the Empire's behest. There seemed no escaping the claws of her eagles.

'Let's go and see Titus,' I suggested to Stumps as our task was completed, and we were relieved from duty for a few hours. 'I need something good to eat, and he's probably the one to have it.'

'Not me. I'm going to sleep.'

And so I walked alone to the quartermaster's department. Alone, that is, aside from the thoughts of Rome, of the puppet master that controlled my life.

'Just get to Britain,' I said out loud.

The quartermaster's building had been built to hold the supplies of a fully manned fort, and was a large wooden building that warranted its own guard force, siege or not.

'I'm looking for Titus,' I asked one of the pair of legionaries at the door. 'The QM,' I added.

The soldier looked me up and down. No doubt he was on Titus's payroll.

'I was in his section in the forest,' I snapped, my hangover and hunger putting me in no mood for games. 'Is he here or not?'

'Nah, he's not here,' the man eventually answered.

I tried to read his lined face. I had no idea whether or not he was telling the truth, but what did it matter? I wasn't about to start throwing punches to get to Titus for conversation and food.

'Tell him Felix was looking for him.'

I considered asking the man where Metella was operating

out of. Instead I decided to give up. I would return to the barrack block and follow Stumps's example of sleep.

It was a female voice that stopped me in my tracks.

'Felix.'

I turned, seeing the German girl who had talked to me as I'd washed the blood of the night raid from my arms and face.

I opened my mouth to speak . . .

But I'd forgotten her name.

'Linza,' she answered for me.

I smiled to cover my embarrassment.

'You look lost?' she asked, smiling too; do all women enjoy a man's discomfort?

'Looking for a friend,' I explained.

'Did you find him?'

I shook my head. 'In all honesty, I was more interested in his food than his company.'

My words were meant as a joke, but Linza's face took on an earnest expression. 'I have food.'

'What? No. I couldn't. I'm—'

'Come. I have food.'

And without waiting for my reply, she took hold of my arm and led me into the fort's alleyways.

We were silent as we walked, my mouth kept shut out of fear of further embarrassment. Embarrassment that this woman had taken such pity on my skeleton-like body that she needed to feed me. My discomfort wasn't helped as other civilians shot us looks as we passed, doubtless convinced that it was my cock guiding me, and not my stomach.

Linza ignored the looks. She was either oblivious to

them, or didn't care, and we soon arrived at a barrack block that was being used to house civilians.

'Wait here,' she instructed me, disappearing within.

As I did, I watched a group of young children playing in the dirt. Two young boys waved sticks at one another, the German warrior and the legionary. It was a game now, but if the siege broke . . . I could only hope the end would be quick for them.

'Here.' I opened my eyes to see Linza had returned with a bowl of stew and a handful of biscuits.

'I can't take this,' I protested.

'We'll share. Come on,' she said, gesturing that I join her on one of the barrack block's steps. 'The others were happy to give it. They like having a soldier around.'

'Why?' I asked, sitting back against the wood.

'You know why,' she replied with a dark expression.

We ate silently for a while after that, dipping the biscuits into the thick stew. It was good. The siege was only days old, and Caedicius had not imposed rationing on either civilians or the fighting men.

'Where are you from?' she asked me through a mouthful.

'The Seventeenth Legion.'

'No. In the world.'

I had known what she meant, but was hoping I could sidestep the question. I looked at her, and saw a face that was open and without guile.

'Dalmatia,' I replied, and found myself smiling. Speaking a word of truth somehow made my shoulders feel lighter. After years of deceit, a brief moment of honesty warmed me like sun on my face.

'It's beautiful,' I told her, feeling that heat as if I were there. Remembering what it had been like to grow up in a sun-drenched port city.

'You miss it,' she stated. My feelings were easy to read.

'I do.'

'How long since you were there?'

'A long time,' I answered as I took another bite of biscuit. 'And you?'

'From Batavia. I followed the army this summer to Minden. My first time from home.'

Linza's missing husband was a Batavian auxiliary in Varus's army, and so, like so many other loved ones, she must have followed him that summer on campaign. No one in the Empire expected that the intended show of strength would degenerate into the massacre of an entire army.

'You'll be home soon.'

'Maybe.' The girl shrugged. 'But without my husband.'

'I'm sure he got out,' I offered lamely.

She gave me a tired smile, thanking me for my effort. 'Tell me more about Dalmatia,' she asked me, apparently to steer us clear of grieving waters. She had no idea that her question would lead me to my own heartache.

'I've got watch tonight,' I apologized, getting to my feet. 'Let me give you some coins for the food.'

I was relieved when she refused my offer; I had none.

'You can bring to me next time.'

'This is where you live?'

'Yes. And my name is Linza. So you don't forget again.'

She had a good smile. I couldn't help but get swept up in it. 'Thank you.'

I walked away, and made for my own barrack block. As I picked my way through the space between the wooden buildings I thought of home, and Dalmatia. I thought of Linza's smile, and how it had reminded me of a woman I had left there.

My woman.

I put my face in my hands, and tried not to scream.

# 23

There was a sharp chill in the night's air, but my section was mobile, the thick cloaks draped over our armour catching the heat from our movements, and warming all but our faces. The tramp of hobnails was punctuated by sniffling noses.

'For fuck's sake, Dog, breathe through your nose,' Stumps begged.

'It's blocked.'

'I can feel your breath peeling off my skin.'

'It's not that bad.'

'You don't have to smell it.'

Stumps's insults were a signal of high spirits. It had been a good day. Arminius's army had shown no sign of growing, and the men of the section had enjoyed the labour of tearing down the buildings and then an afternoon of rest before this night duty. With three of the other sections we were assigned to rove below the walls, vigilant for break-ins from outside or theft within. It was a typical duty for a frontier soldier. Enforcing the law was a far more common order than to close with, and engage, the enemy. Of course, I knew that administering Rome's laws could be just as bloody as any battle.

'I saw a ghost once. On a night duty.' Dog spoke up, doubtless wanting to steer the topic of conversation away from his breath.

'A ghost?' Micon asked, his face suddenly animated in the torchlight.

'Yeah. On the walls at Mogontiacum.' Dog was referring to the stone fort there, which sat beside the Rhine. 'It was walking the walls, and wailing.'

Statius snorted. 'Bollocks.'

'It's the truth.'

'It was probably just some pissed soldier.'

'Nope. It didn't have a head. It was a ghost, I'm telling you.'

'Probably shoved his own head up his arse so he didn't have to smell you,' Stumps said provocatively.

'You don't believe in ghosts?' asked Dog.

'Not really. How many goat-fuckers are dead on the other side of that wall? They'd all be running around here, wouldn't they?'

'Only unhappy spirits are ghosts,' Dog argued.

'Yeah, and I'm sure they were really happy dying from their wounds in a stinking ditch.'

'I believe in ghosts.' I spoke up, surprising my men.

'What?' Stumps's face creased beneath the brim of his helmet.

'I believe in ghosts,' I repeated. 'But not like Dog thinks he saw. I think that ghosts live in our heads. They come with us from battlefields. Those dead Germans in the ditch? Their ghosts went back with their friends. Some of them are in the heads of the men who fought on the wall.'

Stumps chewed over my words, doubtless thinking of the voices he heard inside his own mind, and the images that were painted there. 'That makes sense,' he agreed.

Brando and Folcher were also slowly nodding.

'Not many of us to carry the ghosts out of the forest,' Brando considered. 'A lot to fit in a few heads.'

Folcher rubbed at his face, almost as if he was trying to feel for a presence within. 'If that is true, I would be happy to see these things. To have my comrades still with me.'

His words hit me. I had carried my ghosts, but I had always considered it a curse. Could it be that through my own suffering, I offered my comrades a taste of immortality? Was that not a price worth paying in pain?

When the scream echoed through the night, I almost thought that they were answering me, but moments later, a trumpet began to blare from the direction of the headquarters building.

'They're su-sounding the assembly,' Balbus said. The distinction was important; this was not a stand-to. We were not under attack.

I led the section at a jog-trot towards the trumpet. The other sections of the night's watch converged with us. The crest of Centurion H appeared from the door of the headquarters building.

'With me!' he shouted, and led off at a run.

I recognized our direction. We were going into the part of the fort that had been turned over to the civilians. I wondered why, but heard my answer before I saw it: angry shouts; cries of grief. So deep in the night, they could only mean death.

The alleyway between buildings was packed with three dozen civilians. Most were adult women, and the ones that were not crying hissed insults at whoever was in their midst. I saw then flashes of shields – soldiers were in the centre of the crowd.

'Close shields,' H ordered us. 'Keep weapons sheathed. We'll push them off if we have to.' Then he ordered the civilians: 'Move back!'

'Fuck you!' a young woman spat back.

'Last chance, darling.'

The noise of the crowd dropped as the civilians finally began to realize the power of the overlapping shields, and the centurion's intent to use them.

They moved, and as they pulled away they revealed a section of soldiers who had closed in a circle. As the crowd gave them space these men opened their formation, revealing a body in their centre.

It was a young girl. She was shy of her teens. A quick look was all I needed to see that she'd been butchered like a pig.

'Felix, use your section to close off this stretch of the alleyway. Make some space around her,' H ordered, gesturing to the slaughtered girl. He then moved his other sections, and very soon the girl's body was in the centre of an island of calm. On the edges of that space, angry faces spat and cursed at the soldiers who kept them from the body.

'It's those fucking Syrians!' I heard a male voice shout repeatedly. I identified him in the group to my front, dark-skinned and bearded. Likely a trader who had followed Varus's army on campaign, but had escaped its destruction.

'Come here,' I ordered him.

I had to repeat my words more forcefully before the man stepped forwards.

'Syrians did this?' I asked him.

The man's volume decreased as he stood closer to me

and my men, but his words were thick with bile. 'Of course they did. Look at that poor girl! They butchered her.'

'You saw them?'

'No, but it *was* them. Look at her!' he implored me. 'Of course it was the savages!'

H joined me on my shoulder. 'You witnessed this?' he asked the man.

'No, but—'

'Then shut your mouth and fuck off. You're wasting my time. Did anyone see what happened?' he asked the crowd.

No one had.

'Anyone here family? Anyone know her?'

Two pairs of hands crept up. They belonged to a girl who was about the same age as the victim, and a terrified-looking mother with wild blue eyes.

'Come here,' H ordered them, gesturing that they come forward. I moved aside to let them through, and then cocked my head to listen in on their conversation.

'Who is the girl? Is this your friend? Daughter? Who is she?' H asked.

'My Latin not good,' the woman answered eventually.

H appraised her blue eyes and fair hair, then turned to Brando. 'Brando. Is she German?'

Brando let loose a string of words in his native language. When the woman replied, H gestured for the Batavian to join him.

'You'll translate,' he told the man. 'Who is the girl?'

Brando delivered the words in a voice of stone. The woman's own words were guilt-ridden and tear-filled. 'Her family was lost with the legions. Her father was a legionary. She came here with them. Her name was Frida.'

149

'And what happened to her?'

'I don't know. She must have gone to the latrines. I woke and she was gone. Then I heard the scream as some-one found her.'

'It's not your fault,' H assured her, understanding the emotion if not the language. He asked his next question delicately. This was a young girl lying dead, but the world was sick as well as cruel, and so H asked what needed to be asked. 'Was she . . . was she selling herself? Was some-one else selling her?'

The woman shook her head strongly.

'Do you think I have no shame?' Brando translated.

'Wait with them,' H ordered instead of answering. 'Who found the body?' he asked the crowd.

An older woman with thinning silver hair stepped forward. She seemed unsteady on her feet. She was shaking. Folcher saw it too, and quickly draped his cloak over her bony shoulders.

'Tell me what happened,' H asked her. He had to repeat himself as the woman's wet eyes fixed squarely on the body that lay in the dirt.

'I went to the latrine,' she finally managed. 'It was dark, and I tripped.'

'On her?'

The woman lifted her hands. They were stained with blood.

'It was you that screamed?'

'She's so young . . .'

'Was it you that screamed?'

She nodded slowly.

'And you didn't see anything?'

'It was dark.' Her eyes crept back to the body. 'She's so young . . .'

H caught Folcher's eye, and motioned that he take the woman aside.

'The Syrians did this!' a voice shouted. 'They're not Roman! Get them out of the fort!'

H walked to the front of the crowd. 'Shut up and be calm,' he snapped. 'Did anyone see Syrians here tonight? Have they been around here, watching the girls? Anything like that?'

'I saw them looking at me when I went to get water,' a dark-haired woman called out.

'Where were they?' H asked.

'On the wall. I was filling the buckets.'

H turned from her, doubtless thinking the same as I: the girl was pretty. Syrian or Roman, every bored sentry would have been looking her way.

'But around here?' H pressed. 'Especially with younger girls.'

'I saw some of them playing with children,' an older man put in, his back stooped but eyes livid. 'They're perverts. You've heard what they do in the East.'

'What kind of playing?'

'Chasing them around. Talking to them.'

'Did they touch them?'

The man struggled to find a moment in his memory when they had. Slowly, he shook his head.

H let out a sigh of frustration. 'Did you think what they were doing was strange at the time? Before this?'

The man shook his head once more.

'This is going nowhere,' H whispered behind my

shoulder. 'We'll hold a cordon until Malchus gets here. He can decide what to do.'

It was some time before the cohort commander arrived. Some remained to gawp and point blame, while others returned to the comfort of their bunks.

'What a fucking mess,' Malchus surmised as he looked at the girl. 'Ripped her clean open.'

'Every one of them's blaming the Syrians,' I heard H mutter, gesturing towards the crowd.

'This wasn't the lizards.' Malchus dismissed the theory. 'They like little boys. Probably one of the perverts in our own ranks, H. What do these civvies expect?' He spoke with bitterness. 'That the blokes can rape and pillage in the name of Rome, then turn it off when they're told to?'

'That's discipline, sir,' H countered.

'It is, H, which is why we're not all running around here like a bunch of fucking pirates, but it only takes one or two of the men to fall through the cracks. Keep a close eye on your blokes. People's brains start to boil under siege.'

The cohort commander was right. Any battle brought with it its own pressures, but there was a release from that in bloodshed – a relief. If battle was a quick beating, then siege was slow torture: the agony of never knowing when there would be danger or where it would come from; the constant companions of fear and hunger. It changed people. A lucky few came out of it vitalized and with the ability to then attack any obstacle, but most became withdrawn and fearful. Some broke and took their own lives, or the lives of others.

Looking at the butchered girl in the dirt, I knew that she would not be the last victim to die within the walls.

# 24

I pushed open the doorway and stepped into the courtyard. Sunlight bounced back from the white walls. Alongside paths of painted tiles, perfect lines of flowers shimmered in their ranks like armoured soldiers.

I walked to the centre of the square garden, dipping my hand into the cool water of the pond. As I moved, my eyes searched for an ambush that I hoped would come swiftly.

There was nothing.

I looked into the pond's calming waters. In the reflection I saw a handsome young man, skin darkened by sun, eyes set alight by life.

I smiled. I was enjoying this game.

I went through the house room by room. It was quiet. My family had gone to visit friends and were not expected back until later that night, when they would be soaked with wine and witless. The slaves had been relieved of their duties for the day, and so my footsteps echoed in the deserted building. There was haste in my footfalls; I wanted to make use of this unexpected privacy.

Twice I searched rooms where window veils played gently with the ocean breeze, dappled light falling across furniture polished as dark as my father's beard. Twice I searched, and twice I was beaten.

I left the house and walked on to the street. I could feel the heat through my sandals, but the breeze drew its fingers across my neck like a caress. A prelude to what I searched for.

Despite the heat, I ran. Sweat began to stain my white toga, but I was young. An athlete. My breath was steady and my limbs were loose. The coast appeared before me, golden sand and a glittering sea. Hot sand pushed between my toes. I looked left and right along a beach that knew my deepest secret.

I was alone. The game was wearing on me, but I was young, and competitive. No matter the sport, no matter the challenge, I did not lose.

I looked at the ocean. The wet prow of a galley glowed golden as the oars beat their way out to sea. I took a moment to indulge my imagination, thinking of her destination. Of Rome. Of endless possibility.

The ship had left the port of my home town, and now I knew that this was where the game would end.

I ran along the sand, stamping it from my feet as I reached the paved streets, picking my way between olive-skinned merchants and haggling slaves. A child caught my eye, and smiled for a coin. I threw him two. I wanted my happiness to be a disease. Contagious. I wanted everyone in the port to feel the same thumping heartbeat of anticipation as I did. The same thrill that flushed my skin, and carried me like an emperor above the heads of those around me.

I knew where the game would end – on the stone pier that drove out into the ocean. It was the closest point we had to Rome. The point where we would sit and dream.

Today would be the day that dream became reality. Today, when the game ended, a life would begin in its place.

I turned a final corner between fishing baskets, the smell of salt and olive oil filling my nostrils, and then I saw the pier. It was a scrum of men, women and children. Sailors loaded a galley that was sitting deep as its hull was filled. Old men cast lines into the water for their dinner. The pier was packed, and yet to my eyes it was empty.

She wasn't there.

Somehow, I had lost the game.

I turned for home. Deflated, my eyes were on the cobblestones as I walked into my father's thick chest, the bristles of his beard pushing against my face.

'Father?' I asked, confused. Confused because he was supposed to be with his friends. Confused because, for the first time in my life, the man looked down at me with disappointment.

And then, he told me how the game would end.

## 25

I was used to waking to my screams, not tears. I felt them roll across my gaunt cheeks as I rose from my bed and swung my feet on to the barrack-room floor.

I felt hollow. As gutted as the girl who'd been butchered three nights earlier. My body was still, not fighting violently as it did against my night terrors, but my spirit had fled. I was so calm and empty that, for a moment, I wondered if I'd died in my sleep.

Comrades snored in their bunks; this was not the afterlife. Regardless, I wanted to be free from it.

I took hold of my cloak, pulling it over my shoulders, and stepped out into the night air. The moon was low, and my section was relieved of duty until dawn, when the entire garrison would stand to, prepared for any assault – a daily ritual. Not wanting to return to the dream that had drained me, I walked towards the centurion's quarters, which were situated at the end of the block. When the century was off duty, one man would remain at his post there, keeping a log of the soldiers' whereabouts.

'Felix, Seven Section,' I told the man on duty. 'I'm going to the quartermaster's.'

'Meeting your mate, are you?' the soldier asked, bored and hoping for conversation.

'I'm sorry?'

'Stumps. Seven Section. He's gone to the same place.'

I hadn't noticed Stumps's bunk was empty, and suddenly felt glad that I would have his company. Despite the enemy camped on our doorstep, our life within the fort was taking on the routine of rest and guard duties, and in that discipline Stumps seemed to be finding some sense of order, and a return to his sarcastic self.

'I'm here to see Titus,' I told the two men that stood sentry at the quartermaster department's door.

'Yeah, he's in there,' one of them answered whilst warming his hands over a crackling brazier.

I stepped inside.

Flickering candles lit the room. Placed lower than the man's towering height, they turned Titus's already imposing face into a figure of dread.

'Fucking glad you're here,' he grunted. 'Thought I was gonna have to carry him on my own.'

I looked at the floor. By Titus's feet lay the prone figure of our comrade.

'Drunk?' I asked.

'Drunk was hours ago. I'm not sure what I call this. He's fucking pissed himself too, so watch your hands when you grab him. I'll take the arms.'

'Don't you have stretchers?'

Titus laughed. 'Sometimes I forget there's more to this place than a front.'

'Business going well, is it?'

'Yeah, and you could be a part of it.'

'I could use some coins,' I confessed. 'I lost everything in the forest. A loan though, not work.'

'Shut up, you tart,' the man chastised me, shoving a small purse into my hand.

'I'll pay you back,' I promised as Titus pulled a stretcher from storage.

'We'll take it from your share of the chests. Come on. Help me roll the fucker on to this.'

I did, Stumps mumbling something as his arms flopped over the sides of the stretcher.

'Did he say what I think he said?' Titus asked.

'Chickenhead,' I confirmed. 'He's been struggling since the forest. I thought he was getting better, but . . .' I looked at the limp form between us, at the crotch stained dark with Stumps's own piss.

'Well, he can't do this every night. Only so much wine in the fort.'

We carried the stretcher out of the door and to the barrack block in silence. There wasn't much conversation between myself and Titus that could be had without privacy.

'I wish I'd known he was like this,' Titus admitted as we reached our destination. 'I'd have come see him. I will do now. I'll come and see him tomorrow.'

'Put it down here, and we'll carry him inside.'

'Fuck,' the big man snarled as we entered the barrack room. 'You smell that? He's fucking shit himself, too.'

He hadn't. It was Dog's breath. I tried to catch the laugh, but it was too late, and enough escaped for Titus to catch it.

'What?' he asked.

I told him.

'Don't start laughing,' he whispered, and I could tell he was holding back his own giggle. 'You'll wake them all.'

Perhaps I could have held it, but then Stumps murmured

his way back to life, the cloud of his drunkenness rising just enough for him to slur.

'You fucking bastards,' he accused us. 'You pissed on me!'

It was too much, and laughter ripped through the room like cavalry into broken ranks. It drove us to our knees, leaving us breathless.

'You took me out of bed and pissed on me!' Stumps moaned sadly, adding to our fits.

Eventually, my section had thrown enough curses and objects that the laughter dried out, and there, as I collapsed on the floor with a piss-soaked comrade and a murderer, I remembered for a moment how it felt to be truly happy.

Dawn's stand-to came and went. I walked to the civilian blocks, trying to ignore the sidelong glances that came from alleys and doorways. Following the recent murders, the fort's streets were thick with suspicion and scorn. All knew that there would be more blood spilled on dirt and cobblestone. None but the killer knew when.

'I'm looking for Linza,' I told a skittish child. 'Do you know her? Tell her Felix has come to see her.'

Doubtless eager to escape the scarred man in front of her, the child slipped away and inside. Linza appeared soon after.

'Breakfast?' I asked. 'Where can I buy it?' I held out two coins, and after saying hello, Linza led me to where a trader was selling bowls of thick stew – *suspiciously* thick.

'I think sawdust's part of the recipe,' I half joked, hoping I was wrong. 'But at least it's hot. How are things around here, after the girl?'

It was not the happiest topic of conversation, but we were besieged by an enemy bent on our deaths or enslavement – it was not a happy time.

'People are scared of the Syrians,' she told me. 'You know in the East, they do this to their own families? Also the men fuck the men.'

I could see in her wide blue eyes that she believed it. The march into eastern Germany was likely as far as she'd ever been from home. The idea of civilizations in the desert was a concept beyond the comprehension of the untravelled mind, no matter how intelligent or open – seeing was believing.

'All men are capable of evil,' I replied.

I had meant the words as comfort, but saw from her look that I had blundered. 'I'm sorry. I didn't mean it like that. There are good people, too.'

'No. You are right.' She shrugged, then switched direction. 'You look tired,' she observed, although without judgment – there was something about the Batavian manner that was friendly and yet uncompromisingly direct. I had noticed it in Brando and Folcher.

'I don't sleep well,' I found myself saying before I could stop.

'Why?'

I didn't reply, instead talking to her of Stumps, and how I had found him at the altar. I don't know why I told her, only that her eyes encouraged me to be open.

'He misses his friends,' she said when I finished, recognizing the same pain she no doubt felt for her husband.

'He does.'

'Did you have a day for them? Have you made sacrifices for them?'

I thought about how Stumps had angrily poured wine into the dirt beneath the altar.

'Not really,' I confessed.

'You should.'

I ate on in silence, knowing that she was right. After I had said a fond farewell, I walked quickly from the civilian part of the camp in search of Titus.

'I'd like that,' the big man agreed as I made the suggestion. 'I'd really like that. Let me sort it out.'

And so the next day, we remembered our dead.

# 26

On the day of the service in memory of our friends, a strong wind raked itself off the river, bringing its chill into our throats and nostrils as we stood guard on the southern wall.

I watched the brown waters jog by, thinking of how the river's banks would froth and rage when winter set in. Even now the river provided us with a barricade that matched a cohort of soldiers for deterrence, and in reality my section was here for us to use our eyes, rather than our swords.

My men were spread out on the wall and I was alone. The solitude was almost welcome, as I needed time to think. I needed time to turn words over in my mind, and to try and find the ones that would do justice to the fallen of the forest if I took my turn to speak, though I was not sure if I would even be invited to open my mouth; Titus and Stumps had been long-time brothers of the veterans who fell, and Micon had been thick as thieves with young Cnaeus.

And yet, still, I *wanted* to speak. I wanted to tell them how Chickenhead had helped me in the darkest nights. How Rufus had shown me that there was something bigger than ourselves. I had little good to say about the xenophobe Moonface, that was true, but he was a comrade none the less. An ignorant bastard of a comrade, but so perverted is the nature of camaraderie that I would have died for him.

It had been a long time since I had stood in front of a formation of men and spoken words of thanks for the life and the sacrifice of friends and comrades. At times my audience had been hundreds. At others, a handful of desperate renegades. Never was it easy.

And then I thought about the comrades whose only remembrance had been inside my head. There was no eloquence in those memories, only pain and violence, regret and guilt. Who had spoken for my oldest friend, Marcus? Who had buried him?

I thought again of ghosts. I had no doubt that Marcus's spirit, restless and vengeful, had slipped inside my own mind.

'I'm sorry,' I muttered to the fields beyond the wall and river.

Those abandoned pastures were empty save for a knot of horsemen in the distance – scouts who would warn the Germans, should the garrison take the desperate path of escape through the waters. The besieging forces, reduced as they were, straddled the roads that led inwards towards the fort. These encampments were set a mile back from the fort, the distance seeming to confirm that the German prince was happy to watch and wait.

Of course, I doubted that Arminius himself had remained. Two-thirds of the army had left – whether to follow Arminius or to desert him I could only guess – and Arminius would surely be at the head of this force if it still existed, looking for a place to strike Rome and to shore up his tribal alliances by regaining the momentum he had won in the forest.

The sound of hobnails on wood gave away the approach

of the relieving section. I gave a short handover report to their section commander, and then gathered my men.

'You don't have to come to this,' I told them as we stripped arms and armour in the barrack block; Brando had been inquisitive as to our plans for the service.

'But can we?' he asked.

Folcher also looked at me for permission. The Batavians had lost their own comrades and soldiers in the forest. I had seen one of them killed with my own eyes at the hands of our German captors.

'Of course,' I told them.

The three newcomers to the section remained in the block, happy to escape the wind that was racing between the fort's buildings.

'How long until winter sets in?' I asked the Batavians.

'Real winter?' Brando shrugged. 'Two months. It will be like this a lot now, though. Maybe some sun in six months.'

'Fuck this life,' Stumps cursed.

'You've been in Germany before for winter?' I asked him.

'Yeah, but in a stone fort on the Rhine, and with nice big fires.'

We arrived at Drusus's altar. I had expected to find Titus waiting, but the presence beside him surprised me: Metella, former proprietor of the section's favourite inn at Minden, and now Titus's business partner in black-market trading.

'Stumps, you arse.' She smiled fondly at her old friend. 'I heard you pissed yourself.'

'You know there's an army outside waiting to kill us?'

He smirked. 'I would have thought there were more inter-esting things to talk about.'

'Nah. I hope you've changed your loincloth since then.'

'I don't wear one. They haven't built one that's up to carrying my beast.'

'So that's why the Syrians have been walking around wide-legged?'

Stumps opened his mouth for another round of banter, but Titus beat him to it.

'Come on, we came here to do something.' All sets of eyes fell on the man who had been our leader in the forest. I realized then that the Batavians were unknown to him, and made the introductions.

'Look,' Titus began, a little awkwardly, 'I'm not a priest or an officer, but I don't think we need one to do a service for our mates. Metella's brought the wine, so we were thinking we'd pour some for the lads who aren't here. Then we can say something about them, and then we drink the rest.'

I'd never seen Titus look so uncomfortable; one of his big paws was rubbing at the skin behind his neck as Metella brought forth a trio of wineskins.

'It's the best stuff here, no fucking around,' she boomed. 'A worthy offering to the boys.'

Titus took the skins from her hands, holding on to one himself and passing the others to Stumps and Folcher. Together, they poured the red liquid into the dirt.

The ripe smell of it lifted my nostrils. The sight of it lifted my stomach, because it brought back a memory. A bad one: I pictured the old man of the Pannonian village, and how he had trembled on his knees before me. How his grey hair had felt in my hand as I pulled back his head and sawed open his throat. How his blood had pattered on to the dirt as his family screamed. And then, how they had followed their beloved into the afterlife.

'Felix?' Brando was looking at me, his thick brow knotted in concern.

'I'm all right,' I lied.

As the wine continued to pour into the ground, the men spoke the names of comrades lost to the forest. Some I knew. Most I did not. Titus and Stumps had served in the legion for years, whilst Folcher's entire cohort had been massacred – there were a lot of names to recite.

Once the names had been spoken, it was time for intimacy. A time to reflect in detail on those who had been closest to us.

Folcher went first. To give due honour to his comrades he spoke in his native tongue, the words coming with pride and fire. I heard the name *Ekkebert* amongst the German, before Folcher turned to Latin to conclude his passionate tribute.

'They died for Rome,' he told us. 'They died for a dream. Because they make a sacrifice, now others also can dream.'

Brando bowed his head at the patriotic words. So too, I was surprised to see, did Metella – the Empire's most devout followers were often found in its most unlikely places.

'He has spoken for us both,' Brando answered Titus's invitation to speak, giving his comrade a proud pat on the shoulder.

'All right then,' Titus grunted, stepping forth to the front of the small assembly himself. 'Most of you knew

Rufus,' he began. 'Some of you know that he saved my life years ago, not that he'd ever talk about it. He wasn't like that. Not in any way. They offered him a century, you know? But he turned it down. He just wanted to get along, and be with his family.

'Rufus taught me a lot about family,' the big man continued. 'The way he was with his kids, he brought that with him into the ranks. It's not always about having the loudest voice or the hardest punch. Sometimes you have to put yourself in your kid's sandals, and see things how they look at it. Being a soldier isn't an easy job, after all. Rufus just made it look like it was.'

Titus opened his mouth to speak again, seeming to prepare himself for a revelation or story, but then his shoulders sank down, and he let out a breath. 'I'll miss him,' he finished.

'We all will,' Stumps confirmed.

Silence fell over our assembly. In the distance were the playful cries of children, the sound of hammering and the barked orders of an angry officer.

Eventually Titus looked up from the dirt, and to Stumps. 'You want to talk about Chicken and Moon?'

'Just Chicken,' Stumps answered quickly. 'We don't know if Moon's dead.'

Titus gave his comrade a patient smile. 'You're right,' he allowed, though I could see by his slumped shoulders that he thought otherwise.

Stumps walked to the front of our group. I could see the nerves in each step, his gait tight.

After a moment to compose himself, he opened his mouth to begin. 'Chickenhead was my—'

167

He didn't get any further than that, a racking sob coming from his soul to utterly consume him. Stumps tried to break through the waves, but his grief was upon him now, and within a moment he was sobbing. It was Metella who came forward first, placing a motherly arm about his shoulders. He pushed his head into the woman's embrace, and wept.

I saw Brando turn to Titus. The Batavian's look asked for permission to speak. Titus gave it with a nod.

'Stumps is my comrade,' Brando announced, his voice low and firm. 'If he were to grieve like this when I die, it would be the greatest honour.'

The flow of tears slowed at the words, and Stumps looked up; his face was red, his nose thick with bubbling snot. The memory of war and its pain sometimes reduced killers to infants.

'Micon.' Titus's voice startled the boy. 'Would you like to speak for Cnaeus?'

The young soldier gave a nervous nod. I could see Stumps fight to control himself and give due respect to the words and speaker. I didn't know what I expected from Micon, but the youngster stunned all with his oratory and adoration.

'Cnaeus was a hero,' he recited from well-rehearsed memory. 'He was a born soldier. When everyone else ran on the bridge, Cnaeus turned and faced the enemy. Cnaeus and Felix drove them back, and saved our lives. In the forest, Cnaeus told me it would be all right. He told me I would live. He told me that he would die for me, and no matter what, he would make sure I made it home. Cnaeus was a hero.'

There was not a solitary tear; Micon's usual blank mask was infused with pride. I imagined then the conversations that the two young soldiers must have had in the forest: Cnaeus, terrified as he was himself, promising to see his friend through it. I let out a sigh as I pictured the youngster dying at my feet, his hands clutching desperately at the wound in his throat, eyes screaming for help as he recognized that his wound was mortal.

A lump of ice stuck in my throat.

'You spoke well, lad.' Titus smiled, embracing Micon as if he were his son. Metella followed suit, and soon, Micon had been pulled tight by every member of the assembly.

'What now?' Stumps asked, wiping away snot with the back his hand.

Titus was ready with his answer. 'Let's get drunk.'

We did.

We drank. We laughed. We remembered. Eventually, however, the stories had to come to an end. There was time for a few snatched hours of sleep, before sentry duty in the dead of night.

All was dark and silent beyond the wall. The cold wind brushed against my skin, flushed from wine, and I welcomed it. I pictured how I would fall gratefully into my bed once our watch was over, and sleep until I was forcefully pulled out of it. Then, as the night lifted and dawn came to the fort, I panicked for a moment that I had committed the greatest sin in the legions, and fallen asleep at my post, for surely what I saw in front of me was a dream?

Because the fields were empty.

The enemy was gone.

## 27

It was almost three days before we got our first indication of what had happened to the enemy who had vanished from sight; Centurion H called for his optio and his section commanders to join him in his quarters, a series of rooms situated on the end of the barrack block. One acted as the centurion's office, and it was here that he gave his briefing.

'Anyone notice that Centurion Malchus has been missing?' H asked, and men shook their heads. The cohort commander could be counted on to be found where fighting was thickest, but during the monotonous days of siege he was often out of sight.

'He's been over the wall since the goat-fuckers pulled out,' H explained. 'He went to find out where they've gone.'

Murmured words of admiration tumbled out from the assembled men, veterans all.

'I know.' H smiled. 'He's a tough fucking bastard. The good news is that we couldn't ask for a better cohort commander. The bad news is that the hairy bastards haven't gone home. They've just moved.'

Shoulders slumped a little at this news. The centurion gestured that we join him at a sketch map stretched out on his desk.

'Here're the fortresses on the upper Rhine' – he pointed out with the vine cane that was a symbol of the centurion's authority – 'where the river's crossing points are.

'We're here.' H pointed out to a lonely point within hostile borders. 'And what the clever bastard Arminius has figured out is that he doesn't need to sit on top of the fort to contain us.'

'So where are his men?' an old sweat asked.

'Here.' H pointed to a position between the fort and the Rhine. 'Malchus found them sitting on the road that leads to the Rhine, about twenty miles away. It's a few thousand men, so more than enough to outnumber us and keep us bottled up here. It's also far enough from the crossing that they're not antagonizing anyone into coming over the river and attacking.'

'Where's Arminius?' I asked. 'Where's the rest of his army?'

'No sign of them.'

The century's second in command, H's optio, spoke up. 'If Arminius is gone, and there're just a few thousand of them between us and the Rhine, we need to get word to the lower Rhine legions. They can cross and smash them out of the way.'

H nodded. 'Malchus had two men with him on his recce. He's sent them to the Rhine. If they get through, they're to ask that the legions clear the road from the bridge to here.'

'They won't do it if they don't know where the rest of Arminius's army is,' a voice grumbled. It belonged to a man named Albus, a veteran I could sense was interested in his own survival above all else. 'It looks like a trap, doesn't it?' he pressed.

H blew air from between his lips. 'Prepare for a long winter,' he answered. 'If they come, they come, but let's rely on ourselves to get out of this.' He smiled, trying to spin the situation to the best of his cheerful ability. 'Look, we've got stores, we've got shelter, and – for now at least – we're not facing attack.'

'How long will our supplies last, boss?' the optio asked.

'We were good for two months. I expect the prefect will be announcing rationing soon, though.'

'Will the archers be on reduced rations?' Albus grumbled.

'Of course they will. The civilians too.'

'Don't need the archers if there're no attacks,' the man countered sourly. 'That would be a few hundred less mouths to feed.'

'You hear what they did last night?' A veteran grinned. 'Fourth Century boys found three of them outside the building the civvies use for washing. They'd cut a bit of wood out of the wall for a peep, and were having a good tug when the watch found them.'

Someone laughed. 'Surprised they didn't join in if they were Fourth Century. Fucking animals.'

'Well, makes a change for the Syrians anyway,' the veteran concluded his story. 'Didn't know they were interested in women as well as boys.'

'Doesn't matter who they fuck.' H shook his head. 'We'd be getting our bones picked clean if it wasn't for them. Now listen. On the subject of corpses, I've got some great news for you.'

I heard myself groan with the other men. Now that the imminent threat of German attack was gone, I knew what that great news would be.

'We've got to clean out the ditch.'

*

It had been over a week since the first of the Germans had died in the ditch, and the smell of decay hit us before the eastern gate had even been opened. When the wood did creak back, a century in full battle dress marched out to form a screen a hundred yards away from the fort. Dressed simply in tunics, the men of our own century now filed out beneath the gatehouse. Two dozen archers came with us, the Syrians looking to salvage what arrows they could.

'Don't be shy, lads,' H smiled, his words muffled by the neckerchief tied over his face. 'Grab a German friend, and carry them to their trenches. Once they're all in you can have the rest of the day to yourselves. You're in your own time, now.'

'Why can't we just bury them in the ditch?' Statius grumbled.

'Because it wouldn't be a ditch then, would it, you dickhead?' Stumps snapped.

'Lu-lu-look at this one.' Balbus pointed; an arrow had gone through an eye and clean out the back of the tribesman's skull. Like the other corpses around him, the German's skin was sagging and patterned with decomposition.

'I feel desensitized to this smell,' Stumps grunted as he lifted the dead arms of a stick-thin German boy. 'Thank you, Dog. I didn't realize what a service your arse-breath was doing for the legions.'

'You're welcome.' Dog smiled, Stumps's insults washing over him.

It was unpleasant work: rancid gas escaped from dead lungs; rotten limbs tore from their sockets; insects and larvae crawled and wriggled inside wounds and eye sockets emptied by crows.

The same jokes crept up, those spoken on battlefields the world over: 'he's 'armless', 'he's legless', 'he got the point', 'he lost his head'. The humour was cruel, dark and necessary. As the graft wore on, some soldiers lost their breakfast, but none seemed to lose their mind.

One German tried to change that.

Statius squealed like a pig and jumped back from the corpse he had been reaching for. 'Fuck! He fucking moved!'

'You're a soft cunt.' Stumps smirked. 'It's just air leaving him. You never seen a body before—Fuck me, he moved!'

I joined the veteran and we gazed down into a grey face. Lack of beard made me think that the corpse was young, but the skin was drained of life.

Not so his eyes – they moved. They were looking at us. The lips twitched.

'Fuck,' Stumps whispered again. 'He's alive.'

I looked the boy over. He had a hand on a stomach pierced deep by an arrow. Maggots crawled over his tunic.

I fought hard not to throw up. Statius reached the same conclusion as I had, and lost his own battle.

'He's been eating those to stay alive?' he asked me, hoping that I would tell him otherwise.

The boy's blue eyes burned into mine. He yearned for life. He had done unspeakable things to cling on to it.

I drew my dagger, and ended his hope there. I could not meet the eyes as the blood drained from him.

No one made jokes after that.

# 28

I was lying in my barrack room. The air was warm, a gentle breeze creeping through the window. I was looking at the ceiling, my eyes following a fly as it crawled and hopped on the concrete. It was trapped, unable to navigate, unable to work out the simple puzzle of the open window. The concrete was barren, and the fly would toil against its surface until it expired.

I had been watching it for hours.

Initially I had begun by cheering it, rooting for its freedom. The window was there, so close, fully open! Go!

Then, as time wore on, I began to resent the fly. I began to hate it. How could a creature be so stupid? How could it not see the opportunity? How—

I smelt smoke. Not the ever-present camp smells of cooking, but the thick noxious type that came from burning timber and plaster.

'Stand to! Stand to!' someone shouted from outside.

Then came the screams—

I shot up in my bed, panting, sweat turning instantly cold against my skin.

'Stand to!' the voice called. 'Stand to!'

'Stand to!' I echoed automatically.

In the darkness, my men repeated the order, some with enthusiasm, some still half-deep in slumber.

'Get your kit on! Form up outside!'

With practised motions I began to pull on my arms and armour. The movements were as automatic as breathing, and so I let my mind go to the possibilities of the stand-to: fire? Enemy at the walls? Enemy inside of them?

As I entered the night outside the block I saw the other sections spilling into the torchlight, centurion and optio marshalling the men into formation.

'Section commanders, report in when you're complete!' H ordered.

'Seven Section complete,' I shouted a few moments later, my men still pulling at straps as they trotted into formation.

Over the sound of shuffling feet and chinking chain mail I listened for the signs of battle. I heard shouting from within the fort. Shouting, but no screams.

'Century, right turn!' H commanded. 'By the centre, double march!'

We took off at a slow run, H in the lead, the only man who seemed to know our destination and purpose.

'What's going on?' Statius asked no one in particular.

Stumps sneered. 'What the fuck do you think's going on? We're going to get stuck into a shit show.'

'What kind?' Statius asked, undeterred.

'Hopefully the kind that gets you killed, so you can stop wasting my time with stupid fucking questions.'

A century in full battle dress doesn't move quietly when it runs. Metal banged against metal; shield against shield; hobnails tramped the dirt; and breath escaped loudly from the lungs of men confined within walls. Even so, it was possible to hear the sound of the shouts growing louder. Angry voices, and a lot of them.

Balbus spoke up. 'So-so-sounds like a riot.'

He was right.

'Century, halt!' H called. 'Move from column to line!'

The head of the century wheeled to its right, the tail of the unit following like a snake so that the width of our body now faced forwards, and gave me my first look at what was ahead of us.

A barrack block of the Syrian archers was under siege. Scanning quickly, I guessed that no fewer than three hundred civilians had surrounded it. They threw stones and insults at the windows set in the wooden walls, cursing the men who had taken refuge within.

'Look over there,' Stumps said to me.

I followed his eyes. There was a body in the dirt, now a plaything for young boys, who poked at the dark-skinned man with nervous curiosity.

'Looks like a Syrian,' Brando noted.

Centurion H positioned himself at the front of his men. Elsewhere, other centuries were arriving in formation. The people who had surrounded the archers were now surrounded themselves, save for one road that led away into the fort. I expected that we were to be the sheep dogs that drove the civilians through that gate.

Two figures strode out from the ranks and towards the braying masses.

'Silence,' Malchus called on behalf of the fort's commander. 'Silence!'

The crowd would not oblige him. A few worried faces appeared in their rear ranks, but most were turned inwards, consumed by passionate fury.

Malchus had a remedy for this. 'Centuries!' he bellowed. 'Ten paces forwards.'

We obeyed his command, tramping our feet heavily. More heads turned to face us.

Malchus carried no javelin, and so he drew his sword, and began to beat it against his shield. The men of the centuries picked up this rhythm, an unmistakable drum of war.

Now, all heads turned. Seeing the ranks of soldiers lit and shadowed by torches, anger faded from the civilian faces, and fear appeared in its place. They knew that if they were declared an enemy of the Roman peace, then they could die by our blades just like any other foe.

Malchus held up his hand for silence. He got it, save for the beating of a shield by a solitary soldier: Micon.

Stumps silenced him with a kick. 'Enough, you idiot.'

Prefect Caedicius stepped forwards. 'Return to your quarters. You are confined to the western side of the fort until further notice. Any of you found within a hundred yards of these barracks will be cast out of the gate, and you can take your own chances. Go!'

Individuals began to peel away at the command, but the host of the body shifted, uncertain. They had come for something, and were reluctant to leave without it.

'We just want justice, sir!' a voice called out.

'Justice for what?' Caedicius demanded.

'For the girls! These men are savages, sir!' the voice called back to a chorus of approval.

Girls? So there had been another found butchered?

'I am the commander of the fort.' Caedicius spoke forcefully. 'I alone decide when, and how, to dispense

178

justice. By coming here, you have threatened the security of the fort I have been entrusted by the Emperor to protect. If you want to see justice, how about I choose a dozen of you and take your heads from your shoulders? Is that the justice you would like to see?'

'They keep killing our girls, sir!'

'Enough!' Caedicius roared. 'Three of my archers are dead, which means that there are murderers amongst you! Murderers and idiots, because that's three less bows on the wall when the Germans come back. And they will be back!'

The prefect paced up to the crowd now, staring them in the face, daring them to defy his rule.

'Three dead archers, a dead legionary, a dead woman and a dead girl. Are you trying to do Arminius's work for him? Are you trying to kill each other and save him the fucking bother?

'No more! The next display like this, and I will pick you out at random and take your heads myself! Get back to your barracks now. Stay there, or take your chances outside of the walls. Either is fine with me, but do not test my mercy by acting like this again! You should be ashamed to call yourself Roman!'

The mass of civilians began to melt away. Their anger was not so quick to dissipate, and I could see it held in tight shoulders and vengeful eyes. Despite Caedicius's threats, there would be more bloodshed within the walls, I was certain. Grudges are not easily let go of during the best of times. Under siege, with the stress of death ever present, a person was far more likely to act on vengeful instinct.

'Centurions to me!' Malchus ordered. 'Optios, return your centuries to barracks or duties. First Century, Three and Four Sections, stay here and put guards on these barracks.'

'Section commanders,' H said before departing, 'wait for me in my quarters. I expect we'll have some talking to do later.'

He was right.


It was some time before H returned from Malchus, and in that time the century's section commanders threw about their theories of who could be behind the murders of the young girls. Soldiers love to speculate and gossip, and never more so than when violence is involved.

'Six dead,' H confirmed, 'including the girl that started it all. Probably be a couple more soon. There're a dozen wounded and some are bad. Malchus was arguing they should be left to die, to prove a point, but the surgeon's working on them.'

'I love Malchus.' Two Section's commander spoke up. 'He doesn't give a shit.'

H grinned with admiration for his superior. 'No, he doesn't. Anyway, the long and the short of tonight is this – except to carry out duties on the wall, the archers are confined to the east of camp. The civilians are confined to the west. The north–south road through the camp's centre is the boundary. If you see either where they shouldn't be, detain them and alert your centurion. That's me,' he added with a flourish.

'H?' a veteran queried. 'I've got family here. What's going on with this killing? Is it the Syrians, or what?'

'Malchus says there's no one who's actually seen a Syrian around a body, or with the girls before they died, so no one knows.'

'Can we at least put guards where the civvies are?' the man pushed.

'There're going to be roving patrols. A section will get that duty every night.'

'Just one section?'

'We've got a lot of wall to cover, and without wanting to sound like a bastard, Arminius and the goat-fuckers are our biggest concern, not the civvies. Happy?'

'Not really,' someone grumbled. 'Either the Germans come and try and kill us on the walls, or our families are getting butchered here, and we're just sitting on our arses. It's fucking bollocks.'

'Well then, I've got good news for you, my friend,' H smirked. 'Because I'm looking for volunteers.

'Caedicius has ordered a raid.'

# 29

The request for volunteers shifted the room into uncomfortable silence.

'Relax, you campfire heroes.' H laughed, enjoying the trap that he'd set. 'Malchus is taking his own century, and sixty archers.'

I saw shoulders sag a little in relief.

Two Section's commander spoke. 'I was gonna volunteer.'

'Of course you were, darling.' H smiled. 'All right, that's enough for now. Go get your heads down, and I'll send the runner around if I need you once I work out this new guard rotation. Felix, hang back a moment, please.'

The other men eyed me as they shuffled out of the door. I was still an oddity to them. A stranger from a vanished army.

'What is it?' I asked cautiously. The looks of the departed men had put me on the defensive.

H's smile disappeared and he squirmed slightly. 'I don't know how to put this gently, so I'll just say it. Prefect Caedicius thinks it was you who was responsible for the murders.'

The accusation hit me like Titus's fists. I had no words, and stood there open-mouthed.

H choked out a laugh. 'Sorry, Felix, that was my attempt at humour to try and lighten what he's really after. He wants to take your Batavians out on the raid. He thinks their German could come in useful.'

I thought of Brando and Folcher outside the safety of walls they had fought so hard to get behind. I knew that both men would volunteer for the raid without hesitation.

'They've done their bit,' I said. 'There must be someone else in this fort who can speak German. How long's the legion been based out here?'

H shrugged his armoured shoulders. 'I've thought about that myself, you know? I've been here a long time, but all my German's good for is bartering with whores and buying shit wine. You'd think they'd teach us, wouldn't you?'

I had my own theory on why the legions were keen to keep their men separated from local language and culture: they were there to occupy, not to integrate. Easier to stamp down on dissident thoughts and voices when you don't understand the words that beg for mercy.

'I'm sorry, Felix, but Malchus is taking them whether they volunteer or not,' H concluded.

'Can I at least go with them?' I asked on impulse.

It was an automatic, desperate duty that compelled my words; Brando and Folcher were my friends, and I did not want them facing danger without me. There were only so many ghosts that could fit within my head.

H seemed about to deny my request, but he recognized determination when he looked into my sunken eyes. 'Fuck it, you've earned the right to decide your own death.' He shrugged. 'Ask Malchus.'

His words seemed to be a dismissal, but his voice stopped me at the door. 'Felix. You know why the other section commanders in this century have almost seen out their twenty years? It's because they keep their mouths shut when I ask for volunteers.'

There was no denying the good intention or the truth of those words, and so I simply nodded my head and stepped outside into the growing darkness.

The raiding party gathered before dusk, a century of fully armoured legionaries drawn up beside sixty lightly equipped archers. Brando and Folcher had said little at the news of their inclusion in the raid, but I could feel the anticipation coming from them now that the hour was near. They were looking forward to the chance of spilling blood. The remainder of my section had seemed happy enough to be spared the action. Only Stumps had remained sullen, refusing to talk to me when he had learned of my volunteering. It was not the way I wished to part with my friend, but the time had come, and now I sought out the transverse crest of Centurion Malchus.

'Felix,' Malchus greeted me, eyeing my full battle dress. 'You want to come along, you animal?' He grinned. 'Why not? We had good fun last time, didn't we? You and your German lads join on to One Section. Stay close to me.'

'Thank you, sir,' I murmured, dropping the speech I had been rehearsing all day to compel him to include me, now redundant.

'We leave an hour after full darkness,' Malchus then told me. 'Goat-fuckers are bound to have scouts watching our gates, and we don't want to go giving them time to lay on a welcome.'

'You think they expect attack, sir?' Folcher asked.

Malchus's crest shook from side to side. 'They underestimate us, lads. They think we're going to sit in here with our cocks up our arses, waiting to die.' He laughed. The sound was brutal. 'Let's make some orphans tonight, boys,' he finished, moving away to check over his troops.

Clouds that had threatened suddenly burst, the heavy rain bouncing like lead shot from helmets and armoured shoulders. Caedicius had chosen the night for a raiding party well, and the rain would work to dampen not only our tunics and equipment, but the sound of our footfalls. I welcomed it because of this, but grudgingly; being cold and wet brought with it more than just a physical discomfort, and I thought of how we had huddled as a section beneath a sodden blanket in the forest, our rank breath thick beneath the cover that had been our only protection against the storms.

I passed the wait to depart in unhappy silence. Beside me, Folcher and Brando spoke casually in their native tongue. As darkness fell, my eyes were drawn to Malchus's prominent silhouette as he moved from man to man, offering words of advice or encouragement. A solitary figure appeared, spoke to the centurion and then joined the ranks. I expected it was the runner, as soon Malchus ordered that all torches be extinguished; the rain had already executed that command on all but the most protected flames. Then, after giving our eyes time to adjust to the night, the gates yawned open.

'For Rome.' Malchus spoke, calm and confident. 'For each other.'

We marched out, our ranks double spaced to avoid a giveaway through collision of shields or equipment.

No one talked. Mouths trapped tighter still as the smell of rotting flesh greeted us. We were passing the trench in which we'd dumped the bodies, and the stench was sickly sweet. I'm certain that I wasn't the only soldier picturing how my own body would look if the worst happened, knowing it could be a reality before dawn.

As we marched through the dripping darkness, I replayed the briefing that Malchus had delivered as the cold sun had set. He had surprised me by demanding that his men take prisoners: 'The only thing that will scare them more than dying is disappearing,' the fierce centurion had snarled. I couldn't fault his words, and thought of our time in the forest. How the unknown of trap and ambush had been far more terrifying than any open field skirmish. There was fear in death, but there was also certainty. Imagination could be as deadly as any shield wall. Rumour could break an army with the same devastating effect as artillery. I had seen it with my own eyes. How words had spread like a blaze, and gutted a town to the same effect.

Now wasn't the time to think of that place. Now was the time to concentrate on the present, and how I would live through it. I felt almost naked to be outside of the fort's walls, even within a formed body of men. There was comfort in the presence of my comrades about me, but we were fewer than 150 in a province that had turned against us.

I became caught up on that thought: to turn *against* Rome, Germans east of the Rhine would have had to have been, at some point, *with* the Empire. Had there ever truly been such a relationship? Or had Rome assumed it by dropping legions on to the locals' heads and demanding that they bend the knee? I expected that this was the case,

186

and that this violent explosion had been growing since the first hobnailed sandals had tramped across the bridges over the Rhine and into new territory.

'Slow down,' Malchus whispered, and the leading ranks slowed just enough so that men would not crash into the backs of the soldiers ahead of them.

'Halt.' The formation came to a stop. Malchus began to ghost along its flank, passing down his orders. 'Get off the track and into the ditch. I'm going ahead to take a look.'

We were close, then. With the other men, I slithered into the dark maw of the ditch beside the dirt road, my sandals sinking into ice-cold water and slime. White eyes peered over shield rims as men strained to see into the black. Breath was hushed. Muscles were tight. Soon, Malchus returned.

His teeth were bright beneath the clouds. He was grinning. 'They're asleep.'

It was time for a slaughter.

## 30

Malchus ordered us to place our shields and javelins down in ordered rows on the dirt track. Even with their waxed covers the shields had grown heavy with rain, and their weight would be an unnecessary encumbrance for what Malchus had planned.

'Archers to stay here with the kit. Be prepared to loose volleys on my command,' the centurion whispered.

I wondered at the temperament of the men who would be watching our backs. Legions won battles because brother would die for brother – even those they had never met. Would this hold true with auxiliaries who had been accused of rape and murder by those they would be called to fight alongside? Claims that had led to their own comrades being killed by an angry mob?

I hoped it wasn't a question we would need answered.

'My boys, short swords only,' Malchus went on. 'They're asleep, lads. They think we're cowards. They think we're going to sit in the fort and wait to die. They're going to learn the hard way about the Nineteenth when we creep in there and slit their throats.'

Satisfied that his men were now unburdened, Malchus turned to myself and the Batavians and smiled. 'Let's go.'

We followed him along the unpaved road, our footfalls soft and padded. A light wind carried rain into our faces, but no sound that would betray us to the enemy.

Were they truly off guard?

Taking a shallow bend, lights suddenly appeared ahead of us. They had been screened by trees as we approached. To be still burning in the rain suggested that they were in some way sheltered, which supported the notion that Arminius had settled down to starve us out, whilst the number of fires suggested that this was the main body of enemy troops. Sentries should have been posted beyond the bend and trees, but no one had stirred at our approach. So effortless was our advance that a warning began to sound in my mind that we were crouching our way into a trap. But then I looked at the silhouette of the centurion ahead of me. Malchus was a born killer. He was a wolf, and if there was a snare waiting for us on that track, he would have smelt it.

The wax hide of tents was pale by the firelight. Rain drummed from the shelters in a rhythm that was almost hypnotic. I saw no movement. No tell-tale flickers. No dark shadows against canvas.

My heart began to thump. Imposed silence could be louder than any clash of armies.

Malchus stopped and began to gesture to the men behind me. Section by section, his troops peeled away into the darkness. As we crept to the fringe of the enemy encampment, I began to see Roman soldiers slipping between the tents like wraiths.

Malchus stalked forwards and then held up a hand. We were beside a sagging tent. Beneath the patter of rain I could hear snoring. My heart beat faster still. I tilted my head back, desperate to catch moisture for a throat parched with nerves. Malchus took hold of the tent's flap and, with the delicacy of a lover, opened the canvas. He stopped then, smiling at me. Giving me the honour of the kill.

I forced my breath down into my lungs, willing my heartbeat to slow and my hand to be steady. I stepped within the tent, a waft of stale sweat and ale assaulting me. My eyes were already adjusted to the night, and so I could see the four dark shapes on the ground. Snores and heavy breaths guided me to their heads. I gently reached down with my hand and felt hair, long and lank. The man was sleeping on his front, and so he made it easy for me. I felt for the point where his spine met his skull, and drove my dagger within. What noise came from his death was covered by the snores of his comrades and the rain on the waxed hide. One by one, the tent's occupants died in bliss.

I stepped out into the wet air.

Folcher now held the flap; Brando and Malchus were out of sight. I assumed the centurion had run out of patience, and wanted to indulge in his own killing. I could hear the sounds of it now: the slashing of blades and cut-off chokes. It wouldn't be long until the Germans woke.

'Prisoners,' I whispered into Folcher's ears, gesturing to the next tent. We crept over and then, slowly, the Batavian pulled back the flap. I looked within, seeing two forms that suited my purpose perfectly.

And then we waited. We waited, until a scream signalled that the time for stealth was over.

'Now!' I shouted to Folcher, pouncing on the prone figures.

Shocked out of slumber, the Germans instinctively began to kick and jerk violently. The resistance was expected, and I pummelled my fists into a skull over and over until blood flowed, cheekbones cracked like eggs and the struggle ended. I felt the warmth of piss as my terrified prisoner lost control. Beside me, Folcher had subdued his own captive.

'Let's go,' I grunted, as much to my prisoner as to Folcher, who now began to let loose a savage torrent of his own language, doubtless telling the prisoners what would happen if they thought to resist.

We pushed the staggering figures out into the open. Screams and challenges were beginning to echo. Many of the Germans were waking to blades at their throats, but not enough – we were outnumbered, and Malchus was not going to risk being cut off as we had been on the raid for wood.

'Back! Back! Back!' he called.

My feet slipped on the wet soil as I obeyed the command; I only regained my balance as I gripped the arm of a passing legionary. Even in the night, there was no mistaking him.

'Stumps?'

'Shut up and run!' he shot back at me.

It was not a time for questions, and I moved off on his heels. By the light of the German campfires, I now caught my first sight of the man who was my prisoner. The *man* was a boy, barely into his teens. His partner in Folcher's grip would have had a grey beard had it not been stained bloody crimson, and I could tell by the terrified animal look in his eye that he was the boy's father.

It was not my place to pity them. Instead we pushed them onwards, converging on the road where I saw other soldiers dragging their captives by hair or shirt. One offered enough trouble for the legionary holding him to tire of the effort, instead ramming his sword so deep into the German's stomach that it appeared through his back.

'Have it your way then, you prick,' I heard him spit as he stepped on to the corpse, the blade pulling free of the body's suction with a wet slurp.

Legionaries were all about me now. We were running, though there was no sound of pursuit at our backs. I looked over my shoulder, and saw none of the tell-tale signs of moving torches that would signal the enemy preparing to follow. Perhaps it was simply the rain dousing their flames, and they would attempt vengeance in the darkness. Either way, we would not wait in place to aid them.

Panting, we rounded the bend in the track, a straight run then to where the archers had been left with our kit. We made it without incident, the only danger the uneven surface of the road. Men cursed as they hit rain-filled pot-holes, but the only violence on the track came in the soldiers' language.

'Who's got prisoners?' Malchus called as we reached the Syrians and our shields. 'Bring them here! Quickly! Hurry!'

With Folcher I pushed my captive towards the centurion's voice. Beside his silhouette I found a gaggle of Syrians. They had rope in their hands, and quickly went about binding the captured enemy. Tied together, the Germans became vertebrae of the same miserable spine.

There was no time to catch the breath that burned in my chest, and within moments I had a shield and javelin in hand. In the darkness, I felt more than saw the century forming up on the track. All was in good order. There were panting gasps, suppressed giggles of nervous laughter and the loud clearing of nostrils, but no moans from wounded men.

I dared to hope that we had got away clean. Malchus wanted to make sure of it.

'Archers,' he hissed. 'Three volleys. Creep the range. Loose!'

I heard a strange voice translating the order, and then the first of the arrows whistled out into the night. It wasn't until the third and final volley that the fire was greeted by a scream; there was a pursuit in the darkness, but Malchus had now given the Germans something to think about. I hoped it would be enough. We were a long way from the fort.

'Century,' Malchus ordered. 'Jog-trot.'

We moved off, fear and excitement pushing our pace a half-step quicker than regulation. The rain grew heavier; sandals slapped and tramped into wet dirt. Amongst the sheets of the downpour, teeth flashed white as men dared to hope that we had made our escape so easily.

'How many you get?' a buoyant young voice whispered to a comrade in the darkness.

'Ten.'

'Bollocks! I bet you never even got three. You can't even cut your dinner, you dickhead.'

'Keep the fucking noise down,' Malchus's optio growled beneath his breath.

We trotted on to the steady chorus of hobnails, shifting equipment and the rap of rain against steel. At pauses that seemed to be random and unplanned, Malchus would order archers to loose arrows along the track behind us – there were no screams. No hoof beats. There seemed to be no enemy on our heels, and after hours of sweating into tunics already soaked by rain, a thick black line appeared against the lip of the horizon.

It was the fort.

Unable to contain the release of nervous energy, a young voice spoke up as we passed beneath the welcoming gateway: 'Piece of piss.' And then he laughed.

I couldn't blame him for his relief. We had put our heads into a bear's jaw and survived. With what seemed like little loss to ourselves, we had killed, and we had captured.

I looked at those prisoners, now visible in the torchlight. Most shook with nerves; a reek of piss and shit came from them.

'Bring the prisoners to me,' Malchus ordered. As he paced the fort's dirt, rain dripped from his helmet's brim, framing a face filled with hate. His eyes were ablaze as he took in the pathetic sight of his foe. 'You wanted to get in here, you goat-fucking cunts?' he taunted them. 'Well, welcome. Make yourselves at home! We're going to have lots of fun together.'

I looked at the miserable captives, and knew that their lives had run their course.

So be it. My comrades were safe for another night, and my concern was for no one but them.

Such was war.

## 31

As the prisoners were led away by fresh soldiers of the garrison, the men of the raiding party were formed up and counted off by Malchus and his optio. In the shadows beneath the wall and between buildings, nervous civilians looked for the faces of their loved ones.

'We didn't lose a single man!' Malchus announced to a cheer. 'Archers, get back to your part of camp. Nineteenth Legion, great job, boys! We pulled on Arminius's balls tonight. He's going to be fucking sore in the morning. Dismissed.'

Men laughed and smiled as they fell out of the ranks, seeking out comrades with whom to share their war stories. Spared our own casualties, the tales were told with excitement and humour. I overhead these snippets as I sought out my own comrades.

'You should have seen his face when he woke up!' one soldier laughed. 'Old bastard shat himself! Fucking stank! Bet no one will be tryin' to move into that tent.'

His comrade howled with mirth. 'How many d'ya kill?'

'At least three. I left one with his own dagger in his guts. Not goin' to be a good mornin' for 'im.'

That tale, like so many of the others, ended in glee. I wasn't smiling myself – I was looking for Stumps, worried that he had tagged along on the raid without permission, and would not have been counted in the tally.

I let loose a sigh of relief when I found him leaning back against the wall, shielded from the elements.

'Come on,' I told him, offering a hand. 'Let's get back to the block before we get cold.'

He shook his head. 'I'm knackered. Just leave me here for a nap.'

'You didn't come this far to die of the cold. Get up,' I ordered, at the same time hauling him to his feet so that my friend's face was inches from my own, and close enough that I could smell the wine on his breath.

'Are you drunk?'

He shrugged. 'Only an idiot like you volunteers for that stuff sober. Course I was fucking drunk. And I intend to get back that way. All that fucking running knocked me sober.'

'Dry kit and food first,' I told him, leading off towards our barrack block.

Brando and Folcher were already there. Stripped of their equipment and wet clothing, wrapped in dry cloaks, they were beginning to clean the mud from their equipment and the blood from their blades.

'Let us do that for you,' Dog offered. 'You get some food and rest.'

Balbus and Micon quickly followed the man's example, Statius more grudgingly so, his face sour as he took hold of Stumps's mail and sword. Then, as he pulled Stumps's blade free of its sheath, I saw him sneer – the steel was clean. I expected the arrogant soldier to open his mouth, but following his beatings, Statius had the sense to keep it shut.

'Food then sleep,' I repeated to the men who'd accompanied me that night.

'I'm going to see Titus,' Stumps told me instead.

I put a hand on his shoulder. It was a friendly hand, but firm enough to hold him from the doorway. 'Get some rest, Stumps. Titus isn't going anywhere.'

He pouted. 'I want a drink.'

'I've gu-got a wineskin you can have,' Balbus smiled. 'It's bu-behind my bunk. Go ahead.'

After a flare of his nostrils, Stumps did his best to muster a nod of gratitude for Balbus's offer; then he slipped into the bunkroom.

My shoulders dipped a little with relief. I wanted to keep Stumps close. I wanted to ask him questions: how had he got himself on to the raiding party, and why? Having volunteered, why hadn't he drawn blood when the Germans were at our mercy? These were all questions that needed to be asked alone, but for now my greater need was to keep the man in the sight and company of his section. Drunken solitude was increasingly his desire, and no good ever came of such a thing.

My loose gaze snapped from the wall as Dog spoke to me, smiling. 'Go to bed, Felix. We'll take care of this. You look fucked,' he added, clearly with the best intentions.

He wasn't wrong. Nervous excitement had carried me back to the fort, and so I had barely felt the aches and pains that now seeped from within my bones and into my muscles.

I managed to smile back at him. 'I am.'

And so I crept into the bunkroom, which was lit by a single candle. In the near darkness I heard Stumps suckling from a wineskin like a hungry babe.

'Felix,' he whispered as I lay down on my own bed, 'I didn't kill anyone tonight.'

'I know,' I answered, hoping that my words sounded

like a simple acknowledgment, and free of the judgment I had heard in his own. 'We can talk about it tomorrow, if you like?' I offered.

There was a long moment of silence.

'Nah. I'm fine,' he lied.

Brando and Folcher entered a second later. The night's killing, and the talk of it, died with their heavy snores.

Or so I thought.


I shot upright in my bed, my head colliding with the wooden slats of the bunk above me.

'Fuck!' I cursed.

Reeling from that blow, I reached for my dagger as the screams that woke me continued to pierce the night.

'Wake him up!' I then ordered.

Brando grabbed hold of Stumps's shoulders and shook him like a child. My friend's shrieks were long and woeful.

'Out of the way,' I ordered, clapping my hands over Stumps's mouth and nose. His body snapped from its dream state in desperate need of oxygen. As I saw the white eyes bulge open like a newborn foal's, I pulled my hands away.

'You bastard!' he gasped.

'You were screaming and thrashing. I was worried you'd fall out of your bunk.'

'Much better that you suffocate me then, yeah?' Stumps taunted, propping himself up on to his elbows as his chest heaved. 'Where's that wine?' he finally demanded.

'You fu-finished it,' Balbus apologized.

'Fuck's sake. All right. Move out the way.'

Stumps made to get out of the bunk, but I stayed where I was. 'Dawn's still a way off, Stumps.'

'Well, I think it's fair to say I'm wide awake, thanks to your comforting skills.'

Brando laughed at the words, his thick chest heaving as he snorted. Something about the sound was contagious. Folcher was the first to pick it up, giggling like a virgin, and soon even Stumps himself was smiling. Perhaps we would have all fallen back to sleep, if it hadn't been for what we heard next.

It was another scream, but without doubt this howl was born from physical pain, not imagined.

'The prisoners?' Folcher guessed.

'Gods,' Dog swore. 'I've never heard one go for so long.'

Statius smiled in the candlelight. 'Malchus knows what he's doing.'

'What are they du-doing to him?' Balbus swallowed, a dry tongue running over his lips.

No one answered. For a long time our silence held, ears cocked to the sounds of the tormented cries.

Brando finally shrugged, pulling a thick cloak over his head. 'I'm going to sleep.' The other men who had risen from their bunks slowly followed his example. Eventually, I was left to stand alone beside Stumps. He looked at me from his bunk.

'Put the light out and go to sleep,' he told me. 'Your face is hurting my eyes. I'd rather take my chances with the nightmares.'

The insult told me that, for the moment at least, my friend was restored to himself. Lying back on to my bed, I pulled the cloak tight about my ears. I wanted to rest. I wanted to sleep. I wanted to dream about a past life.

The screams didn't care.

They echoed across the fort until dawn approached, and the time to stand-to arrived. They echoed as we stood guard on a wall that overlooked empty fields scarred by trenches. They echoed as we were relieved and filed back to our barrack block with drawn faces and sunken eyes.

'Will you shut up?' Stumps snapped, barking at the sky. This time, when he told me he was going to seek out Titus, I did not try to stop him. The agony of the tortured prisoners was seeping into my own mind, and I would not deny my friend the comfort of drink.

'You coming with me?' he grunted, desperate to be on his way.

I shook my head, hit suddenly by a pang of guilt and embarrassment, for I knew there was a place where I could seek out my own comfort, and a window to my past.

And so I went in search of her.

'That's a different one.' Linza spoke quietly, her eyes on the floor as a shrill wail penetrated the October morning. 'It sounds like a boy.'

I tried to swallow the biscuit that was now like lead in my mouth, thinking about the young German I had captured in the night, and how I had herded him towards his dreadful fate. Would it have made any difference if I let him run? Would sparing his life have cost the lives of my friends? Doubtful.

But then I thought of Arminius. How I had saved his life on the parade square when his uncle had tried to warn Varus of the prince's treachery. How I had spared it when I stepped from the forest, a spear in my hand and the clear target of Arminius ahead of me. I had thrown myself into harm's way to save lives I thought worthy before, and where had it led? Three legions rotted in the forest because of my sensibility. Suddenly, the rush of guilt and nausea slammed into me like a chariot. The half-chewed biscuit stuck in my throat as I choked.

'Are you all right?' Linza asked me as the crumbs fell on to the floor of the empty barrack block.

'I'm fine,' I lied, like every other soul within the fort.

'You turned white.'

'I'm fine.'

'Here, take some water.'

'I said I'm fine,' I spat, angry and disgusted at my actions that had led to this misery, then instantly nervous that my words would be seen by Linza as an attack on her.

I needn't have worried.

'Just don't waste your food,' the Batavian girl warned me, pushing her blond hair back over her shoulders. 'German winters are long. You look like a skeleton. You should eat.'

'Now the fort commander's ordered half-rations I don't think anyone's getting any fatter.'

Linza shrugged and pulled a face. 'There's always someone who gets fat, even when everyone else starves. That's just the way the world is,' she answered pragmatically. 'My father said so. He travelled a lot.'

'What did he do?'

'He was a sailor. I think he died at sea.' She shrugged again. 'Maybe. Or maybe he found a new family.'

Or maybe he was butchered on a foreign shore. Maybe he was taken into slavery, and now pulled an oar as a whip scarred his back. The world was a brutal place, and not many on the fringes of Empire were destined for a peaceful life.

'My father and now my husband. Both lost.' Linza's eyes wandered over the civilians and soldiers who passed us by. 'They could both be alive. They could both be dead. I will never know.'

'It's not too late for your husband,' I tried. 'We made it out.'

'When the army was here, at the fort. How many days since then? Where are they now?' she asked dispassionately. 'No. Better he is dead in the forest. I say that because I love him.'

We lapsed into silence. Linza wiped at an eye.

'It's all right if you want to cry,' I managed feebly.

She snorted. 'I am tired of crying. I want to live or to die.'

'We are alive.' I said, yet I was unsure if I believed the words myself.

She turned and smiled at me as another animal scream rolled towards the sky, the prisoner's agony making her point for her: this was not life. It was clinging to existence, with the hope that life could one day grow again from the ashes of suffering.

'Tell me something funny.' She spoke quickly, taking me off guard.

'Something funny?'

'A joke. A story. Make me laugh.'

'I . . .'

'No one is this serious all their life, Felix. Tell me something funny,' she challenged me.

And so I closed my eyes. I tried to forget the screams. I tried to remember the time when I was always smiling. Always laughing.

'My father,' I told her, remembering. 'He liked to drink,

but he could never remember where the toilet was when he'd gone to bed. One night I heard a crash, and I ran to my parents' bedroom. I thought maybe it was a robbery, and I had my dagger in my hand. I was scared. My heart was racing. But when I burst through the door, I found my father on the floor, tangled within a table. He'd tried to piss through the window, but the table had collapsed underneath him. There was piss everywhere.'

Linza's smile was growing. 'Your mother must have been so angry.'

'She was used to it.' I smiled myself, the fondness of the memory warming me. 'She wouldn't get up to help him. "I told you you were getting too fat for that," she was moaning as he tried to untangle himself.'

Linza's smile was bright now. My own stretched the cracked skin of my cheeks. 'That's funny,' she snorted. 'Do you miss your father?'

'No,' I answered quickly, the smile gone in an instant, that bright memory eclipsed by the clouds of others – memories that were dark, savage and brutal. 'I have to go.'

'Felix . . .' she tried.

But it was too late. She had reminded me of that stolen life, and I left her in my wake. Her smile behind me. I marched in search of the one constant of my adopted life. The one thing that had distracted me, as a soldier, from the memories I had left behind.

I sought out pain.

I sought out the screams.

## 32

Familiar as I was with the unchanging layout of a Roman encampment, I knew that the screams were guiding me towards the blacksmiths. The rain of the past night had gone, but the ground was still slippery beneath my feet, the air cracked with cold and the promise of the coming winter.

They would be lean months. No one – save Arminius – had foreseen the massacre of three legions, and the forts on the Lippe had been provisioned with rations based on the idea that there would be trade with the locals, and resupply from the legion's stone-walled bases on the Rhine. The fort's position on the river had been chosen to allow barges to ferry in supplies, but the Germans would have blocked the channel up river. Any attempt to clear it would be met with battle, and the Rhine garrisons had shown no inclination to pursue such an outcome. There was not a single enemy warrior within sight of the walls, but the fort was cut off and besieged as well as if the German tribes swarmed against our gates.

The screams were growing louder as I closed in on their source. Between the cries, I could now make out the bellow of angry interrogation. I watched as two young children crept forwards, building up their courage to witness the cause of such misery. Something in their manner made me think back to a time when it was I and Marcus who prowled the streets together like feral cats. Boys are the same the world over, and war and death hold an irresistible attraction for us. Only the most brave, stupid or desperate to prove their worth would actually go on to become an army's fighters and killers – at least by choice – but death itself was an inescapable part of life. Just by reaching these young years, the children had done well. How many brothers and sisters had their parents wailed for? How many times had they heard screams of anguish that surpassed even the prisoner's cries of pain? Some say that one can become inoculated to death and misery, and that once you have seen so much, it affects you no more. That has not been my own experience. True, a mind can become numb in order to survive, but the pain is always there, ready to rear its head in an angry second. We live amongst death, and we fear it more than anything else. If it held no terror for us, then why would men desert the legions on eve of battle? Why would they shit themselves at the thought of it? Why would mothers tear and rend their own skin through grief at the loss of a child they had never known until the same day of its birth, and death? Accustomed is not accepted. Every death, every loss, shapes a man and his mind. Some become wrecks, others become monsters, but none come away from death's touch unchanged.

The boys must have felt my dark thoughts. Clapping their eyes on me, both twisted on their heels and fled.

I turned the sharp corner to the blacksmiths' yard. There was such a building in every fort, the legion training some of its number to become the specialists who would hone the point of javelins and sharpen short swords. As experts they earned a degree of privilege in the ranks, and were immune from such trivial responsibilities as guard duties and the digging of ramparts, but the stench of scorched flesh in the air told me that it was not steel that was now receiving the careful attention of the red-hot irons.

There was no sign of the prisoners, but outside the building stood a section of soldiers fully armoured and on their guard. They were not the only legionaries present. A dozen or so others milled around, trading gossip. I was not the only one with a curious and twisted mind.

Or a broken one.

'Stumps,' I greeted my friend who sat crumpled in the dirt.

'What you doin' ere?' he slurred.

'I came to find you,' I answered honestly. Indeed some sense had told me that Stumps would be drawn to the suffering as I had. I took in the sight of him now, more wine than man, his uniform filthy. Without doubt he had been sleeping in some muddy alleyway between the buildings.

'Come on. We need to get you back and cleaned up before you get disciplined.'

'Where's Chickenhead?' he demanded instead, confirming that he had passed beyond any normal state of inebriation.

'Chickenhead's dead,' I told him gently.

'I know that, you arsehole.' The veteran waved his hands. 'I mean, where's his body? We need to bury him. And the cat. We need to bury them!'

'We will,' I lied.

'Today?' he asked hopefully.

'Today.'

'All right.' He nodded, a little happier. Then: 'Felix, I'm out of wine. I think someone took it.'

A child would have been able to wrestle Stumps's possessions from him. He was lucky he still had the tunic on his back.

'Where's your helmet?' I asked him. 'Your armour, Stumps? Where is it?'

'Left it with Titus,' he managed before belching. A second later, powerful red vomit bounced from the dirt.

Behind us, I heard a pair of soldiers snigger.

'What's your fucking problem?' I snapped at two legionaries barely out of their teens. They said nothing, but one shot Stumps a contemptuous look. It was enough for me to leave my friend's side. Hand on the pommel of my sword, I crossed the short distance to them at speed, seeing the fear etch into their faces as they recognized the murder in my own.

'You have a fucking problem?' I repeated, gripping one by his red neckerchief and pulling his face towards mine.

What did he see? A once handsome face that was now a patchwork of cracked skin and scars. Deep-set eyes that had seen too much, now nothing but empty pits. Rage that could drive my blade into an ally's stomach as soon as an enemy's.

'We're sorry,' the second boy managed. 'We didn't mean to offend.'

'What are you doing here?' I snapped at him, shoving the other boy backward as I released him. 'You enjoying the show?' I gestured to the building that housed the prisoners, and their screams.

The young soldiers said nothing. Like the tens of thousands of citizens who crammed into arenas across the Empire, the boys had come to see suffering as an escape from boredom. I couldn't blame them for it any more than I could blame a snake for its venom, but I knew that, once they had seen and endured enough anguish of their own, the fights of gladiators and the execution of criminals would no longer hold any allure. That every death, every scream, would echo the ones given by their dying comrades. By their friends.

But how to tell a young soldier that?

'Just fuck off,' I said to them instead. 'Get out of my sight. If you ever laugh at my friend again, I'll cut you open.'

The boys were hurriedly moving away when I was struck by a better idea.

'Get back here!' I called, and they turned nervously to face me. 'Pick him up.' I gestured at Stumps, who was now passed out on his back. 'That man's killed more men and seen more battle than you could ever fucking imagine. If you drop him, or even graze his arse against the floor, I will kick your fucking brains out through your arseholes. Do you understand me?'

They did. And so Stumps was carried to Titus.

'He's goin' to drink me dry, this fucker,' Titus snorted, casting a concerned eye over our friend who now snored heavily in the quartermaster's stores. 'I had to smack a couple of lads around when they complained that Stumps was getting more than his fair share.' The big man chuckled at the thought. 'Fair? What the fuck does that even mean, Felix?'

I shrugged my shoulders. Like Titus, I had learned through experience that it was an empty concept. Life was about avoiding suffering, and accumulating power. As long as he did not upset the most senior leadership, Titus had enough of his own within the camp to do as he pleased. The man's sheer size silenced most critics. His monstrous fists did for the rest.

We were alone, but loud voices came through the adjoining wall. They were excited. Animated.

'Business?' I asked.

He gave a gruff nod as he pulled a blanket gently over his comrade's sleeping form.

'Why the fuck did he go to the prisoners?' Titus shook his head. 'And volunteering for a raid? That's not like him.'

'I don't think he even volunteered.' I shrugged my shoulders. 'It was dark. I think he just joined on.'

'Why? You, I can understand. You're one of these fucking idiots who thinks they can unfuck the world. But Stumps? What's got into his head?'

I shrugged again. Clearly the experience of the forest had shaken Stumps's mind, but no soldier reacted to war in the same way. And so, instead of offering guesses, I tried to put forward a solution for keeping our comrade away from the fighting.

'I think I can swing it with my centurion that he joins you here. Shouldn't be a problem, if you pull it at your end.'

'Yeah, good thinking,' Titus agreed, pulling a huge hand across his jaw. 'He's been injured enough times that they won't hold it against him.' It was common practice in the legions that the men who saw the most action, or who suffered the most wounds, should get the pick of the more comfortable and desirable positions within units.

'What did you do to those young fuckers who carried

him in?' Titus smiled, suddenly amused. 'Thought one of them was goin' to start crying.'

I waved the question away. Instead I filled the big man in on the news that the boys had been eager to spill to ease my temper. The news that had dribbled from the trembling lips of the tortured prisoners.

'Arminius is mopping up everything east of the Rhine, Roman or allied to the Empire,' I told him. 'The blocking force that we raided is the only thing between us and Roman lands.'

'Enough though, isn't it?' he grunted. 'And once Arminius is done he can come back here. Finish what he started.'

'Maybe.'

'You don't think so?'

'Why lose the men when he can let winter do it for him?'

Titus had nothing to say to that.

'The Germans seemed to think the Rhine garrisons have been bolstered,' I offered.

'Probably the lower Rhine legions moved up. No good to us unless they cross the fucking river though.'

'They'd have done that already if that was the plan, wouldn't they?' I asked glumly.

He nodded slowly. 'Winter's coming, and you don't fight a war in German winter.'

'You're going to get skinny,' I teased, trying to lighten the mood.

Titus grinned. 'You're the legion toothpick. I'll be fine. Our lot will be fine. Don't worry about winter, Felix. I've got us sorted out.'

'How?' I asked.

'I'll show you.'

# 33

Titus pushed open the door to the rear of the quartermaster's building. Instantly I was assaulted by the heat of bodies crammed into a tight space, and the opposing cries of gambling: joy and despair.

I shook my head in wonder at Titus's industry. 'It looks like a circus.'

The long building had once been a storeroom, but now stacks of supplies had been removed to make room for games of dice, casks of ale and wine, and a wrestling ring surrounded by benches. The ring was currently empty but the seats full, and I expected some spectacle was soon to begin. Until then, Roman legionary and Syrian archer busied themselves with drink and a dozen whores.

'There must be a century in here?' I asked Titus.

'I tell the lads on the door not to let in more than sixty, but they probably take a few coins and forget how to count.' He shrugged. 'They're infantry, after all.'

'Is it like this every night?'

'Not really. Got busier since Caedicius ordered half-rations. Nothing makes a man gamble like a bit of hunger.' Then Titus turned to a knot of soldiers, pointing at an inebriated man in their midst. 'Oi. You lot. He's gone or you all are.'

The men moved quickly to obey him and eject their drunken friend as, from the corner of my vision, I felt the approach of someone whose shoulders were twice the thickness of my own.

'Hello, boys.'

'Metella,' I replied.

'Come for the wrestling?'

'I don't know.' I looked at Titus. 'Have I?'

The man grinned. 'He's come to see that he won't be going hungry.'

'A friend of Titus is a friend of mine.' She smiled too, through broken teeth, catching Titus's meaning before turning back to him. 'You want to get started?'

'This is your show, darling. I'm just the humble quartermaster.'

'All right then.'

She walked away to the centre of the wrestling ring that was drawn out on the storeroom floor. The eyes of the drinking soldiers caught the movement, and there was a noticeable drop in volume as they watched her take centre stage.

'Shut up then, you tarts,' Metella ordered the few soldiers who had yet to quieten down. 'Same rules as last night. You register over there with Plancus. Price of entry is a day's rations. You'll get matched up against someone your own size, and winner takes the scoff. You want to bet for coin, it goes through Plancus and me, or my fist goes through your fucking head, understood? You can bet in your groups, but house takes a twenty cut. Don't like it? Fuck off. We've got plenty more who want to come in.'

There were no dissenting voices. The soldiers on the benches had come to win food or make money. So had the whores whose arms were draped about the men's necks.

'Right,' the burly woman concluded. 'Plancus? First two names.'

An old soldier stepped forward as Metella moved away into the crowd. He walked with a severe limp, his hip dropping low with each step.

'Met him a couple of years ago,' Titus confided in me. 'Solid bloke. Worked with us in Minden.'

I thought back to Titus's black-market trading in the army's summer camp – how his deal with the Seventeenth Legion's quartermaster had led to Roman blades in German hands. Titus's twisted sense of honour had compelled him to kill that man for his deceit, and so I could only imagine that he had found Plancus to be innocent of any part in it.

That grey-haired veteran now called out a pair of names belonging to men of the Nineteenth Legion. Plancus's voice was as tired as his legs: the man must have been close to sixty, pushing two terms of enlistment within the legions.

'What do you get out of this?' I asked Titus as two muscular soldiers entered the ring. Both carried themselves with confidence, flexing shoulders as they eyed their opponent.

'Besides entertainment?' he grunted. 'Half of the door,' meaning the money that was collected for entry. 'And half of what the house takes on bets.'

I didn't need to be a mathematician to see that it would be a profitable night for him. 'That's a big cut. How did you get them to agree to that?'

The big man smiled. 'Metella's an old friend. And she might be built like a war galley, Felix, but this is a man's world.'

I had little to say to that. There was no doubt in my mind that women played the tune of men's hearts and heads, but in the world's eyes only a man could stand to the fore in business or power. Roman society was built on subjugation, and that extended to gender as much as social class or nation of birth.

'Coin on the dark-haired lad?' Titus then offered me.

'Why not? It's your money, after all.'

We lapsed into silence and watched as the two soldiers went at it, both content to dispense with caution and to charge at their opponent, looking for the quick opening and win. Wrestling was a mandatory part of training in the legions, courage and strength being highly valued virtues, and both fighters were looking for victory through those means, rather than tactics.

'My bloke's got this,' Titus grunted, assured. 'Look how the other lad keeps trying to duck out from under his grip. He's goin' to end up on his face.'

The wrestlers stood locked in a vice-like grip, the veins of their biceps like pipes as they clutched at each other's necks and shoulders, each fighting for the leverage that would allow them to flip their opponent on to the floor. Sure enough, my man looked as though his neck was buckling.

'Loser's going to be a lot more hungry than if he just stayed on half-rations,' I noted.

'That's what makes it interesting.' Titus was clearly proud of his ability to turn a profit from disaster. 'They'll double down then, and be back for the next one. They'll hold grudges. They'll get desperate. We're under siege, Felix. People aren't goin' anywhere, and so for distraction they'll pay anything. With or without those pay chests, I'm going home rich.'

'To find your son?' I asked, trying to keep my tone casual. Titus had shared a secret with me as the army had died: that his boy, thought lost with the navy, had surfaced alive, but in trouble. I had never referred to it since.

Titus said nothing. If it was possible to make silence violent, then he did so. His face grew taut. I saw the warning signs of his anger, and let my curiosity die.

'You were right,' I said instead as the dark-haired soldier finally tripped his opponent, sending him sprawling on to his front and giving up his back so that he was quickly pinned to the floor and defeated.

Titus simply grunted as cheers came from the bet's winners, and jeers from the angry losers.

Plancus hobbled back to the fore as the defeated wrestler stormed away in disgust. 'Next one's a treat!' the veteran announced. 'Come up Macro, Nineteenth Legion, and . . . Fuckin' 'ell. I'm not gonna try and read this name. Something foreign. Who's the Syrian?'

A lithe archer raised his hand and stepped forwards, doubtless taking his cue from the look of puzzlement on Plancus's lined face. The archer was tall for an Easterner, and measured up well against the smirking Roman who now rubbed chalk into his hands and spat on to the boards for luck.

'Smash him up, Macro!' a man called from the benches, and others soon followed his example.

'Put him on his arse, the cunt!'

'Hammer the raping bastard!'

I looked at Metella, and saw a satisfied smile tease her

215

thick lips. The animosity towards the archer was palpable, easily drowning out the support of the dozen or so of his comrades. Amongst these angry taunts were calls for bets, coins changing hands rapidly. No matter the outcome of the match, Metella and her associates would harvest a pretty profit.

'Fight!' Plancus called, hobbling quickly to be out of the way.

Unlike the first pair, both men began to circle at a low crouch, eyeing their opponent. They would be judging distance, and speed. Power and strength. Calculating if an opening in their opposition's guard was a weakness or an invitation to a counter-attack. Watching them, I thought back to my own days in the wrestling circle, and how my stomach had tightened with anticipation and excitement as I eyed my challenger as a wolf does a sheep. How my chest would swell with pride as my father would pull me from the ring, and lift me on to his thick shoulders, victorious . . .

'Ten on the Syrian,' I offered Titus.

I was ignored. Titus's eyes were fixed on someplace far from Germany, led there by my asking about his son.

The Roman made the first move. It was a quick lunge for a leg, but the Syrian was quicker, spinning out of harm's way. It was a risky play to open up his back and his blind side, and I wondered if the Roman would have the sense to see it, to feint, and to take it when offered again.

He did, and half lunged.

Just as the Syrian had wanted.

This time there was no spin. No evasion. The Syrian held his ground, and the Roman, only half committed to the lunge, didn't have the momentum either to fully pursue it, or to pull back. Instead, he caught the Syrian's knee fully with his jaw.

'He can't do that, the shit!' a man roared as the Roman hit the floor, unconscious.

'That's fucking bollocks!' another shouted.

'That's bullshit!'

'Cheating bastard!'

Soon the air was thick with accusation. The Syrian had the sense to leave the ring, narrowly ducking a mug that was thrown at his head.

'Shut it!' Metella ordered with a thunderclap, stepping into the ring as if she would fight any dissenters. 'He won fair and square. If you have a problem with it, you can stick your name down to fight him tomorrow!'

Plancus was then almost overwhelmed in a stampede, as a half-dozen indignant Romans rushed to him for just such an opportunity, anxious to restore both legion and national honour.

'You're a clever bastard,' I grunted to Titus, watching the frenzied circus that he had whipped up with his comrades.

The big man shrugged. 'We're out here on a limb because it puts coins in senators' pockets,' he said, rubbing a hand over his granite jaw. 'We've lost this war, Felix, but you don't have to be on the winning side to be on the winning side.'

I knew those words were accurate, but also how they held true in the opposite case; where was victory for the soldier who died in supposed glory for the profit of an emperor and his senators?

'Just be careful,' I warned my friend. 'You rub two sticks together long enough, you'll get a fire.'

Titus waved my worries away with an open palm. 'You can get in on it too?' he offered.

I shook my head.

'All right then. So what will you do?'

I had no good answer for him. Whether the enemy was in sight of our walls or not, we were under siege in a hostile province. Freedom of action was something that Arminius had taken from us, and so what choice did I have?

'I'll wait.'

# 34

I rubbed the chalk into my hands, the fine powder falling like the snow that now clung to the hillsides. Winter had come, but the gymnasium was hot from bodies and breath, my skin shining with sweat.

'Again?' my opponent asked me.

'Again,' I confirmed, and then stepped into the wrestling ring.

The fight was over as quickly as the last. The man was like the sea, always moving, and with a grace that belied his power. There was no doubting that strength now as he kicked my legs from under me and drove my snarling face into the dirt.

'You're too angry,' he told me as he pulled me to my feet. 'You come charging in like a boy that's seen his first pair of tits. Control yourself, Corvus.'

I said nothing. I *was* angry. I woke angry, and I fell to sleep angry. Every moment of the day I was one wrong word or look away from lashing out. It made me angrier still that my friend could be so calm, so perfect, and yet beat me in the ring as if I were a child.

'I used to be the one doing this to *you*,' I grumbled. 'I hate losing, Marcus, even to you.'

My oldest friend saved me the mercy of pity. 'Times change. Concentrate on wrestling instead of trying to take my head off, and maybe you'll have a chance.'

'You know it's not *your* head I want.' I spoke darkly, taking the offered cup of water.

'I know.'

Our conversation lapsed there, but my mind was not so easily pushed into silence. Voices – all of my own creation – fought as angrily as I had wrestled to be heard: *You're a coward. Why are you here? You're weak. You're pathetic. Why did you—*

'Again,' I snapped at my friend, desperate to fight, knowing no other way to shut off the voices.

His eyes narrowed as he took in my battered face. 'Corvus, your nose is already ruined. Let's just call it—'

'Again!' I boomed.

And so we fought. I let the anger consume me. I charged at my best friend with every intention of breaking his bones, and he used that weakness against me, turning me inside out with feints and lunges, planting blows against my skull that only enraged me further, causing snot and blood to bellow from my shattered nose.

'Let her go, Corvus,' he told me as a jab crashed into my eye socket.

I would not. Instead I roared. I charged. Without knowing how I got there, I was then on my front, the weight of my friend pinned against my back, driving the air from my lungs and the blood from my face.

'Let her go,' he said with a calm that had no place amidst the violence.

'Fuck you,' I spat into the dirt.

'Let her go.'

'Fuck you!'

And then I felt the fingers on my windpipe. I felt it

close. I felt the breaths becoming ragged, and the panic in my mind as my vision closed in.

'Fuck you. Fuck you,' I gurgled, blacking out.

And then all was silent.

# 35

I couldn't breathe. My mind was racing. Terrified.

*I couldn't breathe.*

I was dreaming, I knew I was, and yet there was no escape. I was trapped within my mind, and with each rapid heartbeat, each shallow breath, I knew that I was panicking myself towards death. I tried to scream, but the sounds died in my closed throat. I tried to call out for my mother, for *her*, but there was no sound except the pulsing of blood in my skull.

I didn't want to die like this, but if I didn't wake up, I knew that I would.

Somehow, my mind, conscious yet locked in its dream state, knew how to wake. Arms flailing, I fought for the edge of my bunk. With all my strength, I pulled myself out and crashed on to the floor.

I woke. I cried for *her*.

Brando leaped to me and took hold of my shoulders. My chest began to heave as painfully as if I'd been kicked by a horse. My eyes were wild.

'Felix!' Brando said urgently. '*Felix!*' he pressed, trying to pull me back into his world.

I heard the words, conscious now, but all I could think of was *her*.

'Who was she?' Stumps asked me.

We were atop the wall, yet another watch that stretched

the day's hours into an endless tedium. The fields ahead of us were empty, the only movement the birds that sought out scraps of tribesman in the abandoned trenches.

No answer was forthcoming, so my friend shrugged, his eyes on the crows. 'It could be worse, I suppose.'

Still I said nothing. My own eyes were fixed on the cold horizon, where the endless forests appeared like spilled ink.

'Titus says you've sorted it for me to go and work with him in the quartermaster's?' the veteran tried instead.

I gave a shallow nod.

'I appreciate that, Felix, but I can still fight. We all have bad nights.'

I opened my mouth to speak, but the words fell away. Finally: 'I'm so fucking tired of this,' I confessed. 'We can't ever get away from it, can we? You close your eyes, pretend it doesn't happen, and then it finds you in your dreams.'

'We can drink?' my friend offered helpfully. 'Seems to be working all right for me,' he bluffed.

'Until it runs out.' I shook my head. 'What life is that, Stumps? Crawling around pissed like the village idiot. Is it what you pictured when you signed up to soldier?'

His look told me that it wasn't. 'What did you picture?'

'I didn't.' It was the truth. 'I didn't know what I was joining, just what I was leaving.'

'Her?' he tried at last.

I didn't answer.

We watched the feeding crows.

*

Days passed with guard duties and half-empty stomachs. Moods grew as dark as the brooding German skies. There was an unseen enemy beyond the horizon, but the soldier's concern now was the battles he fought against appetite and boredom.

'This is shit,' Stumps grumbled after yet another stint on the walls. The previous day, Balbus had been sent to the surgeon when a cut on his hand had turned septic. Unable to hold a javelin, he was currently relieved of all but light duties, and so Stumps's transfer to Titus had been cut temporarily short.

'Better than being in the forest,' Folcher said, trying to lighten the mood.

'Forest or fort.' Stumps shrugged, climbing for his bunk. 'All the fucking same. People out to do us in, no pubs and no women.'

'There're women here,' the Batavian offered.

'You seen a decent one? They only managed to sneak out of the forest because they looked like boar.'

'The one that Felix talks to is nice.' Folcher smiled. 'The Batavian,' he explained, wondering at my sudden unease.

'I like her company,' I explained to Stumps's sly look.

'The company of her tits in your face,' he leered. 'Good for you, Felix. At least someone's getting some fanny.'

'Not like that,' I answered, pulling off my sandals. 'I haven't even seen her for days.'

'Probably found some new cock, then,' my friend teased me, enjoying my discomfort. 'Maybe young Micon here? You look like a fine swordsman.'

The boy soldier, an admitted virgin, blushed at the attention.

Brando smirked. 'There're whores in the fort.'

'That's why you have stopped fucking your mattress?' Folcher laughed.

'So it's mattresses as well as goats for you lads, is it?' Stumps grinned, leaning over the edge of his bunk. 'I'll keep that in mind when I retire and open my brothel.'

'You'd retire in Germany?' Dog put in.

Stumps recoiled in horror. 'Fuck me, Dog, we're supposed to be on half-rations. How come it smells like you've eaten a sack of onions? And no. The only way I'm staying in this shithole is if some goat-shagger nails my head on to a tree.'

'They do that.' Micon spoke up without emotion.

'They do, my friend,' Stumps granted. 'Civilization for me. Back to Italy. No more forests. No more snow.'

'I'll come and visit.' Folcher laughed again, enjoying the fantasy. 'I will show my children Rome.'

'Why not?' Stumps rolled on to his back. 'A nice picnic whilst we watch a few executions in the arena. A proper Roman family day out.'

'Felix,' a voice called from the barrack room's doorway. It belonged to a young soldier. Dressed in helmet and mail, he was acting as the company runner. 'Centurion H wants all section commanders to his quarters for briefing.'

I looked down at the pair of sandals I had unstrapped from my feet. Sleep would have to wait.

Stumps snorted. 'Privileges of rank. Ask him if I can go back to Titus.'

'Missing life in the stores?' Brando asked.

'Those blankets won't stack themselves,' Stumps

answered as I left the room and made my way to the centurion's accommodation.

'Get comfortable, lads,' our centurion offered to the small assembly of section commanders. His tone was reserved; H was usually a genial soul, and I wondered at the cause of his change in humour. Whatever the reason, I doubted that it would be good.

'Right, lads. General situation is still the same. Only sighting we've had of the enemy is a few mounted scouts, and we expect they're keeping eyes on us constantly from Bald Crest Hill on the northern flank. Visible fires at night seem to confirm they're in that area, but not in any force that we need to worry about.'

'Any news from our own scouts?' a section commander asked, referring to the two men who had left the camp with Malchus a week before, and who had been sent onwards to the Rhine in an attempt to rouse the legions there into effecting our rescue.

'You'll know if there is,' H shrugged. 'It'll be like a triumphal march by the time everyone comes out to hear what they've got to say. But no, I'm afraid. The situation's the same, boys. Germans out there. Us in here.

'Now look,' he went on, his brow creasing. 'It should be that, with us in here, and them out there, nobody in this fort is dying. Well, that doesn't seem to be the case. One of the First Century lads got stabbed by a mate of his last night, and bled to death in the barrack room. He died because he was complaining about someone's fucking snoring – don't laugh, you fuckers – and we cannot afford to be losing blokes for that kind of bollocks.'

'Noted, boss.' One of the veterans smiled. 'Beatings only for snoring.'

'I'm fucking serious,' H warned, trying to suppress his own dark grin. 'I don't want to lose men to the Germans. I sure as fuck do not want to be losing men over shit like that.'

'First Century lads have always been nuts,' the veteran offered, and H shrugged in agreement.

'Even so. Keep a close eye on your boys. Keep the discipline. I'm not one for bullshit, you know that, but I'm going to start doing snap inspections of the block and the lads' kit. Extra duties for anyone who's not up to standard. Section commanders included,' he added with a smile.

After a few dramatic groans from the veterans, the men were dismissed. I hung back.

'He can go back to the QM's once you get Balbus back from the hospital,' H told me in answer to my question on Stumps's transfer. 'Could be a few days though. His finger looked bloody horrible when I went to see him.'

It did not surprise me that H would visit one of his men in the fort's hospital, even for an innocuous injury. His leadership pushed me to chastise myself for not calling in on Balbus myself that day.

'Got it from a splinter,' I told him as I turned for the door.

'Hang on a minute, Felix.' The centurion's tone was friendly, but it was still an order. 'I've got my own question about the QM.'

I held my tongue.

'It's all through the cohort that you can have a good night in one of the stores down there – wine and tits – but no matter who I ask, everyone's pretending like it doesn't exist.' He paused then, trying to read me. I knew that my face would be nothing but a scar-crossed mask.

'I'm not stupid, Felix, I know why they don't want an officer turning up, but officers need wine and tits too. Seeing as you arranged your friend's transfer so easily, I'm wondering, if you and the QM are such old pals, whether maybe you could vouch for me? Leave rank at the door, and all that good stuff.'

'If I can,' I began, keeping up my guard, 'then I'll be glad to.'

'Good man.' H grinned, his spirits seemingly restored. 'If we can die together we can drink together is the way I see it. Not that I plan on the first eventuality. Tomorrow night then, if you don't mind? We've got the walls tonight. Try not to let any of the boys fall asleep or kill themselves out of boredom. It's going to be another dull watch.'

He was wrong.

# 36

No one knew when the girl had died, only that her young life had come to an end in a bloodstained alleyway, her corpse then dragged and stuffed into a latrine. Gruff soldiers laughed and joked that the civilian who found the body had shit herself.

I was not one of the men laughing.

Our section was on the walls when the news of the latest killing spread around the fort, the army's chain of whispers leading from the patrolling soldiers who attended to the girl's body, to the guard commander of the watch, and finally to the eager ears of the men on the battlements.

I might not have been laughing, but I was the most enthusiastic amongst the guard to hear every detail of the body, no matter how grim, and my hurried questions drew peculiar looks from my comrades, who must have wondered why I wanted to know such things. Doubtless they thought me deranged, but I was not seeking the sickening facts from morbid curiosity, but from fear. Try as I might, from the moment I had heard the first whisper of death, I had not been able to shake the idea that the butchered girl was Linza. No matter how hard I tried to push the images away, the picture of her cut-up body floated in front of my eyes.

'You sure she had brown hair?' I pressed the soldiers who were relieving us of our duty.

One of the veterans shrugged. 'That's what everyone's saying.'

'Who's they?' I pushed him.

'Fuck's sake, I don't know. Everyone. I won't bother saying anything next time, if you're just gonna grill me over it.'

I brushed past the man towards the battlement's stairs. I moved with speed because I knew that the soldier was wrong. He was wrong, and the girl's hair would be blond. She would be German.

She would be Linza.

'Felix,' Folcher called after me as I reached the bottom step and broke into a run. 'Where are you going?'

I ignored him. I ran past our barrack block, not wanting to waste a single second by stripping off my kit. Instead I carried my shield and javelin as my sandals slapped against the dirt. My haste and my armour drew looks of flushed panic from the civilians and curious frowns from soldiers, but I ignored them all as I concentrated on finding Linza. By the time that I had sprinted to her block on the west side of the fort, sweat was running into my eyes and my chest was heaving beneath the heavy chain mail.

'Who was the dead girl?' I asked a crone who backed away at the sight of my desperate eyes.

'Where's Linza?' I shot at a pair of frightened children. 'She's Batavian. Linza? Do you know her? Linza?'

'Felix?'

I turned.

She stood in the alleyway, a bucket of water held in both hands, a look of confusion on her face. She was alive.

'Linza,' I breathed, my relief followed instantly by

regret at jumping to morbid conclusions, 'I was worried you—'

She sliced off my feeble words: 'Are you my friend?' she demanded, catching me off guard, her blue eyes now lost beneath a frown.

'Of . . . of course,' I stumbled.

Linza placed the bucket down. Her fingers ran through blond hair dirtied by labour. 'You only come to look for me when I'm dead?' she finally accused. There was no heat in her tone, only disappointment.

I said nothing. I had nothing to say, because it was true.

'I'm sorry,' I mumbled, cursing my stupidity. Cursing my warped mind. 'I . . .'

Why did I think this way? Act this way? I had thought about this woman for days. She was here all of that time, literally trapped within the same four walls as I was. Why had I made no attempt to see her – to talk to her – until I thought that she was a cut-up body dumped in a latrine?

What the fuck was wrong with me?

'I'm sorry,' I repeated, my words heavy with self-reproach.

My apology was honest. Linza saw that. Her frown softened, but she held her distance.

'Do you only talk to dead people?' she pressed me sadly, before realizing that the handful of civilians were watching our exchange avidly. 'Come with me.' She gestured towards a building, tired of their scrutiny.

I followed her away from prying eyes. 'I didn't come here to upset you,' I told her once we were in the privacy of a wooden awning.

'Do I look upset?' She shook her head. 'I am worried.'

'I can teach you how to look after yourself, and how to fight?' I offered quickly, desperate to be a help and not a burden. 'And I know a safer place for you to stay. My friend is the quarter—'

'I am worried for *you*,' Linza confided. '*You*, Felix, when you run around looking for death. Looking for hurt. You have friends. They are alive and they are here, but when do you *live* with them? When do you think about *living*, and not *dying*?'

'I—'

'Shut up,' she told me gently. 'I don't want you to speak. I want you to think. I want you to enjoy.'

'But—'

'Fuck!' She laughed with frustration. 'Shut up, Felix!' she ordered me, waving her arms to drive home her point. 'I am not stupid. I know I can die here. I know I can die out there. We can all die. We *will* all die. I don't need to think about it every. Single. Hour. And neither do you,' she offered with a smile.

I had the sense then to hold my tongue. Silence fell, and with it, unease. I felt as though I had walked into an ambush. A killing ground. I was a yard away from this woman who had cost me sleep and caused me panic. If she were an enemy, I could cross that space and kill her before she breathed. Being who she was, that yard was as great an obstacle as the blue sea where I had sat on the pier and dreamed.

'You remind me of someone,' I admitted, thinking back on those blissful days.

'You too,' she slowly confessed.

I didn't dare meet her pale eyes. 'Your husband?'

I saw the smallest of nods in the corner of my vision.

'Who?' she then asked as she reached out, her fingers falling on to my shoulder, her gaze irresistibly drawing my own.

Looking up, I saw comfort in blue eyes. Comfort and love. It was not born of lust, but kinship, the recognition of a fellow wounded soul. That compassion took me back to a life before war and suffering. To a time where I had looked into eyes like hers, and known that each breath, each touch, was a blessing to be cherished.

'I'll tell you,' I promised.

And I did.


The century stood in formation. Afternoon was turning to dusk, and, as was the wartime ritual within the legions, all fighting men of the garrison would man the walls or wait as fully equipped reserves should the Germans choose to appear and attack in the twilight. No man expected such an eventuality, but no commander wanted to be the one who overlooked the procedure and woke to a blade in his guts.

I was exhausted. Opening my soul to Linza and telling her of my own lost love had drained me more than any forced march could do. My head felt muggy and heavy; my shoulders ached beneath my mail. I was exhausted, but despite the fatigue, I felt fresh. As if, in some inexplicable way, I had accomplished something. Like the times that I had left the gymnasium battered and bruised, I knew that I would wake in the morning and feel the pain, but that ache would be a welcome signal that I had improved myself.

I looked to the front of the formation. Centurion H was there and caught my eye. He smiled at me, hopeful that I would vouch for him later that evening so that he could enjoy a night of 'wine and tits' at the enterprise of Titus and Metella.

Suddenly, I saw the conspiratorial look on the centurion's face change, the smile slipping as the brow beneath his helmet creased with question. H was no stickler for discipline, and so I allowed my neck the slightest twist to follow his look.

Centurion Malchus approached with purpose. The cohort commander was dressed for war, his gaunt face tight, shoulders rigid. He was clearly in the mood for killing.

'Century,' H called to his troops. 'Atten-shun!'

Malchus made a hurried gesture, and H turned his back so that the hushed conversation between the officers was screened from their men. It was a short briefing, and when the centurions turned back to face the formation, H's face was as grim as the man's beside him.

'This isn't good,' I heard Stumps whisper.

'Fifth Century.' Malchus spoke in a tone of iron. 'In the last two nights there's been three rapes and two murders in this fort. It's a fucking disgrace, and shits all over the discipline that makes us who we are. We are Romans, not barbarians, and if you want to act like animals, then there will be fucking consequences!'

My stomach tightened at the implied threat. The imposed discipline of Rome's legions could be harsh, quick and lethal, and I wondered what measure Malchus was threatening, and why. It was true that rape was common in the world, and murder a fixture, but it seemed now that Prefect Caedicius was attempting to stamp out all and any forms of unrest. The prefect was charged with bringing the fort through the siege, and to do so he required strict order. In the Roman Empire, that order was bought through blood. With every other man in the ranks, I awaited Malchus's next words with a knot in my guts.

'If there's going to be killing,' the man snarled, 'then it's going to be out there.

'The prefect wants a raid on the hairy bastards, and this century's drawn the honour. We march out as soon as it's dark, and we don't come back without some heads. Lots of fucking heads.'

'You heard the cohort commander.' H stepped forwards after leaving a moment for Malchus's threatening order to sink in. 'When I fall you out, section commanders get amongst your blokes. Strip your kit. No shields, no helmets. Blacken up whatever shines. Anything else, sir?' he asked the cohort commander.

Malchus shook his head. There was nothing but killing on his mind, and so H opened his mouth: 'Century, falllll out!'

After we made the standing right turn and the formation broke up into shouted commands and hurried whispers, I hustled across to my centurion. H caught my eye, and raised an eyebrow in question.

'My man, Stumps,' I began, 'can he get back to the quartermaster's?'

H gave an apologetic shake of his head. 'We need every man in the century for this, Felix. Balbus can't soldier until further notice, and so your boy is going to have to march out with the rest of us. I'm sorry. I don't pretend to know what you guys went through in the forest, but orders are . . .'

I gave a glum nod, resigned.

'No hard feelings?' the centurion asked. I knew well enough why he was anxious for my approval, seeing me as the scarred and dangerous veteran who had cut his way out from the enemy trap when almost all others had fallen. Malchus saw the same, thinking me the blood-thirsty hero. If only they fucking knew.

'Of course not, H.' I was forgetting rank for a moment, pretty certain that he would approve of me using his nickname.

'Been a while since I did something like this,' the man admitted, smiling to cover his nerves. 'Drew some blood on the walls, but . . . different when there's nothing between you and them, isn't it?'

It was.

'I should get to my section,' I said. 'Good luck tonight.'

'Look after my lads,' H told me, offering his hand. I took the strong grip, and then went to join my comrades.

The barrack room was filled with my men and their industry, but talk was reduced to the bare essentials: the requests to pass something out of reach, or to help tighten straps and sharpen blades.

'You tried to get me off it?' Stumps greeted me with a little accusation.

I shrugged my armoured shoulders. 'You're coming.'

'You still tried though,' he grunted. 'I haven't forgotten how to soldier, you know.'

Nothing good could come of the conversation, and so I ignored my friend, instead addressing the section as a whole, and repeating the orders that H had issued.

'When you think you're done get outside and jump around,' I then added. 'Anything loose that makes a noise, strap it down or leave it here.'

'You didn't have any casualties last time, did you?' Statius suddenly piped up. He was slower than the other men in his preparations, and I noticed his eyes had grown a little wider. He reminded me of a rabbit that had caught a scent.

'We didn't,' I confirmed.

'That was last time,' Brando grunted. 'We got them with their trousers down. Tonight won't be so easy.'

'Ready or not, we'll gut them all the same,' Folcher spoke up confidently. 'Arminius has gone to fight. He's left behind the fat and lazy. We'll gut them, Brando. It will be a good night.'

Brando did not argue, and I could see that both of the Batavians were eager for the raid. They were true warriors, these German-born, and I wondered how long Rome could contain their cousins to the east of the Rhine.

Attempting nonchalance, Statius opened his mouth as he put away his shield. 'I could go to the hospital, and see if Balbus is fit for duty?'

The idea reeked of malingering, and Stumps recognized the purpose of the words as easily as I had. 'You'll strap your sandals up and earn your pay, you mincing little cunt,' he sneered. 'Try and pull your half-arsed soldiering out there tonight, and I'll dry fuck you with this blade.'

'I was only asking.' Statius spoke sullenly to the floor.

'Fifth Century, form up!' came the inevitable call from outside. 'Section commanders, get a grip of your blokes. Let's go!'

'Here we go then.' Dog tried to smile, and I felt the eyes of the section turn towards me – some were scared, some were eager, some were vacant, and yet all looked to me for guidance, and survival. Perhaps a great leader would have fired them up with words and promises, but I was not Marcus, Malchus or Titus. I was just me, and I was terrified. What the fuck was there to say?

'All right,' I offered to the uncommon band of brothers. 'Follow me.'

## 37

The dry leaves pushed against my face as I edged my way through the copse. Flickering light danced in the distance; the sound of German voices was clear in the still night.

My throat tightened. Nothing about this raid was aligning in our favour. Our last assault had been unexpected, cloaked by heavy rain and wind. Tonight the land was tranquil, the enemy alert. Malchus had reconnoitred the enemy camp, finding no soft underbelly. We were now in the trees because it offered the best chance at concealment, and perhaps a few seconds' surprise. There had been no talk of abandoning the mission, and when the archers had been left in position to cover our extraction, the faces around me had been grim and sullen beneath the half-moonlight. It was not the place for words, but men clasped hands and squeezed their friends' shoulders, the comradely gestures an acknowledgment that some of us would not live through the night.

I looked at my own section. They crept beside me through the foliage, lifting feet high to avoid rustling the leaves that had fallen with the approach of winter. Even amongst the trees I could make out their wide eyes in faces darkened by dirt. So familiar were we after hours of nocturnal duty that I could pick out each man by his silhouette. I noticed Brando and Folcher at the fore, the Batavians eager to strike and spill blood.

At our rear was Statius. This was to be his first real taste of combat. He seemed loath to meet it, but who could fault him for that? Likely he was the sanest soldier in the section.

I forced the thought away. Now was the time to think of nothing but the most basic of instincts, and stealth: the placement of sandalled and swathed feet; penetrating looks into darkness; filtering the sounds of danger from a backdrop of nature. Forests are a noisy place, if you stop and listen, but an expert ear would hear death approaching above the creaking of old branches and the taunting crackle of dying leaves.

A hand signal to halt passed down the line. Eventually, the loose formation of soldiers came to a halt. I went on to one knee, the bone pressing into dirt still wet from earlier rains. I swallowed fear, knowing that soon the earth would be enriched. I could only mutter an oath that my men would not be the ones to fertilize the German woodland.

I looked through the last few yards of trees, my vision blocked partly by the tangle of bushes. I swore to myself, knowing that these would hinder my progress when the command to attack came, and I would be forced to run the hundred yards to where the first tents of the enemy's camp were pitched. Constant roving patrols of German tribesmen rendered stealth impossible once the trees were cleared, and so Malchus had issued orders that were as brutal and simple as his manner.

'Stay in your sections and sprint to the tents. Put your blade into someone – man, woman or child. When you hear the whistle, move back to the rally point on the other side of the trees.'

Malchus was no coward, and for him to issue orders for killing with such economy, I knew that he feared the futility of this mission as much as I did. We were a tiny force attempting to assault an army of thousands. They were alert, and would fall on our attack like a landslide. Every inch of my experience told me that this was an act of stupidity, and lethal. It told Malchus the same. Maybe even dim-witted Micon could see it.

But what did it matter? We were soldiers, and the command had been given. We would not be the first to charge forward with doubt about our orders in our minds. We would not be the last.

'Let's go,' I heard whispered from the darkness, then the wraith-like figures uncoiled from the forest floor.

'Stay together,' I urged my own men, hoping that I had suppressed the fear in my voice.

Within a moment I reached the bramble bushes at the forest's edge, the barbs snagging and tugging at my tunic, ripping at my skin. I pushed through, hearing other men curse beneath their breath as the vines gripped their shins like attention-starved children.

'Get through,' I urged, my voice higher now that the adrenaline was coming. 'Get through,' I said again, clearing the last of the bushes and stepping out beyond the trees' reach.

The German camp was clear ahead of me now, braziers throwing warm light against the canvas of dozens of tents. Glancing left and right, I saw the black figures of ghosts racing across the open ground, their footfalls padded, breaths rapid.

I looked over my shoulder. Enough of my section's

silhouettes had made it through the natural barricade. We were falling behind the others. It was time.

I ran. Like every other idiot in the raiding party, I pushed away my reservations and rational thought, and instead sprinted headlong at an enemy encampment where I knew that death awaited me.

Why did I do this?

For Rome, the city I had never seen? For the Emperor, a man who had wrested power and kept it through violence and civil war? For glory? What was that? Something celebrated by people who had never experienced the cost of buying it.

No. None of that. I sprinted towards the enemy and death because, if I did not reach it first, then one of my men might, and if they died I would be racked with shame, guilt and sorrow. I charged at the enemy because my comrades did. They charged at the enemy because I did. If one of us had pulled out, then perhaps we all would have done, but the army relies on pride and the bonds of brotherhood to drive soldiers into the jaws of death, and so we ran willingly towards our fate.

We were almost at the tents when the first cries of alarm rang out. There was no need for Brando and Folcher to translate the words, and I knew that the enemy would now be rousing and rallying to meet our attack with their own counter. Our lives were now measured in seconds. We had entered death's domain, and to climb out we would need to kill.

'Into the tents!' I ordered my men, all need for stealth gone now as we finally crossed the open ground. I ran with Folcher and Brando to the closest canvas, Folcher stepping forward to pull back the flap so that we could charge inside and butcher the occupants. Instead, in a split second of spurting blood and a gargled cry of pain, Folcher stumbled back from the tent's opening with a spear-point in his throat.

'Folcher!' Brando cried, reaching for his friend, all thoughts of attack forgotten as Folcher crashed on to his back.

Three Germans burst from their tent in the same moment. Half-dressed and unarmoured, the seconds of warning had been enough for them to pick up weapons and shields. Now, the trio of bearded warriors came at me as a howling pack.

If I had an advantage, it was that my muscles were already loose and my eyes adjusted to the darkness. An inch marks the divide between life and death in battle, and I was able to step out of the arc of a swinging blade, lunging to my right and driving my javelin into a thigh. The man went down but he took my weapon with him, and so I was still pulling my short sword free of its sheath when the other two came at me, roaring threats and murder.

Brando fell on to their exposed backs like a violent landslide. He held no weapon, instead grabbing fistfuls of hair as he bit at the men's faces and plunged a thumb into a German eye. That warrior cried in agony as Brando pushed it in deeper and deeper, and the Batavian's teeth sank into the flesh of a cheek. Brando's rage had consumed him, and it was almost a look of relief that passed over the second German's face as I drove my freed blade into his heart, and saved him the savage fate that had befallen his partner. By the time that Brando backed away, the dead German at his feet was as mauled as a bear's victim in the arena.

I moved past my comrade, desperate to seek out the rest of the section. Free of my own immediate life-or-death struggle, I now became aware of the shouts and screams that were ringing out around us, and, above it all, a whistle.

'We have to go!' I told Brando, grabbing him.

Despite the gore on his face, the man's eyes were sharp and focused. 'Help me with Folcher,' he told me.

I followed him to the dark shape of his friend. Instinctively, I knew that he had passed.

'Help me get him on my back,' Brando urged me.

'He's dead, Brando.'

'I know that he's dead,' the man told me with the calm that precedes a warrior's grief. 'But I'm not leaving him here. Help me.'

I did, pushing the body of our friend on to the Batavian's wide shoulders. My hands came away warm, and wet.

'Get to the rally point,' I told him. 'I need to find the others. Go.'

Brando broke off at a run, adrenaline compensating for the burden of his comrade's body. The whine of the whistle still pierced the night, but it was moving now, towards the trees. The clash of blades had dropped, but the screams were growing. So too the German commands and challenges. Had the raid become a rout?

There was no way for me to tell: I was between the tents, and my world was confined to the few yards around me.

'Seven Section!' I shouted. 'Seven Section!'

No voice returned my call. No figures appeared around me.

'Seven Section!' I tried again. This time, there was movement to my right.

Germans.

A pair of swordsmen. One carried a torch in his left hand, and by the glow of those flames I saw the excitement etched into their hungry faces. With a sudden sickening realization, I realized why.

My hands were empty.

They charged at me, eager to butcher such idiot prey. On instinct I turned, and ran.

I'm not sure which body tripped me, but I tasted blood and dirt as my face drove into the floor like a spade. The golden light and shadow cast by the torch told me that a blade was on its way into my back, and so I rolled sideways. It bought me a moment to push away, but the torchbearer saw my eyes on an escape, and broke from his partner so that they faced me from both sides.

I looked quickly from one man to the other, needing to know which would be the first to attack. Both were young, and grinning. Both were eager for the kill.

They came at me in the same moment. Trapped in the alleyway between tents, I was left with no other option. With all my strength, I threw myself against the tent's canvas, and prayed that the tent pegs had not been driven so deeply into the wet soil that the lines would take my weight.

They didn't, and the canvas buckled beneath me, rope snapping free of the dirt as the tent's side collapsed. Already I was moving, needing to free myself before they recovered from the unexpected. I escaped a swipe of a blade by inches, coming off the canvas like a sprinter at the games. The Germans were on my heels, but my arms were empty, and I used them to power my steps, charging between the tents, knowing that if there were any Germans in my way I would have no other option but to try and run by them. I was under no illusion that such a tactic would leave me gutted from a sword's swing, but what choice did I have?

And so I ran. I ran from the camp and into the open ground between the tents and trees. This space was now a hunting ground, tribesmen whooping with glee as they chased down the fugitives who had dared set foot in their camp a second time. The whistle was gone, replaced by screams and the drumming of hooves as a half-dozen horsemen whirred amidst the chaos, chopping blades into exposed backs and driving spears into heaving chests.

It was a nightmare and a blur. I ran with blinkers, my sight and focus on nothing but the blackness of trees that offered at least the smallest chance of survival. Why did I survive the massacre in the open ground where others did not? Why had I come through such things before, when many had fallen? I could not speak to that. Maybe the name that Arminius had given me was true. Maybe I was the lucky one. Whatever the reason, I plunged into the barbed bushes of the forest as if it were the most inviting Mediterranean waters.

Caught up in the easy slaughter of the open ground, the trees seemed empty of Germans. I took no chances and moved at a crouch towards the rally point that I was certain must be deserted.

Cries of pain and barked orders echoed through the

branches as I quickly stalked my way to be clear of the carnage. I hoped that Brando had had the time to get clear before the enemy were fully roused, but what of the rest of my section? I hadn't set eyes on them since I had turned to the first tent, and Folcher had moved to the flap.

Folcher. One moment he had been alive and vital, the next he was dead. I had seen his end, and yet I hadn't. The memory was so vivid, and yet a blur.

I shook my head. Now wasn't the time to mourn him. I was unarmed and with an enemy army at my back. So far as I knew I was the only survivor from the century. If I allowed myself to stop and to consider what that meant, then I would not live through the night. Despair would overcome me.

The sounds of battle – of massacre – died as the wall of trees grew behind me. Soon I reached the rally point. I forced out a breath, telling myself that it was only what I had expected. What I was accustomed to. I was alone, I thought.

But then I heard the sound behind me, the slightest scrape of steel.

There was someone in the trees.

I was being hunted.

## 38

I held my position, and trusted my instincts. I was being hunted, and I would let myself be caught.

'How did you know?' Malchus whispered, slipping through shadows to join me at my side.

'I can smell soap on you, sir,' I answered honestly.

'I sent the rest of them back,' Malchus explained.

From his tone, I took it that 'the rest of them' were pitifully few.

'You can catch them up,' he told me.

'What are you doing, sir?'

'I'll take my chances here. More of the boys could be lying low.'

His tone betrayed his true feelings, but Malchus was an honourable officer. He was not about to abandon hope for his men.

'Listen,' he instructed me, and we lapsed into silence, attempting to distinguish the sounds of the forests from the noise of the enemy camp, now fully roused. A few cries of pain echoed in the night, but largely what we could hear was the mumble of raised voices.

The enemy would be organizing search parties, I was certain. I could only hope that they would wait for the dawn, cautious in case the attack had been a ruse to draw them on to the blades of a larger force.

After a while, Malchus spoke. 'There. Listen.'

I heard it. Footsteps. They were timid and careful. Not the sound of a German warrior flushed with victory.

'Wait here.'

The centurion returned soon. With him was a legionary. His silhouette was alien to me, and I knew that he was not of my own section. He was injured, his breathing shallow as he clutched at his shoulder.

I had questions that I burned to ask him, the need to know the fate of my comrades gnawing at my chest, but I held my tongue, placing our survival first. Malchus left again, and returned with another soldier. The third time that the centurion left my side, he returned alone.

'I don't think there's anyone else,' he announced quietly to straining ears. 'Follow me.'

We turned our backs on the victorious chants of the Germans, and slid into the black undergrowth.

We followed the cover of trees for as long as we were able. When we broke into open ground, Malchus was blunt in his orders.

'We're not going to take the track. Whether they attack our boys or not, there're going to be cavalry scouts out there. We'll make best speed through the fields. That means we fucking run. If we're out here when daylight breaks, then we're dead.'

No one commented.

'Dump your mail in that ditch. I'll make sure the quartermaster doesn't bill you for the equipment loss,' Malchus joked darkly. 'Let's go.'

So began hours of burning legs, aching muscles and scorched throats. Running through the night was abject misery, but no man complained, for what was the choice? Instead, I tried to do what Linza had told me. I tried to think about life, and not death. I promised myself that if we made the fort, then I would not wait until murder struck to see her again. That I would meet her friendship with my own.

'You're doing good, lads,' Malchus encouraged us. 'We're getting close. Listen. There's the river. Not even a couple of miles to go. We'll make it; just keep going.'

I had to marvel at our leader. After the bloodshed and despite the exertion, his tone was calm, his breath steady. Malchus was a born warrior and leader. Perhaps, if the three legions that had entered the forest had been commanded by this man, then the bodies of more than fifteen thousand would not have been picked over by crows. But what chance was there of that? Malchus was not a senator. He was a soldier who had fought his way up the ladder, each step a testament to his prowess as a killer. Rome's borders held and grew due to men like him, and yet the warrior would be no more welcome in the senate than a dog. Malchus was a tool that fit a purpose, and though the upper classes would laud him and heap praise on his armoured shoulders, he would never be seen as anything but a pawn to the men who controlled Rome. And yet, I knew deep down, he would die for them and their city.

Why were we soldiers so blind and obedient?

'The fort,' Malchus announced, jolting me out of my mutinous thoughts. 'Made it, lads.'

With salvation in sight, nervous bursts of laughter broke out amongst us. Despite the death that we had left behind, relief at having survived overtook us, and I saw the white of smiles in the darkness.

Malchus announced himself to the guards on the gate-house, and confirmed the night's watchword. 'Where's the raiding party?' he then asked.

The confused reply left me sick.

'It's not you?'

There was a moment of heavy silence. I thought I heard Malchus's teeth grate.

'Get inside,' he said to me. 'Get these men seen by a surgeon. I'm going back to find the others.'

'I can come with you, sir,' I offered, my relief overtaken by guilt as the centurion turned me down.

'I move faster alone. Get them to the surgeon, and then report to the prefect. He'll need briefing,' Malchus ordered, and with those words he was lost to the night.

## 39

I broke the cohort commander's instructions as soon as the gates opened and we were met with the torchlight and nervous faces of the guard.

'Where's the rest of you?' a salted centurion asked, his eye appraising wounds and the blood on our skin.

'I need to brief the prefect, sir,' I told the officer. 'Can your men see these two to the hospital?'

'We can see ourselves,' one of the survivors answered gruffly. Having come so far, they would not be carried this final distance.

By the torchlight I met the man's eye, admiring his courage. Now safe ourselves – at least for the moment – I knew that sickening worry for our comrades was about to come crashing down.

'Go,' the centurion told me. As I broke into a run, I heard him call orders to bring stretchers and surgeons to the gate. If – *when*, I forced myself to think – the century arrived, then the centurion and his guard would be ready.

The pounding of my sandals and my blood-coated arms caused civilians in the streets to run in panic. I did not even know if they were aware that a raid had been launched, and now panicked rumours would spread like a disease. The gossip would worry some, and thrill others. Here was a break in the monotony of the siege, paid for in blood.

'I need to see the prefect!' I called to the guards as I

approached the headquarters building in the centre of the camp. 'Centurion Malchus sent me,' I explained between ragged breaths.

The soldiers were understandably wary of my appearance, and held their ground as one called inside for the guard commander. The veteran appeared quickly.

'Who are you?' he demanded.

I rattled off my particulars, moving straight into the reason for my appearance, and my need to see the fort's commander.

'They're still out there,' I finished.

I found myself in front of the prefect moments later. From the instant that he took in my desperate state, Caedicius's face was drawn and grey.

'You say Centurion Malchus has gone back?' he asked me again.

'Yes, sir.'

'And Centurion Hadrianus?'

'I don't know, sir. After the fighting, I only saw the cohort commander, and the two men we came back with.'

That left a century and sixty archers unaccounted for. Caedicius's jaw twitched with anger.

'Shall I ready the men to march out, sir?' a grey-haired centurion asked. 'Screen them back in?'

Caedicius shook his head without hesitation. 'No. No one leaves the fort. They'll make it back by themselves.' He offered the words up as if they were a prayer.

The prefect then gestured to me. 'You can go, but remain here in headquarters.'

A clerk came forward to lead me from the now silent room. I was offered a stool in a small room that acted as a mess for the headquarters staff. 'Can I get you food? Water or wine?' the man asked me kindly.

I said nothing.

'I'll get them all.' He smiled and returned in moments. I greedily snatched the water from his hands. The man took no offence, and I chugged deeply, draining it in moments.

'I'll go and get you another.'

The wineskin was also empty by the time the clerk returned. My indulgence was born not from thirst, but fear. With every moment that passed without news, the knot of terror in my stomach was growing. The grip of grief about my throat was closing.

My section. My friends. Could they all be dead?

I looked at the food in front of me, and pushed it away. I knew that it would be chalk in my mouth.

'Was it . . . bad?' the well-meaning clerk ventured.

My eyes told him all that he needed to know. As he looked into them he shrank back as if I were a growling dog.

'It was bad,' I confirmed, not wanting to scare away the one soul who was my company.

'Would you like more wine?'

I thought for a moment. There was something I wanted more. 'Could you do something else for me?'

The clerk was eager to help. Moments later, he was leaving with my messages. As he left the room, I realized that I had done all that I could. I was useless now, a piece cast aside and out of the game.

All I could do was hope, and pray.

I sneered at that thought, and instead got to my feet in search of wine, and oblivion.

# 40

By the time my message had been delivered, and Titus had joined me in the headquarters building, a second empty wineskin lay at my feet. The huge man dumped my requested replacement of armour and weapons alongside it.

'Stumps?'

I shook my head. 'I don't know. I didn't see him go down, but the century's still out there.'

'How bad was it?' the big man asked, drawing up a stool beside me.

'Chaos,' I told the floor. 'The whole mission was fucked from the beginning. No rain? No cloud cover? What the fuck did they think was going to happen?'

'Keep your voice down,' Titus warned me, conscious of where we were.

'I don't know what happened to them, Titus.' I shuddered. 'What if . . .'

What if the Germans had taken them alive? What if the Germans were killing them by inches? Raping them? Skinning them? Burning them?

'I should have died with them,' I croaked, overcome with guilt and pity.

I didn't see the hand coming. One second I'd been miserable and hunched on the stool, the next I was on the floor, my head singing from the blow.

Titus lifted me to my feet by the scruff of my tunic. 'Finished feeling sorry for yourself?'

'I shouldn't have—'

He hit me again. I tasted blood in my mouth. Anger built to replace self-reproach.

'What am I supposed to do?' I spat at the man. 'They're out there, and I'm here! What do I do if they don't come back?'

'What the fuck do you think you do?' Titus shook his head. 'You remember them, and then you pick up your sword and you kill for them. This isn't your first bad night, Felix, and you're still standing.'

'Well, maybe I don't want to stand any more!' I shot back.

'Stop talking like a fanny. You were born to kill, whether you like it or not. And it's still dark. It's not over.'

'And how am I supposed to wait until dawn? Tell me that, Titus? How am I supposed to sit here with my thumbs up my fucking arse while our friends are out there, dead or dying? How the fuck do I do that?'

'I can help you, if you like?' he asked me earnestly.

I gave him a pleading look. I just wanted to know. I wanted it to be over. I couldn't stand the agony. The wait.

'Please,' I asked him, wondering what miracle he could work.

I saw nothing but a blur, and then his huge fist crashed into my jaw.

# 41

I woke in my barrack block, excited calls from the walls the first signs of the raiding party's arrival, these heralds followed closely by the pounding tramp of sandals as soldiers and civilians rushed to the battlements, every soul within Aliso desperate to set eyes on the returning formation.

At least, what was left of it.

Reaching the top of the battlements, my heart dropped into my stomach. By the grey light of the dawn I saw a skeleton of a century limp its way towards the gate. Roman supported Roman, and behind them, arrows nocked as they crept backwards, were the Syrian archers.

'Open the gates!' a voice called from the walls. 'Stretcher parties out! Surgeons, triage and then get them to the hospital!'

I went to join them, but something – someone – held me back.

Linza. My heart leaped and sank in the shock of seeing her.

'Let them do it, Felix. You're too tired,' she told me, and from the ease with which she had stopped me, I knew that she was right. Instead, I searched the faces of the returning soldiers for men that I knew. Still cloaked by the last dregs of night, and the shadows of their helmets, I recognized only one man amongst the few dozen, his wide shoulders and height raising him above his comrades.

'Brando!' I shouted, my voice cracking. This time, there was no way for Linza to stop me, and I reached my comrade as he set weary feet inside the fort's gate, throwing my arms about his mailed back as if I were a child.

'Felix?' he asked, puzzled, seeing a ghost. 'How . . .' His words trailed off. Instead, the Batavian embraced me.

I looked quickly for the other faces of my section, shrugging off the mystery of arrows that protruded from the bloody wounds of some of the raid's survivors.

'Felix!' I heard, and in the scrum of bodies I turned to find Stumps, his arm over the shoulder of a bloodied Micon.

I pulled them both close to me, their heads touching mine. I was not the only soldier who let loose tears at this reunion between comrades.

'Micon.' I was worried, seeing the blood thick on his arms and face. 'Are you hurt?'

The boy soldier shook his head. 'Not mine,' he mumbled.

'How did you get back?' Stumps managed. 'We waited, but . . .' His voice trailed away, racked with guilt.

'It doesn't matter,' I told him, meaning it. 'Where are the others?'

'Folcher's dead,' Stumps told me, his eyes on the fort's dirt. 'Dog, too.'

I pressed the heels of my hands into my eyes.

'Dog.' I breathed out. 'How?'

'Took a spear in his chest,' my friend told me, swallowing at the memory. 'It was over for him quickly.'

'Statius?' I asked.

'Around here somewhere. Arrow sliced his arm.'

'An arrow?'

Stumps's face turned grey as he shot a look at the Syrian archers. These men were unbloodied, their heads bowed. Under command of a Roman centurion, they were being quickly shunted away. For the first time now, I noticed that abusive cries in Latin followed in their wake.

'Sleep with your eyes open!' one veteran of the Nineteenth called after them. 'You're gonna be waking with open throats!'

'What happened?' I asked Stumps, noticing now half a dozen Romans being loaded on to stretchers, the shafts of arrows sticking out of their flesh. With horror, I saw that Centurion H was amongst them.

'When we left the rally point, H ran us to where the archers were waiting,' Stumps explained, his voice dark. 'He called out his part of the watchword, and we got an arrow back instead. It hit someone, they screamed, and then the next moment there were arrows everywhere.'

I swore, imagining the chaos. The terror.

'Eventually they realized what they were doing,' Stumps concluded, spitting pathetically on to the dirt. 'But by then we had men down everywhere, the fucking lizards.' He snarled.

'Fifth Century!' came the shouted order, cutting short my friend's tirade. 'Fall into formation. Don't worry about sections, just get into three ranks. Move!'

The words had come from Malchus, and he cajoled the weary soldiers into obeying his orders. Within moments, those of the raiding party who could still stand were formed up in formation before him. Casting a quick eye over the ranks, I estimated that less than half of the century had escaped death or wounds to the point where they could still stand.

'Century will form open order,' the cohort commander then called. 'In open order, march!'

The front rank took a pace forwards, the rear a pace backwards. Now, there was space for Malchus to walk by the men one by one. As he came closer, I heard words of encouragement. Praise for their deeds. He would not let the survivors of the raid slink away into the barracks like whipped dogs. He would remind them that they were soldiers. Killers.

'Show me your blade,' I heard him ask a young soldier, congratulating the young man on the steel painted red with German gore. 'You made him dance, didn't you?' Malchus encouraged him. Then: 'Did you lose a friend tonight?' he asked.

'I did, sir,' the boy answered, attempting to rouse his courage.

'Remember him every time you ram that blade into German guts. Make them pay for it. Every one. Understood?'

'Yes, sir.'

'And what about you?' Malchus asked Stumps beside me. 'Missing fingers and an ear? You're not a stranger to this, are you, soldier? Show this young lad your blade. Show him what it means to be a man in this army.'

For a moment, Stumps did nothing.

'Did I speak into the wrong ear?' Malchus asked, an edge of amusement to his iron tone. 'Show him your blade.'

Stumps drew the short sword from its sheath; it was clean.

'I like to stick them on the javelin, sir.' Stumps covered, feigning confidence. 'I like to see them wriggle on it.'

'Good man.' Malchus grinned, slapping him on his shoulder.

And then he came to me. We exchanged no words, just a look. A look from veteran to veteran. A look which acknowledged we had been fucked that night, and that the chances of the fort's survival had ebbed along with the blood from those men who had been lost beyond the walls, and those who now screamed in the hospital as the surgeons set to their gruesome work.

It wasn't long before Malchus had spoken with each man, and returned to the front of the formation.

'We lost brothers tonight,' he told us, without a hint of weakness in his voice. 'We'll lose more before this is all over. Being a soldier is about suffering, boys. It's about these nights. What separates us from every other army in the world is what we do when we bleed. Others will run and hide from it. Not us. We'll lick the blood from our blades, and we'll go after these cunts again. We'll go after them harder. We'll go after them without mercy. By the time this war is over, every one of the Germans in that camp will be dead. Every one of their women will be raped. Every one of their children will be slaves. Do you understand me?'

'Yes, sir,' came the chorus of croaking voices.

'Your centurion's in the hospital, and your optio died with glory,' Malchus went on. 'We'll restructure the century, but for now, go to your barrack rooms. Eat and sleep, but don't you dare think about doing either until your kit is cleaned, and you're ready to fight again, understood?'

'Yes, sir!'

'Good. Fall out.'

*

Walking back to the barrack block, I felt as though I were waist-deep in water and my legs were lead. Beside me, the men of my section moved like similar ghouls.

*My section.*

What was left of it? Brando, head on his chest, the Batavian grieving for his friend Folcher. Micon and Stumps were unhurt, at least in body. I suspected that the blood-free blade of Stumps was caused by an injury just as dangerous as any flesh wound. Balbus was already hospitalized with the corruption to his hand, and now Statius had joined him. Dog, a soldier I had liked but had never truly known, had died out of my sight from a German spear. Battle is a brutal blur, and it is fantasy to believe that a soldier witnesses the end of his comrades. As with Dog, the news of their end usually comes from a hushed comment, and sunken eyes.

'Brando.' I placed a hand on my friend's shoulder. I hoped that in that word he would know how I grieved for him, and for Folcher. I hoped that my eyes were enough.

'He was my best friend, Felix.' Brando sighed, his big chest heaving. 'My best friend, and I couldn't bring him home. I left him in the trees.'

'You did all you could.'

'Do you know what they'll do to his body?' Brando asked me, exhausted.

We both did.

'I should have carried him home.' He meant to the besieged fort that we clung to like limpets to rocks.

'And died yourself? Folcher wouldn't have wanted that.'

The Batavian nodded at the truth in my words. 'But it doesn't make it easier, does it?'

We cleaned our equipment in silence. Linza came and went to bring bowls of hot water, barley and soup. She spoke to Brando in their native tongue, and I knew that the language was a comfort to him. A tie to the comrade he had lost.

I expected Titus to arrive and to squeeze the life from his oldest living friend. I was wrong; his business partner Plancus hobbled into the room in his place.

'Titus has to reissue equipment and organize the funeral rites,' the old veteran informed us. 'Two of the wounded died under the surgeon.'

'Was one called Statius?' I asked.

'Doesn't sound familiar. Anyway, he said he'll come see you when he can.'

Then, equipment cleaned, and exhausted by exertion and grief, we fell back on to our bunks. At first I thought it was a dream when I felt the woman's presence beside me, her arm over my shoulder, but then I saw blue eyes beneath strands of blond hair.

'Sleep,' Linza told me.

I closed my eyes.

# 42

When I woke, Linza had gone.

Daylight lit the room, but Brando and Micon snored on. Stumps fidgeted fitfully in a sleep that I was certain was full of bloodshed.

In search of water, I stepped outside of the barrack block. The fort was eerily quiet. The sight of the ravaged century had sent a shock of fear throughout the place. Arminius had pulled his troops from under the walls' gaze and, out of sight, they had been out of mind for many of the fort's occupants. There could be no such blissful ignorance now. Not whilst graves were being dug. Not whilst the unsanctioned families of the soldiery wailed over the loss of their loved ones.

I caught the eye of a veteran of my own century. A survivor, like myself. I had no idea of his name, but what did it matter? In many ways, this stranger was closer to me than the family I had been born into.

'Hard to sleep, isn't it?' the veteran offered.

'Thirsty,' I told him.

'I've got wine?'

And so, moments later, we sat in the shelter of the wall's lee. We didn't talk, not even to ask each other's names. We simply drank, slowly, comforted that we were not the only creature to be suffering. We sat there until a knot of soldiers approached, bandaged and grim. Centurion H was at the head of them.

'It's good to see you, sir,' I told the man honestly. His smile was gone. Instead, H's lips were drawn into a grimace. Half his century had not returned, and this was not the kind of officer who looked for glory or opportunity in that loss. His clouded eyes told me as much.

'Your man Statius is still in the hospital,' the centurion informed me. 'Balbus, too. His corruption's getting worse. I don't know when you'll get him back. To be honest, Felix, I don't know if there's a century any more. I expect that we'll be split up amongst the others,' he concluded sadly.

I noticed a red stain that was spreading through the centurion's linen bandage. 'I don't want to overstep, sir,' I offered, 'but shouldn't you be in the hospital, too?'

H slowly shook his head, and then looked at the men around us. They took his hint, and left.

'I'm telling you this because, after all you've been through, you deserve to hear it. Last night was a disaster, Felix, nothing less. We can't afford to take losses like that, which means no more raids. No more proactive patrols, or attacks. We're going to sit here in this fort until we're rescued, or until we starve.'

'Are supplies that low?'

'They will be. German winter's harsh. Have you seen many cats and dogs around recently? People are preparing already. Everyone's about to go hungry. That's why the prefect's ordered that we release the prisoners we captured last week.'

'Release them?' I asked, surprised at the mercy.

The centurion shrugged. 'Better they eat the enemy's rations than ours.'

I understood that logic well enough, but the clemency confused me. Why not kill them, and let them feed the crows? Dead men didn't eat.

H read my thoughts. 'It's not as simple as that, Felix.' The man shook his head. 'We're taking a burden of hungry mouths from us and putting them on to the goat-fuckers.'

I licked nervously at my cracked lips, knowing what was coming next. 'But we're not about to hand them soldiers, are we?' I asked.

H met my own dark eyes. 'Caedicius wants to take their hands, Felix,' he confided in me, spitting at the dirt. 'And he wants what's left of our century to be the butchers.'

We formed up in full battle dress and marched to the centre of the camp and its parade square. The ranks were silent and sullen, men grieving over the loss of their comrades from the raid not yet a day old. It was this grief that Prefect Caedicius and Centurion Malchus hoped to tap into. The opportunity to give men who had been beaten – for what else was the botched raid but an abject failure? – the chance to strike back at the faces of their enemy. To draw blood, and bring forth screams. To avenge the comrades that they had left behind.

And this demonstration was not only for those who had taken part in the failed assault. Leaving a skeleton guard force on the walls, the entirety of the garrison had been formed up in ranks to watch the coming punishments. Civilians, whether drawn by order or by morbid fascination, jostled for space to witness the proceedings.

There were ten German prisoners. Naked, haggard men, on their knees, heads hanging, their bodies a map of torture from where Malchus and his men had extracted their information some days ago. Once proud warriors were now a pathetic sight, drained of all spirit and humanity.

Our century drew to a halt in front of them. Malchus, as imposing as ever, quickly strode forward to our ranks, tossing four pieces of rope to soldiers at random. One such length was dropped by Micon, but the young soldier scrabbled quickly to pick it up. I noticed that there was a noose at one end.

'Those of you with rope, step forward,' Malchus ordered, his eyes like caves. 'Take an arm or a leg and put the noose around wrist or ankle.

'This one first.' He pointed to a fair-haired German who was silently weeping. So timid and shattered from captivity was this enemy that it took only moments to subdue him: the ropes around his limbs pulled outwards under Malchus's instruction so that the German was spread-eagled on the parade square's dirt, his wriggling limbs held fast by Micon and the other soldiers. As if the gods were watching and casting judgment, the skies chose that moment to open, and a light rain began to patter against our armour and the victim's naked skin.

A squat legionary then walked forwards and handed Malchus an axe. Malchus used the tool to gesture at an arm, and the burly soldier knotted rope around the elbow – he was creating a tourniquet. Once finished, the squat soldier stepped away, and Malchus spat into the face of his enemy. Then the axe swung down. With a sickening chop the lower arm came free, and Micon, who had been holding that rope, stumbled backwards as the anchor of flesh was severed.

The screams came moments later. They were universal in language, and dreadful. Tired of the sound, Malchus drew his dagger and knelt over the man. Within a breath, a tongue lay discarded on the floor.

Malchus snorted. 'Tongue first for the rest of them. Can't hold their pain like men, the fucking scum. I suppose if you fuck enough goats, you start to bleat like them.'

The centurion's taunt was followed by laughter from the hardest of his men, and the most nervous – those who were keen to hide their own perceived weakness behind the terror of others.

I looked at Micon, who held a rope with the severed hand at its end. I tried to read the boy's expression, wondering about his sanity. In the forest he had turned green at such sights. Now his face was without a trace of emotion. Why should I have expected differently? Only weeks ago, he had seen his best friend die beside him. He had seen men and women killed in the most unimaginable and horrendous ways. This teenage veteran had never known a woman, and yet a severed hand and cut-out tongue were now nothing out of the ordinary to him.

'Next four,' Malchus ordered, taking the rope from Micon and the other soldiers who had held down the condemned prisoner and tossing them towards the ranks of our depleted century.

Brando snatched one from the air as if it were hewn from gold.

The second German victim whimpered like a dog as he was pushed into the dirt, and I heard the big Batavian plead with Malchus as he strode to his side.

'Let me gut the bastard, sir,' Brando begged, and I suspected Malchus would have agreed, had Prefect Caedicius not answered for his more bloodthirsty subordinate.

'Send them alive and unable to fight, and they become a burden on their own people, soldier. If you kill him, he's just food for the crows.'

Brando stood to his full height. He was an imposing bastard. Respectful of his seniors, but imposing. 'Then let me do it slowly, sir. Please. They killed my friend, sir. They killed my whole cohort in the forest. Please, sir, let me send him back with a lesson.'

Eventually, Caedicius gave a slow nod. Malchus took the rope from Brando, and handed the Batavian his blade.

The German writhed as if he were possessed by spirits. It did him no good. Brando took his tongue first. He was savage in his work, and most of the man's lips came with it. His ears were next.

'Hurry this up,' the prefect ordered, eyes on the rain clouds, and Brando hacked at both of the man's wrists until they were ragged stumps. As blood pooled into the dirt, the prisoner rolled on the floor like an eel gaffed out from a stream.

One after another, the German prisoners were pulled forwards to similar fates. Eventually, one of the pieces of bloodstained rope found its way into my hands. From a long acquaintance with death and fate, I knew without looking who the victim at my hands would be: the young boy I had dragged from his tent. The young boy that I, with Folcher, had brought to this place.

'You want to cut him?' Malchus asked me, seeing my gaze linger on the boy's thrashing eyes.

'He's young,' I tried, feigning indifference. 'Don't we need slaves, sir? Maybe he's worth keeping.'

Malchus shrugged, oblivious to my true intention. 'Not with winter coming. Take hold of his arm, Felix. Hold him still.'

And so I did, watching as Malchus's dagger bit into the red meat of the boy's tongue. Through the rope, I felt every lashing second of defiance. Every wild jolt of panic. Malchus soon tired of the boy's resistance and rammed his fist into his face. The boy didn't know it, but the punch was a mercy: he was barely conscious as the gore-painted axe head chopped into his thin wrist and took his hand.

I fought down the bile that rose in my throat. What good was a sign of weakness now? What good was pity? Mercy? I had to think of my friends. I had to think of Linza. This boy and his comrades belonged to an enemy that wanted us dead. That wanted Linza raped and enslaved. Now, at least these ten were no longer a threat.

'Send them out of the camp,' Caedicius ordered, loud enough for the assembled troops to hear. 'Let this be a lesson to them, and to anyone who dares take up arms against Rome.'

'I have a suggestion, sir,' Malchus quickly put in with a grimace that touched on a smile. Prefect Caedicius listened, and agreed, and so it was that the prisoners were freed with their hands after all, or at least one of them, stuffed into tongueless mouths. Of the ten prisoners dragged on to the square, only six survived the initial shock of their injuries to stumble in agony from the gates, their moans stifled by their own amputated flesh. Another dropped before barely clearing the gates.

'They won't survive more than a few days,' Stumps said to me later, dispassionately. 'Drain on the enemy resources, my arse. The prefect knows he fucked up, and he wants to pretend we didn't leave forty of our blokes out there, where the same thing's happening to them.'

I kept my mouth shut. Stumps had spoken for us both and, sure enough, the enemy were quick to make their own point, for later that day a large body of horsemen arrived and pulled to a halt beyond bow range. Their horses were trailing something, and the soldiers with the keenest eyesight told us that they were the bodies of the raiding party. The German riders then fell on these corpses with glee, hacking until there was nothing remaining but a pyramid of chopped limbs and skulls.

I knew that amongst that carnage would be the bodies of Folcher and Dog. One of those men was a friend that had escaped slavery with me. The other, a soldier I had barely known, yet I had been responsible for. Both men had lived for families, and dreams. Now they were reduced to food for crows and foxes.

'Fuck war,' Stumps snorted angrily beside me, and I did not know if I had ever heard words so heartfelt and true. '*Fuck war.*'

# 43

We slept for a long time after the raid and the mutilation of the prisoners. It wasn't a good rest for some, and men cried out and shook in their sleep, fighting unseen battles, losing the same friends over and over. I wasn't the only man to wake more exhausted than when I'd fallen into sleep.

'He's not here.' Brando spoke sadly, looking at the empty bunk that had been occupied by his closest friend. 'I've been awake for hours, but I didn't want to open my eyes.'

We were alone in the bunk room; I presumed that Stumps was drinking with Titus, and had taken Micon with him like a cherished younger brother.

I rose from my mattress and put a hand on the Batavian's shoulder. He didn't need words, or promises from me. He just needed to *know*.

'I don't think he would blame me for leaving him behind, Felix.' Brando rubbed his hands together as if he were milling wheat. 'He knows I would have died with him if he was breathing.'

I nodded at that truth.

'I tried to hide his body in the trees. Maybe they didn't find him?'

Maybe. Or maybe Folcher's severed head and dismembered limbs were in the pile of bodies that the Germans had stacked beyond the wall. Prefect Caedicius had sent a work party to recover the fallen so that they could receive a proper burial, but German horsemen had burst from the trees. They had baited the trap with our need to give the men a decent burial, and the work party had narrowly escaped with their own lives.

'He's in a better place,' I told my friend. How many soldiers had heard that promise?

The door to the barrack room pushed open then.

'Balbus,' I greeted the man at the threshold.

'I'm su-sorry it took me so long to get back,' the soldier told me, head bobbing in earnest, his eyes struggling to meet my own. From experience, I could see a familiar slope in his neck and shoulders where shame had gripped him. Shame that he had been spared the slaughter when others had fallen.

'How's the hand?' I asked him, hoping to pull him from those thoughts.

'It's fu-fine,' he bluffed.

I stood and took it. Beneath the bandage I could feel swelling. Balbus tried to mask a wince as I applied pressure through my fingers.

'You're a good man, Balbus, but a shit liar,' Brando said from the edge of his bunk, recognizing the hurt and the reason for hiding it.

'I'm su-sorry about Folcher,' Balbus answered with feeling. 'He-he was a great bloke.'

'He was,' Brando agreed, standing so that he could meet Balbus's eye man to man. 'Dog, too. He was long a friend of yours?'

'Tu-ten years,' Balbus confirmed.

'Then he wouldn't want you trying to fight with one hand, would he?' the Batavian pressed gently. 'This siege isn't going anywhere, my friend. Get your rest. Get it for us, and for Dog.'

'I'll walk with you to the hospital,' I put in, ending the matter. Balbus's cheeks reddened with shame at being dismissed, but he did not try to argue.

We walked through the camp in silence. My mind was elsewhere, and I suspected his was on the friends that he had lost, and the shame that he had been spared that carnage because of a splinter picked up during a work party of no consequence.

Good soldiers blame themselves for the death of their comrades, no matter how ridiculous the accusations. Neither I nor Balbus had control over even our own lives, and yet we would beat ourselves mercilessly because we had not saved others. *What if* was the veteran's greatest enemy.

'Don't leave here until the surgeon gives you the all-clear,' I ordered the man as we reached the high-sided building of the hospital. 'I'm going to look in on Statius.'

I half expected Balbus to offer to join me, but he left quickly enough. I expected that he did not want the shame of confronting a comrade injured in a fight he had taken no part in himself.

The stink of blood and bodily fluids hit my nostrils as I entered the hospital. The building was quiet but for the bustle of slaves and the specialist assistants who worked beside the surgeons – those who would have screamed from their wounds had either died or were now battling to recover.

Finding Statius was easy enough. He had the strong accent of the Empire's capital city, and I heard it carry along a hallway as he boasted of a whore he had once known on the Rhine.

'Statius,' I greeted him, throwing a nod to the two bandaged men who sat with him on their cots.

'Felix?' he replied, a little puzzled. A little alarmed.

'I thought I'd check in on you,' I said, and Statius's companions had the acuity to leave the room. 'How's the arm?' I asked.

Statius shrugged. He looked uncomfortable, whether from wound or from scrutiny, I could not tell.

'It's a struggle to lift it,' he finally offered when I said nothing. 'One of those fucking Syrians.'

I looked into his eyes, then. I don't know what compelled me to do it. Perhaps it was because of the way his voice had shifted from bravado with his hospital comrades to piteousness when he saw me. Or perhaps, after living a life of duplicity, I knew how to spot a fucking liar.

I smiled. 'Let me take a look.'

'I don't know if the surgeons—'

'It's fine, Statius. I want to take a look. I want to see what those fucking Syrians did to you.' There was no room for compromise in my tone, and the man held his tongue as I unwrapped the bandage covering his arm and looked at the wound: a clean cut through the flesh of his upper left arm. Within a moment, I was certain.

There are many things in my life that I am not proud of, and one of these is that I have seen and inflicted wounds with almost every blade and weapon imaginable. From this dark experience, I knew now that Statius was a liar. He claimed to have been struck by an arrow, but from the thickness and direction of the sutured wound, I knew that it had been done by his own hand – his opposite hand dragging a dagger across his own flesh.

I smiled at the coward as if I were his greatest ally. 'It looks clean,' I told him. 'Missed the muscle?'

He gave a reluctant nod.

'Good. You can come with me back to the section. We need every man, and they'll be glad to see you.'

Statius hesitated, desperate to remain within the hospital's walls. 'The surgeons—' he began.

'—are here to patch us up so we can fight,' I finished for him. 'And they've done that. Get your equipment together. You're coming back to the section.'

'But—'

My patience ran out at that moment. It was one word too many from his sewer of a mouth, and as the image of Folcher's torn throat flashed into my mind, I drove my fist into Statius's startled face. My hands were on his neck a second later.

'You want to stay here, then I'll give you a reason.' His face was growing as purple as the Emperor's robes. 'You can stay here and die, or you can find your fucking balls and act like a soldier.'

When his eyes begged hard enough, I let go of his windpipe.

'I'm sorry,' he gasped. 'I was scared.'

I stood back from him. 'We were all scared,' I spat. 'You're out of chances, Statius. The next time you put your own life ahead of the others, I'm taking your fucking throat.'

The time for pity was over. The death of men under my care had seen to that, and now there was only one thing on my mind. One thought for the men that depended on me.

Survival.

# 44

Statius followed me from the hospital like a whipped dog. I felt his eyes on my back. Did he hate me? Undoubtedly, but I knew that hate was born not from my actions, but his own – no man wanted to discover himself a coward. In a world that placed virtue and courage above all else, what was there for the soldier who found that he was unable to control his fear? Pity was for the women and children. Sympathy for the wounded. For the coward, there was only contempt.

'Felix,' Centurion H called, catching sight of me as I passed the window of his quarters.

I waited by the doorway for my superior to appear.

'Cohort commander's stood us down for forty-eight hours,' H told me, eyeing Statius but making no comment. 'Time to lick our wounds and remember the boys. You still have a friend in the quartermaster's?'

I gave a shallow nod.

'Then get your section. I'm buying. Can't take the shit with us, can we?'

It took little to convince Brando to join us. I considered leaving Statius behind. The more malicious part of my mind wanted to put him to work cleaning latrines, or the equipment of men who had stood and fought. Instead, I decided that his shame would be a secret held between him and me. There was nothing to gain by dividing a section already depleted. Already in grief.

'How's your wound?' I asked H as we walked to the quartermaster's department.

'Not fatal.' He managed to smile. 'Which is the only thing that matters, when you get down to it.'

'There is that,' I granted.

'The other lads, though . . .' The centurion trailed off. 'Keep an eye on your blokes and the Syrians, Felix. I've done enough years to know that these things happen, but it's not like things have been great as it is. I keep thinking that all Arminius needs to do is sit back, and we'll pull ourselves apart easier than he could have ever done.'

I nodded. 'A siege does things to men.'

'Not like any of us were sane in the first place, is it?' H tried to grin. 'Got to be a lunatic to sign up for this, haven't you?'

I said nothing.

'I can still remember the recruiter,' H told me, enjoying the memory. 'He was a hard-looking bastard, and threw coins around like he was Marc Anthony. Course, I thought, that'll be me in a year or two! My dad beat the shit out of me when he found out, but it was too late by then, wasn't it? Marched away the next morning, and it's been sixteen years since I set foot south of the Alps. Haven't seen much of that coin, either.' He laughed.

We had reached the quartermaster's department. The guards recognized me and moved aside. We entered the long storeroom that doubled as the site of games and gambling, but all was quiet. Three men sat alone at a table.

'Titus. Boys,' I greeted my friends.

'Where the fuck have you been?' Stumps slurred, his eyes then settling on Statius. 'And what the fuck's he doin' 'ere?

Better grow your hair if you're lookin' to sell your fanny. Oh, 'ello, sir,' he added quickly, spotting his centurion.

'Relax, Stumps,' H smiled. 'I just want to get shit-faced. Can I buy in on that wine?'

'Your money's no good here,' Titus interjected. 'The blokes have spoken up about you, sir. You're my guest. Drink what you like.'

'You're a gentleman, for such a scary-looking bastard,' H conceded, and then laughed. 'I suppose the wine fits into our daily ration?'

'There're forty less mouths to feed, boss.' Stumps spoke without humour. 'I don't know about the Nineteenth, but in the Seventeenth Legion, that ration goes to the lads who made it, so we can give them a good send-off.'

H nodded, solemnly. 'We do the same, and we're all Nineteenth now, boys.' He raised his drink. 'Here's to the boys who can't raise a cup.'

We echoed the toast, and drank deep. Titus poured again, the wine splashing over the brims like bubbling wounds.

'Another one,' the big man ordered.

We drank, and then we drank some more. In what seemed like moments, my eyes began to swim, my words catching on my tongue.

'Tell me more about the desert,' H pressed Titus when Stumps had revealed something of his friend's past.

Titus shrugged. 'Sand and camels.'

'What about the women?' H encouraged him. 'How do they stack up compared to the Germans?'

The big man thought over his answer. 'They're slighter. Smaller tits. Dark eyes. Dark hair.'

'But who fucks better?' Stumps asked eagerly.

Titus considered for a further moment before answering. 'The Germans.'

'Thank the weather for that.' Brando laughed. 'It's so cold here in winter no one wants to keep their clothes off. Get it done wild and fast.'

We laughed at that, wine spilling over our lips and on to our tunics. Only one man sat unmoved.

Statius.

'What's wrong with you?' Brando asked the man. 'You've got a face like a donkey's bollocks. Drink some wine, man. Relax.'

'Why?' the Roman asked, simply.

Brando's thick brow creased. 'Why? Why the fuck not? Because we could be dead tomorrow, and so enjoy. Enjoy this time.'

There was a chorus of applause at that, cups rapping on tables. I looked at young Micon, and saw that even his dull-witted face was twisted upwards in amusement. He had seen the evidence and learned the lesson: live for the moment.

'But it's all bollocks, isn't it?' Statius said suddenly and sullenly. 'Die tomorrow? Yes. And if not tomorrow, then soon. And for what? We'll die in this fort, or outside of it, and for what?'

The question was met by silence, and dark looks. Micon was the first to move, slurping noisily at his cup. It was Titus who opened his mouth to speak.

'What would you like to die for?' he asked plainly.

Statius had no reply.

'There must be something?' Titus shrugged his massive shoulders. 'You want to die for fame? For money?'

Statius shook his head. 'I don't want to die at all,' he admitted, his eyes on his drink.

'Picked the wrong profession then, didn't you?' Stumps scoffed, before a look from Titus shut him up.

'No one cheats death,' H put in, his words slurred from wine and blood loss from his still-leaking wound.

'All right then,' Statius conceded. 'I don't want to die for this.' He gestured at his uniform. 'I don't want to die so someone can put a mark on a map. I don't want to die so a senator gets new lands. I don't want to die so a general can have poets suck his cock and say what a brilliant mind he had, losing only hundreds of men like us, and not thousands.'

'You joined the army,' Stumps sneered. He couldn't help himself. 'The army didn't join you.'

'Yes, I joined the fucking army,' Statius snapped back. 'I joined the army because I wanted food in my stomach. I joined because I didn't want to die a beggar in the streets.'

Stumps was like a dog with a bone. 'You have a roof over your head now, don't you?' he demanded. 'Food? Even if it is half-rations.'

'Yeah, and for what price? So that I can watch friends die? So that I can be skinned alive by the goat-fuckers? How many friends did you lose in the forest, Stumps? You're not screaming the barracks down and getting pissed every night because you love what you do.'

'You have no fucking idea,' Stumps warned darkly.

'Then enlighten me,' Statius pressed. Somehow his fear of death had given him the confidence to confront the absurdity of his position. 'Are you going to be one of these lying bastards who tells the stories of smiles and laughter as we march off to get fucking slaughtered? I may not have seen much, but I've seen enough to know that the only ones who talk that way are the ones who have never drawn a blade! Three legions gone in that forest, Stumps! Felix, you were there. Are you telling me that you went through it all thinking of glory for Rome? Do you wake up screaming thinking of eagles and triumphs?'

'Of course I fucking don't. And you know nothing about it, so hold your tongue now. We came here to remember friends,' I warned.

Statius shook his head. 'Bollocks.'

Titus saw me rise, but held out a hand – he wanted me to let the man speak.

'You came here to forget,' Statius insisted. 'To drink, and forget. You all know it's a fucking sham. Glory is just something they invented to suck us in. If it were true, then why would they need to enlist us for twenty years and more? Who'd want to leave if it was like they said it was?'

No one answered. I could see on the faces of my friends that they hated Statius for his words, but that hate was born from the realization that, in some aspects at least, he was right.

'Are you honestly telling me you're all right with all of this?' the man pressed on. 'Do you not see how fucking ridiculous it is?'

Titus then stepped in, placing his cup on the table, his words measured. 'Of course we do. But the world is a hard place. Open your head a bit, and you won't see the army as a prison. You'll see opportunity.'

'Easy for you to say, when you're running the black market,' Statius sneered.

Titus was unblinking as he delivered his calm threat. 'You've obviously got eyes and ears, and some brains between them. Learn how to keep them all where they should be.'

'And there's more to this than money and lands, Statius,' Brando put in diplomatically. 'There is something bigger than us all here. We are small parts of greatness. We are parts of Rome.'

'What do you know about Rome, Brando?' Statius asked, swirling the red liquid about his cup. 'I'll tell you about Rome. Swarms of mosquitos so thick you can walk on them. Streets running with piss and shit. Every month there's some new fucking disease that's filling holes in the dirt and taking your family. Rome's a curse,' he finished with a cautious eye towards his centurion.

H shrugged. 'There's no rank here,' he said, his tone suggesting that his mind was aligned at least in part with that of his bitter subordinate.

'You're wrong, Statius,' Brando countered, shaking his head. 'Rome is no curse. The Empire is a *cure*. My father. My grandfather. They lived in chaos before Batavia was taken into the Empire. The system is flawed, I'll give you that, but it *is* a system. It brings law and order. On the frontier, of course, life is hard, but our sacrifice as soldiers means better lives for others.' There was real passion in the Batavian's voice. 'That is why I would give my life for Rome. And that is why Folcher gave his.'

'Then you're a fucking idiot,' Statius mumbled, and I saw Brando's nostrils flare like an enraged bull's, his muscles bunching. Perhaps, if Statius had held his next thought within himself, then the bigger man would have let the insult pass.

But he could not, and the fateful sneer fell from his lips.

'Open your eyes, Brando,' he hissed. 'Folcher died for nothing.'

Not even Titus had the strength and speed to stop the Batavian. Brando crossed the table like a leopard, taking Statius down in a flurry of thrashing arms and legs. He was pulled away within seconds, but those short moments were enough – blood pooled on the floor.

'Fuck, Brando!' Stumps shouted. 'What have you done?'

I looked down at Statius. He lay frozen on the floor, blood on his lips, dark eyes fixed and rigid.

'Brando . . .' H whispered, his shocked gaze on the dagger that had been driven deep into the Roman's heart.

Statius was dead.

# 45

Titus was the first to recover his senses, and to assess the danger of the situation that had now presented itself on his doorstep.

I wondered what was running through the big man's mind. The death of Statius was a murder, nothing less, and Titus was surely weighing up the chances of avoiding attention being brought to his enterprises through a cover-up. Inevitably, that brought his eyes to Centurion H, the one man who had not been through it with us in the forest – Brando was one of us through companionship in enslavement. H was the weak link. A good man, but an outsider. An unknown quantity. A danger to our tribe.

I saw Titus's hand creep towards the dagger at his belt.

'How do you want this to play out?' he coolly asked the officer.

Moments ago, H had been drunk. Now, with the body of one of his soldiers at his feet, the man was as sober as rock. 'I join him if I try and report this, don't I?' he answered pragmatically, knowing what was on Titus's mind. 'Gods, Brando, did you have to kill him?'

The Batavian grimaced. There was no trace of remorse on his face, or in his words. 'You heard what he said about Folcher. Fuck him. If he was still breathing, I'd cut open his throat.'

'I'll just tell that to Malchus and the prefect, shall I?' H shook his head. 'You know what they'll do to you for this?'

Brando knew. 'I'm not afraid to die.'

'No one's dying,' Titus cut in.

'No one else, anyway.' Stumps tutted, looking at the leaking corpse. 'Fuck him, anyway. He was a piece of shit.'

'This is the legions, Stumps,' H said with a heat that was at odds with his usual passivity. 'Killing someone because they are a piece of shit is a little outside of fucking regulations!'

'So what do you want to do?' Stumps countered. 'Lose Brando, too? You want to see him lose his head?'

'Of course I don't.' H cursed, knowing that the penalty for the murder would be death, and nothing less. 'And even if I did want that, I'm not stupid enough to think I'd be leaving here alive.'

Silence prevailed over the scene. It told H that his dark prediction was accurate.

'There's no need for that,' Titus eventually said. 'So long as we use some common sense.'

'Common sense being that we forget we were ever here?' H guessed. 'That's great, Titus, but there's this little problem lying at our fucking feet.'

'Easy enough to make him disappear,' Stumps piped up.

'Do you have any idea how a legion runs?' H chided the veteran. 'It's ledgers and accounts, Stumps. He can't just "disappear".'

I had listened to the conversation up until now with near disinterest. Blood and death were the constant of my life, and the brutal truth was that I had not liked Statius, and my only regret for the end of his life was that it endangered a man that I cared about – a brave man, who did not deserve to lose his head for silencing the insults of a coward.

'Statius was a shit.' I spoke up, surprising the others. 'And he was a coward. Look at the wound on his arm, H.'

After a moment's hesitation, H began to unwrap the bandages on the body's arm. Statius's limbs were limp. It would be some time until his body hardened.

'Look at that cut,' I told my centurion. 'That's from a dagger. You can see how he would have drawn the blade across. He did it himself to get out of the fighting.'

'He said it was a Syrian arrow.' For the first time, H looked at the body with a trace of contempt.

'I knew he was a fucking coward.' Stumps spat, his spittle landing at the body's feet.

Titus met my eye, then. He knew that I'd brought up the self-inflicted wound for more reason than to heap shame on to a cooling corpse.

'You want to stick this on them?' he asked me.

I nodded. 'Everyone except us thinks he took a Syrian arrow. Won't be hard to believe he went looking for payback.'

'Not like he could keep his fucking mouth shut,' Brando grunted.

'I don't know.' H shook his head. 'Half the garrison's at the Syrians' throats as it is. A fuck-up during battle? Maybe that they can understand. But this?'

'What's the alternative?' Titus asked. 'Either way, the civvies and half the Romans here hate the Syrians. What's to be gained by you losing a good man?'

'I'm not afraid to die, Titus,' Brando stated again. 'I'm glad that I killed him. When I die, I'll laugh about it with Folcher. If saving my head means more fighting in the fort, then that isn't something I want. I did what I did, and I'll take my punishment.'

'No one's asking you, you dense German dickhead,' Stumps dismissed the Batavian. 'I'm not losing another mate.'

The harsh silence fell again. All eyes rested on Statius, and the dagger in his chest.

'What will it be, H?' Titus finally asked the officer.

H continued to look at the floor for a long time. 'You'd take your punishment?' he finally asked of Brando, raising his gaze.

The Batavian met his look with unblinking eyes – he would.

'And I believe you,' H conceded, with more than a little admiration for the killer. 'But if you lose your head, Brando, I've got a feeling that I'd be joining you in the afterlife soon after.' He cast his eyes over the assembled, grim faces. Brando's comrades. His family. Men who would kill for him. Even an officer they admired.

'You're a good man, H.' Stumps shrugged, trying to shake off the truth of our primitive instincts.

'I'm a realistic one,' the centurion snapped. 'Statius isn't coming back, and if he was a coward, then fuck him. But this is the legion, boys; we kill who we're told to, not who we want to.'

He was right, of course. Kill a thousand and you would be a hero, but cut the wrong throat and you would be condemned a murderer.

'I can't be with you lot after this.' H shook his head, touching his fresh bandages. 'I'm in no shape to fight anyway. I can't promise I can keep you together – you and what's left of the century will probably get split up to boost the others.'

'You're not a bad soldier for doing this, H,' I offered, seeing that he was coming to his conclusion, and one that sat badly with him.

A ghost of the man's former smile crept on to his weathered lips. 'Good or bad doesn't matter on the frontier, Felix. Are you alive, or dead? That's all that counts.'

Those words were true, and Statius was now amongst the fallen. With tight faces and nervous movements, we set about ensuring that his end would be attributed to others.

'Here.' Titus returned from a storeroom, a saw and an axe in his hands. 'Stumps, take Micon and watch the front.'

H grimaced, taking in the tools in the big man's hands. 'Time for me to go.'

Titus shook his head. 'You stay until it's over.' What did rank matter when murder was concerned?

'I can't be a part of this,' the centurion asserted. 'There has to be a line somewhere.'

Titus shrugged. 'Turn your back, but you don't leave my sight until this is over. Afterwards, you'll never have to see me again.'

H hesitated for a moment. Then he took a wineskin and walked away, sinking on to his heels when he was clear of the blood that had run from Statius's body. It was as well for his own safety that he stayed. I knew from experience that Titus was not opposed to killing officers, and Brando was one of his wards, now – the Batavian's kinship to myself and Stumps had seen to that.

The former auxiliary stepped forwards now, and held out his hand to Titus. 'Pass me the axe.' Then, blade in hand, he straddled the body of the man that he'd killed. 'You said Folcher died for nothing,' he snarled at the corpse. 'Well, what did you die for, you cunt?'

Titus looked at me. 'Are you ready to do this?'

'What choice do we have?' I asked him.

There was none, of course. To protect the life of one comrade, we would have to butcher the remains of another.

Titus knew that truth. His eyes were as grim as his words.

'Start cutting.'

# PART THREE

# 46

There are a lot of ways that a soldier can die, and death at the hands of a comrade is not an uncommon one. In fact, when the legions require the most malevolent form of discipline, army commanders can enact the punishment of decimation, where lots are drawn between men of a section and a single man is then condemned to be beaten to death at the hands of the men he called brothers. Funny, how an enlightened civilization keeps its soldiers in check.

Murder was a staple, too. Sometimes pre-meditated, but more often as a result of a drunken brawl or a bull-headed grievance. Fall the wrong way, hit your head in the wrong place, and a man's lights could go out, never to be relit.

Then there were the accidents. During times of peace – or at least, when not prosecuting campaigns – the army was the Empire's corps of engineers, and building bridges and aqueducts carried with it the inherent risk of injury. A dropped stone from above or a wobbly piece of scaffold could see a soldier dead or, worse, crippled. Reduced to be a beggar in the streets, living amongst the filth and surviving on scraps.

Of course, soldiers were not immune to the plagues and diseases that were a constant of every civilization. Even senators had to fear the unseen killers, and for the men of the legions, often travelling into new climes, death was more likely to come from a sweated fever than an enemy spear. The discipline of the legions ensured that its men did not live in filth and squalor, but even so, a tightly packed mass of men often seemed too tempting for the gods, or whatever force, to pass by. Entire legions could be reduced without a blade being drawn. Even the baths, a benchmark of Roman enlightenment, were an invitation to death for a man with an open wound.

Boredom could be fatal. Many soldiers were young men, and young men do stupid things. In Pannonia, I recalled watching a soldier who had been challenged by his friends to leap from one rooftop to another. He failed miserably, his life ending as a heap of fractured bone and skull.

Thinking was no good for a soldier's health, and was to be discouraged. Think too much about your place in the army, and the army's place in the world, and you might well become a deserter, and deserters died painful deaths. Think about what you had done in the name of glory and perhaps, as I had done, you would consider taking your own life. Then there were men like Statius. He had been stupid enough to give voice to his thoughts, and his dismissal of purpose in Folcher's death had been enough to bring about his own end.

I thought a lot about that murder during the weeks that followed. The way the saw had ground against Statius's bones. The way that his blood had soaked the sacks into which we'd shoved his dismembered body. The pant of the hungry dogs that had followed us through the darkest parts of the fort, and the way that they had pulled an arm free from the sacking before we had a chance to run breathlessly clear.

I thought a lot about the murder, and the butchery, but it wasn't with guilt or shame that I looked back on it – it was with anger. Anger at myself that I should have ever allowed the killing to take place. Anger at myself that I had not dealt with Statius's cowardice in my own way.

True, I had disliked Statius and his malingering, but he didn't deserve to die for that spinelessness. I did not want to be like the legions, sentencing to death men who had seen sensible reason to keep their blades sheathed. The punishment was unjust, but once Statius's heart had stopped beating, his body had become mere flesh, and nothing more. There was no way to turn back time. Brando, my friend and comrade, had then become my only concern. It was for him that I had played a willing part in the gruesome cover-up, and for him that I suffered the shame in the eyes of Centurion H, a man I admired.

After that night, I realized that my mind was becoming as hardened as the chain mail that hung over my shoulders. A war was being fought inside my head, and the darkness had taken the advantage. In a way, it seemed almost a blessing – my nightmares were becoming less frequent. The death of Statius was now an afterthought in my own life, and in that of the fort's – a murder attributed to the Syrian archers.

The fallout of that revelation had been predictable enough. Fortunately, as it was assumed that Statius had gone looking for revenge for his 'wound', Prefect Caedicius had not been proactive in his search for a scapegoat. If anything, he used the Roman's death as an example of why the men and civilians under his command should remain within the boundaries that he had drawn up. It came as no surprise to find that Statius had been short on friends, and no acts of vengeance were carried out in his name. I was almost coming to believe that the death was free of consequences, when a grim-faced Brando rushed into the alleyways of the civilian encampment.

He found me with Linza. I was scrubbing my mail, and smiling. Smiling until I saw the look on my comrade's face, and I knew that tragedy had come with him.

'What?' was all I asked. Beside me, I felt Linza stiffen.

'Balbus. The corruption has spread up his arm. The surgeon's amputating now.'

I dropped my mail and ran with him, Linza left behind in our hurried wake. As my sandals beat the cold dirt, my stomach churned – I knew what this was. This was our punishment. This was justice for our butchery of a comrade.

'This is because of me,' Brando breathed, thinking the same.

'The corruption was there before . . . that,' I tried to console the Batavian, and myself.

'No, Felix.' Brando was adamant. 'This is the gods. This is it. The beginning of their punishment. I should have died like a man, Felix. Now . . . now this . . .' His voice trailed off.

We reached the hospital. Balbus's screams rang out from within.

They were terrible.

'Wait in the barracks,' I told my comrade.

He shook his head. 'I wait here.'

We stood in silence. A breathless Stumps and Micon arrived soon after.

'Should we go in?' Stumps asked, wincing at the sound of the screams.

I shook my head. 'Let the surgeons work.'

'This is—' Stumps began quietly.

'I know,' I snapped. 'Enough.'

And so we waited, each one of us stumbling over doubts and accusations and thoughts of divine justice. I had never seen Brando shaken, but now there was a tremor in his hands and jaw.

It seemed like an eternity, but eventually the screams died away. I hoped that Balbus's life had not gone with them.

'You his mates?' a bloodied surgeon's assistant asked us as he emerged for air.

'His section,' Stumps answered. It was a good answer. We all sensed that Balbus was a good man, but we had not lived and breathed beside him long enough for him to become family.

'He's alive,' the man told us, with no trace of happiness at that fact. 'Bled a lot, though. Prepare yourselves for the worst.' He shrugged as he ducked back inside the building.

'Not a word,' I told the men, seeing Stumps and Brando on the verge of self-reproach and recrimination. 'Not a *word*,' I forced again. 'We wait.'

And so we did.

The night had long settled before a slave appeared from the hospital and summoned our huddled figures inside.

The copper tang of blood hit my nostrils as we were led into the candlelit building. We passed the open door of an operating room and saw a slave on his knees, scrubbing away what must have been the blood of our comrade.

'In here.' The first slave gestured, and we entered an open ward of beds. Only two were occupied. Standing next to Balbus was a man whose once red hair was losing the fight with white. He introduced himself as Balbus's surgeon. Though not unfriendly, the man's tone was clipped and dispassionate, a necessity of his profession.

'He won't make the morning.' The surgeon confirmed what I already knew. One look at Balbus had been enough to tell me that the soldier was on death's door. His skin was grey and waxen, like tent canvas. Despite the thick blankets about him, he looked cold to the touch.

'Lost too much blood in the operation,' the surgeon explained. 'Had to take the whole arm. There're not many who come through from that.'

It was Micon who spoke. 'Thank you for trying, sir. We know you did your best.'

The surgeon gave a curt nod. 'Stay as long as you like.'

I watched the man leave. Then I felt Brando's eyes on me.

'This isn't our fault,' I said to him as he placed his hand on Balbus's shoulder.

But the Batavian ignored my words. 'I'm sorry, Balbus. This is my fault. I'm sorry.'

'Is there nothing we can do?' Micon ventured.

'Sure. Donate him your arm,' Stumps lashed out, regretting the insult instantly. 'Sorry, Micon.'

The youngster shrugged. 'It's all right.'

'What do we do?' Stumps asked me then. 'He must have other mates here? He was Nineteenth Legion a long time. They'll want to see him off, won't they? He's a good bloke.'

He was right. 'Half the garrison's on the walls,' I answered, 'the other half's asleep. The centurions will have runners posted at their quarters, though. Try them. It's the least we can do for him.'

'All right,' Stumps agreed, turning to Micon. 'You come with me.'

'You too, Brando,' I told the crouched figure.

'I want to stay with him,' the man protested. 'This is my fault.'

'Go and get his friends,' I said. There was no room for argument in my tone, and not long after my friends had departed did the reason for that forcefulness walk into the ward.

'Sir,' I greeted Centurion H.

'Felix.' Framed by candlelight, I saw nothing but sorrow and dread in his features. Hard to believe this was the man who had worn his humour so openly.

'I sent the others away,' I explained. 'I thought you'd come here.'

'Balbus was – is – still one of mine,' H agreed, coming to stand beside the bed and looking down at the unconscious soldier. 'Was one of mine when he was hurt, anyway. Can you believe a splinter did this to him?' There was as much wonder as grief in his voice. 'A fucking splinter, and a good man's life is over.'

'There's no reason in death, sir,' I offered, having spent years searching for it. If I was honest with myself, I was still looking.

'Maybe it's a blessing.' H seemed to be trying to

convince himself. 'I just came from a briefing with the prefect. Rations are to be cut again from tomorrow. I'd actually forgotten I had ribs.' The man attempted to smile.

I liked this officer. Shame burned me for what I had done in his sight, and the desire for his approval pushed me to speak. 'Better hungry stomachs than the Germans, sir,' I said, and that was true – cavalry scouts aside, there had been no sighting of a body of enemy troops for weeks. Neither had there been any sight, or even word, of our own.

'They won't leave the Rhine.' H's words mirrored my thoughts. 'They'd be mad to. Three legions gone, Felix. We're on the defensive now. There's no need for forts on this side of the Rhine. We're the dregs of Varus's barrel, and we're not worth scraping out.'

I tried to find some ray of hope. 'A lot can happen in a few months.'

The centurion shook his head. 'We don't have a few months. Could we split the rations down further, and make it through winter like skin and bone? Maybe. But the fort will pull itself apart before that, Felix. There isn't a united group here. Everyone's in it for themselves.'

I shrank a little with shame at the man's words.

H saw my disgrace. 'I don't blame anyone for it,' he told me, and I could hear his honesty. 'Arminius did more than win a battle, didn't he? He *wiped out three legions*, Felix, and when he did that, he pulled away the blindfold. We know that we're not invincible any more. There're fewer than a thousand of us here, and Varus had more than fifteen! Why should anyone believe we can come through this?'

Did he hope that perhaps I, a survivor of that massacre, would have an answer for him? 'There's always hope,' I said, but my voice was weak.

H looked down at the dying form of Balbus. Resignation was etched into the centurion's face, this man who had been so full of life and purpose. Like Balbus, he had given up his own fight. When he spoke, his words were soft, but as lifeless as rock.

'Hope died in the forest.'

Soon after, Balbus followed in its wake.

# 47

Balbus wasn't the only person to die in the fort that night. The other was an aged civilian who had lived outside of the camp since its construction, but sought refuge inside when the rumour of war had spread. Linza told me this as we walked away from the graves. We were outside the walls; our enemy was distant enough to spare us the necessity of having to bury the dead alongside the living.

Linza shrugged. 'The old die first, in times like this.' There was experience in her voice, and I did not wonder at that. Lean times and famine were commonplace in the world. Blighted crops could starve a family as well as any besieging army.

'It just doesn't seem real this, does it?' she asked me as we stopped ahead of the open gate, savouring the promise of freedom of movement, and choice.

It was an illusion.

'The cavalry beyond that wood-line are real enough,' I told her. 'There're not many of them, but enough to stop what you're thinking.'

She shook her head, pushing a strand of dirty blond hair from her face. 'I'm not trying to leave this place, Felix. Not like that. Better hungry than dead.'

We walked beneath the gateway. Some three dozen had attended the funeral of soldier and civilian, and now the thick wooden gates were closed behind us. There was a fatalistic finality as the heavy locking bar was dropped into place.

'Funny, isn't it?' Linza smiled wryly. 'That we only get to leave the walls for death? Either raids, or burials.'

'I hadn't thought about it.'

She laughed a little at that. 'It's all you think about,' she teased me lightly.

But the woman was wrong. Perhaps my mind had orchestrated its own successful defence of a siege – a siege of horrors and hopelessness – because for the first time in months I was sleeping without nightmare. I was waking without screams.

I knew that the woman beside me was a part of that. Perhaps the entire part. She was a window to my past, but she reminded me of the good memories, not the bad. I had laid my early story bare to her, and with the revelations a weight had been lifted from my shoulders. I could breathe more easily. I could think more clearly. I did not dare to allow myself to hope, but I fought to honour her request to not only survive, but to live.

'Thank you.' I smiled at my friend, taking her by surprise.

'For what?'

I waved that away. She would understand in time, if she did not already.

'Shit,' Linza suddenly grumbled. 'It's starting to rain.'

I had learned quickly that German rains could move from a dribble to a downpour in an instant, and so it was with haste that we moved to my barrack block. Centurion H had been wrong when he guessed that we would be reassigned to another century, and our reduced numbers were now overseen by the newly minted Centurion Albus. Having survived the botched raid by the skin of his teeth, Albus's sole concern was now to live through the siege and retire with a centurion's wage and pay-out at the end of his service. As such, he made for a lenient commander.

'Hello, boys.' Linza smiled at Stumps and Micon before speaking to Brando in their native language. Brando was sullen, as he had been ever since Balbus's death. The Batavian had never struck me as more religious than the next soldier, but now the tall warrior spent much of his time in prayer at the fort's shrines.

'I'm going to the shrine of Donar,' he told me. 'I'll let the company runner know where I am.'

'We have the watch tonight,' I said. 'Be back well before last light.'

Brando said nothing, but stepped out into the rain.

'I've spent more time on watch than anything else in my life,' Stumps grumbled from his bed. 'What is it tonight? Walls or patrols?'

'Patrols,' I told him. A consequence of our diminished size was that our century was easily rolled into patrolling the fort's roads and alleyways, rather than being stretched thinly on the walls.

'Hope it stops raining by then,' he moaned.

It did not, and we passed the next few hours in banal conversation. Linza was a good listener, and Stumps was an Olympian talker. Between pulls from a wineskin he told us of his colourful childhood and family.

'First time I met my dad was when I punched him in the face,' he asserted as Linza giggled. 'I'm telling you! He was dancing on a table with his balls between his legs – balls that I come from, not that I knew it then – and he kicked a cup of wine all over my woman. Couldn't have that, could I? So I pulled the fucker's legs out, and then I punched him in the face.'

'How did you find out he was your dad?' Micon asked, an eyebrow threatening to move on his statue-like face.

'Only a young lad, wasn't I?' Stumps explained. 'Innkeeper held me back until my mum came down. Then my dad got a second punch in the chops.' He laughed.

It had been a good afternoon. I could see that Linza's presence was sucking the poison from Stumps's soul as it was my own. I suddenly realized that the man never woke with night terrors on the days that she had sat laughing at his rambling stories.

'Will you come and see us tomorrow?' I asked her, acknowledging to myself that I wanted her to be drawn here for me, rather than any other. There was a little guilt at the thought, but . . . we were friends, and I was well aware that my mind was, if not mending, then bandaged tightly by this woman.

'Stay out of trouble.' She smiled as she took her leave.

Stumps gave her a moment to clear out of earshot before his eyes locked on to me, a conspiratorial smile creasing his face. 'Please tell me you're shagging her,' he begged.

I shook my head. 'You ask me this every day.'

'Yeah. I live in eternal hope that you remember what your cock's for,' my friend leered. 'Seriously, Felix, she's a good-looking girl and she's fucking lovely. Why are you dick-dancing around her? Just shag her already.'

I said nothing.

'You don't think she's tasty? Because if that's it, and you don't mind me—'

I cut him off. 'Of course I think that, but she reminds me of someone,' I admitted. The tone of my voice told Stumps that it was a painful reminder.

'Ah.' He sighed. 'Well, all right then, mate. I'm just saying, as your brother, that you should maybe think about securing it before someone else does. Don't know if you've noticed, but it's not a great ratio in this fort. Even with these looks I'm struggling to get any.'

I looked at my friend, and a laugh choked out from my throat. Stumps was grinning like a lunatic, the maniacal smile only made ridiculous by the botched sewing that had reattached his right ear.

'I didn't do a great job of that, did I?'

'Nah, you didn't, you cunt. Looks like I've got a pig's tail on the side of my head, but I know you did your best.'

We said nothing, then. What else was there to say? I had been through everything with this man. Only months before he had been a stranger. Worse than that, a stranger who hated me as much as I distrusted him. Now he was as close to me as a brother. I would die for him, he knew that, and I knew that he would do the same for me. Perhaps that's why he finally found the nerve to voice a confession.

'I haven't killed anyone since the forest,' he admitted, still trying to smile. 'On the raids, it just . . . I don't know if it just didn't happen, or I didn't want it to happen?'

'What does it matter?' I asked my friend honestly.

'It matters if I can't kill someone, and one of my mates dies.'

I hoped that dark humour would be the cure for his

worries. It was a remedy used by all soldiers. 'You don't have many mates left, Stumps, so the odds of it happening are pretty slim. You'll be all right.'

'Yeah,' he finally breathed, appreciating my effort. 'I just . . . Nah, forget it. It's all right.' He tried to smile, and I knew from experience the tide of reproach that would be washing over him now. The guilt and the shame that he had exposed a weakness. The self-loathing that he possessed such a flaw to begin with.

Stumps climbed from his bunk, and moved towards his arms and armour. He was right to, as dusk was approaching, and with it our watch, but I held my friend by his elbow and swallowed back the stumbling clumsiness of my words.

'You're a good bloke, Stumps. I don't want anyone else with me if things go bad.'

To speak those words – and to hear them – was as terrifying an ordeal for us as to face an enemy shield wall. We swallowed the sentiment down with curt nods and broken eye contact.

'Let's get on parade,' I added hurriedly.

'Yeah,' my friend agreed. 'Twelve hours of sticking my thumb up my arse and wishing I was on an Italian beach.'

The image made me laugh, and the tension of our heartfelt words was broken. 'You're an idiot,' I smiled, avoiding a thumb that was shoved towards my face.

But it was I who was the fool. I who should have learned to be suspicious of such moments of happiness.

Later that night, we found her body.

# 48

It was Micon who was the first to realize something was amiss in the night. The young soldier's eyes were far sharper than his mind, and through the downpour of chilled rain he had seen the movement of a dog as it emerged from an alleyway. Micon had called to it playfully; dogs were a rare sight since rationing had come into force. He was eager for its companionship, and such was his gentle nature that the creature allowed his approach.

'There's a hand in its mouth,' the boy soldier then told us, as if it were the most natural thing in the world.

Stumps carried the section's torch; the flames spat in the rain as he used it to light the alleyway. We saw a set of legs poking out of the shadows.

'Gods.' Brando grimaced. 'She can't be more than ten.'

'Get the guard commander,' I ordered Stumps, anxious to have him clear of the sight. He passed the torch to Brando and made off at a sprint, sandals slapping in the rain.

'You think they're still around here?' Brando asked me cautiously, hand on the pommel of his sword, eyes on the long shadows.

I shook my head. 'They're spreading fear. They don't want an even fight.'

'Who does this, Felix?' the Batavian pressed me. 'What's wrong with these fucking Syrians?'

So he bought into the angry bile of those who blamed the archers for each of the gruesome deaths.

'I don't know,' I answered honestly, though I had my suspicions, which were that the killer had been born in the West, not the East. What better way to weaken the garrison's resolve than by sowing fear and discontent amongst those that dwelled within the fort, and relied on each other for survival?

'I think Arminius has men inside here,' I finally concluded.

'Warriors?'

'No. No one could hide this long. It's someone in the garrison. They either sympathize with him, or they're getting paid.'

Arminius had shown in the forest that he was a master of tactics, and so surely he would have known that the forts would have to fall after the legions? To that end, there was ample time for him to insert saboteurs, spies and assassins.

And yet . . .

Something troubled me. The theory was solid, but Arminius hadn't come to Aliso expecting a fight. He hadn't expected a siege. Surprise had been Arminius's ally as he took down the forts along the River Lippe. Was he so thorough that he had considered all eventualities, including a garrison being prepared for his arrival? His lack of siege ladders and ability to storm the fort's walls would suggest not.

'Guard's coming,' Brando put in, the rushed tramp of hobnails announcing the arrival of the fort's quick-reaction force, a half-century of men.

'Another girl?' their centurion asked me. 'Report.'

I did. All the time the man's eyes were on the girl and her wounds. I wondered if he had his own children, and was picturing them cold and dead in the wet dirt.

'You and your men wait here,' I was then ordered. 'Send for Centurion Malchus,' he told a runner.

'Don't we need more men, sir?' a veteran asked of his officer. 'Last time the civvies caused a right fucking riot.'

The centurion shook his head. 'The fuckers are sleeping, and even if they're not, they won't be coming out in this.' He gestured to the heavy weather. 'Best thing to stop a riot's some rain.'

It wasn't long until the imposing silhouette of Centurion Malchus appeared in the darkness. 'Another?' His voice carved out the question.

'Younger,' the centurion answered. 'Looks like this one's been raped, sir.'

'Hmm.'

Malchus noticed me then by the torchlight, but made no acknowledgment – his face was tight with anger. He was a tethered lion, held from its prey. The fact that a murderer was loose on his watch could only further fuel his rage.

'Get her out of here,' he instructed the centurion. 'Find somewhere to keep her dry, and tell your men they'll pull a triple duty if one word of this gets out before the prefect says something himself, understood?'

'Yes, sir.'

Malchus spat into the dirt, water falling from the crest of his helmet as he turned on his heel. 'I just want a war,' he growled. And then the beast slipped away into darkness.

# 49

The young girl's death began a pattern as dark as the night her body had been found.

First there was the revulsion, fear and panic that such a crime could take place within the walls that were supposedly our bastion against such violence. Then came recrimination, and the primal urge to find and punish the source of such terror. Civilian blamed Syrian archer. Syrian archer blamed Roman legionary. Roman legionary blamed the civilians themselves. As the girl had been butchered, so too was the fort's garrison carved into tribes full of suspicion and hatred.

'If Arminius comes again, we'll all be fucked.' Stumps spoke up gloomily from the edge of his bunk.

Linza was with us, sitting at the end of my own bed and feeding sticks of wood into a small fire that was seeing off the worst of the autumn chill. Hard cold had followed the rains that had masked the young girl's death, but flame and the warmth of bodies did enough to take the nip from the barrack-room air.

'They wouldn't come again though, would they,' Linza stated rather than asked, the light of the flames rippling over her stoic face.

Every person in the garrison could see the truth of that now. Winter would do what Arminius could not. Through stockpile and the stripping of surplus buildings, there was enough firewood in the camp to survive two winters. But food was at a premium; even fishing in the river was doing little to bolster rations now that winter was placing its icy hand on the German lands.

'You know what I miss?' Stumps grumbled in an attempt to lighten the mood. 'A big, fat, wobbling arse. Even Brando's looks like a plank of wood now.'

The Batavian, whose face and long limbs had become considerably leaner, was in no mood for humour. The death of his best friend Folcher, and the guilt that he felt for the fate of Balbus, had silenced him in all but prayers and the acknowledgment of orders. And yet I had hope for the man.

I looked at Stumps. After the forest, he had been a shell of the man I had known in the summer camp of Minden. Having escaped slavery, Stumps had then wanted to do nothing but drink, and escape his memories. Linza was beginning to change that, I could see. We were far from being happy with our lot in life, but we were finding a reason to live with the memories, rather than to try and drink or fight our way into forgetting them. She was a reminder that there was more to our existence than as parts of death's machinery.

Of course, I was aware enough to know that there was another reason I wanted the blond-haired woman around.

'You got any sisters with fat arses?' Stumps smiled at Linza, the question a happy and oft-repeated staple of their conversations.

'You're too short for them,' the Batavian girl answered as always. 'They like tall men. Real men,' she teased, and I caught Stumps's knowing look – I wasn't much taller than my friend, and Linza was not far from my equal.

I let the two continue their usual dialogue of finding a suitably fat-arsed wife for Stumps. Though it was days since discovering the dead girl in the rain, my mind continued to slip back to that alleyway and my thoughts as to the identity of her killer. The more I mulled over the murders, the more I became certain that it was a servant of Arminius who had carried out the crimes – terror was splitting a garrison as well as any breach in the fort's walls could have done.

I thought again of approaching the garrison's command with my suspicion, but quickly dismissed the idea. To begin with, a soldier does not simply walk to the headquarters building and ask for an audience with its commander – I would have to go through my chain of command, and that meant Albus, my new centurion. Albus, a veteran long in the tooth, would look on any such venture as more work for himself and his century. The old soldier's maxim of 'never volunteer' held just as well for information as it did suicidal missions.

I chided myself for my thoughts then, and wondered at my hubris. Prefect Caedicius had not reached his station through incompetence, and Malchus lived and breathed war in all its forms. Both officers would have come to the same conclusion as myself. Appearing at their door and rubbing it into their faces – because what else was it, when they had found no solution? – would do nothing to stop the terror and the internal hostility of the garrison, and do a lot to see me on latrine duty until the end of my days.

'Welcome back,' Stumps smirked, seeing me emerge from my considerations. 'He does that a lot,' he said to Linza, who was sharing the same grin. 'Have you noticed?'

She poked me. 'Maybe we are not good enough company?'

I laughed it off. My laugh was cracked and quiet, but it was a laugh. I was proud of that. 'A lot on my mind.'

'Ah, the dizzying heights of section commander!' Stumps cackled. 'That why you're always so quiet, Micon? Lot on your mind?'

'What?'

'Exactly.'

'I should go now,' Linza announced. 'It's almost time to draw the rations.'

'I'll come with you,' Stumps offered.

'You have forgotten the menu? I can carry it in one hand.'

'Yeah, but I haven't seen Titus in a while. He's a scary-looking bastard, but he can't sleep unless he knows I'm around to look after him.'

Linza frowned. 'You saw him yesterday.'

'Well, anyway, I'll come with you. Too nice a day to stay indoors.'

Linza looked at me, the corner of her lip twitching as she wondered whether she should smile openly, or pretend casually that she did not mind leaving me. I knew what was on her mind, because I was thinking the same. We settled on half-smiles that must have looked moronic to our friend.

Stumps then turned to me as the pair left the room, and I met his eyes with a look of thanks – he wasn't going to see Titus, but was acting as escort for our friend. Should something happen to Linza, we both sensed that what was left of our sanity would flee. Linza was more than a companion to us, she was our anchor, and with that peaceful surety as comforting as any blanket, I lay back on to my bunk, and happily closed my eyes.

I knew that the nightmares would not come for me.

## 50

The nightmares did not come for me, but Centurion Albus did.

'Oi. Felix. Oi! Wake up, you bastard! Oi!'

'What is it?' I asked, sitting up quickly.

Our century was not on duty that night, but the veteran's worried tone was beginning to unnerve me. Yet there was no sound of an alarm. No clash of battle.

'Just come with me.' The man gestured, hurriedly.

'I'll get my kit—'

'No time for that, just follow me, for fuck's sake! Come on!' he urged as I tied my sandals, grabbed my sword belts and pulled a cloak about my shoulders.

The cold air slapped me in the face as we stepped into the darkness. The air was dry, and I felt its chill pull at my skin.

'What's going on, Albus?' I asked, seeing that we were the only men to emerge from the barrack block.

'Your friend's gone and stepped in it,' was all that he told me as he took a blazing torch from its mounting on the wall. 'He's really fucking stepped in it.'

'Who?'

'Stumps, you arse,' he hissed. 'Now hurry up. Follow me!'

Albus broke into a run, and I kept pace alongside him. As we sped through the deserted streets of the fort, a hundred questions bounced inside my mind as to what Stumps could have stepped into. The answer was clearly

315

trouble, but what kind? I prepared myself for the worst, expecting that my friend had got drunk and spilled blood in a brawl.

I could not have been more wrong, nor could anything have prepared me for what I saw as we took the corner into the alleyway behind the fort's empty stables.

Stumps had not spilled blood, but, javelin in hand, he was prepared to – the point of his weapon was aimed at the throat of a soldier.

Centurion Malchus.

Such was my confusion with the scene before my eyes that it took me a moment to register Linza's presence in the shadows. She was panting, Stumps's short sword in her hand. The blade was bloodied, and I followed her eyes to two snarling veterans who stood at Malchus's back. Their own blades were sheathed, but one soldier was clutching a wound on his arm.

What the fuck was happening?

'Felix,' Stumps breathed, seeing me in the periphery of his vision. 'He's the fucking killer. He tried to grab Linza!' he shouted.

The words, like the sight before my eyes, made no sense.

'What are you doing?' I grilled my friend, certain that he was suffering a hallucination caused by his embattled mind. 'That's your cohort commander, Stumps! He's no German! Put your weapon down!'

'I know he's not a German!' my friend cried back, his voice breaking with stress.

'Put your weapon down,' Malchus growled.

'No, sir!' Stumps shouted back, unwavering. 'Not until the guard arrives!'

I looked at Linza. She said nothing. She didn't need to – I could see her fear. She was under no illusion. She knew whose throat my friend was holding a blade to.

But why?

'Stumps, don't do anything stupid,' I urged.

'No one do anything stupid,' Albus put in, seeing that one of Malchus's veterans was slowly reaching for his blade. At Albus's words, the soldier moved his hand clear of his weapon.

And so we stood, my friend's javelin at my commander's neck, a scene as terrifying as it was bizarre – I knew that any moment could bring death, and that even when the weapons were lowered, the promise of bloodshed would not be silent.

My muscles quivered as we awaited the arrival of the guard force. I almost dropped in relief when I saw Centurion H at their helm.

'What the fuck . . .' he said, as uncomprehending as I had been.

'H. Get this idiot's javelin from my throat, or ram your blade into his thick skull. Either's all right by me.' Malchus spoke evenly, his savage eyes burning into Stumps's own.

'What are you playing at, Stumps?' said H. 'Lower your weapon. Do it now.'

'He's the killer, sir,' Stumps insisted, unmoving. 'We set a trap for him.' My throat turned dry at the revelation. 'We used her as bait, and he took it, sir. He tried to kill her. On the honour of the Seventeenth, and all the dead of my legion, he tried to kill her!'

'You're out of your fucking mind,' Malchus snarled.

But one look at Linza told me that he was not. She had seen the fear on my face when Stumps had revealed how they'd trapped the man in front of them, and my fear had revealed her guilt. Guilt that she had kept me in the dark. Guilt that she would risk herself when she knew that I – selfishly – needed her.

I looked at Malchus, a man I admired. The embodiment of a soldier. I saw his eyes, then, and they were like a shark's, empty of all emotion, filled only with the need to kill.

I knew then that it was all true.

Perhaps H saw the same. Perhaps that was why he drove his fist into Stumps's skull, and not his blade. The second that my friend began to crumple, Malchus was drawing his own sword.

So were the two men on his shoulder.

So was I.

'I can't let you kill him, sir,' H protested, straddling the man he had downed, his empty hands held up for calm.

My eyes met those of the two veterans on Malchus's shoulder. My look delivered the same message as H's, but there was nothing peaceful in my own stance – I'd gut them if they closed on my comrade.

Slowly, Malchus raised his hate-filled gaze to fall on to my face. I knew that he was sizing me up; he had enough respect for my fighting skills to take a moment to consider how best to kill me. I readied myself for that attack, but instead, the centurion let heavy words drop from his mouth.

'Walk with me,' he ordered, lowering his blade.

After a moment's hesitation and a glance towards Linza, I followed.

## 51

Keeping myself clear of the reach of his sword, I walked with Malchus into the darkness of the stables. The building reeked of stale straw and dung, but the animals were long gone, their meat salted for winter. It was not a good place to die, and I was glad to see that the silhouette of Centurion H had followed us into the shadows.

I had expected that Malchus wanted me dead. Once I was silenced, it would be a simple matter of sentencing Stumps to death for attacking a superior officer. Linza could be killed at will. The incident would be forgotten, or at least hidden in the minds of those other men who wished to stay free of cold graves. H's presence in the stables, however, now made me wonder whether, instead of bloodshed, it would be explanation that freed Malchus from his entanglement.

The one outcome I did not expect was that the centurion would casually admit to his crimes.

'I was going to kill her,' he said carelessly. 'What does it matter?'

Such was his candour that it took moments for either myself or H to recover our senses.

'Sir, it matters . . .' H finally managed.

'Why?' Malchus asked without heat. 'Have any of them been citizens? They're all goat-fuckers, H. They just happened to end up on this side of the wall. We probably killed their sisters and cousins when we raided the camps. Did anyone care then?'

I had no words.

'A soldier is a weapon,' Malchus explained slowly, as if we were boneheaded children. 'A blade. He has to be kept sharp. And how does a soldier do that? How does he keep sharp?' he asked. 'He. Has. To. Kill.'

'Not our own people,' H protested.

'Have you not been listening, H?' Malchus chided him. 'They're goat-fuckers. I wouldn't touch a citizen.' The cohort commander sounded as if the idea appalled him. 'But if a few dead hairies keep the garrison on its toes and vigilant, then what's the fucking problem?

'We're under siege, but there're no warriors at our walls. You think the Syrians and the civvies will observe the rationing if they forget we're cut off out here? You think our own boys do? I've had three punished for stealing rations just today!'

I had lived and breathed war for years, and in that time I had developed the mind of a warrior. The mind of a killer. I had had to, to survive, and that voice inside my head now stepped forth to speak.

*He's right,* it told me. *He's doing what needs to be done.*

There was part of me that believed that, as much as it disgusted me to admit it. Perhaps, if it wasn't for the thought of Linza lying dead and butchered, the cold-hearted part of me could have accepted the words. After all, tens of thousands were already dead in this war. How many would follow? Was the death of half a dozen girls worth it to keep a garrison alert, and fighting? We were

Roman, after all, and wasn't the offering of sacrifice a corner-stone of the culture and the Empire's religion?

I was saved from having to voice such dark words by the intervention of a better man.

'Malchus, this has to stop.' H spoke, deliberately dropping his superior's rank. 'It's un-Roman.' That was the term coined for anything the Empire deemed unseemly, and beneath them.

'There's nothing more Roman than killing barbarians,' Malchus grunted. 'And I'll do as I want.'

'Citizens or not, you've still broken the law.'

'And who applies that law here? You think Caedicius will lose me to avenge a few girls? Grow up, you soft bastard.'

'He'll have to if enough people ask for your head,' H insisted, unwilling to back down. 'You've helped put this garrison on a knife-edge, Malchus. The people have torn down tyrants that ruled empires. They can tear down the second in command of a forgotten fort.'

Something in those words struck Malchus. It was a long time before he spoke.

'The man who put his javelin up,' he eventually rumbled, sour at the memory and the fact that H was correct in his prophecy. 'He has to go. The girl too. That'll be an end to it.'

'There's no need for that,' H asserted. 'He's just battle-mad from the forest, and you love your soldiers enough to forgive them. There's no one who wouldn't believe that, Malchus. And the girl doesn't matter. No one will believe her without a soldier's voice to back her up.'

Malchus considered the idea; then he looked at me. 'Can you shut your friend up?'

'I can.'

There was another drawn-out silence. I could hear Malchus's jaw grind in irritation.

'One word, and he dies,' he eventually pronounced. 'That goes for you pair, too. You've always been a soft bastard, H, but don't let that get the better of you.'

'I won't, sir,' H answered.

'And you'll take care of your friend?' Malchus pressed me again.

'I will, sir,' I promised the murderer.

And when I returned to the barrack room, I did not disappoint him.

## 52

Stumps's head crashed into the wood of the bunk. I gave him no time to breathe, driving my knee into the side of his skull and stamping down on to his heaving chest.

'Stop it!' Linza screamed at me, trying to pull me back.

I cast her aside like an afterthought, grabbing Stumps by the scruff of his tunic and hauling him to his feet. Blood and snot ran from his crushed nose. His eyes were unfocused. He was already broken from the beating I had given him, but my sense was lost to anger, and so I drove his skull once more into the wooden frame of his bunk.

'You could have got her killed!' I screamed at the same time as I pushed away the woman I was so desperate to protect. 'You cunt, Stumps! You cunt! You could have got her killed!'

'Felix!' Linza screamed. *'Felix!'*

I took hold of her shoulders and pushed her down on to a bed. She came back at me like a fury, swinging a punch that rocked my jaw.

'What were you doing?' I screamed into her face, discounting the blow and sending another kick into Stumps's ribs. 'What did you think you were you doing?'

'Felix!' a voice bellowed from behind me.

I ignored it.

'Felix!' Brando yelled again, grabbing at my shoulders.

Planning my sentence for Stumps, I had calmly sent

the Batavian and Micon on a fool's errand. They had returned to find me transformed, our bloodied comrade at my feet, Linza as consumed with rage as I was myself.

'Stop it!' Brando tried. 'That's your brother!'

But I would not stop. I kicked, I punched and I roared oaths. Eventually, Micon returned with some men of the century and the scrum of bodies held my thrashing form to the floor and beat me into compliance. By the time that I began to pass out, one of the people I cared for most in the world lay bloodied and beaten by my hand. The other looked at me with hatred.

The calm that I had begun to know was over.

I was returned to myself.

# 53

The salt water washed lazily over my toes; it was warm. Sun bounced from my bare shoulders. I looked out at the sea, seeing its power radiating from the waves.

'I love you,' she told me, feeling that same energy and purpose.

'Is he all right?' she then asked, her fingers touching my arm as she looked back behind us to where a young man waited beyond the sand's reach.

'Marcus is a big boy.' I smiled. 'He can stand to be alone for a little while. He loves the sound of his own voice more than anyone else's, anyway.'

'That's not what I meant.' She pushed me, and I saw the quiver of unease pull at her lips, attempting to take away the smile that was my reason for breathing.

'He's fine about us,' I told her honestly. 'He's my oldest friend,' I added after a moment to give her confidence – I needed that smile. I did not want a single slip.

'I love you,' she said again, and in those words were captured our strongest desires.

'I love you too.'

I kissed her. Another wave ran over my feet; it was hot. I looked down.

Blood.

Panic overcame me in an instant. I looked at her face

for comfort, but found only terror – her skin was grey, eyes sunken. Flies danced on what had been her smile.

I backed away.

'Marcus!' I screamed, helpless. 'Marcus!'

I looked up the beach, to where my friend had stood.

'Marcus?' I pleaded when there was no sight of him.

'Look at what you've done,' he hissed, appearing suddenly by my side, the carnage of his jaw flapping beside his lolling tongue. 'Look at what you've done,' he challenged me again, and I followed his pointed finger to the ocean, seeing blood-red waves crashing, hundreds of bodies churning in the red foam. I saw faces amongst the ruin: Varo, Priscus, Octavius, Chickenhead, Rufus, Cnaeus, Folcher, Statius.

The tide of death was endless.

'Do you see what you've done?' Marcus asked me.

I turned my tear-filled gaze back towards the man who had been my greatest friend.

He was not alone, now. Stumps stood beside him.

'How many dead is your life worth?' he asked, nose twisted and bloodied from the beating I had delivered.

'Let it go,' Stumps urged, 'before you take more of us with you.'

His words were calm. Without hesitation, I followed his outstretched arm – and his forgiveness. I began to wade into the bloodied waters that churned about me, amid the bodies of my comrades carried by the tide to bump against my legs like ghost ships in a dead harbour. Soon, chest deep, I was surrounded by the carnage of my own creation.

'Let go, Felix,' Stumps told me from the shore.

'Let go, Corvus,' Marcus rasped.

I put my head beneath the waters.

# 54

My eyes blurred open. I saw Linza. Her face was as tight as hide on a shield, lips drawn and eyes narrow. In her hand was a wet cloth, and she used it to wipe at the cuts on my face.

'I should choke you with it,' she said, and though I could see that she wanted to be angry, there was something that held her back from reproaching me.

It was pity, I realized.

'You scream a lot,' she told me quietly, sensing that I recognized her true feelings. 'Last night I wanted you to die. Now I think I love you.'

There was no warmth in the words. She knew as well as I did that love was a curse.

'I know why you did what you did. It wasn't you. It was war.' Linza looked at her hands as she wrung out the wet cloth. 'Your eyes, even, were not the same.'

'I'm sorry,' I croaked, exhausted from the night, my nightmare and her revelation. 'It would be better if I wasn't here,' I murmured. 'I should have died in the forest.'

The wet cloth came back to my face with force. Her words stung as much as the cuts to my face. 'Don't talk like that,' she snapped. 'It's pathetic.'

'I'm sorry.'

'You feel sorry too much,' she snapped, on the offensive now, her cheeks flushing. 'You are so *lucky*, Felix.

Fuck, you are making me so angry! This pity for yourself. What is wrong with you? Be a man!'

'You have no idea—' I began quietly.

She cut me off, blue eyes wild as her anger began to bubble over. 'I have no idea? My husband is dead, Felix! I will never see him again! My friends? Gone. My family in Batavia has war coming to them. My brothers will fight, and maybe die. My cousins. Don't tell me I have no idea! You think because you hold a sword you are the only one who can speak about war? Fuck you! You see one side of it. One part. War is not all about *you.*'

'I didn't mean—'

'Shut up. Shut *up.* You make so angry!' She threw the cloth at me then. It slapped pathetically against my face as she crashed from the room.

'*Fuck!*' I screamed after a moment, sinking down. 'Fuck . . .' I groaned through hands clapped tight on to my face.

Depression washed over me like the waves of my nightmare. Linza had called my self-pity pathetic, but she was wrong. *I* was pathetic. How else could a man go from having a woman admit her love of him, no matter how grudgingly, to her spitting oaths and storming from his company a few seconds later?

*She loved me,* I then cursed myself. *Loved* not *loves.* I had that chance to take hold of her feelings, and I had let it fall through my grasp through my own self-loathing. Loathing that only grew stronger and heavier now that I looked back at my weakness. I cursed myself for a fool. I cursed myself for a coward. In my dream, Stumps had been right; how many people needed to die for me? Had I earned their sacrifice? Had I earned the right to live when they had died?

Of course not.

I wanted to lie in my bed, then. I wanted to lie there, and to forget about walls, and sieges, and soldiers, and enemies. I wanted to lie and sleep, forever. I didn't want to wake up. I just wanted it to be over. I couldn't take care of the love who had been everything to me when I *had* everything. How was I supposed to protect Linza, and be a man for her, when I had nothing but a head full of nightmares?

'Enough!' I shouted through clenched teeth, desperate for it to be over. '*Enough!*' I screamed again, before lapsing into silent misery.

'Felix?' A timid voice broke through. 'Can I come in?'

I opened my eyes. Moved the fingers that were pressing with hatred into my skin.

Micon.

'Is it all right if I come in?' the boy asked again. 'Stumps asked me to come and get some of his things.'

Stumps. My friend. What had I done to the man? When I had left Malchus, there had been nothing before my eyes but rage. Seeing Linza threatened, I had known that I loved her, just as I loved my friend. A friend that I had beaten without mercy for putting Linza's life at risk.

'How is he?' I forced myself to ask.

Micon shrugged, eyeing me nervously. I had protected him in the forest and fort, but now the young soldier looked at me with respectful fear, as if I were a snake on a path.

'Where is he?' I asked.

'With Titus.'

'And Brando?'

'With Titus.'

'I suppose you're with Titus, too?' I asked, hatred for myself redoubling.

'He said we should give you some space,' Micon explained. 'So you could sort things out. With her.'

'Titus said that?'

The boy shook his head. 'Stumps.'

My chin sagged to my chest. Even after what I had done to him, my comrade was selflessly looking to my own interests.

'Wait,' I urged the young soldier as he moved to the doorway. 'Can you help me put my mail on? I'm coming with you.'

# 55

'So you saved his life, then tried to kill him?' Titus greeted me as I entered the building that served as the centre of his black-market racket. It was quiet, a few groups of off-duty soldiers and archers playing dice or talking over watered-down wine.

'I don't really remember,' I answered honestly.

The man let out a snort, taking in the injuries I had sustained myself, my century having had to beat me into unconsciousness to put an end to my swinging fists and gnashing teeth.

'Do you think he'll see me?'

'Doesn't have a choice. He's not running fast in the state he's in.' Titus smiled darkly. He then offered a shrug of his huge shoulders. 'Girls make us do daft things.'

'He should never have used her like that,' I argued, feeling the anger tighten my chest as I thought of Linza being put in danger.

'You known many women?' Titus asked, catching me off guard. 'If you had, you'll know it's not us who pulls the strings. Look at her.' He gestured across the room towards Metella. 'I could get into business with anyone, Felix, but I do it with her.'

'Why?'

'Because one way or another, she'd get what she wanted. Better I'm cut in on it.'

'You and her, are . . . ?' I asked, a little surprised.

'No!' the man scoffed. 'But they see things we don't. The gods made us different for a reason. If it was just about fucking we'd have our own dick and hole, wouldn't we? It's about this,' he explained, slapping me across the head and grinning. 'You've got some miles on you, Felix, but you're still a clueless bastard. Come on.' He gestured. 'Let's go see him.'

Titus led me through a door into a storeroom that was stacked high with engineering supplies. There was a brazier set in its centre, and around the warming flames were the shapes of Brando, Micon and the shrouded figure of Stumps.

'You made some mess of him,' Titus remarked as if it were a casual observation.

I looked at my friend, seeing his eyes dark and his lips swollen.

'Looks like an eastern whore with his eyes like that.' Titus smiled, gently easing the mood. 'Sit down, Felix.'

I could not. 'Stumps . . .'

'It's all right,' he mumbled from between his thick lips. 'I know why you did it.'

I sat then, heavily, facing my friend, forcing myself to meet his forgiving eyes.

'You two.' I sensed Titus gesture to the other men. 'Come help me set up for tonight.'

And so we were left alone. The silence held for a long time, and within it, my self-recrimination grew.

'I think I love her,' I eventually offered as my defence.

My friend tried to smile. 'I worked that out when you stuck my head through the bunk frame.'

He chuckled then. I was a second from following, but then I saw him wince in pain, and shame fell heavily upon me.

'She reminds me of someone,' I told him, anxious for him to know why I had behaved the way I had against him. 'I don't know if I love her, or if it's the old love. Does that make sense?'

'Course it makes sense. But Linza's a great girl in her own right. I'm sure it's that,' he offered.

I knew that I had to tell him more. It was a duty to a friend. A debt I had to pay for my crime against him. And yet the words stuck in my throat like the barbs of arrows. My chest tightened, and my head swam.

'I couldn't protect the last one,' I confessed, letting my chin drop.

For a moment Stumps said nothing. I hoped that my admission would be enough for him to understand why I had reacted with so much rage to seeing Linza placed in harm's way.

'Felix, I'm not saying this to start trouble, but I need to tell you because I would never put someone you love in danger.'

I lifted my gaze.

'It was Linza's idea, Felix. Not mine. I'd never do that to you.'

I struggled to accept the words. They sounded almost like a betrayal.

'It was her idea?' I finally said.

Stumps nodded, wincing at the pain from his bruised spine. 'When we went to get the rations. I just wanted to humour her a bit. She'd cooked up the idea with another of the Batavian girls. It was her I sent to get Albus, and you. I thought he'd bring the whole century, the twat,' he added with a curse.

'Why would she do that?' I asked, suddenly uncertain that my friend was telling me the truth.

'Put yourself in her position,' Stumps urged. 'Her husband's missing, Felix. Which, let's be honest, means he's dead in the forest. She's got no control over that.

'Then there's an army at the walls, and she's days away from getting raped to death. She's got no control over that. All right, the hairy bastards have pulled back now, but we're still cut off. She's got no control over that.'

'And then the killings in the fort,' I whispered, beginning to understand.

'Exactly. Imagine it. She's got no control over any part of her life, but she's a fucking strong girl. She's a fucking fighter. She found a way she could hit back.'

'You still shouldn't have let her do it,' I accused.

'Let her?' He laughed. 'If you think you can control this girl, then you're in for some sleepless nights. The bad kind,' he added with a wry smile.

I said nothing. Instead I thought back over Stumps's explanation. Of course he was right. Linza was no one's to control, and she was a fighter. Those were the qualities that had pulled me into love once more, and so why should I be surprised by them?

'You just don't like other people sticking their necks out,' Stumps piped up, reading my face and thoughts. 'You're obsessed with control, Felix.'

I shook my head. 'I'm not.'

'You are,' he insisted. 'Dangerous mission? Yes please.

Suicidal mission? Oh yes. Trying to keep everyone else from danger except you? Oh, shit, yes!'

'It's not that . . .'

'I remember your face when you found me on that raid, like I had betrayed you by going. You tried to keep Brando and Folcher from them too, I know.'

'And look what happened to Folcher,' I countered.

'Ha! There! See? There it is. You think you can save everyone, you daft old bastard.'

'I don't,' I told him, remembering the day when that truth had been taught to me.

'Well, you try to,' my friend told me gently.

He was right, I realized then. He was right. It all began with her, and my failure to keep her safe. As if a bandage was unravelling before my eyes, the purpose of all my later actions began to show clear.

'You want to tell me about her?' my comrade offered with a smile.

'I do,' I admitted.

But then I heard a door crash open, and the rasp of blades being drawn.

Stories would have to wait.

We were under attack.

# 56

I moved quickly to the door, holding a finger to my mouth to silence any question from Stumps. Outside, I heard the bark of challenge. Of command.

The voices were Roman.

'Lie face down on the floor!' one voice shouted. 'Hands away from your weapons! Face down!'

I suddenly realized that it was a raid, not an attack. There was scant relief in that fact, because we were on grounds that – though tolerated until now – broke legion law. More than this, my friend Titus was the architect of the flagrant flaunting of regulations.

'It's a raid,' I mouthed to Stumps, who hadn't moved from his position.

Courses of action ran through my mind as I listened to the sound of barked orders and furniture being turned on its head. Black markets and drinking holes had existed within the legions for as long as the eagle standards had been carried, and the clampdowns that came against them were a periodic reminder from the hierarchy not to overstep. As such, I wasn't particularly worried about our physical safety – I was certain that our punishment for being caught in such a place would be nothing more severe than extra work duties on some unsavoury task. I was about to suggest to Stumps that we walk out openly, until I heard one voice raised above the others.

'Get them lined up against the wall.'

Malchus. I looked at Stumps, who had turned ashen as he heard the murderer's voice, and for good reason: Malchus would use any opportunity to break the man who had held a javelin to his throat.

I quickly searched our surroundings. The sole window was high, and would have been a struggle for Stumps to reach even if he were fully fit. As it was, I had beaten my friend to the point where he moved like a cripple.

'Over here,' I mouthed silently.

'What are you doing?'

'Help me move these.' I gestured to stacks of pick-helves on a shelf; then I started lifting the bundled tool handles and placing them gently on the floor.

'Why?'

'Just do it,' I urged.

It took only moments to clear the space that I needed.

'You're going in there,' I told my friend.

'Have you lost your head?'

I didn't answer. The voices outside were growing nearer. With a sour look, Stumps pulled himself into the cleared space.

'Felix—' he tried, but I was already piling the bundles of wooden handles back in front of the man, my heart beating faster as the angry calls from the outside dropped away. It was the signal that they had gathered together their culprits, and that they would now begin searching. I hurried to place the last bundle of helves on to the shelves, and then lunged for the brazier, desperate to distance myself from my comrade's concealment.

The door opened a moment later: two soldiers. They

held wooden staves in their hands. They had come to beat, not to kill.

'Who are you?' the older of the pair asked.

'Friend of the quartermaster's,' I answered. 'We were Seventeenth together.'

'You one of the ones that got out of the forest?' the younger man asked, interested.

I nodded.

'What was it like?'

I had no time to reply as the older of the pair waved the question away.

'Come with us,' he ordered me. 'Anyone else with you?'

'No. I was having a drink here and waiting for him to come back. I heard the noise outside and thought it better to wait here.'

'Smart bloke,' the veteran conceded. 'We did have to crack a few heads in there. No need for that if you play along though.'

'Of course,' I answered earnestly before placing my hands on my head and walking towards the pair. They moved to the side of the door, and as I passed between them I saw the effect of Malchus's raid – not one piece of furniture was left unturned, and with their noses against a wall were the twenty or so men and women who had been enjoying wine and dice until the doors had crashed open.

'Over to the wall,' the older of the pair instructed me.

'You,' I heard growled then. 'Why the fuck are you here?'

Malchus again. His predatory eyes had fallen on me instantly.

'I was with the QM in the Seventeenth, sir,' I explained. 'The same century.'

Malchus's jaw jutted out as he bit back and accepted my reason. I reached the wall, my nose pressing into the cold wood.

'All of you,' Malchus then ordered. 'Turn around.'

We complied. The tall centurion was flanked by two dozen men of his own century. Standing beside him was a soldier I recognized as one of Titus's doormen.

'Who runs it?' Malchus demanded.

The doorman's hand began to raise.

'You fucking snitch!' a voice called out, only to be silenced with a blow of the wooden handles, the sound like slapping leather.

'Keep your mouths shut!' one of Malchus's veterans barked, as much of a hound as his leader.

'Point them out,' Malchus snapped. The doorman's hand raised again. As his finger indicated each target, a pair of soldiers came forwards to pull the accused from the line-up, and bound the culprit's wrists behind their backs.

Plancus was the first, the man's pathetic hobbling drawing a grimace from Malchus. Next came Metella, her head back and indignant. Finally, Titus was fingered as one of the racket's three ringleaders.

'Centurion,' Titus greeted the cohort commander in a voice as calm as a dead sea. 'It's a pleasure to see you here. Your lads have been quite the regulars.'

Malchus scoffed, showing his disinterest in how his men spent their time. 'So the quartermaster's bent?' he said instead. 'Who'd have fucking thought it.'

'Just trying to make a living, sir,' Titus appealed, strong man to strong man. 'Happy to help others make theirs.'

Malchus smiled darkly then. It was a terrible thing to see. 'I couldn't give a fuck if every man gambles away their last coin,' he said, approaching Titus. 'But there's one thing I won't put up with,' he added calmly. 'And that's being fed FUCKING DOG MEAT!'

The sudden blows landed a second later. Against Titus's thick muscle and skull, they sounded like artillery hitting stone battlements. The big man had the sense to go down.

'Feeding me fucking dog?' the centurion snarled, standing over him. 'Putting dog on the plate of the FUCKING PREFECT? Are you out of your minds, you greedy bastards?'

From the floor, Titus spat blood and words. 'Plancus!' He roared. 'I'll fucking kill you!'

Every set of eyes turned towards the stooped veteran – there was no disguising the look of guilt that hung over his weathered face.

'You cunt!' Metella roared, charging for the man.

It took four soldiers to hold her back. As she was restrained, Malchus watched her struggle with a smile. Then he turned to a veteran beside him.

'No need for names and units of the others in here. Just rough them up a bit, but not enough that anyone has to miss a duty.'

'Yes sir,' the veteran replied, before stepping forwards to carry out the order. 'You heard the boss.'

He then addressed those of us standing against the wall. 'Just suck it up and we'll be done in a second. Now face the wall,' he commanded and, like well-trained animals, we turned our backs, and tightened our muscles against what was to come.

The punishment arrived a moment later, the wooden stave crashing against my hamstrings, pain singing through my legs and into my back. Anxious to avoid a second blow I dropped to my knees, submitting to the legion's discipline, and the power that it held over every part of my life.

'You're done,' the veteran announced after a second blow had landed. My punishment received, I pushed myself up on to throbbing legs. The beating had been merciful, and yet as I looked around me, I now felt nothing but sickness and fear in my stomach.

Because Titus was gone.

# 57

Titus was not the only familiar face missing – Metella and Plancus had disappeared with Malchus and his soldiers, and that could only mean that there was further punishment planned for the ringleaders. Titus would certainly lose his rank, but beyond that? I had no more time to think on it.

'Brando,' I called. 'Micon. Come help me.'

They followed me into the engineering equipment room, puzzled at first as to why I was pulling the bundles of staves from the shelves.

Stumps smiled with relief as he saw our faces. 'I'm quite comfortable in here. Shut me back in and let me sleep.'

We said nothing. Levity slipped from our friend's voice as he recognized the warning signs.

'Titus?' he asked, immediately worried.

'And Metella and Plancus.'

'Shit,' Stumps groaned, gasping as we uncoiled him from his hiding place and placed him on the ground. 'Gone with Malchus? That can't be good.'

There was no reply to be made to that.

'What can we do?' he asked.

'I don't know,' I told him honestly. 'But we've got the walls tonight. If we don't report for duty, we're in bigger shit than Titus.'

'We could talk to Albus? Maybe he'll do something?' Brando asked.

'He'll do nothing.' I was certain. 'He just wants an easy life.'

And so it proved when we returned to the barrack block.

'Centurion Albus wants to see you,' the century's young runner summoned me.

'Felix,' Albus greeted me in his quarters. 'Look, this is nothing personal,' he then began. 'I know you've got shit-loads of experience, but you were the last one here to get made up to section commander, and we're half a century. I need to consolidate the sections, and so you guys will go into what will now be Two Section, under Livius. The good news is that it's just the three of you. I pulled some strings and got your mate Stumps back into the quarter-master's.' Albus smiled, unaware that Titus was now likely in chains.

'Thanks, sir,' I muttered, my mind elsewhere. Albus took my indifference for offence.

'It really is nothing personal,' he insisted. 'But last in, first out. I can't be fairer than that.'

'It's fine, sir,' I told him. 'I'll get our kit moved across before watch.'

'No need for that.' He waved my suggestion away. 'We're only a half-century, so may as well use the space we've got. Just pop your head in and link with Livius.'

I did. Livius was an athletic-looking soldier in his mid-twenties. From the little that I had seen of him, he seemed capable. He was also acute enough to smell the salt on me, and know that I was as experienced as any man in the fort.

'I think there's a lot I can learn from you.' The man had smiled, attempting to soften the blow of my demotion.

I couldn't have cared less for the loss of position. My mind was pulled in every other direction within the fort – what was happening to Titus? Where was Linza, and what was she thinking? Was she thinking about me, and if so, in what manner?

I got the answer to at least one of these questions as I stood watch on the darkness of the battlements, the German cold whipping across my skin and tugging at the scarf I had pulled tight about my face.

I was stamping my own feet to move the blood when I heard other footsteps approach – Centurion H, his face framed by moonlight.

'That is you under there, isn't it Felix?' he asked, and I pulled the scarf down to show him.

'Why are you up here, sir?' I asked, puzzled.

'I thought you should be told before the parade in the morning,' he explained. 'You'll be going there as soon as it's light, and the watches are changed.' H's tone was grim, and my stomach tightened at the implication.

'What parade?' I managed.

'Punishment,' he told me heavily. 'They're putting your friend to death.'

## 58

I struggled to comprehend the centurion's words – Titus, sentenced to death?

By the grey moonlight, H saw the fear and confusion that danced across my cragged features.

'Prefect Caedicius wants to make an example of him.'

'It's just gambling,' I protested. 'It's in every legion!'

'It's not that.' H shook his head. 'They were taking the good ration of meat for the officers, and selling that on. Replaced it with dog.' He grimaced, doubtless thinking of what rested inside his own stomach.

'That wasn't Titus,' I swore, certain of it. 'He's no fool.'

'Wasn't the woman, either,' H agreed. 'Titus's partner Plancus has copped to it, but it doesn't matter. Prefect wants an example. I expect Malchus just wants someone to die because he was tricked, and ate it.'

I placed my javelin against the wall, and pulled my hand across my face, willing my emotions to quieten. Dawn was only a few hours away, and the death of my friend would come with it. There had to be some way out.

'How will they do it?' I forced myself to ask.

'Beheading,' the centurion answered coldly. 'It's a mercy, compared to what Malchus wanted.'

I didn't ask what that was, but H told me anyway.

'He wanted to gut the man alive so that the dogs could eat at him. Poetic end, he said.'

'Gods,' I swore. Even after I had seen what Malchus was capable of, he had still managed to surprise me.

'The man's a fucking monster,' H agreed. 'I looked up to that bastard.'

That was no surprise – who hadn't? Aside from the few that knew the truth, Malchus was still a hero to all in the fort.

'Caedicius wants discipline but he's not sick,' H summarized. 'And he's not stupid, either, Felix. I could see tonight that the fact Romans are eating dog – intentionally or otherwise – has shown him how truly fucked we are here.'

'He doesn't think we can hold through winter?'

'He knows that it doesn't matter if we *do*. No one's coming, winter or spring. Where are the legions going to come from – the Emperor's arse? Everyone is pretending that we didn't lose three legions in the forest. There is no relief coming, no matter when. The Rhine is the frontier now, and if it isn't coming to us . . .'

'. . . we have to go to it,' I finished, for the idea was simple. It was the execution that mattered.

'I have a plan,' H told me then. 'An idea to get your friend out of his execution, and to get us to the Rhine.'

I could hear in his tone that he believed both things were truly possible. What I could not understand was why he was telling me this on the fort's walls, instead of putting them into action.

I looked at his face, which had once held nothing but humour, but was now a mask broken by war.

'Why are you telling me this, H?' I asked.

'Because I need you, Felix. I need you to volunteer for something that you shouldn't expect to come back from.'

*

346

Dawn crept over the horizon like a cloaked assassin, thick clouds heavy against a dark sky. There was death coming with the rising gloom, and I had thought of nothing else since H had left me on the battlements to set his plan in motion.

The replacement sections joined our own on the walls. We stood double watch as the darkness slid away, once again revealing nothing before us but frostbitten fields and forests – the terror today would come from within our camp, not without.

It was with a sour stomach and swimming mind that I marched with my century to the parade square. So far as I knew, I was the only one aware of what would await us there. I considered warning my friends, but what would be gained by telling them? No, I'd rather spare them a few moments' worry in a life that was already soaked in it.

'This had better not have anything to do with cutting rations again,' Stumps grumbled. He was walking as stiffly as a corpse from the beating I'd delivered.

'Can't cut them any more.' Livius, our new section commander, tried to smile. 'My belly button's already poking out of my back.'

'Things will change when I get into the QM's,' Stumps promised. 'Consummate professional, I am.

'What's up with you?' he asked me then, irritated at the lack of conversation.

'Tired,' I lied, my limbs alive with nervous dread at the thought of what was to come.

'Bollocks.' He spat. 'I've seen that look before. You're either gonna do something stupid, or you're feeling sorry for yourself. Maybe both. Is it the girl?' he pressed.

'Yes,' I lied again. The truth was that my mind had been so full of worry for Titus, so full of nerves at what H had proposed, that I had had little time to think over my romantic failure.

'Century!' Albus called as we reached the parade square. 'Halt!'

Hobnails tramped down into the packed dirt, frost cracking beneath our feet. Our halt was ragged, a reflection of our state of mind.

'That was a fucking abortion,' Albus barked, though I doubted he was in any mood for drill practice between the endless rotations of guard duties.

Limbs soon began to cool as we waited on the square. Coming off watch, we were one of the first subdivisions to arrive. Gradually, the space at the camp's centre began to fill with blocks of legionaries and archers, and the scattered mass of civilians – the men on the wall aside, all within the fort were obliged to witness what was to come.

'Maybe the Emperor's dropped in to boost morale,' Stumps quipped to a few chuckles amongst the men.

I was silent, my eyes on the headquarters building whence I expected the officers and the condemned to emerge.

They came not long after, Caedicius and Malchus at the fore, the stone-faced pair followed by two sections of soldiers. It was impossible for me to glimpse the prisoners in their midst. When they came to a halt in the centre of the parade square I cursed my position – I could see neither Titus nor his partners, surrounded as they were by shield and armour. What I could see was the wooden block that was thumped menacingly down in front of the fort's commanders.

Immediately, the men around me either drew breaths or forced them out, muscles tightening as they realized what the block implied, shoulders then sagging as they remembered they were safe within the ranks.

The square was as silent and unkind as the clouded sky.

Caedicius stepped forwards. 'I told you I wanted discipline,' he began, his deep voice booming and bouncing from the cold wooden buildings that surrounded us. 'I told you this. I told you how we should behave as Romans. How we needed to behave to survive.

'You have failed me.' He spoke sadly. 'You have failed yourselves. But worst of all, you have failed Rome.'

A long silence held over the square then, broken only by unruly children who shuffled irritably in the arms of their parents. Gripped by cold, a baby at the far end of the square began to wail. It was a long, plaintive cry. When Malchus stepped forwards, I wondered if he was enjoying the child's discomfort.

'These prisoners', Malchus began, his voice cutting over the cries of the baby, 'have been seeking to profit through selling and trading rations that were intended for the garrison as a whole. For that—' He stopped then as the baby doubled its efforts. 'Get that fucking baby off my parade square!' he roared, and I saw a woman run from the ranks. Despite the imminent death, or because of it, a ripple of laughter broke out amongst the soldiers.

Malchus heard it. 'You do not fucking laugh!' he bellowed at the assembled troops, his hand pointed like a blade. 'You do not speak! You do not eat unless you are ordered to! You do not shit, until you are ordered to! *This* is what happens when you think of yourself first, and not

Rome!' He swept out his arm. At the gesture, a limp form was dragged forwards by two soldiers.

Plancus. The man's neck dropped heavily on to the chopping block. Perhaps fear had taken over his limbs, for any fight seemed to have left him. More than likely, Malchus had already beaten every inch of his body.

Prefect Caedicius stepped forwards. After a look at the shaking man before him, he addressed his words to the parade. 'Legionary Plancus is guilty of stealing rations from his legion during a time of war and siege. For this crime, he is sentenced to death. Centurion Malchus, carry out the sentence.'

Malchus drew the blade. I could only imagine the look of savage contentment on his taut face.

I could have looked away then, or shut my eyes. I don't know why I didn't. Instead, I watched Malchus bring the longsword over in a looping arc. Instantly I – like every other seasoned soldier in the ranks – knew that it was a bad stroke.

The blade bit across the back of Plancus's shoulders. A hideous scream cut through the assembled ranks like a chariot's scythed blades.

Malchus pulled his weapon free of flesh, and I had no doubt that he was smiling now, exacting his vengeance. He was too good a swordsman for such a poor stroke, and the look on Caedicius's face told me that he knew it too. I saw the prefect's lips move, and I wondered if he was urging the man to finish the job quickly.

The blade swung again. This time it bit the neck, but the strike was weak. There was no scream, and I expected Plancus's spine had been broken. The man yet lived, though, and his gurgled coughs spat out across the cold dirt.

Caedicius spoke to Malchus again. The words were hidden, but there was no mistaking the urgency in his face.

Malchus swung. It was a beautiful strike, and in its arc was delivered a message: those who crossed Malchus would die terribly for it. I could only imagine what restraint it took the man to hold back from kicking the severed head across the square, and hacking the body to pieces. Instead, Plancus's leaking body was loaded on to a stretcher and carried clear.

'Next one,' Malchus called.

My stomach knotted into a ball of stone. Blood beat against my skull. Finally, I chanced a look at Stumps – my comrade's face was white. He was no fool, and the plot of this play was now obvious. Stumps knew that Titus could be the next man to kneel before the bloodied block.

'Please, no,' I heard him murmur through shaking teeth.

His wish was granted. It was Metella that they brought forwards. She carried herself like the bravest of soldiers, and as she approached the block, she sent a stream of violent spittle towards her executioner.

'Try that on me, you bastard coward!' she boomed at Malchus. 'Easy to kill someone when they're on their knees.'

'Be silent!' Caedicius ordered. 'Die with some decency, woman.'

'Oh, fuck off,' Metella snarled instead. 'I'll see you all soon, anyway!' she shouted as she was shoved hurriedly to her knees. 'This fort's fucked! No one's coming for you, darlings! You'll starve to death here, or die out there!'

Malchus wasted no more time in shutting her up,

shoving Metella's throat against the block with such force that the woman's final words were choked from her.

This time, the stroke was quick; Metella's head rolled across the dirt, crimson splattering the frosted floor in a final act of defiance.

Plancus's death had caused revulsion in the ranks. Metella's had brought fear – not from her death, but from her prophecy. She had voiced what all but the most optimistic in the fort feared deep down in their souls: that the fort was beyond help.

Caedicius could smell the panic. 'Do not heed the words of a criminal,' he began. 'No one will starve here. There is a plan of action! It is a secret one, but something that you will all hear of soon, I promise. For now, continue in your duties. Continue to uphold the traditions and expectations of Rome!'

There was a finality to those words, and as I heard them, the first spear-point of hope began to push its way into my chest.

I felt eyes on me. It was Stumps. We shared a look: Titus?

Malchus paced forward to stand beside his prefect. My heart caught in my throat. I knew that the next words from the killer's mouth would mean the death or salvation of my friend.

'Parade!' Malchus growled. Time seemed to stand still as his first command echoed in the crisp air.

'Parade!' the executioner called again.

'Dismissed!'

# 59

I have marched across nations to war, and I have crossed a continent to escape one, but I have never felt a march so long as the one that followed our dismissal from the executions. The few hundred yards from parade ground to barrack block felt like an eternity.

I had almost collapsed in relief when the order to dismiss had passed through Malchus's snarling lips. The cohort commander and his bloodied sword had trailed the prefect from the parade square, the prisoner's escort following in their wake, stretchered bodies carried behind them. In none of this was there any sight of Titus.

Returning to the barrack block, I felt as though the regulation marching pace was like wading through tar. I wanted nothing more than to break ranks and sprint, but I had no choice but to force my worry back into my chest.

Stumps, having little idea of my conversation on the walls with H, had none of the same concerns, seeing only that Titus had seemingly escaped from death's grasp once more.

'He's a slippery fucker.' He beamed at me as we marched. 'Like a fucking eel, he is. Wriggles his way into and out of everything. Shame about Metella though. I liked her.'

'Me too,' Brando agreed. 'She went out well.'

'By fuck she did, didn't she?' Stumps laughed with pride. 'Spat right in Malchus's face, the cunt!'

'Keep your voice down,' I hissed.

He gave me an apologetic look. 'She did die well though. Bigger balls on her than most men.'

Albus called us to a halt outside our barrack block. The movement was observed far more crisply than it had been earlier that morning – the executions had had the desired effect of sharpening minds and attitudes. Overall, though, I sensed a feeling of disquiet in the air. Stumps was buoyed up by the fact that his friend had escaped the fate of his fellow ringleaders, but Metella's last words had struck a deep chord with the fort's garrison, and it showed in their stooped postures, and the absence of good-natured insults and laughter.

Albus was as glum as any of the men. 'Fall out,' he told us, already walking to his quarters. 'Next duty's at noon.'

I was already sprinting to our room.

'You missed your bed that much?' Stumps called after my back. I ignored him, pushing open the door and pulling back the partition to our living space.

A familiar figure was lying in my bed.

'All right?' he grunted.


Titus lay back on my bed, chewing a piece of dried meat. He was not alone in the room. Centurion H leaned back against the wall, his arms folded.

'How was it?' he asked me.

I shook my head. 'Malchus is a bastard,' was all I said.

'I'll miss Metella,' Titus said, getting to his feet. 'Plancus deserved what he got, the fucking idiot.'

I was about to tell Titus that no one deserved such a death as Plancus had suffered, when what was left of our section began to enter behind me.

'Brando,' H put in quickly. 'Watch the door.'

'You slippery bastard,' Stumps smiled, pushing his way through and hitting his friend across one of his massive shoulders. 'How the fuck did you pull that off?'

'Ask them,' Titus grunted, with just a nod of his head towards myself and H.

'We're not out of the fire yet,' H explained, frowning. 'But the prefect's seen enough to know that we can't stay here forever. We've had no instruction or word from the garrisons on the Rhine, so if they have sent any scouts they're not making it past the goat-shaggers.'

'What's this got to do with Titus?' Stumps asked, pulling a face.

H shrugged. 'In return for his life, Titus has volunteered to go on a scouting party of our own. We're going to search out their army, and find a way to bolt around them to the Rhine once we get a heavy enough storm. I convinced Caedicius that the best people to come with me and do it are the ones who got away from Arminius in the forest.'

'H is going to lead us,' I put in. 'Me and Titus, anyway.'

My friend's face darkened. 'Having your own little picnic is it, you fuckers? Well, what if I want to come?' Stumps was clearly desperate not to lose sight of a comrade he had only moments ago thought condemned.

'You're in no state to lower yourself on to a latrine, never mind fight,' Titus told him – truthfully.

'And I need you to look out for Linza,' I added. 'Micon and Brando, too. You've seen what Malchus is, Stumps. I can't leave her alone here when he's got a blade to grind.'

'I'll trade places with you,' Stumps pressed defiantly.

'Won't work.' H shook his head. 'Caedicius has a high

opinion of Felix, and Malchus can't go back on his old praise, either. We're taking a few others with us to send word to the Rhine about our intentions, but you're in no state to be a runner, Stumps.'

'Ah, fuck the lot of you anyway,' our comrade cursed. 'Go and get yourselves killed and I'll stay here and keep warm. You're the fucking idiots, not me.'

'There's my boy.' Titus grinned, ruffling Stumps's unkempt hair as if he were a child. 'What now?' he then asked H.

'We draw rations and kit. Leave as soon as it gets dark.'

'Enjoy your dog,' Stumps grunted from his bed, his back turned to us but mind fully in the conversation.

'I think I'll lie low here,' Titus said to me. 'Don't want Malchus having second thoughts, so it looks like you've lost your bed.'

There were plenty of empty ones in the room. After a moment, I caught my friend's meaning.

'I'll go and see her before we leave,' I promised.

'Now,' he said, and I felt the eyes of my other friends burning into me, telling me to find my balls.

'Now,' Titus urged again.

'Don't tell me you put my head through a bunk for nothing,' Stumps rumbled from his bed.

Titus laughed.

'I'll go—'

'Now!' my comrades shouted in unison.

And so I did as I was ordered.

I left to find Linza.

# 60

Walking through the fort I felt the same edge of fear that had descended on to the parade square following Metella's final words. It clung to every person in the fort. Shrouded figures moved sullenly from building to building, avoiding eye contact at all costs. There were no thoughts of the greater good, only of their own person, or the smallest band of brothers and sisters.

Such pessimism made finding Linza difficult. My questions were met with suspicion and scorn. Combing the grid-like layout of the fort, I eventually found her cutting wood with a dozen other women, their faces ruddy from effort and biting cold.

'Linza,' I said.

There was no happiness in her expression when she saw me. I felt as though I was being watched and judged for intention, the way a horse warily eyes a dog.

'Felix,' she finally said, walking clear of the prying eyes and ears of her group. 'What do you want?'

'I want to speak to you,' I answered, as though it were the most obvious thing in the world.

'*To* me?'

'With you.'

'About what?'

I faltered then. Even her tired look of annoyance

brought back memories that I treasured – did I truly love this German woman, or was I chasing a ghost?

'I'm not sure,' I finally said. 'I'm going away for a while,' I added, as if it explained everything. Perhaps it did, because I saw the tension in her shoulders soften.

'What the prefect was talking about on the square? He has a mission for you?'

I nodded. She shook her head as if disappointed with a child.

'I suppose you volunteered?' she accused me.

'I had no choice,' I tried, recognizing a deep note of worry hiding amongst the simmering anger.

'Of course you did. That's why it's called volunteering.'

I said nothing. How to explain to her the ties of comradeship when I could not understand them myself? Titus was a friend, and putting my own life at risk had been the only way to give him a chance of survival. There was nothing heroic or glorious in those actions. They simply happened because they *had* to. There was no other choice.

'Do you know what a snowball is?' I asked, earning a look of contempt.

'I'm Batavian.'

I blushed a little at my foolishness. 'Volunteering is like a snowball,' I tried to explain. 'You do it once, roll it once, and it just keeps getting bigger. Once you volunteer for one thing, they'll always expect you to do it the next time. It gets to the point where if you don't volunteer, you're not standing still, but pulling back.'

'So it's about pride?' Linza snorted. 'What a surprise. Stupid of me to think you weren't as arrogant as the next Roman.'

'I'm no Roman,' I told her, meaning it.

'You dress like one. You kill for them. Now you risk your life for them.'

'I'm not doing it for Rome,' I told her honestly. 'Fuck Rome. I just want to see my friends get home alive. I want to see you get home alive.'

'Why?' she pressed me.

And I knew then that she wanted me to kiss her. To take hold of her. To be a man.

But I could not. I could not, because I was looking at a ghost, and she was looking at a husband lost to the forest.

'Stay with Stumps and the others when I'm gone,' I urged, watching the moment sail by me as I had once watched the ships leave the pier of my home.

'What do you think is going to happen to me?' she asked. She was angry with me. Angry with our place in the world.

'You'll be all right with them.'

'I'll tell you what will happen to me, Felix.' Linza spoke over me, closing in so that her flushed face was inches from my own. 'If Malchus doesn't rape and kill me here, another man will. German, or Roman. That's my place now. That's what you soldiers see me as. Plunder.'

'That's not true,' I urged, but I could hear the frailty of my words.

'Of course it's true,' she snapped. 'Sooner or later this fort is falling. I will not fall with it, Felix,' she vowed. 'I will take my own life before that.'

Her words hit me harder than any blow I had suffered at the hands of Titus. The thought of a man forcing himself on Linza revolted me, angered me and filled me with shame in the same moment – shame that I could not protect her. Guilt that I had failed before.

'I can show you a way to make it quick?' I tried.

She laughed at me then. It was a bitter, furious laugh. Instantly, I knew that I had failed a test. My soul and manhood had been on trial, and both had now been condemned.

'You think that's what I wanted to hear?' She shook her head, her face made ugly by bile. Resentful that she had let her shield and defences down, as I had my own.

'Go and fuck yourself, Felix,' she snarled at me. 'Go and look for your war.'

She walked away from me. Defeated, I made no attempt to follow. No attempt to call out. Instead, I vowed that I would take her guidance, and do what I had been doing since the first moment I had known loss, and true pain.

I would look for my war.

# 61

It was dark by the time I joined Titus and H in the barrack room. Neither soldier was surprised, assuming that my time had been spent doing what every soldier wants to do when he sees the end of his life hanging by a thread.

'That much fun, was it?' Titus smiled, his teeth yellow in the flame of the room's flickering stove.

'Where are the others?' I asked.

'Guard duty.'

My stomach turned sour. My self-pity had cost me the chance to say goodbye to my comrades.

'Get your kit and let's go,' H instructed me. 'The runners are waiting for us at the gate.'

We joined them soon after. Having ruined my farewell to both Linza and my comrades, I was anxious to be free of the fort and to place myself in danger, where my thoughts would be occupied with survival and not recrimination. The two runners were young men, and carried themselves with confidence. Both had been known and trusted by H for years.

'We're not in any rush to get there,' H told us as we let our eyes adjust to the darkness. 'Priority is to get the runners clear to the Rhine. Once that's done we'll lie up, and start working out the goat-fuckers' positions and routines.

'Any final questions?' H asked. Once we left the gate, we would only speak when strictly necessary.

'Don't you mean last words?' One of the runners grinned, keen to show indifference towards the danger that lay ahead.

We chuckled darkly at the joke. That was the soldier's way.

H turned to the men of the guard. 'Open the gate.'

Without armour and shield we moved quietly through the night. The air was cold but not vicious, and I felt beads of sweat trickle down my lower spine. I had a blanket rolled and looped over one shoulder and down to my waist, and alongside that rested a bundled pack of drinking-skins and rations. There was little weight to either – we would be returning to the fort in a fortnight, or we would be the ones providing meals to nature's creatures.

It was a still night, and the moon was low and shrouded. We knew that Arminius had scouts watching the fort, but we didn't fear them. The land surrounding Aliso was vast and the number of enemies in close proximity few. Should we happen to stumble upon them, then the more pious amongst us would take that as a message from the gods that the mission was doomed to fail from the start.

My own thoughts on a chance meeting were a little different. If we found the enemy then we could steal their mounts. As far as our reconnaissance was concerned, it wouldn't be helpful to announce our presence thus, but the beasts could carry the runners to the Rhine more quickly than their feet. However, before leaving the gate, H had been fast to veto my suggestion of hunting the enemy scouts for such a purpose.

'If we unsheathe our blades, something's gone wrong,'

he told me. 'Don't be in such a hurry, Felix,' he added, sensing something in my nervous energy. 'There'll be killing to do if we're ever to reach the Rhine.'

He was right about that, of course. He was also right that I wanted to draw blood, I then realized. I wanted to fight. I wanted to lose myself in that chaos. That savagery.

There was nothing savage about the way we crossed fields and woodland. Our approach was calm and methodical. H led from the front, and we followed in a loose single file. I brought up the rear, pausing often to watch and listen that we were not being tracked.

There was no need or room for words. We took our lead from our centurion: walking where he did; stopping when he did. There was little of this, as we aimed to cover twelve miles in the darkness. The Roman soldier marches at four miles an hour with full equipment, and is expected to cover twenty miles a day in such conditions. Though unburdened, we were required by stealth and terrain to moderate our pace, and so pauses in our advance west were limited to the time it took to piss, and to draw a few gulps of water from our skins.

The spectre of dawn was threatening the sky when H broke from a farmer's trail and led us towards the darkness that promised the refuge of trees. We found what we wanted there, and so we set about building our hide. Fallen branches formed the support for blankets. Each had thin rope stitched into the corners, and we used pegs to stretch the material tight, as we would a tent. We then covered this structure with the decaying leaves that autumn had left thick on the woodland floor.

'Everyone inside,' H whispered. 'Get some rest. I'll

take first watch, and check the hide and position once it gets lighter.'

With the others, I slithered inside our temporary home. Titus struggled to enter without shaking leaves free, and I knew that the big man would be cursing inside his head. There was little room for personal space, nor did we want it – following our labour, sweat was now growing cold. Our collective body heat beneath the blankets was our best defence against the German chill.

We were not out of danger, but we no longer had to have our senses on high alert, and so thoughts that I wished left in the fort began to fight to be heard. I wanted none of them. Fortunately, the day and night had been long, and my emotions were as exhausted as my feet. I tucked my chin against my chest as Titus began to snore. It wasn't long until I followed his example.

The daylight hours passed without incident. I was woken sometime in the afternoon by Titus, and took my turn at the opening of our hide, my eyes and ears tuned to the autumnal woodland and the shuffling of bronzed leaves, the dank of wet earth and mulch rich in my nostrils.

There was no escaping my mind as I lay beneath the trees. As the coming winter stripped the branches above me, so too were my thoughts laid bare.

I loved Linza. I loved her because she had told me to go and fuck myself. I loved her because she was scared, but she was defiant. I hadn't understood it at the time, but after she had got so angry I had come to realize that she didn't *need* me, but that she *wanted* me. I was as certain of that as I was that my misreading of her emotions had cost me my chance.

A chance at what? I chided myself. Had I forgotten where I was, and who? Even if I survived the reconnaissance of the German force, we would still need to slip by the enemy army eventually. Even the most optimistic soldier in the fort could not expect such a thing to happen smoothly. At some point, there would be bloodshed.

And what if we did survive? What if we did make it to the Rhine? What then? Since Linza had reminded me of the better part of my past – at least, until it had been taken from me – I had forgotten who I was, and fallen into the role of the soldier. The legionary. But the bases on the Rhine were not my final destination; Britain was. Would that change if I were with Linza? Would she love me once we were free of imminent death, and away from the compressed and chaotic world of siege? Would she come with me to Britain if she did?

I had a head and heart full of questions, but only one certainty – I knew that I had failed her.

Knowing that sleep would now evade me, I kept the watch until darkness was falling. Under its blanket we rolled away our own, and H led us westwards. We were like animals now, grunts and looks all that we needed to know our pack leader's intention.

The ground was cold and hard, and so we made good distance on that second night. H and one of the runners had bands of beads threaded with cords, and these they used to measure our distance in the darkness. To achieve this they had walked a hundred yards within camp, counting the steps it took them to cover the distance. Now in enemy territory, they counted their steps and moved one bead for each hundred yards covered. It was a skill they had practised, and became an automatic rhythm that was as natural as breathing.

I had no beads, but experience of my own had made me a good judge of time and distance. I estimated that we had made fifteen miles that night, putting us roughly halfway between Aliso and the Rhine.

Once more, H led us to a place beneath branches and shrouded by undergrowth. Once more we made our shelter and rested concealed in our hide. My time on watch was again one of questions without answers, and it was with relief that we began the third night's march, and then the fourth.

It was that night that we reached our closest point to the Rhine. It was beyond our sight and hearing, but H estimated that we were within ten miles of the waters that separated the Empire from the enemy.

'Make another few miles tonight,' he whispered to the two runners. 'Lie up, then cross tomorrow. Good luck.'

Titus and I added our own farewells through pats on the men's shoulders. After leaving what rations they had with us, they took their leave.

'We've got a long spell ahead,' H murmured once the quiet rustle of the men's movements had died away. 'We'll lie up here tonight. It's a good spot.'

We formed our hide in silence. Titus took the first watch, and I was still in the laze of near-sleep when I heard him speak up. I kept my lids tightly shut, willing my mind to disengage, but it caught like a hook on the big man's conversation with the centurion.

'You look surprised to see me,' he said, his whisper like a forge's bellows.

'Not really,' H replied. 'But I am glad to wake up alive, at least, so thank you for that.'

For days we had stayed silent, but I could tell by their surprised words that both men needed the closure of this conversation. I feigned sleep, not wanting to become an intruder.

'Why would I kill you?' Titus asked, bemused. 'You saved my life. Dragged it out a little longer, anyway.'

'What happened with Statius,' H explained. 'You don't strike me as the kind of man who likes witnesses, Titus.'

'It wasn't my crime. You were as much a part of hiding it as I was.'

H had nothing to say to that.

'How did you know I wouldn't run?' the big man pressed.

'You didn't run a black market to go home poor, and you're not weighed down with coins.'

'You bet I want those coins more than my life?' Titus asked, amused.

'No,' H conceded. 'But you'd never leave without Stumps and Micon, would you?'

There was silence then. With certainty, I knew that Titus would be picturing the moment he had chosen to walk away with a legion's pay chests rather than to stand and die alongside his comrades. The situation had seemed hopeless, and yet I was sure the shame of that moment gnawed away at his core. Titus was more complicated than he seemed.

'I wouldn't leave them,' he admitted, and there was steel in that promise. Titus had been given his chance for redemption, something I had always been denied. He would not spurn it.

'You're a good man, H,' Titus added after a long moment. 'I can see that this shit with Statius, the raid and Malchus eats at you. That's the problem with being a good bloke. But you are one, and I just wanted to tell you that.'

'Before we die?' the centurion asked darkly.

'Of course,' Titus answered, unashamed.

When darkness fell we left our shelter and the men's words behind. We went forth, and sought out the enemy's army.

# 62

For ten days we lived like animals in the undergrowth that touched the encampment of the blocking force. The German army was where it had been the night of our failed raid, straddled across the paved road that led to the crossing on the Rhine twelve miles distant – far enough to avoid tempting the Rhine garrisons to battle, close enough to make escape for us impossible.

We hoped to make a fool of Arminius's claim. To that end we skulked in depressions in the earth during daylight, watching the enemy from tree-cloaked ridges and hillsides. At night we emerged alongside fox and wolf, creeping so close to the enemy positions that we could smell the ale on the cold air. We heard the bored voice of their sentries. We heard their laughter, and farts. We were close enough to kill them, but we watched, we noted, and we learned.

The force Arminius had left behind was a considerable one, a few thousand men, but it had grown lazy. Stagnant. There were no challenged passwords, simply spoken greetings that even we could understand. The patrols were infrequent, predictably timed and lacklustre. The German tribes had shown themselves to be brutal and fierce in combat, but given the tedium of the grind of campaign, they now showed their amateur nature.

'Germany breeds warriors,' I had once been told by a veteran of the early campaigns. 'Rome trains soldiers.'

I saw the truth of that distinction now. Without the strict discipline that was the backbone of the legions, the German army appeared as nothing more threatening and hostile than any gathering of peoples.

Of course, that would change quickly if we were caught in the open.

The coming winter proved our ally in avoiding such detection. The nights grew bitter, and men clung to flaming campfires that warmed their hands but ruined their night vision. Tribesmen and camp followers stuck to their tents, leaving only when they had to. Frequent downpours washed away the enemy's will to patrol.

But nothing comes without a price. We had no tents to retreat within. Instead, hides of branch and leaves were our refuge. We lived in sodden clothes, dank and miserable. My nose was a constant spout of snot, my greatest fear of detection coming from a wayward sneeze or cough. We were becoming sick men, our stubbled beards dusted with frost on the harshest of mornings. Needing to maintain our silence, there was no means to complain. No means to encourage.

It was not a happy existence, but we watched, we noted, and we learned.

Eventually, H decided that we had learned enough. I knew this because that night, following the fall of darkness, he began to lead us eastwards. We walked for miles before we stopped, resting on our knees within the slippery confines of a woodland ditch.

'Seen enough,' he told us. Words were almost unfamiliar to the man after ten days of near total silence.

We covered another eight miles before we stopped to

build our hide, H anxious to make good speed and deliver our news to the fort. We were also on the last day of our rations, though there were plenty of icy streams to drink from.

On the second night of our withdrawal, H stopped us with hours of darkness remaining.

'Don't want to turn up in daylight and get picked off by their scouts,' he explained. 'Not after this.'

And so we spent our last night in the dirt. It began to rain, the stripped trees offering no protection from the wind-lashed hail that struck our skin. We huddled together, sleep an impossibility. Instead we thought of hot water. We thought of baths. We thought of food, and firelight, and dry clothes. We thought of our friends, and I thought of Linza.

The next night, we returned to the fort.

## 63

Watchwords were called. The guard commander was summoned. The gate creaked open, and we stepped inside the walls.

Torchlight greeted our arrival. What did those soldiers see by the flames? Weathered faces bearded like our enemy and as filthy as the lowest beggar in Rome. Clothes torn from bramble, soiled and repulsive.

But it was our eyes that made them tense, for they were both wild, and sharp. They took in everything, and nothing. They were the eyes of men stripped of civilization, returned to their most primal. The soldiers knew that we were animals, and they had opened the gate to let us in.

H led us at speed to the headquarters building. Already I saw word of our return begin to spread from the soldiers present. Soon, the entire fort would know that a trio of individuals had entered, barely recognizable as soldiers, yet possessing the watchwords that Malchus had ordered every man of the centuries to learn by heart.

The guard commander escorted us inside the building at the fort's centre. A nervous-looking clerk showed us to an empty room where we were to wait until the fort's leadership could be roused.

'Food and wine,' Titus growled at the clerk, who went scurrying in search of it.

Prefect Caedicius arrived moments later. His face had thinned, but his eyes were alive.

'Did you find us a way out?' he asked, desperate to know if there was an escape from Arminius's trap.

It was H who spoke.

'We did.'

Dawn had come and gone by the time that we had finished our debriefing at the headquarters building. Malchus had arrived soon after Caedicius, and to both officers we had reported on all that we had witnessed of the German camp, and their movements.

'We just need a storm,' H concluded. 'We get that, sir, and we have a chance.'

'How are the skies looking?' Caedicius asked of Malchus.

'Good, sir. Cloud's building. Winds are picking up. Could be as soon as tomorrow.'

'Don't waste any time, then. Get the garrison ready to move, and increase the patrols around the walls. Spread the word that anyone attempting to leave before I order it will be put to death. We can't have word getting to the goat-loving scum.'

'Understood, sir,' Malchus grunted. 'Is there anything else?'

There was not, and Malchus left. If he had praise for Centurion H and the information we had brought, he took it with him. Caedicius noticed, and smiled apologetically.

'The cohort commander, as do I, knows that you have suffered hardship to bring us this information. Titus, you can consider this your slate cleaned. For you two' – he turned to myself and H – 'when we reach the Rhine, I'll be recommending you both for the Golden Crown.'

The Golden Crown. An award for valour which brought with it the doubling of pay. Our commanders knew that the promise of financial gain was the best way of encouraging soldiers to commit deeds that they paid for in blood.

We murmured thanks. Coin was not in our minds now. Fresh clothes, our beds and food were – Titus had thrice dispatched the frightened clerk to fetch us more bread and wine.

'You're dismissed, men.' Caedicius put out his hand to shake ours one by one. 'You've given us a fighting chance, and that's all a soldier can ask for. Take the time to rest. I'll send instructions that you're exempt all duties and rationing until we get our storm. Take the rest, and build your strength.

'We're going home.'

The prefect was wrong. I would never return to my home, but I was now in the closest thing that I had known to it – a barrack room with comrades.

'All right, lads?' Stumps spoke up nonchalantly from his bunk as we entered. 'Did one of you shit himself?' he asked disgustedly, sniffing the air. The act held for a few moments more before our excited friend sprang forwards, taking us in an embrace that drove the air from our lungs. Brando and Micon followed soon after, adding to the crush.

'Seriously, though.' Stumps grimaced, stepping back. 'I've never smelt anything so bad.'

'Sorry if it offends you,' Titus replied, before lunging

quickly towards his friend, grabbing Stumps's surprised face and shoving it into a rancid armpit.

'What was that?' Titus asked as cries of muffled horror and laughter echoed about the room.

Stumps gasped as he was let free. 'People have been condemned to the arena for less than that.' He scowled. 'Nice beards though. Yours looks really good, Felix.'

'You like it?' I asked, feeling at the dark whiskers.

'Of course I do.' He smiled. 'It covers your face.'

Laughter erupted anew, relief in every note.

'What can we do to help?' Brando offered.

'Stoke that fire up,' Titus told him. 'I'm going to wash, then I want to feel like I'm back in the desert.'

'Where's H?' Stumps asked, but he wasn't concerned. Doubtless the rumour mill had already informed him that three men had entered the fort that night.

'Gone to his own quarters. Wanted some peace.'

'Probably wanking himself silly after two weeks.' Stumps laughed, full of humour now that his friends were returned to him.

'Maybe,' Titus countered. 'Why don't you go offer him a hand?'

'I see you got funnier on your picnic.' Stumps rolled his eyes. 'I hate to think what you lot were doing to stay warm. But look, what happens in the field, stays in the field. Worked for the Spartans.'

Titus shook his head. 'You done?'

'I could probably scrape out a few more.'

Titus snorted. 'If your mother'd scraped out more I could be sitting by a hot stove now, instead of talking to a dickhead. Now be a mate and get those flames going.'

375

Stumps obliged with a smile. His eyes were on the fire, but I knew that his next words were meant for me.

'I can see that you're gagging to ask.'

'I am,' I admitted.

My friend turned to me, brother to brother, and grinned. 'She looks as bad as you do.' He spoke warmly. 'Minus the beard, of course. She's been worried about you, mate, and you know what that means.'

'I should go and see her,' I confirmed.

'Well, yeah, but . . .' His voice trailed away as he took in the dishevelled figure in front of him. 'Probably not when you're looking like you just crawled out of a grave.'

I laughed, and took the wineskin that Micon held out to me.

I was home.

# 64

Hot air with my comrades was followed by hot food, hot water and hot shaves. Stumps had already acquired clean clothing for our return – a symptom of his friendship – and I now pulled these on to my gaunt frame as our comrades quizzed Titus about our mission.

'Just let me sleep, you bastards,' he growled from his back, lids shut.

'You see a theatre around here?' Stumps asked his friend. 'We've been standing like spare pricks on the wall. Give us some entertainment.'

'Shouldn't you be in the quartermaster's?' Titus rumbled back. 'Go stack your blankets on the hand carts ready to leave.'

'Tell him about that, Stumps,' said Micon with a rare smile of mischief.

Stumps's own face turned sour and curdled. 'Had to bribe the bastard Albus to reverse the transfer.' His voice was forlorn.

Titus kept his eyes shut, but his thick chest bounced with laughter. 'You got the job you always wanted and you paid to come back here? You soft bastard.'

'Someone has to look after the suicide section,' Stumps countered. 'That's what the rest of the century calls us, thanks to you lot. Especially you, Felix. Volunteering for everything like you're tired of living. I'm starting to think you're one of those strange ones that likes women to hit his balls.'

I allowed my friend a smile for that insult. Amongst my friends, and soon to set things right with Linza, a quiet confidence had settled over me. Perhaps it was the power of hot water, but I felt invigorated and full of life. I was under no illusions that there were trials to come, but for now I was content to take Linza's advice and live in the moment, rather than fear the possible, and the inevitable.

'Titus!' Stumps exclaimed dramatically. 'You missed it! He smiled, and you missed it!'

'I'm going now,' I told them.

'Have fun.' Stumps smirked before turning back to Titus. 'Come on, mate, give us one bloody story.'

As I pulled back the partition to the equipment room I heard a groan as Titus gave up his battle for peace and began to tell his friend how a group of foraging German women had come within twenty yards of our hiding place.

'One of them was the most delicious thing I've ever seen,' Titus explained as I opened the door, the cold instantly assaulting my freshly shaven face. 'I'm not going to lie. I was seriously considering certain death, just to have a go with her.'

Stumps's reply was lost to me as the door closed quickly behind me, taken by the wind.

I turned and made my way in the direction of the civilian quarters. I wondered what I would find there, now that word would have reached them of our intended departure. The men of the legions were drilled in such decampment, and they would have prepared their kit and equipment within hours, the labour made easy by Caedicius's order that only a day's ration and fighting gear would be carried. The message in such an order was clear – this was an evacuation, not a relocation. I wondered if the civilians would understand that.

'Felix,' a voice called from behind me.

Livius, the section commander to whom I was now accountable. Titus had been incorporated into our section too, which now numbered nine men. I worried that this anomaly was the reason that he approached me now, about to break the news that our circle would be split up, and one of us moved on to a section of strangers.

I should have prepared myself for worse.

'We've just been moved up to immediate notice to move. Prefect's orders,' the soldier told me.

His youthful face was excited at the prospect of our attempted escape. My own had turned to stone.

I knew what that notice would mean.

'No one can leave the barracks.'

I re-entered the room a different man than I had left it. My comrades saw as much in the defeated slope of my shoulders.

They grimaced in sympathy for me when I told them why.

'Albus wants us all in armour, helmets on, ready to go.'

Stumps spat at the order. 'Takes all day to put a helmet on now, does it? How big's his fucking head? We can be good to go in no time. We're all packed. Not like we turned up with a villa's worth of furniture, is it?'

'I'm just telling you what he said, Stumps.' I spoke

tonelessly, suddenly drained by the knowledge that I was kept from Linza, with her so close.

'Yeah, sorry,' Stumps apologized, sensing my disappointment. 'You'll see her when we get to the Rhine, mate,' he offered. 'We may get stood back down anyway. You know how these things go.'

But the strong winds flirting with the barrack block told me otherwise. Soon rain was lashing against the walls.

'It's got legs,' Titus opined, having opened the doorway to look at the sky.

Brando had joined him. A native of the lands, he knew the German seasons better than any of us. 'We'll go tonight.'

But darkness was a long time away. To leave in daylight would be suicide, offering the German scouts ample time to ride ahead and warn their army, and so the order to remain in barracks chafed at me like a rope around my neck.

'I'm going to the latrines,' I told my comrades.

'I'll keep you company,' Titus offered. 'Sound of this rain has me pissing like a horse.'

'Oh yeah?' Stumps smirked. 'Develop some new friendship whilst you were away, did you, boys? Well, enjoy,' he joked, hoping to lift my mood.

It didn't work.

I stepped outdoors, the rain whipping across my face. Its touch was cold, and violent. I savoured it.

'You don't need to keep an eye on me,' I told Titus as we walked to the latrines.

'It's not that.' He shook his head, surprising me by coming to a stop. We were short of the latrines, fully exposed to the elements.

'Not a good place to piss?' I spoke up, wondering at what was in the man's mind.

'I don't like the odds on this one,' Titus confided in me with a look towards the shrouded skies. 'There're still chests full of coin in the forests, Felix. You can take the chance to get them if you make it out.'

A legion's pay chests. A fortune.

As the approaching storm assaulted me, I thought of what those coins could buy: a ship; a home; a new beginning.

'Where?' I asked my friend. I had been born with a sense of direction and distance, and my time in the legions and escape from that service had only honed the talent. I trusted in my ability to find what Titus was offering.

'You sure you don't want to write it down?'

'I'll remember.'

And so, closing in so that his words would not be lost to the wind, Titus told me where I could find a fortune. When he was finished, I repeated the directions back to him.

'It's a needle in a haystack,' Titus acknowledged. 'But at least we know the haystack.'

We said nothing as we went to piss in the latrines, our thoughts caught up on that day when three eagles had tumbled, and Titus had walked into the forest alone, leaving his comrades behind him. It had been a day of misery, and bloodshed.

Tonight would be no different.

# 65

Wind carried rain below the brim of my helmet and into my eyes. It forced it into every crack of my armour. Every space between clothing and flesh. The rain felt all the harder for its coldness, the fat drops like the pebbles I had thrown at Marcus as a child, back when we had fought our first war as toddlers on the beach.

Marcus. I would see him soon. The certainty of it gnawed at my conscience like a rabid wolf. It was not a reunion I was ready to embrace.

I was not the only man to stand miserable in the pelting rain. We had formed as a century at the excited calls of the company runner. His cries of 'Prepare to move!' had sent us reaching for shields and weapons. Men had streamed from the barrack rooms to form up before the block, some bolting quickly to empty bladders before the formation was fully formed.

'It's still fucking daylight,' Stumps had scowled.

By that light I saw the faces of the men about me scratched red by the cold. We stood impotent, awaiting an order to move and lurch forwards towards the gate. All that we knew was that we were leaving. The details were in the minds of our commanders. There was nothing for the foot soldier to do but stamp his sandals, blow air on to his hands and think.

It was the final action that caused me the most hardship.

I had learned to live with the brutal conditions of the continent, and I fancied that not even a German winter could match those I had endured fighting on Pannonian mountainsides. I could master shaking limbs, quivering jaw and chattering teeth, but what I could not master was the chariot race of thoughts that wheeled around my skull as if it were the Circus Maximus: an endless loop of reproach and regret.

'Tell me a story,' I told Stumps, desperate for distraction.

He looked at me with surprise. I'd never asked for such a thing before. 'I'll tell you a story. It's about a soldier who stands shivering his balls off in the cunting rain whilst his dickheaded officers sit in their quarters drinking wine and dreaming up new ways to fuck us over.'

'Cheer up, Stumps. We'll be at the Rhine in two days,' Livius tried, the youthful section commander yet to realize that the time to worry about a soldier like Stumps was when he was *not* complaining.

'Yeah, I can just see us doing that,' Stumps scowled. 'I mean we've had great preparation for it, haven't we? Standing on a wall. And then there're the civvies. I'm sure they're all great fucking athletes. Olympians. We'll probably reach the Rhine by morning.' Sarcasm dripped from him with the rain.

'Don't you want to get home?' Titus tried instead, his words as hard and as flat as hammered steel.

'Course I do,' Stumps allowed.

'Then save your energy for the road.' His friend was firm but gentle.

'Here comes Albus,' Brando noted, and I saw the curdled face of our centurion appear before the ranks.

'Stand down. Back to your rooms,' he ordered.

A chorus of groans and questions was launched like arrows in return, demanding why we had been kept shivering in the elements.

'I don't fucking know!' Albus answered. 'We stay on immediate notice. Fall out.'

Entering the room, Stumps made straight for the stove. Its embers were still glowing, and he hastily set about reviving them.

'What the fuck was that about?' he grumbled. '"Oh, go on lads",' he mimicked. '"Go stand out in the fucking rain. Not like you've got anything better to do!"'

'Maybe Caedicius got cold feet,' Brando suggested, stripping off his sodden cloak.

'I've got cold balls, never mind feet,' Stumps shot back. 'My cock's halfway inside me.'

'Makes a change from fully inside a Syrian.' Titus smiled as he slapped his friend gently over the head. 'I don't think he got cold feet,' he went on. 'Him and Malchus probably just wanted to test the garrison. Make sure every unit was ready.'

'I think the fact that we're all half frozen is proof of that,' Stumps replied as he stepped back from the growing flames of the stove. 'What do you think, Felix?'

I expected that Titus was right, and Caedicius had wanted to test the readiness of his men. Such a trial was unwanted – even considered an insult – by those who had sprung ready when summoned, only to have to stand shivering, but there were doubtless some in the garrison who would not have reacted as smoothly to the order, and they could now be put on notice, and watched. It was just another part of life under the eagles, another part of war, and I hoped that my sullen answer would explain as much to my comrade.

'It's soldiering,' I told him.

And then our wait began anew.

If confusion about the conspiracies of our commanders was a part of soldiering, then waiting was what was at the profession's core. 'Hurry up and wait' was a common refrain for a reason, and a legionary would spend far more time in his career passive and immobile than he would in the thrust of a campaign. Even invasions of enemy territory were preceded by long periods of inactivity, then broken with a few short moments of frenzied action. In battle, a soldier could stand looking at his enemy for hours before the commanders made their decision to attack, their orders were passed, and the men found the courage to close the distance and fight. Then it would all be over in a horrid, blood-soaked blur.

Titus knew the truth of all this, and absorbed the delay like the veteran he was, unquestioning and uncaring. Stumps occupied himself with second-guessing our leaders and doubting the ethics of their sexual practices. Micon and Brando passed it in silence, while the Batavian broke it mostly to offer prayer to his gods, who he still feared were angry with him for the murder of Statius, the subsequent death of Balbus being just a part to their punishment. Brando would be far from the only one within the camp to offer prayer, and more, and I expected that the space beneath the altars would be thick with gifts and offerings for the gods, beseeching them for deliverance from what was to come.

Knuckles rapped on the door of our barrack room. 'Prepare to move,' a voice called over the wind and rain.

'Here we go then.' Stumps smiled. 'Think this one's the real thing?'

'It's getting dark,' Titus answered. 'We go now, or it won't be tonight.'

We didn't tell each other good luck. We didn't say good-byes. We simply met the looks of our comrades. We all knew what was in our minds. A knowing nod or a touch on the arm was enough, and then we stepped forth into the storm, and fell into the ranks of the century, Livius checking all the men of his section dutifully for the correct equipment and its proper carriage. All, that was, except for myself and Titus. Livius recognized us as the most salted men in the century, and that experience both awed and frightened him.

I knew what was in the young man's mind. I had once been him, the ambitious soldier with potential. I had looked at the veterans' cragged faces, cold eyes, and wanted to know what had made them like that. I wanted to know how *I* could become like that. A person to be feared. A person whose reputation could, by itself, protect all those around them.

The wind and rain had kept their strength, but the light of day was losing its battle. Black storm clouds were growing darker still as dusk came over the soon-to-be-abandoned fort, a blanket pulled over a corpse.

Rain bounced from the dirt that was already slippery beneath our feet. I caught Stumps's smile and look; *remind you of anything?* I read in his dark eyes.

There were no torches. No lights. Centurion Albus made

constant headcounts of the men in front of him – a nervous tic. He was not the only one in search of ways to distract his mind from fear, and despite the rain the ranks were thick with the sound of dark jokes and forced laughter.

I looked at our centurion, and wished that it was H who would be leading us into the night. Lying in the dirt with someone for two weeks – even in near silence – breeds a strong bond, particularly when it is under the nose of an enemy army, and it was with sadness that I was denied a chance to see the good man before our departure. H's place was in the van with Caedicius, and I could only assume that the scouting knowledge of myself and Titus was now deemed either irrelevant or unworthy, because alongside a quarter-cohort of Syrian archers, our century would form the rearguard.

'Century.' Albus spoke in the darkness, catching me in my thoughts. 'By the centre, quick march.'

With those simple words, the Fort of Aliso was abandoned.

# 66

We abandoned the fort like a guilty lover. Only because we had been told as much did I know that we were the last men to pass through the western gate and to strike out towards the Rhine. What was ahead or around us was nothing but a guess, the night's storm robbing me of awareness of all but what was within two javelin lengths of me.

The ranks were silent now. There was time only for panted breaths, and no need for words of harsh encouragement from the officers – we all knew what the penalty would be for failing to cover a backbreaking distance. Dawn would expose us on the wrong side of the German army, and then we would die.

Even making it to the west of the enemy was no guarantee that we'd see out the daylight. At best we could hope to have a few miles between us and the forces we had slipped past, but they would be fresh, and fierce. Cavalry would harass and slow our advance. Eventually, bands of spearmen would crash into our exhausted ranks. There would be no drawn-out battle. It would be over in a blood-soaked hour.

Unless.

Unless the runners that Caedicius had dispatched to the Rhine had prepared the legions for our attempt. Unless they were ready to cross the bridges and come to our aid. I had no sure knowledge that this was the message the prefect had sent with the men, but what else was there to say? What else was there to beg for? Without their help, we would be dead by noon.

Sixteen hours of life. Best then to savour the savagery of the storm. Best then to embrace the burning in my muscles, and the throbbing ache of my knees. The alternative was thought, and I had no wish to spend my dying hours cursing myself for the mistakes I had made when life had been an open road ahead of me.

Hour past hour. The storm held. So did the pace. It was steady, short of panic, and still I wondered how many civilians would have fallen by the wayside. How many would be making their own paths in the darkness, hoping that the fat target of a beaten garrison would distract the enemy from their own escape?

Enough of that. Concentrate on one foot in front of the other. Concentrate on the dull steel of the helmet in front of you. Concentrate on keeping your shoulders loose for when the time comes to draw your blade.

I told myself this. Over and over. Did I listen? Of course not. Instead I tortured myself. Relived my life, mistake by mistake, death by death. Perhaps this was my way of preparing for the end. So deep was my anger, so overwhelming my distress, that I would almost have welcomed an enemy blade in my guts.

Almost.

Stumps. Titus. Brando. Micon. H. Linza.

Six reasons I would parry that blade, and shove my own into the enemy's chest.

Things had changed, I acknowledged. They'd changed in the forest, and now they'd changed in the fort. The hope of my future wavered between the dream of what could be in Britain, and the company that I was within.

*Maybe we would make it,* I dared to think.

Hour past hour. The storm held. So did the pace.

The civilians did not.

Panicked calls began to echo in the night. They were shrill with fear, shouted in Latin.

Titus spoke up, his voice like the rumble of thunder in the storm. 'They must be losing the vanguard.'

'They'll be losing more than that if they don't keep up,' Stumps hissed. 'How far you reckon we've covered, Felix?'

'Eight miles? Nine?'

'Fuck,' Stumps swore, realizing what that meant.

We were on the wrong side of the enemy army, and the cries of the terrified civilians were cutting through the din of the storm, their harried voices like the bleat of frightened goats with the scent of wolf in their nostrils.

'Fuck!' Stumps cursed again, this time loudly, because now there were more voices in the darkness. Commanding voices, loud and angry.

'That's not Latin,' Titus growled.

And then the wolf attacked.

## 67

Wind carried death's symphony to our ears: the clash of blade on blade; the cry of orders; the screams of pain.

Stumps grimaced. 'Vanguard's getting it.'

The panicked cries in Latin were louder now. Moments later, we began to see the fleeting figures of fugitives streaming by our century, the lashing rain doing nothing to hide their terror.

'They're running back to the camp?' Brando guessed.

'They'll die if they do,' Titus grunted. No one pointed out that they could well die here – the sound of crashing shields spoke well enough to that.

'You see that?' Stumps shouted. 'One of those civvies was running with half a villa in his arms!'

Peering into the darkness, I saw more figures escaping towards the false comfort of the fort. Many carried burdens, some even chests. With such loads, there was no way the untrained civilians could have kept pace with the vanguard of soldiers.

'Fell behind and woke the goat-fuckers with their singing,' Stumps sneered. 'Fucking civvies. Should have left them in the fort. Linza excluded,' he added quickly. 'We'll all get it, now.'

Was I worried for Linza? Of course I fucking was. I was worried for her, and for all of us. That's why I looked to our flanks as we continued to push onwards. So far the noise of battle remained distant, but that would not hold for long, I was certain, and I braced myself for the rush of spear and shield I was certain was coming.

'Form square!' Albus called from ahead, his crest lost to me in the darkness.

'Form square!' section commanders repeated above the winds.

Hindered by the elements and a few figures of fleeing civilians, the century's movements were sloppy, and Albus and his optio screamed oaths at anyone who threatened the tiny formation's integrity. Our section found itself on the left flank, which meant that when we moved, we would be taking side steps to our right, our eyes always forward to the formation's flank, and away from our direction of travel. It was a disorientating way to move, but gave us the all-round protection we needed.

'Slow march!' Albus ordered, finally satisfied, and the formation began to creep in the direction of the fighting ahead. After the forced pace of our march, the slow step was agony on minds now fuelled with fear.

We were the rearguard, and I knew what the slow march and square formation meant: Caedicius was using us as a lizard does its tail. We would occupy the attacker as the body made its escape.

'Keep your shields up,' Titus warned. 'Be ready.'

'Shields up,' Livius echoed the veteran's words. His voice had climbed an octave since battle had been joined ahead.

'First time?' Stumps asked, hearing the same.

'I was on the raid,' Livius offered.

'So it's your first time,' Stumps told him, and I could imagine his playful grin. 'You'll be all right.'

As we crabbed towards the Rhine, still agonizingly distant, I took in the comrades by my side. Stumps was on my left shoulder, his face twisted into a mad man's grin. I felt good that he was there, knowing that I could trust him with my blind side. He would die for me, I knew with no doubt, and I hoped that Micon to my right knew the same of me. His head was made of clay, but I was certain his heart understood that he was beloved of his comrades.

Titus's bulk was a blur to the right of Micon, but beyond that I could make out nothing but vague shapes of shield and armour. Behind my back was the second file of the section, men I neither knew, nor, in all honesty, cared about more than any other soldier, or man. They were unknown to me, Livius the only one I knew by name. If we survived this battle, then likely I would know them as well as family. War created brothers with far greater speed than a mother's womb.

Silence had fallen in the ranks. The sound of our steps, and of the bump of our weapons against shield, was lost to the wind and the cries it carried.

I stared on into the darkness.

There were orders being shouted in the black.

The sideswipe of my right foot hit something hard, and I glanced quickly down at the obstruction. It was dark, but it appeared to be a child's toy: a whittled horse.

'Watch your feet,' I whispered.

A voice spoke. 'Torches.'

The light of the flames moved across our vision like fireflies. They were distant enough to pose no immediate threat, and numerous enough to know that, when they did, it would be fatal.

'What was that?' a nervous voice asked.

Fear began to stalk our ranks as certainly as the enemy.

'Are they all around us?'

'Keep quiet.'

'What was that over there?'

'Did you see something?'

'No. Did you?'

The voices fell. Wind drove the rain into my eyes. I tried to blink the drops from my vision to clear the murky blur.

And then I saw the grey vision for what it was – ambient light bouncing from the armour of chain mail, the iron boss of shield and the steel of sharpened blades.

With a vicious roar that humbled the storm's savagery, the enemy attacked.

# 68

One moment there had been empty darkness, the next there was an ink spill of enemies across the night's black canvas.

They were on us before even half an order could leave a mouth. There was no time to think, and instinct carried the tip of my javelin into a bearded blur, the shock of the blow ripping through my wrist as the German skull lost its battle with iron.

I pulled the weapon back, bringing the man's face with it, and then I was driving it forwards again, feeling more than seeing, sensing the strike against wood, or flesh. Then either German body or hands wrenched the weapon free of my grip. The wooden shaft was only a moment clear before I was drawing my short sword and driving it into the waist of the enemy swordsman biting chunks from Micon's shield, splinters from which were scratching against my face.

By my strike that tribesman went down, but another soon filled the void. I saw the light shine from Micon's blade, and felt the hot blood against my hand as the German fell back towards me, the reek of his breath and his opened bowels now thick in my nostrils.

That was the final moment of the action that etched its way into my consciousness. Automatic movements took over my body, thousands of hours of drill and their refinement in battle now put on trial once again. One slip would be enough to be my last. One split second of struggling to pull a blade from ribs. One inch of a shield lowered as biceps burned and screamed as loud as the howling enemy.

I had danced this dance before. Cut, parry, thrust. Plunge the steel into flesh in the space in front of me, pull it free, and repeat. It was the work of a butcher. Bloody, panted labour.

'Halt!' Albus called over the madness, his voice cracking. '*Halt!*' he shouted again.

I let my sword arm drop beside me.

The enemy had gone.

Like the men to my sides, I stood panting, muscles and lungs burning. There was no time to speak, only to draw ragged breaths into a body that yearned to live a few moments longer.

We waited for them. We waited for the enemy's next push. We heard the shouted commands in the darkness, and waited for the black void before our stinging eyes to fill with snarls and spears.

Instead trumpets blared in the distance.

'The double march.' Livius spoke up from somewhere behind me, my first indication that he still lived.

'But who's calling it?' Titus spoke, and my panted breath eased knowing that he was still with us.

The German shouts came again, closer now. Some were excited. Others angry.

'Brando,' Titus called along the line of shields. 'What are they saying?'

For a moment, there was silence.

Then: 'Brando's dead,' Stumps shouted against the rain.

The words were a gentle slap in my face, and nothing

more. We were still in the killing ground. Fear and excitement were making my limbs tingle with nervous energy. The enemy would come again, and more men would die. Now was the time for survival. Like the crows, grief and guilt would come when the battle had broken.

Trumpets blared once more.

'Century!' Albus hollered against the winds, deciding that he would follow the trumpet's order. 'Form into column!'

'Form into column,' men answered automatically, and section commander and veteran went about pushing men into place, their actions hurried and nervous, knowing that we were weaker in this formation if the enemy chose to attack again.

'Prepare to double!' Albus called. 'Double march!'

And so we began to run, my shield and gaze turned out to the left, certain that the German warriors would smell this weakness and close in for the kill.

But there was nothing.

'The torches are coming closer!' someone shouted, and I watched as the beads of light danced and weaved in the darkness.

'They're getting near,' Stumps warned, and I could hear him choke back fear. 'Does Albus think we can just run home?'

Perhaps the centurion did, for as the trumpet's notes continued to wail ahead of us, we passed the first band of torchlit German warriors. Some of their bearded faces looked our way, hurling oaths and spit, but most of the tribesmen had their eyes fastened to the ground, uncaring of our retreat.

Because there was loot to be had.

The ground about us was scattered with the discarded possessions of the civilians, and on to this windfall the tribesmen fell. As I watched the thick carpet of torchlight in the distance, I realized now in which direction the enemy horde was moving.

'They're going to loot the fort!' I shouted against the storm. 'They're going east!'

East – away from the river and its bridges. Away from Roman lands. The enemy blocking force had chosen loot over battle, and no man contested our hurried formation with anything more deadly than a cruel smile or a stream of curses.

The trumpet's call was closer now, the sound of clashing blades and screams a memory carried away by the wind.

Instead, we heard the rumble of hoof beats.

'Cavalry front!' Albus called instantly. 'Form square! Fucking move! Form square! Go! Go! Move!'

No man wasted a moment, and shield overlapped shield, men in the front ranks calling for javelins as they knelt in the mud, and we prepared to receive either an enemy's charge, or our own deliverance.

'Make or break,' Stumps snorted.

The hoof beats came closer.

'If I don't make it back,' Titus said into the darkness, 'I buried my and Metella's stash under the granary.'

Stumps snorted. 'Now you fucking tell me.'

'Brace yourselves,' I urged my friends.

The horses were upon us.

## 69

Roman cavalry.

Dozens of them, their beasts' nostrils snorting in the night. The smell of fear and panic made them skittish, and the cavalry officer's steed shifted nervously beneath its rider as he shouted against the storm.

'Keep going!' he ordered. 'Follow the road! We've cleared it, and the legion's coming! Keep going and you'll run right into them!'

'How far?' Albus called.

'Eight miles, but they crossed an hour ago, coming at the double! I'll send twenty of my blokes with you!' the cavalryman shouted. 'Just follow them and the road!'

The century was already forming into column before Albus could order it.

'Double march!' he bellowed.

And we ran to meet the legions.

We found them in less than an hour of scorched lungs and aching shoulders. Muscles pulled and burned, but no man complained – we were a final effort from sanctuary. A final push from home. The hobnails of our sandals had sounded like music as we had hit the paved road that ran west, its stony course leading us into the wide front ranks of the imposing First Legion, the faces of its soldiers etched with disappointment when they saw that it was

Romans who arrived with the dawn, and not an enemy they had burst lungs to meet in battle.

Looking behind us, it seemed that they would be denied their moment of combat, for the lightening horizon was empty but for the galloping scouts of the Rhine legions.

'They've all gone east!' one called the news as he thundered by. 'You're clear, lads!'

'Fuck me,' Stumps murmured, wiping sweat and rain from his eyes. 'We made it.'

Not all of us.

'What happened to Brando?' I asked as the inevitable grief crashed into my chest like a boulder.

'I don't know,' Stumps replied, chin dropping to his chest. 'One moment he was there, the next he was gone.'

'The Batavian?' a soldier asked, his name as unknown to me as Brando's was to him. 'He took a spear in the chest,' he told us. 'I'm sorry.'

'You get the one that did him in?' Stumps asked after a moment.

The man nodded.

'At least that's something. Thank you.'

I looked at our surroundings. The light of day struggled to break free of the storm, as we had done ourselves. Wind and rain still scoured our skin, but I saw the thick ranks of the First Legion stretching as they took up position on a crest that straddled the road, their imposing cohorts a bulwark between us and the enemy. We were truly safe. Looking at our own ranks, I saw that Brando was one of only a few to fall.

'I just can't believe it,' Titus said to me, seeing the same.

'They went after your coins,' Stumps grunted.

'They won't find them. But they're welcome if they do. We made it from the forest to here. I'll take that.'

Fatigue and orders kept us from further words. Having checked in with officers of the First, Albus marched us onwards, moving along the ranks to pass news to men with anxious faces awaiting tidings of comrades in the cohort.

'All the centuries made it back,' Albus said when it came our turn to hear the words. 'First and Second caught it badly. The others not so bad.'

'What about the civvies?' Stumps asked on my behalf. My stomach was like ice as I awaited the news. 'Did they all leg it?'

'Only some,' Albus answered. 'We'll find out on the Rhine.'

'I'm sure she made it,' Stumps offered to me. 'She's not an idiot. She'll have stuck with the troops.'

I believed that, but not all of the troops had survived. With the First and Second Centuries badly mauled, what chance was there for an unarmed civilian?

'She'll be fine,' Titus added. 'You don't help her or yourself by worrying.'

But what else was there to do? And so, for those final miles, I thought of Linza. I thought of her body alongside Brando's. I thought of the enemy emptying their pockets, and crows emptying their eye sockets. I thought of maggots wriggling in their flesh, and wolves gnawing their bones. So it was that, as the storm slipped into the distance and my sandals hit the wood of a pontoon bridge, I thought of nothing but death, and my failure prevent it.

'I can't believe we made it back to the Rhine.' Stumps grinned, slapping my shoulder. 'Cheer up, Felix, we made it!'

But Brando had not, and I was certain of the same fate for Linza. I opened my mouth to say as much, but as the brown waters of the Rhine swirled beneath us, my eyes fell upon someone who *had* survived the night, and who now stood smiling on the western bank of the river.

'Welcome back, boys!' H called to the men of what had once been his century, delighting in each face that he recognized.

As my own feet left the wooden boards and hit the soil that was the Roman Empire, H fell in alongside us. His smile slipped as he saw that Brando was absent from the ranks, but he fought to be positive. To make it a moment of victory, and not defeat.

'It's good to see you, boss.' Titus meant it. His words were echoed by those around me.

'I'm glad you're alive,' I added quickly. 'Have you seen Linza?'

The man shook his head. 'But most of the civvies made it, Felix, and she's a young one with a brain. She'll be fine. I mean it,' he added, seeing my face sour and chin drop. 'She'll be fine.

'You've got hot baths and hot food coming, boys,' H said to the other men about me, and I followed his gesture to where the stone walls of the fort of Vetera loomed ahead, the powerful bastion overlooking lands that were now unquestionably under the power of the tribes and their leader Arminius. We had slipped from the German's grasp, but the man I had once called a friend was victorious – all Roman presence east of the Rhine had been wiped away, and Arminius sat atop a powerful army that had tasted victory.

'They won't stop at Aliso,' I said.

H shook his head. 'They'll have no choice, Felix. The commander of the lower Rhine has brought the First and the Fifth legions up here.'

I felt his confidence, but believed none of it. 'Arminius killed three legions in the forest.'

'In the forest, yes,' H agreed, with a slow nod of his head. 'And he defeated three legions, but he won't beat five.'

'Five?' I asked, puzzled. There were only two on the Rhine. Varus had led the other three to ruin, and for a moment, I thought that fatigue had robbed H of his memory.

But I was wrong and, as we marched into Vetera, the centurion gave me my answer – it turned my guts to the same stone as the gatehouse above me.

'The war in Pannonia's finally put down!' The Roman smiled. 'The last of them have surrendered, Felix, so Tiberius is leading his legions to us!'

My step faltered. The Pannonian legions, coming here?

'Are you all right, Felix?' H asked, concerned because he was seeing a ghost, now – white-skinned, my breath held in unmoving lungs.

'Which legions?' I finally choked.

He told me with glee.

I heard only one.

The legion I had betrayed. The comrades I had abandoned.

*The Eighth.*

H beamed. 'They're coming here!'

My throat was lead, my stomach ice. The eagle I had

once carried for Rome was now marching to the Rhine to bring vengeance against the turncoat Arminius, but my former legion would find another traitor in their path. A traitor they despised more than any other.

*Corvus.*

'Felix, are you all right?' H was worried. 'What's wrong with you?'

At first I said nothing, but then I laughed at the sky, bitter and angry.

'*You're* wrong,' I told him. '*You're* wrong, H!'

And so he was.

All the miles, all the fights, all the pain – I had thought it was carrying me away from a treasonous life. From a poisonous war that H thought was over. But the Eighth Legion now marched towards me and the treasured beginnings of a new life I had found amongst comrades.

They would not take it from me. I would not run again from what had started on bloody mountains a continent away – mountainsides where my friends had fought and died. Where Marcus had slipped away in my arms.

It would not be forgotten. Not one misdeed. Not one death. Blood would pay for blood.

'You're wrong,' I said again.

Because the war in Pannonia was not over.

Corvus was alive, and I wanted vengeance.

# Author's note

A quick note on the map – Pannonia and Dalmatia weren't established as separate provinces until after the events in this book, but I've used them for simplicity's sake throughout this series.

Following the destruction of three legions in the Teutoburg Forest, Arminius set about wiping out what was left of the Roman presence east of the river Rhine. In the classical texts of Velleius Paterculus and Cassius Dio, both men wrote that the revolting tribes were able to overrun the Roman forts on the Lippe one by one, often taking them by surprise. This run came to an end at the Fort of Aliso, which was under the command of Prefect Caedicius. Caedicius's men supposedly inflicted a terrible toll on the enemy forces during the German's assault, in large part thanks to the presence of archers on the walls.

The fort then held out for several weeks, and in this time a number of frustrated tribes began to leave the battlefield. Arminius decided that starving the garrison was now his best course, and to this end he left a force between Aliso and the Rhine to block the Romans' way to safety, while he himself left the site to shore up support for his war against Rome.

Aliso's commander Caedicius did not expect that a rescue would come from across the Rhine, or that the garrison would survive winter, and so the prefect planned to break out of the siege. Following reconnaissance by his scouts – who made note of the German dispositions and routines – the Romans waited for their chance to slip away. This eventually came under the cover of a heavy storm. According to Dio, the fort's occupants succeeded in making it past the enemy's first and second outposts before they were discovered by the tribesmen. As I have written it, this detection was supposedly caused by the panicked shouting of civilians as they failed to keep up with the vanguard. Dio says that, surrounded and attacked on all sides, Prefect Caedicius ordered that the civilians should abandon their possessions. When they did so, the Germans became distracted enough by this loot that the Roman force was able to cut its way clear. Dio goes on to say that the garrison in the fort of Vetera – modern day Xanten – learned of what was happening to the east, and sent units across the Rhine to see Aliso's refugees safely home.

Personally, I believe that there must have been some early co-ordination in this. The flight from Aliso took place at night and under heavy storm, and so I have to think that the soldiers on the Rhine would have been at least warned of such a breakout attempt, and stood ready to support it. Given the conditions, and that it took place on the opposite side of the Rhine by some miles, it's hard to think that the garrison at Vetera only became aware of the breakout by chance.

On the subject of distances from the Rhine, there is some debate as to the exact location of Aliso, but Haltern looks like a good bet. For the purposes of this book, I didn't see anything to be gained by nailing my colours to the wall as far as an exact site went. I write stories rather than lessons, and so in this book I have simplified when it suited, exaggerated when it suited, and flat out invented when it suited – there's nothing in the classical texts about murders in the Fort of Aliso. That's all from my deranged little mind, and I implore readers to remember that books like this are *fiction*, and should not be swallowed whole as historical record. There are plenty of excellent non-fiction works about the Roman Army — too many for me to list, in fact. If you'd like to know more about the ones that I use when writing, please feel free to ask me online.

I've used 'supposedly' a couple of times in this note, and for what I believe is good reason. We only have a couple of primary sources to draw upon when it comes to the siege of Aliso, and even these tend to be written decades or more after the date of events. If you want to hear an unbiased opinion about military campaigns in 2018, then I don't think that taking news from a single media outlet is a good idea, and I'm sure that this would have applied a couple of thousand years ago, too. Just because there is a surviving record doesn't make it fact, or even accurate. I'm sure the capacity to bullshit and twist the truth was as alive then as it is now.

The great thing about writing historical fiction is that you get to interpret what we do have — and fill in the blanks of what we don't — with your own mind. I'm sure that there are plenty of other minds that would fill them in differently to how I do, but great! That's what makes things interesting.

Micon, Stumps, Titus, and the rest of Felix's cronies are all fictional characters, but each are rooted in the personalities of soldiers that I was privileged to serve and fight alongside. Nothing gives me more pleasure than to talk with veterans, or to read the accounts that they have left behind, and I am convinced that the spirit and the nature of 'the soldier' transcends time. Regardless of the uniform, regardless of the weapons, there is a commonality to the men and women that bear arms and kill.

And killing is something that Felix wished he had seen an end of, but with Arminius and his army undefeated, and with the vengeful legion that he deserted marching towards him, there's still a lot more blood to shed.

# Acknowledgements

Thanks to Rowland White, Jillian Taylor, Sharan Matharu, the Michael Joseph team at large, and to everyone at Penguin who made *Siege* possible; from drawing up contracts to distributing copies, there are so many people involved in the process and I'm grateful to every single one of you.

Bear hugs to my agents Rowan, Rory, and to the extended family at Furniss Lawton. Lots of love to my flesh and blood in Wales. I wouldn't be able to do what I do without the help of all of you, and I rather like what I'm doing, so cheers!

Finally, thank you to all of the historians and archaeologists out there. Any book like this would be impossible without you.